T0064754

The Chalidang soldiers seemed so filled with blood lust and so confident of an easy victory that they didn't even realize that the mantalike Sanafeans had been drawing them slowly down, at great cost, to the reef below.

Suddenly, as a large number of Chalidangers swooped in to finish off some bleeding stragglers just above the reef, the coral reef itself seemed to erupt. Shapes—nasty, vicious, with huge jaws, wide eyes, and pointed teeth—lashed out from holes and hideaways within the living rock. They looked almost comical, but they were incredibly fast, and they ignored the armor and started chomping on the Chalidangers' tentacles. Soon the thirty or so invaders who were close enough had gaping wounds, and tentacle parts and blood began floating about, yet every time the Chalidangers tried to harpoon or net or otherwise grab one of their large serpentine assailants, there was nothing there. As quickly as they struck, the giant sea snakes could withdraw into the protection of solid coral, only to emerge somewhere else when the victim was right.

Withdraw! Get away from the damned reef! Mochida screamed at them. . . .

By Jack L. Chalker
Published by Ballantine Books:

AND THE DEVIL WILL DRAG YOU UNDER
DANCE BAND ON THE *TITANIC*
DANCERS IN THE AFTERGLOW
A JUNGLE OF STARS
THE WEB OF THE CHOZEN
PRIAM'S LENS
THE MOREAU FACTOR

THE SAGA OF THE WELL WORLD
Volume 1: *Midnight at the Well of Souls*
Volume 2: *Exiles at the Well of Souls*
Volume 3: *Quest for the Well of Souls*
Volume 4: *The Return of Nathan Brazil*
Volume 5: *Twilight at the Well of Souls:*
The Legacy of Nathan Brazil
Volume 6: *The Sea Is Full of Stars*
Volume 7: *Ghost of the Well of Souls*

THE FOUR LORDS OF THE DIAMOND
Book One: *Lilith: A Snake in the Grass*
Book Two: *Cerberus: A Wolf in the Fold*
Book Three: *Charon: A Dragon at the Gate*
Book Four: *Medusa: A Tiger by the Tail*

THE DANCING GODS
Book One: *The River of Dancing Gods*
Book Two: *Demons of the Dancing Gods*
Book Three: *Vengeance of the Dancing Gods*
Book Four: *Songs of the Dancing Gods*
Book Five: *Horrors of the Dancing Gods*

THE RINGS OF THE MASTER
Book One: *Lords of the Middle Dark*
Book Two: *Pirates of the Thunder*
Book Three: *Warriors of the Storm*
Book Four: *Masks of the Martyrs*

THE WATCHERS AT THE WELL
Book One: *Echoes of the Well of Souls*
Book Two: *Shadow of the Well of Souls*
Book Three: *Gods of the Well of Souls*

THE WONDERLAND GAMBIT
Book One: *The Cybernetic Walrus*
Book Two: *The March Hare Network*
Book Three: *The Hot-Wired Dodo*

Ghost of the Well of Souls

Jack L. Chalker

A Del Rey® Book
THE BALLANTINE PUBLISHING GROUP • NEW YORK

A Del Rey® Book
Published by The Ballantine Publishing Group
Copyright © 2000 by Jack L. Chalker

www.randomhouse.com/delrey/

Library of Congress Card Number: 00-190079

ISBN 978-0-345-49030-8

146846710

For Anne McCaffrey

Author's Note

THIS IS THE SECOND AND FINAL PART OF A SAGA OF THE WELL World. I think you'll find it a bit different from the past ones while still keeping the same fun. The first book we called *Currents of the Well of Souls*, and the whole project is The Sea is Full of Stars. You'll see the meaning of the various names as you read.

If, perchance, you missed the first one, it should be available at all reputable booksellers, stores, superstores, etc. Any intelligent, competently run bookselling operation would have it on hand when the second one comes out, so if it isn't there, you know what to say to the proprietor. You *should* read them in the order they were written; otherwise it completely spoils the surprise and, because there is a minimum of recap here, you might even get confused as to who's who. So, please, buy this one now and the first one, too, huh? People who read fiction for pleasure are a vanishing breed of high order intellectual. We need you.

—JLC

South Zone

AMBASSADOR DUKLA'S ALMOST EQUINE FACE PULSED AS HE breathed the water of his longtime ambassadorial home. Most of those he addressed were no more likely to read his mood or expressions than they could read it on a rock's, but there was no mistaking the tone the telepathic translator module carried through to the allied hexes.

"The Chalidang ambassador has been replaced, as you know," Dukla began, sounding cheerful. "My suspicion is that he either did not go home or he is home for good. The Emperor and Empress there are having quite a purge."

Those watching in both air- and water-breathing ambassadorial chambers gave their own equivalents of nods or knowing chuckles. Not only did the Chalidang rulers have vicious tempers, they were known to go into serious rages and eat the nearest person alive, slowly, limb by limb. It wasn't *just* personal, it was almost traditional.

"The official protests, of course, have been coming in fast and furious as well—not just from the Chalidang, but also from the Jirminins and the Quacksans. Both lost quite a bit more in the Battle of Ochoa than the pride their rulers lost—for all that means to the bastards. It centered mostly on my using my authority to allow Ochoan armed troops inside Zone as part of the battle. They are waving the treaty like never before, even though they ignore it whenever it doesn't suit them. They have called for an impeachment of me and my office, and for my immediate recall with censure, and, of course, they want all sorts of reparations. As usual, these things are being negotiated under the table, even as they bluster, but I wanted to let you know ahead of any Council convenings that a deal is already shaping up.

"Technically, the Ochoans were here primarily as a deputized force of the Zone Council—as all of our races who participate do from time to time. They were empowered to prevent hostilities and to prevent Zone's use in influencing the course of a conflict. The complaintants see it differently. The fact that the Kalindans gave over their assignment to the Ochoans is in order, but I'm afraid the Ochoans aren't good for long periods underwater, no matter how well they fish."

The Ochoan ambassador, who knew he owed the continued existence of his nation in part to the courage of this strange creature and its sense of right and wrong, had guessed that this was coming, but he didn't like it anyway. "So they are taking the easy way out, I suppose?" he said. "Much easier than making a moral choice. They justify their action in using Zone as a planned military escape route because of our action, in support of Kalinda's authority, to stop them. The invaders are disarmed and sent home. We are already home, so that is moot, although we did go home fully armed. And you take the political fall."

"That is an accurate summary," Ambassador Dukla acknowledged. "I knew this was probable when I did it. Do not worry. My homeland does not eat its recalcitrants. Fortunately, we are vegetarians. And it shall be nice to be home once more in my native land. I have an estate that is a gorgeous coral reef, nicely designed by me and my kin. I truly have missed it. In a year or two, when things quiet down and memories fade and the rage of nations is elsewhere, I'll quietly be let back into the government, probably as an adviser or deputy minister."

In the Kalindan embassy, the twin-minded Ari and Ming watched while reclining in comfort just beneath the water, along with the very strange one called Core, who appeared to be the self-aware portion of crime lord Jules Wallinchky's computer, designed to run his faraway museum and retreat. For the moment, Core was on their side, but there was no precedent for such a creature, not even in its own memories, and nobody knew just what it might do or become.

"Do you mean that the Ochoans win the war because Dukla had guts and Core had a plan and the guy who made it possible gets kicked in the tail?" This was clearly Ming, outraged.

I thought at least by now you'd have lost that childlike faith in justice and the rewards of goodness in this life, Ari commented mentally.

"Only since I got stuck in the same head as you did, dear," she shot back.

"It is likely that most of the nations of and around the Overdark are secretly pleased," Core commented. "It is expedient that someone take the fall, and the ambassador will fall more softly than others. It is a logical result. The important thing is that we have bought some time."

"Huh? Only that?" Ari responded.

"Only that. No war was won here; please put that idea from your minds. A *battle* was won. The defeat is considerable, but it involved a less than thirty percent casualty rate to the main two nations. Bad, but seventy percent was able to evacuate either via Zone or in ships, so I would expect that Josich now is formulating plans for everyone who caused him this inconvenience and loss of face."

"Inconvenience! He was creamed!" Ming exclaimed.

"Indeed? How many Chalidang troops were lost?"

"Huh? None, I guess, except maybe a few to some sniping around the ships. They're water breathers and this was a land attack."

"Precisely. His surrogates did the fighting and took the losses, and he still has many allies. Take a look at the map."

Core rose, floated over to a wall and checked the labels. She withdrew a large scroll, which she proceeded to lay open on a table and clamp down the edges. A small current was applied, which illuminated the tabletop and therefore the map of the eastern Overdark.

"The Quacksans were not used much because their hypnotic powers do not work well against Ochoans," Core said.

"They were mostly holding troops on the heights. Their army is still intact and barely tested, and their junior commanders now have some real battle experience. The Jirminins took the brunt of the losses, but have well-seasoned troops, who now bear hurt pride and grudges. There are at least eleven more hexes here that either have allied themselves with Chalidang or were easily conquered and turned into allies under some of the relatives of the dear Empress. Still, the bulk of Josich's troops are water breathers. The Olan Cheen are much too far away to be factored in at this time. What other hex is within the field of fire and would provide a near irresistible target for revenge while also serving some practical military use? Take a look—a good look. You do not need to be a general—nor formerly a computer, I should think—to see the answer."

They hovered over the table looking at it. "You think they're gonna come after us next," Ming said.

"Soon, and with everything they've got. They already have some political allies and what historians used to call 'Fifth Columnists' installed, many in high places."

"Fifth what?"

"An ancient term, the origin of which is not worth explaining," Core replied. "It means people of one nation in high positions who seem quite loyal but who have actually sold themselves for potential power to become agents of the enemy. Josich was always good at corrupting the incorruptible. They've already conquered some of the neighboring hexes in that manner. Weak megalomaniacs were placed in charge and given absolute power—so long as they did what they are told if called upon."

"But we're thousands of kilometers from them!" Ari objected. "It's impossible without their tipping their hand way in advance!"

"We are no farther than Ochoa, and our two small islands are the only other land in the entire region. Certainly it's not the ideal placement that Ochoa offered, but let us take a look at who is in between us and the enemy." A claw from his webbed hand pointed to the map. It was so much easier to hover over something than to have to sit around it; all three had begun to take for granted the powers of levitation that being a water creature conferred.

"Chalidang, Laskein, Dauwit, S'Coyd, Jovin, Saluda, Yabbo, Kalinda. Seven hexes, approximately sixteen hundred kilometers, or just one hex farther than Ochoa. But, unlike Ochoa, suppose we had a well-financed gang of ambitious egomaniacs keeping us tied up at home? And what if Bludarch is in their hands, here? A land hex only three hundred kilometers from our capital?"

"But that's a nontech hex. They wouldn't get much use from it," Ari commented, staring at the map.

"Nonsense. The key isn't Bludarch. It's the fact that it's a peninsula surrounded on five sides by ocean. Cromlin, Saluda, Yabbo—all high-tech or semitech. Formidable. And you've never been outside of Kalinda except to Zone, here. You are tending to think, as most do, that because the border of a hex is straight lines, so is its coastline. The Ochoans know better, as should you. Mountain ranges don't stop at these borders, nor do most other landforms, any more than the Karellian Reef stops because it hits our boundary with Yabbo. Saltwater is saltwater. There's some change in the vegetation, true, due to its colder waters and different nutrients, but it goes on for another kilometer. By the same token, Bludarch has a great many ports because its rugged coastline extends irregularly in and out of neighboring water hexes. You couldn't fire a gun or turn on an electric light in Bludarch, but you *could* dock and service any ship under steam or sail. On the Cromlin side, you could repair a fusion reactor if you needed to. A close-up topographic view of the region shows this. He's coming. The only question is *how*, and when."

"You've never been in any other hex, either," Ming pointed out.

"I don't have to be," Core said. "I am used to logic and data and big pictures. However, I also do not have to try some dangerous travel to scout this area. It has been suggested that you might be a very good one to send instead, considering your two for one, um, features—and because the two of you previously had skills in this sort of skulduggery."

Ming sighed. "Uh-huh. And who suggested us?"

Core shrugged. "I did, but the powers above us thought it was quite a good idea."

"And why not you?" Ari asked him. "After all, you have all that analytical power. You've said it yourself. You had to leave data behind, not logic, so why not accumulate more data, by experience for a change?"

"I cannot afford to take the chance, nor can our alliance," Core answered without a trace of modesty. "You see, I have some reason to believe that Josich knows who, or at least *what*, I am. Therefore, I am a priority to be captured, if possible, and killed if not. Remember that Josich was in many ways a confederate and co-criminal conspirator of your—um, *Ari's*—uncle Jules Wallinchky. He, or more properly now, *she*—although that makes precious little difference to a Chalidanger unless they are making more Chalidangers—knew quite a bit about the other criminal empire with which it often had to deal. The Chalidang intelligence network here is as good as those back in our old corner of the universe. Also, I just made a damned fool of them. That counts against me, you know."

"I can imagine," Ming responded dryly. "What will you do? Build yourself an armor-plated prison?"

"Being inside a single room is not the same torture for me as it might be for you," Core pointed out. "Until I arrived here and managed to 'pull this off,' I had never moved at all except in that the planet moves. To one who always experienced everything second- or thirdhand, even a very limited life in an organic body is liberation. We have determined that I will do the most good and be the most secure remaining here at the embassy in Zone. I will be able to make use of this sophisticated if very alien computer system, keep an eye on what's happening, and contact anyone as needed. There is also the pressing problem that all Kalindans who are not already female are turning female. They have been desperately taking sperm from those not yet changed, but analysis seems to show there are no viable male sperm in the samples, either. You can see that if we do not solve that one, the rest is moot. It has been speculated that the Well World master control computer would not permit a species to go extinct, but I believe that this is not true. These were laboratories to prove or disprove racial viability. Dying out is one effect that must be accepted as a valid scientific result."

That was a sobering thought. "Any race ever died out here before?"

"Who knows? None on record, but some have gone in directions where they might as well have, including your own old form. It is possible that we might not be allowed to drop to zero, but what will result will not be the kind of civilization we know, and we will be more than vulnerable to being displaced. No, we solve it or it is probable extinction. Even if it isn't, we must act as if it is true. We have no choice. And we need to know if, as now seems logical, it is genocide that we are facing rather than natural forces. What Josich's scientists can do, we can undo—if we find the agent. In the meantime, we must not put so much in the hands of our enemies. No race should have that kind of control over another.

"No, we have two problems. I must aid in breaking this internal threat, and you must assess the external one."

"So just what do you want us to do?" Ari asked.

"Do a survey of the neighborhood. All six hexes surrounding us are potential paths to our door, not just the obvious. It might not be Bludarch. Josich did not get as far as this or survive this long by being obvious, and the Empress must *never* be underestimated. There are other land areas not much farther off. You don't move forces through this kind of distance without a lot of preparation, and Josich's generals will not make the overconfident error of leaving supply lines vulnerable and stretched again. We have the only land, small as it is, other than Ochoa, between the western continent and the Far East. It is not the best port for them, but it would do. And if an entire enslaved population expanded it artificially, it could become formidable indeed. We need to know how they are coming. We need to know who our friends are, who our enemies are, and how those sitting on the fence will jump if things begin to happen. Follow the preparations. Find the route and follow it. When you have it, get back here and map it out."

"All by ourselves? You must think a lot of us," Ming commented. "We may be two minds, but we're only one body." And *you're sure painting a target on us,* she added to herself.

"You will have an easier time if you do not take a crowd," Core told them. "You will not, however, be alone in this endeavor. Others are working on this. It is best that none of you know who the others are, not names or even races, until and unless it is necessary to know. That way, no one can betray anyone else. However, anyone you feel you *can* trust would be welcome. Simply watch your back."

"I assume that O'Leary and Nakitt will have things going on," Ari said thoughtfully. "What about the angel girl?"

"O'Leary, Nakitt, and their people are not water breathers. They cannot do what you can, but will be doing much the same on land. And as for the angel, unexpected as that was, I believe that she is evolving. And whether or not she will be a help, a hindrance, or an entirely separate problem has yet to reveal itself."

"Huh?"

"If you look at the histories and the old guides, you'll find that even the creatures here—all 1,560 races of both north and south—are not the same as they were in past times. Oh, they're *close*, but the sleek centaurs of Dillia, for example, seem almost like streamlined, stylized idealizations of their coarse, muscular, and far more brutishly equine ancestors. The same goes for almost every race here. The Kalindan of yesteryear could not breathe air at all for any length of time. They were quite rough, mottled, and more leathery than scaly. There may have been a point after that when we were primarily air breathers, and we are now in the process of losing that ability. Certainly we are *primarily* of the water. Unlike the mermaidlike race of the west, our tails are vertical, not horizontal, and we have never lost the dorsal. I can give you almost as many examples as races, save for some of the northern ones where nobody could tell. Evolution did not stop simply because it was a limited population. Given enough time, it continues.

"The Amborans, they are quite a bit different than the much more fragile creatures of their past. The males, who are now basically short, fat groundlings, were once winged as well and sleeker. The females, who now have all the muscular power and the wings, at one time were extremely fragile, and once they mated, they lost the ability to fly. They've evolved into a much more stable, more survivable biological form. Somehow—perhaps it was partly my doing, partly the sheer empty vessel provided and the magic-masked sophisticated biochemistry of the Amboran priesthood—the ongoing process has been sped up. The angel girl is currently a mutation, but in directions that so far indicate that her development reflects what the race may become in tens of thousands or more years. She is not done yet. What is happening to her might have taken hundreds of thousands of years for the whole race. Then again, she may well be a freak, one of a kind. In either case, if she survives, she may well be one of the most powerful single creatures on the face of this planet."

"Oh," was the only thing either Ming or Ari could think of to say.

"We must ensure that she regains or at least retains some toehold, however minuscule, in her past humanity. I hope I did not strip all of it from her. If so, it may well be the Well of Souls that must deal with her, lest she become a god. Until and unless I can be certain of which way she will go, it is essential that she at least feel comfortable with us, that our side is the side of the just. Understand?"

"I think so," Ari replied, and indeed they both saw the threat. "So, when do we leave, and how do we work out reports and contacts with you and the government?"

"You will report only to me, and to those whom I can code to work entirely for me. The message traffic will be to and from Zone only. I do not believe that the whole of the government is reliable. Some of it would willingly sell us out to Josich. A good share of the rest would surrender rather than face genocide—and, frankly, if that were the only choice, who could blame them? For now, we—those of us who come from other places, who came here knowing one another—are the third force on the Well World, and we damned well better keep it that way."

In fact, Ari and Ming were more than eager to get out of the straitjacket they'd been in since arriving on this strange world. Unable to see and enjoy their new, exotic, combined form, they'd been kept effectively prisoner, and treated like freaks—which, both had to admit, they were, under most definitions.

The odd thing was how well the master crook's somewhat bent nephew and the pretty but tough policewoman had gotten along. Of course, the alternative to getting along was committing suicide. Even so, with the truth of each of their backgrounds known to the other, there was a compatibility they would not have expected. Control wasn't much of a question; each automatically deferred to the other whenever appropriate. An observer could not tell which one was in charge at any given time. And the ability to have a full dialogue with the other at the speed of thought, without eavesdroppers, was often quite useful.

There was *one* point of privacy that had driven each of them crazy since they awoke as two different minds in a single body. Neither was ever alone. Ever. Oh, there was a level to which each could withdraw mentally. Nonetheless, the other was always around, always observing. Both felt it, and neither was completely comfortable with it.

Recently, Ming was disturbed by a new wrinkle, one she didn't yet feel confident enough to bring up with Ari. She was beginning to dream his dreams; to dream things that were related to his old experience but not to hers. There was also a sense of memory leakage that hadn't been there at the start. At first it had been hardly noticeable. Now, it was common to be thinking over something when, suddenly, a memory or piece of data popped into her mind from what could only have been his half of the brain. No one had discussed the future with them, but she and Ari had overheard some of the medical and psychological types back in Kalinda when they were still specimens. The near unanimous prediction was that they would begin to merge into one. It was supposed to have been slow, and happen without them really realizing it, but that wasn't the way things were occurring.

Ming knew, and she suspected that Ari did, too.

She didn't want to be a part of him. To her, it was like dying. What was her would be there, of course, but it wouldn't really be her anymore, nor him, either. A person was more than the sum of his or her memories.

Even that poor girl whose physical shell should have contained Angel Kobe's mind but instead had no personal memories at all, Ming thought, was still more Angel than not. Angel's body had been newly created from a shell of an old mind whose personality had been erased before it ever got to the Well World. Yet much of what Jaysu the Amboran Priestess was could be recognized as the essence of the original Angel Kobe—from the search for spiritual heights beyond the material world, and the drive to serve, as well as the ironic physical incarnation of the poor girl's birth name.

How Angel Kobe would have loved being that person!

Ming couldn't help but wonder where those memories, that personality, were now. Most likely nowhere; unlike Angel, Ming never believed in any sort of hereafter or deities.

Core thinks her memories and personality module are still back in the old computer back on Uncle Jules's gallery world, Ari commented telepathically.

Ming was startled. *You heard me musing?*

Yeah. Sorry. Didn't know you weren't doing it for my benefit, or at least without caring if I heard or not.

How much of my thoughts do you get? she asked him, the worry coming back again.

Probably exactly as many as you get of mine. It's gonna happen. Bound to. There's really only one brain and central nervous system here. You heard 'em.

For his part, Ari was as insecure as she was, though more resigned. Many times upon awakening from sleep, it took a while before he could remember which one he was. At least once recently he'd awakened thinking he was her. Only when her own consciousness awoke and was clearly Ming did he realize his mistake and suddenly become "Ari" through and through again. Funny, too—her cultural heritage was eastern and mideastern; stoicism and pragmatism were part and parcel of that upbringing. His background was Latin, Greek, and Slavic—emotional, explosive types, expressive and always fighting against the Fates. For all her lack of belief, Ming was more Zen Buddhist deep down than he was Catholic. Yet, he was the accepting one, while she was fighting like hell.

Of course, "stoic" was a Greek word . . .

You want to go see this dump? he asked her.

Might as well. Besides, if I said "no," you'd go anyway.

Might as well see what the budget is, at least for starters, Ari suggested. *In a way, this could be like old times.*

No, she responded slowly, sadly. *It can* never *again be like old times.*

Ambora

ANGEL KOBE, KNOWN AS JAYSU, RETURNED TO HER HOMELAND
more upset and confused than ever, both about herself and
about the way the world should be.

So many dead. So much evil. The very existence of it, the
depth of it, was upsetting to her. She could feel it, at that
extreme, just being in proximity to the representatives, the
diplomats and soldiers, who served it back in that Zone place.

And that gill monster—the Kalindan they called Core—
she could hardly bear to be close to the creature. Though it
was less evil than an enormous, cold emptiness. It was like
flying over a great bottomless pit and working to keep from
being sucked into it, then falling, falling, falling forever in
the cold and dark. Only in the triangular, leathery winged
ones, the Ochoans, had there been a real sense of the soul.
But the urge to violence and the sense of vengeance threatened to consume even them.

It was a strange sensation to look inside others and interpret what she was seeing. She knew that to cure the darkness
that ate at the souls of the living was a priestess's main job,
but to see it so starkly, so organically and effortlessly, and in
every race—that was something new.

Their tools were the ancient tools of an ecclesiastical society: counseling, prayer, fasting, penances. None of them could
simply reach inside and change what they sensed by an act of
conscious will. But she could, and it frightened her. Gods
might have such power, but not mortals. Certainly mortals
should not, and more certainly not her.

She had spent much of her time by herself in the volcanic

13

beauty of Ambora's wild places, praying, reflecting, to reason it out. She hoped for a sign from Heaven that this was something she should use—or something she should fear and avoid.

The isolation hadn't helped. It had accelerated the continuing changes going on inside her. Priestesses did not fly; although they had those wonderful white wings, they were decorative. The muscles were inadequate to use them properly, and their bones were thickened, almost solid like the men's. Her own snow-white wings were enormous, far larger than any priestess's wings. The feathers had a lushness about them she'd not seen in any others.

There had been a period after she'd drunk the potions, faced the Grand High Priestess, and accepted her vocation, that she'd lost strength and her flying ability. She'd begun to feel progressively heavier; but no more.

Now, standing atop Mount Umajah—its great black, steaming caldera stretched out below her as a demonstration of the power of the gods—she stretched and spread those huge wings. Almost as if on cue, a brisk, cool wind swept across the vast pit below, striking her unexpectedly and causing her to lose her footing. She fell forward into the caldera perhaps a kilometer or more below her. The wings spread, and she *flew*!

She flew, not as the warriors flew, with the speed and nimbleness of the huntress; no, not like them. Instead she soared, majestically, rising up almost without effort, the great wings barely beating every few minutes in response to a change.

This was not supposed to be, but it was the most wonderful thing of all.

It was a sign. It was the sign she'd been waiting for. The gods would not allow a priestess to soar so close to Heaven if this were some evil being worked!

Jaysu began a leisurely turn and took a tour of Ambora. When she flew, it wasn't an ordeal to see much of the country. The wind was with her, and great distances could be covered easily.

She rose up high, and watched the warriors of many clans

swarm and play and hunt below. She did not envy them, but she did take in some of their joy. She also could sense their astonishment when they looked up and saw the strange figure hovering far above them in the highest currents. Curiously, while they were all puzzled at the sight of her, not a single one of them rose to see just who or what she was or how she was able to do this. Some began to do it, then suddenly lost interest.

She wasn't sure, but she suspected it was partly because of her. She already knew she had some power over other minds— which was how she'd remained solitary while she figured things out. These were powers only gods were wise enough to have. Why had they given so much of that power to someone like her?

The others at that meeting at Zone had said she was from where they'd come from, another world or worlds somewhere off in the heavens. Her memories had been left behind, but not her soul. How could that be? The girl they described had been a low-ranking priestess of a church she could not remember or understand. Even those who had told her who and what she'd supposedly been were at a loss to explain who and what she was becoming.

That was the most frightening idea of all. The idea that it wasn't over, that something was still changing her at an increasingly rapid pace. Changing into—what? What more could she become? And to what end?

Still, to discover that she could fly again was the one bit of wonderful news. There was no feeling quite like flying— soaring across the vast landscape, feeling and seeing the wind currents, floating along lazily in thermals that carried her almost like the caressing hands of motherly goddesses. It was so *easy*, not like walking or running along the ground. Up here, gravity was no enemy.

She hadn't realized until this miraculous grand tour how beautiful Ambora was. A peninsular hex, surrounded on four sides by the ocean and on the western two by the continental landmass. Ambora's high volcanic peaks, sheer cliffs, and dynamic if colorful landscape was in stark contrast to the apparent emptiness of the sea or the dark, gray-shrouded lands of the western region. She had no idea what might live there, nor what they could do. The truth was, she'd had little curiosity about them then or now—particularly after having seen so many of the monstrous races that lurked beyond Ambora when she'd been to that gathering place they called Zone. Slimy, dark things that crawled from the sea, serpentlike things that crawled on their bellies in the dust, leathery flying things that were half lizard and half bird with the worst of each, and all the others—no beauty, no grace. Yes, they had souls of the same sort as the Amborans, but they seemed disinterested in exploring the only part of them worth looking at.

Flying around the border of Ambora, she could see that it was virtually walled in. The walls weren't of stone or mud or wood, of course; but to one who could see thermals and sense minor fluctuations in local magnetic fields, they seemed like walls. Cold, rising up to heaven, straighter than anything in nature, dulling vision beyond and shimmering like air above a rushing lava flow. She had no desire to fly through one, even though she instinctively understood that it was possible. What might it be like on the other side? Even in Zone she had felt heavy in one office, light in another, freezing cold and wet in yet another, and nearly boiling in the one next to that. If that kind of variation was to be found there, presumably for the comfort of the other races, then what might it be like just over that boundary? Suddenly too cold, or with the air too thin—or might she drop like a stone when suddenly weighing far more?

And yet there was a very little trade with those who lived beyond the walls. It was precisely because they were so different that they had things Ambora could use but could not make, and for which they would accept Amboran surplus foods and certain minerals. She thought they were probably desperate for what was natural and pure and true. She could see in one of them, across that eerie border, the lights that had no fire and things moving far too fast for nature. The other was one of the in-betweens, but there was belching smoke rising up from their own coastal area, fouling their air.

It did not occur to her that those neighbors found a land smelling of sulfides and belching liquid rock and gases from below the earth as unpleasant and obnoxious as she found theirs. She was growing in power, but not in wisdom. It was something Core had understood but she did not. When one sees herself and her kind as the standard of perfection against which all else is measured, it is impossible to have perspective.

She kept high and to herself during her grand tour, using it as a meditative experience as much as a learning one. She fasted during the whole of it, taking just a small bit of water each evening, and avoided all others until she felt cleansed, renewed, and ready to return.

She wanted to go home to assume the duties of High Priestess and to minister to and serve the Grand Falcon clan. She was beginning to understand that events were not taking the course she might devoutly wish. If the gods wished her to serve in some different way, she could hardly avoid their will.

There were other sensations she was getting—in the air, in the ground, in the water. They seemed as coldly powerful as the gill creature, Core, only more pervasive. They were every-where, and it scared her. Forces she could not understand, pulses . . .

Numbers . . .

It was as if the whole land, the whole *world*, was related to numbers. The strings were far too complex for her to follow, and far too pervasive for her to take in, but she was aware that they formed patterns that wound in and out and through every particle of matter and energy.

The geometry of the gods. It was the universe. It was the rules by which the universe worked. It was what continually stabilized it—and everything within it.

An impossibly complex series came to her. It did not pass out, but instead went through to the very core of her material being.

She settled back on the side of a cliff and closed her eyes, trying to see this personal part with senses other than her sight. She gave up trying to decipher the patterns. Instead she tried to follow them mentally back down to the earth below, and through it, to its origin.

She followed it down, down, through layers of rock and what the rock sat upon, through depths of alien substance that could not be comprehended or sorted, down, down, to a center, a monstrous center, a cold, calculating, horrendous First Source, a Cause with no soul at its center but containing the souls beyond number . . .

She screamed in horror and passed out from the shock. It was more than she could handle, more than she could understand. Worst of all, it had sensed she was there. It had recognized just who and what she was, and it hadn't cared one whit . . .

A test of faith, she told herself. It must be a test of faith. I do not want this burden, but I am only a slave, the property of the gods. It is their will that I must accept.

Security Ministry, Chalidang

BARELY MOVING IN THE DEEP OCEAN WATERS, THEY STARED AT the screen.

Colonel General Sochiz of Cromlin appeared cocky and arrogant as he left his embassy and made his way through crowds toward the Well Gate. He pushed aside anybody who did not yield and ignored the stares. He did not care what anybody thought of him, and his great claws could cut steel rods if he was so inclined.

Josich would be so proud of him! The way they had looked as he had spoken! The way they had simply melted away as he strode off the platform, through the hall and out. That was fear, fear of power, and it felt most excellent.

When it was clear who he was, the others along the route gave way. No one, not even those who were larger and looked meaner than he, impeded his triumphal march.

He turned the corner and saw the utter blackness of the Gate directly ahead, its hexagonal shape unmistakable. He was almost to it when he suddenly realized that for this last, short stretch there was nobody in the corridor.

He stopped, suspicious. This was the way assassins worked. Well, let them come! Let them see he was not afraid of them!

A noise caused him to turn to the wall to his right, perhaps five meters in front of the Gate. It had no shape at first, but then took on a humanoid form that seemed to extrude right out of the wall. It looked like nothing he'd seen—almost like a moving idol from some primitive tribe. It was made completely of dull, rough, granitelike stone—a cartoonish, idiotic, and simplified face carved into it. Only the eyes said it was something more—the burning fire-orange eyes in the tranquil water—and the fact that it walked to him.

"Who are you who would block me?" the Cromlin general shouted. Both forward claws went up; one snatched at the creature while the tail reared up and the syringelike point at the end struck the head of the creature.

And broke off.

The creature reached up with a stony hand. It held the claw immobile, then grabbed the other. As the pain of losing the stinger hit the Cromlin's body, the creature ripped off the right claw and discarded it.

"You know my name," the creature said, in a tone that could only mean it had a translator. "Let it be the last thing you or any of your brothers hear."

"What name?" the creature screamed. "Who are you?"

"Jeremiah Wong Kincaid," came the reply, just before the second claw was ripped away. The stone right hand of the idol-like creature punched through the face of the Cromlin right between the protruding eyes and extended antennae, and kept going all the way into the brain.

It was a slow and messy way to die.

Just before stepping off into the Well Gate, Kincaid—if that was who it truly was—paused, turned, and located the monitoring camera. "Each of you in turn," he said in a tone all the more chilling for being so matter of fact, so cool and emotionless. "Josich, I could kill you at my pleasure, but that would be meaningless. I want you to see how I get the others, one by one, so that you live some time in abject fear. It is still not enough, but it will have to do. Monitor, see that the Chalidang get a copy of this, won't you?" And with that the creature vanished into the hex-shaped blackness.

Colonel General Mochida, Chief of State Security for the government of Chalidang, turned slowly in the water. His two huge yet oddly humanlike brown eyes protruded slightly from each side of his rigid-looking but surprisingly soft and pliant nautiluslike spiral shell. He looked at his subordinates. "Any luck yet on tracing the race?"

"No, sir. It almost has to be some northern race distorted

somewhat in the southern biospheres. There are some races who can do that sort of thing among those in the South, but they don't look like that, and a couple that come close to that appearance but have no abilities to hide or extrude. In fact, none are water breathers."

"Idiot!" Mochida snapped. "The appearance was obviously distorted, probably by some sort of disruptor shield. As to the North—even if we assume that for some reason we don't already know all of them as well as we know ourselves—at least in terms of the computer database, it's never happened. No carbon-based life pattern has ever been recast here as a northerner. No, he is playing some sort of trick on us, and we will have to find out what he is doing and counter it quickly. I want him in pieces! *Pieces!* I don't want any of the Empress's old family or associates, let alone Her Majesty, losing any sleep over this, understand?"

The others waved their tentacles in a manner approximating a Chalidang nod, but it seemed perfunctory and Mochida felt it.

"Perhaps I do not make myself clear," he added. "For every victim from this point on, one of you will die—a random choice. I want this bastard and I want him now!"

That put the fear of the gods into them! Not that they fully understood what fear was. Too many failures, and it would be Colonel General Mochida who would have to explain failure directly to the Empress.

"Enough of this," Mochida said abruptly, shifting gears. "We need to know how many pieces of our puzzle remain to be located."

This was something they felt more comfortable discussing.

"There are eight pieces, General. Three are already in our possession," one of the commanders told him. "Two more are probably attainable without military action. The two that are going to prove *difficult* are to the east—one in very secure circumstances in the eastern ocean, the other an object of apparent religious veneration on the far eastern continent. The last piece, I fear, we still have not located."

"We must find it! If we can secure it and the others, then

the rewards and power that await us will be as wondrous as the punishment for failure will be terrible. All the others were from here and to the east; I see no reason why the last piece should not be within the same region. There must be records, *something,* damn it! It was less than three hundred years ago that it was disassembled and scattered! All the others had some kind of record, some kind of trail."

"But most believe that the Straight Gate is only a legend!" one general protested. "It is difficult even to get taken seriously. Of necessity we must keep everyone outside our inner circles believing that it *is* a mere childish fable. If the others should ever get the idea that it is for real, then a coalition far greater than the one we now face would be turned against us, just as it was in the days of Jaz Hadun!"

"Subtlety is not the strong point of our race," Mochida admitted. "Still, treachery is, and that takes a great deal of talent and care. Let us concentrate on getting the other pieces as we search for this one. Do we at least know what it looks like?"

"Thanks to the drawings of the Empress of the other side, we have a reasonable idea," one of the staff officers replied. "There are only two sections—the religious relic and the highly secured piece—that we do not at least have a description of. That means it must be one of these two pieces, since the others are accounted for."

A tentacle swept over a hidden sensor. The top of a highly polished table, which was apparently made from gleaming coral, suddenly lit up. Another tap on a hidden control panel, and a design appeared as if etched into the table. It was actually a projection, but it looked real.

The design of the full Straight Gate was exotic, even though the interior was in the unsurprising shape of a hexagon with slightly rounded points. Around it was an ornate frame seemingly carved from some sort of ivory. It sat straight upright on a magnificent stylized carved base. There was no power supply; it didn't need one. The remote needed only to be on a world where once the Ancient Ones had lived and which still had an active Well Gate. It drew its power from that, while the one on the Well World side could draw its power from any Zone Gate. The controls themselves, like those in the viewing table, were hidden and obscure. Only one who knew where they were and what they did, and who could operate them as a Chalidanger might, could use them properly.

The colonel at the viewer controls tapped out another code, and the drawing of the Gate changed, reflecting the eight segments that composed it.

"They were afraid to destroy it because of the potential problems for power leakage and disruption," the colonel commented. "They had no knowledge of how it worked and had no one who could tell them. Jaz Hadun had taken everyone, including the designers, with him, and he'd left no known operator's manual, as it were. They broke it up into the eight segments from which it had been built—feeling safe enough to do that—and gave one segment to each of the eight in their alliance to safeguard both from us and from each other. To discourage others from trying to build something similar, they agreed that it would be referred to only as a mythical device, a legend, one that went with their victory but wasn't a part of the reality. If Jaz Hadun was not dead or in some sort of eternal limbo, then they felt this would prevent him and his party from ever returning, save through the Well Gate, where they could be dealt with. You can see how it broke down in the Empress's sketch here."

It was straightforward. The eight segments were assembled by some sort of magnetic system into the whole, but were easily twisted apart when the power was off.

Two segments were outlined—one a piece from the lower left side of the hexagonal opening's border, the other the top part of the base. "These are the two that are missing or are unaccounted for. What is not reflected here is the size of the thing. It's not *huge*, but the eight of us could probably swim through it at once, in a two-four-two formation."

That would make the upper base roughly four to five meters across its long side, and the missing side segment would be about a meter and a half, perhaps two.

Mochida's beak clicked like a telegraph, a nervous habit

when he was in deep thought. Finally he said, "I very much hope that our missing segment is part of the base. It will be much easier to recognize it than that side framing, which could be virtually anywhere and in anything. That makes finding out our secured segment that much more important."

"Well, yes, sir," the subordinate responded nervously, "but isn't that what the previous campaign was all about? Sanafe is a nontech hex in the middle of nowhere. Without Ochoa as a base, how can we hope to get in there with sufficient force and resources to find, or force them to find, what we require?"

"Well, if at first you do not succeed, try a different plan," Mochida told them. "The planning department has decided that if we can not use Ochoa, we must try a different route. Their Highnesses are quite keen on shifting to an alternate target for several obvious reasons, the least of which is the two small islands. You all know that we have a deep score to settle with Kalinda."

"Yes, but high-tech defense against a high-tech attack is risky. They need only hold. That is an ancient lesson learned long ago on the Well World."

"Yes, it is more complex, which is why Ochoa was the preferred route," Mochida admitted. "Still, it is possible. If the air-breather allies can establish themselves in Bludarch, Kalinda is a far easier target. We are already working with some allies there. Their government is weak and corrupt, their society fat, lazy, complacent. With an adequate supply base and simple chain, and the understanding that *this* time they will not be dealing with the limited Quacksans or lock-step Jirminins, but with the best soldiers of Chalidang—I believe it is a *very* attainable goal."

Kalindan—Yabbo Border

DID YOU EVER FEEL LIKE BAIT?

Ari knew just exactly what Ming meant by that. *Frequently. Like now.*

They had indeed had some training back in Kalinda with the police and intelligence agencies, but these only gave them some general idea of what their destinations might be like, and some additional hand-to-hand defensive training for their underwater environment. On the basics, they knew far more than their instructors did, and seemed to have more experience and fewer scruples as well. Still, it wasn't lost on either of them that sending a single unescorted non-native into other countries and environments wasn't the best way to gather information and ensure it would get back to whomever needed it. No, clearly they were wanted out of Kalinda for some reason by both the Powers That Be and Core. Anyone working for their enemies would have no doubt whatsoever why they were there. They weren't even provided with cover identities or a cover mission; in effect, they were simply being sent on a journey to the nations bordering Kalinda to get "experience."

Think anybody is gonna be fooled that maybe we're off on some desperate mission or something and drop all plans to target Kalinda? Ming asked sarcastically.

It seems to me that Josich was known to be ruthless, amoral, merciless, dishonorable, and that's just for starters, but never *did I hear him described as stupid. Nor were his agents incompetent, either.*

Think they expect us to get back alive? Ming asked her partner in mind.

Probably not. I don't think they're out to kill us, though. I think they just don't give a damn.

That was probably the hardest idea to accept. The object was to get rid of them, and maybe distract some enemy agents, but it wasn't in the hope that they could really divine anything of importance. Somebody just wanted them out of Kalinda.

Kalinda's "highways" were marked by varying colored strings of a naturally occurring substance that could be "tuned" to any depth. It stayed in place by means of treating it with certain magnetic properties. The combination of color and depth allowed anyone to travel almost anywhere in the hex without getting lost or disoriented once they had the code. Some were strictly for motorized traffic, others for swimmers. Although Kalindans were not dependent on sight and could be comfortable at depths of at least a thousand meters— depths that would crush many organisms not born and bred to those levels—they were a high-tech people, with the usual overdependence of such advanced races on their technology over their natural abilities. As such, vision was a commonly used sense, particularly at the levels at which the majority spent their lives.

Much of Kalinda was a series of high plateaus and underwater tablelands; while the valleys went very deep, they weren't wide. The cities in which most people lived were, on average, no more than 350 meters down.

Coming from an even higher technological society, Ari and Ming had felt fairly comfortable in the Kalindan cities. Out here there was only the crisscrossing colored lines to show the routings in three-dimensional space.

There was some traffic. Most motorized transport was in the one to two hundred meter range, between towns, so it would be both out of the way of most swimming traffic and also fairly easy to maintain at a decent pressure. And, as in most technological civilizations, ancient roadways that were the underwater equivalent of long-range footpaths did not have very many people on them. Most took the trains or rented motorized scooters.

They were not more than half a day out from the Kalindan capital of Jinkinar and already they were the only ones on the road. Not that they *felt* alone; out here, away from the noise of the city, it was louder than ever.

The water was filled with sounds of all kinds. Loud sounds, soft sounds, clicks, whirs, whooshes, even the sounds of unknown beasts and the calls of bizarre creatures they weren't sure they wanted to meet. These, combined with the rumbles and motor noises and whines from the steady powered traffic a hundred meters above them, made it almost a cacophony of confused tones.

This was where not being a native caused problems. Anyone who was born and raised a Kalindan would know what the sounds were, and which were worth attention. No quick course in Kalindan wildlife could possibly substitute for that experience.

They did quickly learn about some minor noises. The windlike rushing of a school of colorful if exotic-looking fish, for example, was quite handy. Anyone who needed to could eat on the fly. Virtually all the fish in the region—except a few untouchables—were quite edible.

When the Well World made someone into one of its own 1,560 races, it did so with a balance; certain things it gave as if one were native, so that he or she stood a good chance of surviving. Experience, however, it could not give.

Ari decided to test out some Kalindan abilities while still in friendly territory. Closing his large, round eyes, which could convert the smallest light into usable views, he allowed the other senses of their shared body to take control. It was easy to use them, but much more difficult to interpret them.

The sounds were part of it, of course—as much a distraction as a help—but they were peculiarly localized in time and space. Even if he didn't know what was making most of them, he found it relatively easy to estimate how far away they were and in what direction they were moving.

And then there were the sounds he could make. They emanated from a small protruberance on the face, about where a conventional air breather's nose would be, and they were quite distinctive—or, more properly, *it* was quite distinctive. A long, pulsing, high-pitched sound well above the range of their old human hearing, it was caught not just by the ears but by other bodily sensors and sent to the brain for interpretation. It illuminated everything within thirty to forty meters around them. It was constant, like having unblinking eyes that could see in all directions at once. The images the sonar-like system sent to the brain were not interpreted as pictures, but were so recognizable that they might as well have been. Rocky outcrops from below, the route lines, fish, small crustaceans, anything at all was clearly defined. The brain also did some kind of math that neither Ari nor Ming could have done consciously. By simply concentrating on a single fish, they instantly knew its size, shape, speed, and even type. It was easy to track and catch.

Finally, there was what Kalindans called their "sixth" sense. Rather than telepathy, it allowed them to sense changes in both the planetary and even the individual organism's magnetic field. It oriented them and also revealed anything nasty that might be waiting beneath the sand or disguised in one of the reefs or rocky outcrops.

This sixth sense wasn't unusual among water-breathing races, but was unlike anything Ari and Ming had experienced before. Kalinda had long ago been relieved of any predators who could threaten Kalindans, but out in the rest of the world, where things didn't work by Kalindan rules, the sixth sense was one of their most vital abilities.

Why didn't we just rent one of those motor scooters at least as far as the border? Ming complained.

Because they didn't offer one, and we've precious little in the way of money or lines of credit, as you well know, Ari responded. *Besides, I seem to remember someone telling them that it would be good to practice in Kalinda before leaving it, and that they needed the exercise.*

Don't rub it in!

The hardest thing about being a Kalindan, Ari reflected, was thinking in three dimensions. Walking in a normal situation back in the Commonwealth was essentially a two-dimensional affair; he didn't look up unless someone yelled, and he concentrated on one direction at a time. To go up, he needed some kind of aid, such as stairs or a lift. This was more like being in space without the suit. He floated, not on top but *within* the environment, and he could rise or drop as easily as going backward or forward. To do this without a suit or suit controls was unnerving in and of itself.

It took them three days to reach the border, lazily testing out their new abilities, exploring the region, and resting in small towns along the way. Things had sufficient sameness so that Ming began to wonder how they would know that they'd crossed the border at all.

She needn't have worried.

All the senses save sight saw it as a massive brick wall. No matter how wide the spray, sonar bounced off it and gave the impression of a monstrous structure that was both solid and impenetrable. The magnetic-field sense showed it as a single solid shield. There was yet another sense—that the border was a static electromagnetic field.

But sight showed that it was not solid, but some sort of energy barrier. They could see through it, but there seemed little to see. It looked dark and murky, and if there was anything solid beyond, it was blurred and indistinct.

A small Customs station sat on a narrow rock outcrop at the end of the fluorescent "road" they had been following. Clearly, the route and the lighting stopped there, in a small boxy structure that probably provided its initial power. They discovered that the other building was a small inn and Customs processing center combined. Of course, they could easily penetrate the border at routes not covered by these stations, but non-Kalindans stuck out like sore thumbs. They couldn't buy anything or rent a room or even get a ticket without valid encoded visas. They saw that the place was deliberately overly bright on the "wall" side, probably so that anyone coming into the country would see it. Above, other "roads" for more elaborate and motorized traffic converged onto a much larger center.

Yabbo was a semitech hex; no one could use the sleek electric scooters beyond this point, or the big fusion rigs that moved heavy freight.

Doesn't look like there's a similar station on the other side of the barrier or whatever that thing is, Ari noted. *I wonder if Yabbo is as bureaucratic?*

Depends on what the hell they are, Ming responded pragmatically. *Besides, steam engines wouldn't be much use down here.*

That was true, although there were a lot of other things that could be done in a semitech hex, even underwater. Many of the underwater semitech hexes were said to have substantial volcanic activity, for instance, which could be harnessed.

It was in the Customs house that they saw their first Yabban, and they were definitely—different.

It had an exoskeleton, which glowed from some inner light and yet seemed transparent. They could have sworn they were looking at a smudged or unclear X ray. The creature had long, thin, plierlike claws in front that appeared to be mounted on natural ball joints and seemed to be able to turn any which way; the claw itself could also revolve as needed around its wrist joints. Four long, spindly legs, two on each side, were in back of the claws. At the rear, on each side of the back end, was an incongruous-looking pair of flippers. The head seemed nothing more than two independent eye stalks, and beneath them was a round orifice filled with what seemed to be constantly writhing little tentacles, although a close look showed two gill slits on either side.

There were others in the Customs station, and so they could see two Yabban types. One was slightly smaller than the other, and had a translucent waving membrane on top of the head which changed color through a series of pastel hues. Clearly two sexes, although which sex was which was impossible to tell.

"I have been dealing with the Corithian Sons Company since I apprenticed my trade," a Yabban was saying to a Kalindan Customs officer as they drew closer. Ari and Ming had seen pictures and gotten a basic briefing on all the neighboring hexes, but that wasn't the same as seeing a Yabban in the flesh. At least after all that time with the other races in South Zone, the odd workings of the translator modules no longer seemed strange. The Yabban sounded just like a Kalindan to them, even though they could not imagine where any conversational sounds could emerge from it.

Maybe they didn't. Who knew what Yabbans actually sounded like to each other?

"I know, I know," the Customs officer responded, sounding exasperated. "You are a well-known trader, Citizen Slagha. But pending clearance from the Security Service, I must hold you and your family here. It is nothing aimed at you; it is *everybody* who is going through this. We are having a serious problem at the moment and we must take extra precautions."

"Indeed?" the Yabban snapped, those thousands of little tentacles around its mouth almost frenzied in pulsing movement. "And what of *my* customers? We cannot make the level of refined tubing we require, and a whole new subdivision is awaiting the shipment. Suddenly nothing is going out or coming in without going through this horror of a bureaucracy!"

"I'm so *very* sorry, but it's the war, you know—"

"Don't give me that!" the Yabban snapped. "That skirmish is over anyway!"

Ari and Ming decided not to dwell on the conversation but rather to go into the small, nearby café and get the gossip from Kalindans who were coming back home via this road house. It was odd how quickly and easily "us" meant the leathery-skinned reptilian mer-people and how everybody else had become "them."

It didn't take long to get a general picture of where they were going. There were no roads in the Kalindan sense, but Yabbans had laid out a series of markers using a grid system that could be "read" by the magnetic "sixth" sense. The numbers and directional signals would tell how far one was from anyplace in the hex and also the direction to go for major habitation.

The water was said to be far warmer and the sea floor on the whole much shallower than Kalinda's, although there were a few narrow "deeps" which the Yabbans reserved for their own use and which they guessed might have something to do with reproduction. It was suggested that all Kalindans stay away from the deeps. If they proved unavoidable, they should be crossed quickly and at a high level.

There were plenty of nutrients in the water, and the microscopic plants and tiny animals were filling, if not very interesting to a Kalindan. There was a lower oxygen content in the water, but not enough to cause serious problems.

Other than that, the Yabbans tended to be fairly friendly if visitors didn't abuse their hospitality or overstay a welcome. Their rear flippers gave them tremendous sprinting abilities, but they preferred walking across the bottom. Essentially vegetarians, they had long ago gotten rid of the predators that once stalked the area.

Politically, they were a nation of large families, or clans, with a hierarchical structure based on age. There were no old age homes. When a Yabban became mentally feeble, there was a great clan ceremony. The ranking Elder who was no longer capable was taken in, slain, and ritually eaten by his or her clan. It was the only meat they ever ate and, it seemed, the only kind they could digest. It was a sobering end; from lord to lunch.

I don't find growing old in that society to be very fulfilling, Ari commented.

Appetizing, though, Ming shot back. *If you've got the stomach for it.*

Their next step was to cross over into the hex. They wondered if Chalidang activity would be as conspicuous in such a place as they would be.

A friendly salesman gave them a fair route map marked with the main city centers, as well as a decent route to the capital city of Abudan. It also noted the deeps and ways around them—and, interestingly, some large cautionary zones.

"Volcanoes," the salesman explained. "They're quite active in Yabbo. That's what makes things so rich and also provides a lot of comforts. You'll see. And don't worry, you won't be surprised by them—you'll know where not to go without anybody having to yell!"

They stayed over for a last native meal and a few hours rest in one of the road house cubicles, then felt ready to venture outside Kalinda for the first time.

Approaching the hex boundary was intimidating, since all of their senses told them it was an absolute barrier from the sea floor up through and past the surface. They watched as a few Kalindans emerged from Yabbo and headed toward the road house, and some Yabban natives did the opposite. It seemed effortless. There was nothing to do but to try it.

Going through the barrier had, curiously, little sensation. There was only a slight tingling, almost like passing through a very thin wall of cobwebs. Much more dramatic was the sudden shift in all their natural senses.

Kalindan water temperature, comfortable to them, was fairly cold for active ocean water; it varied only slightly, from five to seven degrees C. With their natural fatty insulation under that thick, leathery hide, it felt very nice indeed. But this water was very warm and would take some getting used to. The sounds and smells were different as well. It meant trying to sort out things all over again. There was a kind of distant roar that seemed unplaceable, and many other unfamiliar noises amidst the usual sonic bedlam. The water tasted sulfuric. Vision was okay but slightly clouded. The magnetic field sense, once away from the border wall, showed tiny things all around them, in the millions or even billions, numerous and thick. They felt as if the water was alive.

And it *was* alive. Even those tiniest of pinhead signals was coming from a concentration of microorganisms that seemed omnipresent. They couldn't help but take them in with the water they breathed. As they swam, their stomach and digestive tract seemed to fill with them as well. They had to slow down so as not to choke on the food they were consuming.

Reminds me of Malacanus, Ming commented. *Tropical but so bug-infested you needed a diving mask just to filter out the little bugs. Ever get there?*

No, but I know what you mean. Never thought I'd consider putting in a food screen across my mouth, though.

Going slower was soon something they chose for other reasons as well. There was in fact less oxygen. They didn't really notice it at first, but swimming suddenly required more of an effort. They breathed harder to take in more oxygen, which, of course, meant that they also took in more of the microoganisms.

They began struggling, and the thought in both their minds was that perhaps they should turn around and get back into Kalinda while they still could. They were about to do just that when they heard someone nearby say, "First time in Yabbo, I take it?"

They could hardly reply, but Ari turned and saw a fellow Kalindan floating, who seemed to have no problems at all. Ari managed to nod.

"Put your teeth together so they mesh but don't clench," the stranger instructed. "Let whatever is in your throat settle and go down a bit, and breathe normally through the teeth until you feel more like yourself."

They tried it, and it did help, but it also seemed a temporary solution.

"Once you're feeling better, close your mouth and relax it," the stranger went on. "Don't breathe through it. I know it goes against your instincts, but force yourself. You'll get used to it. Wait a little bit and see what happens. It's a trick they never tell you about."

Little happened at first, and then their slitlike nostrils opened and began taking in water. Since these had heretofore only been used to breathe air into what passed for lungs when they were out of the water, there was a natural tendency to override and squelch this. At the stranger's urging they fought it and quickly discovered that indeed the nostrils acted as a kind of bellows, and the water intake went not to the chest but to the gills. It wasn't like air breathing; there was no exhalation. That function was taken over by the gills. Still, it worked. After a couple of minutes, they found the rhythm and it did seem to get much easier.

"Thank you, citizen!" Ari called to the stranger.

The Kalindan chuckled. "Just remember to swim only with your mouth shut and only speak when you're hovering, and you'll be okay," she assured them. "To eat, just do it the old way. Makes it real cheap and easy to get through here, which is a good thing since we couldn't eat anything the natives do anyway. Take it slow and easy, though. The nostril system does not deliver as much volume as the usual mouth method, and you're dealing with lower oxygen content here as it is."

Ari managed another nod. "Are you going into the country?" he asked the stranger.

"No, coming out. I've been here ten days, and that's more than enough in this boiling kettle."

Ari was grateful to the other for saving them from retreat or worse right at the start, but Ming was already at the next level and took over. The personality differences between them even in casual speech sometimes threw people. If the stranger noticed, however, she was nice enough not to react, or more likely put it down to their recovering from the initial problem and panic.

"Where did you come from, then, if I might ask?" Ming began.

"Abudan," the stranger replied. "We've been designing a new transport line."

"Transport line? I thought you couldn't use any fancy technology here." Both Ming and Ari were intrigued.

"This must be your first time outside Kalinda," the other, an engineer, guessed. "Otherwise you wouldn't confuse innovation with high energy sources. This is a volcanic place, and it's *very* active. Our biggest problem with closed systems is dealing with seaquakes when lava shifts or steam creates new outlets. We can tap that energy, though—it's quite natural, and it's so steady in the volcanic fields that we can do wonders with it. All you need is pressure and a way to control it and you have useful power. Give me useful power and you have machinery that can do a lot. Remember, the limitations imposed on the hexes were originally put in to simulate the properties of other worlds far away so that they might support the creatures who dominate there. Getting around these sorts of environmental handicaps was part of the exercise. Of course, now, and for millennia, we've been on our own, so we can cheat guilt-free. They have shipped massive tons of this seafood garden to Kalinda since we grew too lazy to remain self-sufficient in food, as well as a number of minerals that are nuisances here but very useful in our manufacturing and even medical systems. We make conduits and pipes and other things that make their lives easier here, and can be run using only their technology. We all benefit."

It sounded clear and simple, and gave the best, succinct examples of how the international and even interspecies economy worked.

"Do we do this with all our neighbors?" Ming asked her.

"Well, most of them. And some much farther off. We even trade some things with nations halfway around the world. That's what those anchorages are for up top. There are some hexes, though, that just don't have anything we want or need, or we don't have anything they want or need, or they're just so downright spooky and strange that we can't deal with them. I'm told there are some races that shun all contact, that don't even send ambassadors to Zone."

"That brings up an interesting point," Ari put in. "If you were in Abudan, there was a Zone Gate right there. How come you didn't just use *that* to come home?"

The engineer laughed. "You must work for the government! Most ordinary folks can't use those routes unless it's a life or death situation. If we all did, why, the areas in and out of Zone would be crushed with people from all over and nobody could ever use them in an emergency or for diplomatic work. We *do* occasionally use them to ship delicate or time-sensitive stuff, but we have to set it up way in advance, on off-peak hours, using Yabban crews propositioned in Kalinda. The paperwork alone is a nightmare. No, I'm perfectly happy to go this way. After all, it's only a few hours by tube to Banu City, just a kilometer or so back. After I clear here, I'll pick up a company scooter and be in the office by midday tomorrow at the latest."

"Um—excuse me? *Tube?*"

"Yes. It *does* cost, and you'll have to get your money changed, but it's pretty reasonable. Fast, too. My company built this line decades ago." She looked at the watch strapped to her wrist. "My goodness! Glad to have been of help, but I really *must* be going!"

"Oh, that's all right. But this—tube . . . ?"

The engineer was already heading away toward the hex boundary. "Don't worry. You'll see what I mean! Good fortune in your venture, whatever it is!"

They watched her go, once more alone and regretting it.

So, you want to see what she meant? Ari asked.

Might as well, Ming responded. *Since we're going that way anyway.*

It may have been little more than a kilometer to Banu City, but it took them a couple of hours to get there while they got used to the vastly different and very alien environment and the new way to breathe. Compensating for the lower oxygen content was much like it would have been for high altitude work back in the Terran universe from which they'd come.

I wonder if it's this hard for air breathers to cross a border up top? Ari mused.

I doubt it. Altitude and maybe temperature, but I doubt if there's anyplace where the air is so filled with food that you die of gluttony by simply breathing normally, she replied.

Ain't that *the truth!*

Still, they did make it to the city using the magnetic routing lines and the grids.

Banu City was actually only a small town by Yabban or any other standards, but it certainly was impressive nonetheless.

Impossible to ignore was the smell and taste of sulfurous compounds in the water. They stung the eyes and gills and any minor cuts or scrapes.

It was not a town either Ari or Ming would feel comfortable living in for other reasons entirely. Even in the murky water, it spread out before them in an alien design. Broad boulevards were clearly designed for a species that liked to walk rather than swim. Large but low buildings no more than four stories tall were designed by and for nothing vaguely humanoid. The town was lit in varying colors by what could only be some sort of chemical secretions, whether natural or artificial, that were mixed and matched for shade and brightness and applied where needed. The streets were clearly outlined in bright green lights, the buildings in varying reddish hues. The Yabbans were all over the place, crowding central squares and going in and out of building entrances with such speed and sense of purpose it reminded both of them less of a city—Terran or Kalindan—than of an insect colony.

Of greater interest were numerous long, thin transparent tubes. They went in and out of every building and crossed streets overhead. Things were routed inside the tubes at great speed as they went into and out of rooftop level enclosures. Since they were much too small to be the transportation tubes the Kalindan engineer had been referring to, it took several minutes and a much closer look before Ari and Ming realized what they were.

Some kind of high pressure piping! Ari noted, amazed, as he watched a Yabban at street level insert something into a small cylinder, open a branch tube, put it in, then use a claw to press a lever. There was a hiss and some bubbling and the small cylinder suddenly took off and joined the main route. As it passed the point of the lever, the yellow-painted bar shot back up on its own, closing off the start.

Wonder how it knows where it's going? Ming mused.

Must be in those little houses up top. Somebody's throwing switches, maybe based on color codes. We'll never know, I suspect. Translators allow us to speak to these folks like natives and be understood the same way, but they don't teach us how to read Yabban.

And, as they were learning, just because you heard somebody as if they were a native didn't mean that you could understand what they said. Creatures like the Yabbo were quite alien to Kalindans.

Still, it wasn't its incomprehensibility that made the town one they didn't feel comfortable in, but rather what it was built upon and what lay just beyond it. It was an active volcano, and blotted out much of anything beyond to the south.

Much of the activity was coming off the sides of the mountain—smoking, hissing, and often exploding. It was unnerving, almost as unsettling as the fact that the town was built on a lava flow right up against that mountain.

You think they can predict when it'll go off? Ming wondered.

Probably. I'd say these folks had to be experts if this is the way they live. Otherwise there wouldn't be any Yabbans around by now. They must not hear like we do, though. Those explosions would not only keep you awake, they'd drive you batty.

In a layer of construction between the town and the volcanic activity there were large artificial works: towers, spirals, pyramids, and cubes. Much of it had the look and feel of Kalindan construction. Even through the murkiness they could see how large the industrial works were, and they could also see networks of cables going along the floor of the sea in all directions.

There's the answer. Power, Ari noted. *Natural steam power harnessed and directed through pressure regulators anywhere else they wanted. Pressure to run turbines or move heavy machinery or even generate electrical fields.* The "rules" prevented batteries from working here, but apparently not transformers, as there were several large ones just at the edge of the town. They couldn't store it, but they could use the steam power so long as the volcano and the molten magma beneath them remained active.

Ari and Ming decided to move around the city rather than through it, at least for now. There didn't seem to be much reason to go there at the moment, and the noise was deafening.

I hope all the cities and towns aren't like this, Ming commented. *Otherwise we'll have no hearing left by the time we get through this place.*

Unfortunately, their helpful Kalindan friend had forgotten to tell them to get earplugs or sound dampers. On the east side, though, they did find the tube that their kinsman had spoken about—and it truly *was* obvious.

Just as the town seemed to be shipping small parcels, messages, and the like through a miniature steam-pressure-powered pneumatic tube system, there was another, similar system that was even more impressive because it was designed for people.

That is, for Yabbo's people, anyway.

Although it drew power from the volcanic fields, it did so indirectly via the industrial works and transformers and whatever else was in those buildings. The giant tube appeared to them as a solid gigantic pipe when viewed through most of their senses, although their vision said it was the same sort of translucent material as the smaller parcel network. Clearly, a magnetic substance formed a thin coating inside the tubes. The "cars"—which looked more like oblong shaped pills—also had a coating, but of opposite polarity. When one was pushed by a pressurized rod into position to inject into the tube, it appeared to be just smaller all around than the tube. It hovered, not quite touching the sides. The craft was then in a condition that approximated weightlessness, and it didn't take a lot of force to propel it along those tubes. The vehicle coating itself appeared inert; the tube coating seemed to get some power from a steam turbine. That was how it was controlled. Section by section they could apply power and therefore create an electromagnetic field, or remove power, at which point the vehicle would skid to a halt using friction and perhaps some sort of purely mechanical braking.

It was, in effect, a national train system for moving cargo and people, in a hex that was prevented from employing the highest technology and was also underwater. It was damned clever.

It's also on the least active side of the volcano, Ari noted. *The sea grasses and other growths there go right on up the side of the mountain. This is old lava here.*

Ming was thinking it over, and finally mused, *I wonder how much they want for a foreigner to ride it? And do we have the guts to do just that?*

I don't know about you, but if we have enough money at all, I'm for it. Anything to get away from this land of the constant headache!

Where you go, I go, and vice versa, Ming remarked.

Quislon

IT WAS A BLEAK LANDSCAPE, MORE LIKE THE SURFACE OF AN-other planet than any of the hexes he'd seen so far. The land was reds and yellows and purples, with distorted and menacing shadows. More disorienting was that there were no flat places; he was always going up or down. In some ways it reminded him of a frozen ocean in the midst of a storm.

There was water here, though not a lot of liquid on the surface. Beneath it, water was evident; and here and there on the taller hills and on the distant mountains there was plenty of glistening snow.

Then there was the wind.

It whistled through the cracks and crevices, the dips and valleys, always present, always singing its eerie songs. It actually interfered with his deceptively good hearing. More important, he could *taste* the wind. It brought him a great deal of information, but it was distorted, chopped up and mixed as things should never be mixed by the infinite number of paths that wind took before hitting him. It made the information less useful than he'd have liked.

Still, this was just the sort of place his own kind was good at operating in. Having eaten before entering this desolate hex, he had no particular need of food for perhaps a week or more. He could survive with what little moisture condensed at night on the rocks. His eyes could adjust almost instantly to the changing light from the land and its eerie and unnatural sunlight, or operate by the light of just a few stars.

In some ways Pyrons resembled nothing so much as giant cobras. Certainly the enormous head—with its exotic eyes and pulsating hood—gave that impression, and the tongue—with its added sensors that could literally taste the air and parse its odors—darted in and out as necessary. Beyond the hood, though, were a series of thin, tentaclelike arms ending in small serrated pincers, and along its back were two folded leathery appendages that seemed to be wings. In fact, Pyrons weren't fliers, but could glide from heights if they had to. Their wings were primarily repositories for even more specialized sensory organs, and also had the ability to gather and amplify sounds from very far off. Under optimum conditions, he could receive certain signals specific to him across an entire hex, even if that hex were Pyron itself and filled with millions of his kind receiving similar signals.

He had the wings folded now because the windy conditions here made them more trouble than they were worth. His people had a listening post just inside Quislon that he could use for a help call or to report what he could if he himself was unable to make it back. They would send anything new to him at a prearranged time of day, but that was the limit of his technological abilities here. Pyron was a semitech hex in which only what could be directly powered was allowed. The technology here was very basic indeed. If they had anything as advanced as waterwheels, they were buried well underground, although now and again he'd come across a windmill, apparently pumping water up to usable levels.

The Quislonians didn't much show themselves on this bleak surface, either, although in areas of dense population one could see their pyramids of stone, brick, or mud. The natives had to spend a good deal of time building and maintaining the structures—some of which were impressive in size, but all of which were under constant attack from weathering. He'd seen little activity around, but he could occasionally hear them when going over the ground around a group of pyramids. They made rustling and chattering high-pitched sounds. It seemed as if, just below him, there was a constant rush hour.

Maybe there was. His briefing books said the Quislonians resembled an insectlike hive society, although unlike any he'd ever known. He was assured that a single Quislonian, while remaining part of the collective hive, could still converse on things like the weather or the state of the world's economy. It was just impossible to be sure if he were indeed talking to an individual or to all of them.

Yet that sort of thing wasn't uncommon among all the races of the Well World he'd been in contact with, including his own. He had found the superficial civilization fairly straightforward, but just below the surface there were whole layers of culture and belief systems that he hadn't grasped or been given access to yet.

The Pyrons were individuals, bisexual, and, despite their appearance, warm-blooded. He didn't feel they were nearly as alien as *these* people.

The pyramids sure weren't the kind he'd seen on a hundred worlds where critters instinctively built structures from natural elements as homes or forts. No, the Quislonians clearly built these as *buildings*. However, since their whole city structure was underground, they couldn't be using them the same way other folks did. Although the structures were similar, each one had something individualistic about it. He'd not seen two exactly the same.

Occasionally the top stone would be left off, creating a small flat top; other times there would be a small square or rectangular or triangular building on it. They were made of different materials and used planned color schemes, often with what were, to him, abstract designs on their sides. There were step types, blocky types, smooth types. The best guess from those who'd sent him was that each represented a family or clan or perhaps a complete tribe within the city.

Perhaps each represented a single mass mind within a hive?

That would make the place he was moving into now the home of maybe tens of thousands of Quislonians but only . . . hmmm . . . one, two, three, four—seven "individuals"? Interesting idea, if true. It still amazed him that, after all the hundreds of thousands of years since this world had been built by the Ancients, there were any questions at all about other races and cultures, let alone ones that were neighbors. Of course,

Pyron and Quislon hadn't exactly been friendly for much of that time.

The Quislonians, it seemed, made excellent one-course dinners for the Pyrons.

That, of course, was in the past. Everybody was so *civilized* now. Still, he could understand why Quislonians never felt completely comfortable around the Pyrons, and why, therefore, he was out here in the middle of nowhere all alone instead of with local experts.

If he were some sort of throwback, he might swallow a few dozen of them, but they would overwhelm him. When predator seeks an accommodation with past prey, it's always essential that the former prey at least feel that they have the advantage.

The more he got in among the buildings, the more he realized how large a complex this particular one was. His pyramid count had been shockingly low; coming over a rise, he saw the tops of all sorts of pyramids going out in all directions as far as he could see, flanking a huge mountain right in the center of things.

It appeared to be the remnants of some ancient volcanic extrusion; it was coal-black in a land of reds, yellows, oranges, and purples, and it was a solitary behemoth, rising perhaps nine hundred meters into the sky and stretching out for several kilometers at its base. Although rough-hewn and irregular after being weathered for so long, it kept the vague shape of a pyramid. Whether it had been carved by the labor of millions or it simply had weathered into its current form was impossible to guess, but it gave an idea as to why the shape so dominated here.

There were higher if more conventional mountains in the ranges to the north and to the west, but this was the sort of freak of nature that started religions in places. His briefings said it was called simply the Center, and that somewhere at its base was the Quislon Zone Gate going right into it. Now *that's* one to give a shaman power!

Somewhere here, too, was a sacred relic, something these creatures venerated as much or more than the pyramids and the

Center. Nobody knew why they thought it was sacred, but it always translated that way, with awe and veneration attached.

How did one disguised in the shape of a past enemy gain information about such a venerated object? He wasn't sure. He only knew that agents of the Chalidang had been sparing no expense on research in Zone and elsewhere to find things that appeared to resemble what the old records said was the Quislon sacred object. He had to find out just what this meant before the forces so recently defeated could regroup and move on it.

There wasn't much else to do. Guessing that the three major finishes of pyramids represented specific classes or castes, and that, from the elaborateness of the side designs, smooth outranked rough or steep, he chose the largest tall, smooth, ornate pyramid he could find closest to the sacred mountain. He circled around, using all his senses, spreading his wings for the first time to use everything in his arsenal. After a few minutes he sensed a thermal difference between the rest of the pyramid and the outside air at ground level. There were other such spots all over the place, which probably were vents of some sort, but this one was different. This one, he was positive, had to be a door.

It was shaped like a hexagon.

There seemed nothing else to do. Moving up to it, Genghis O'Leary extended one of his long, thin arms and knocked as hard as he could.

He felt a little foolish doing so; the surface of the pyramid looked and felt like any of the other pieces of polished rock used to sheath the exterior, although it was well off center. The only reason he thought it might be a disguised door was the thermal pattern. Even if it was, who could hear a knock like this on that kind of rock? He was pretty good at crushing, but those old jackhammer fists were history, left with wherever his old body might be, if it was at all.

He could hear, though, that they knew he was out here. Most likely they had some sort of system that had kept him under observation ever since he entered this place, waiting to see what he was going to do. He counted on it, in fact.

There was a pause, as he'd also expected. More rustling went under him and up and into the pyramid's base. The stone seemed to jiggle, then it moved. In an elaborate groove system. It was pulled in and slid into a carved notch in the much thicker stone to his right. There was a sudden blast of warm air, and a Quislonian emerged from the apparent darkness beyond.

It stood about a meter high on all six legs. Its color was an unremarkable pinkish-gray, its skin or possibly soft exoskeleton had a smooth and slightly wet look to it. Its head was on a retractable neck that appeared to be able to turn most of the way around and rise from a notch in the body—elevating the head another thirty or so centimeters or leaving it facing forward as an extension of the body. It was no beauty: there were four horns, two long, two short, atop an oval mouth that seemed to have wriggling worms where teeth might be, constantly in motion and dripping some kind of wet ooze. O'Leary wasn't at all certain whether two of the soft horns were eyes and two ears. In the end, except for the sake of politeness, it didn't really matter.

"What brings you here, Pyron?" the creature asked.

He saw nothing extra move, nor heard much in the way of background sounds save a kind of modulated hum, so he wasn't sure just how these things spoke, either. If they were group minds, it probably didn't matter anyway.

"I'm sorry to intrude, but you leave your embassy empty at Zone, giving us no choice but to enter your land to speak with you," he responded, trying to seem calm and natural. He had the sense and sounds of thousands of these things lurking all around him, not just in the pyramids but also just beneath his feet. They were certainly burrowers and tunnelers. Although he'd had these sensations to one degree or another during the two days traveling here, the danger to him never seemed as acute as it did now. He hadn't felt this nervous since the night he'd arrested the Commonwealth Security Minister in his own office.

"We have no need for much contact with the outside, and when we do, we initiate it," the creature responded.

"You are aware of the war just fought to the west of here?"

"We are. It is none of our concern."

He took a deep breath. "I'm afraid it is. We have been monitoring the communications of the Chalidang Alliance. While much of it is in codes we can't decipher, we have been able to deduce patterns in their communications that correspond to activities by their agents elsewhere. Recently, a good deal of interest has been shown in Quislon."

"Deduced, you say. Nothing more?"

"We are good at our jobs, and some of the finest minds on this world are working on this, aided by the most capable computing devices. Even with some subterfuge to confuse us, we feel confident that they are looking very closely at—at a minimum—Quislon, Sanafe, Pegiri, and Regeis. Do you or anyone in your own authorities know why those four radically different hexes would be of interest to Chalidang? Two land, two sea, none close, none the slightest bit related to one another; the only connection we can find is the not very remarkable fact that none are high-tech hexes."

The Quislonian froze for several seconds, as if thinking or, perhaps, discussing this with others through some kind of link. It startled O'Leary by suddenly extruding two rather hard and mean-looking arms from inside its wriggling mouth. At the end of each of the arms was a series of tiny suckers on softer tissue that extended from the harder mandibles. The Pyron watched in surprise as the creature seemed to begin spitting into the two small tentacles. As it did so, it upchucked a gummy substance which the mandibles furiously shaped and manipulated in a way too fast and too complex to see. Still, between the two softer "fingers," or whatever they were, there quickly grew, well . . .

A rock. No, not a rock. A slate. A slate as smooth and as polished as the sides of this particular pyramid. And on the slate, with sounds like glass cutters at work, the thing was drawing.

It was finished in just a few minutes, but held it carefully. The slate was drying out fast, but still seemed fragile and a bit wet. The Quislonian turned it around.

The drawing, as precise as any blueprint or engineering drawing O'Leary had ever seen, was of a structure that resembled an old-fashioned mirror or faceless clock, or an award one's superiors gave in lieu of a bonus—an antique, ornate-looking frame sitting atop a neo-Victorian rectangular base. About the only thing that seemed to relate it to the Well World was that the center part was hexagonal.

"Have any of your people seen this?" the Quislonian asked.

"I do not believe so," he told the creature honestly. "What is it?"

"It is the most sacred relic of all that has remained in this world," the creature replied. "You take this drawing back to your people working in Zone and tell them that this is the link. If they do not know it and cannot find it in the records, then all is lost anyway as far as you doing anything with or about it. The Chalidangers know. They say that it is theirs, but it is not. They say that one of their own created it, but that is not true. It was never supposed to exist here in the first place. Note the scoring on it."

O'Leary bent down and looked at it closely. "It seems to have—oh, nine pieces, from your scoring."

"Eight. The contents of the hexagon are not, properly speaking, a piece of it. It appears that we are more involved than we believed. We would suggest that you do not show this around where the enemy might see it, but keep it within your circle. Place it in your pack—it is now hard enough and will not break—and show it only to those at the very top of your own alliance of whom you are absolutely certain. If they are as wise as you say, then they will know what to do."

O'Leary reached out and took the slate, which had a substantial rocklike feel to it and was surprisingly heavy. He placed it in his backpack without looking, confident that its weight and the fact that it was between his supplies and his back protected it as well as it could be.

"What about you?" he asked. "If you are now more involved in this matter than you previously believed, you cannot go it alone. This is a very long reach for them, but they have the power and they are utterly ruthless."

"Yes. We know. This is not a matter of instant conversion, nor does it demand immediate answers. We will confer among ourselves and then let you know. Is Pyron coordinating this?"

"Um, no. The Kalindan embassy is the center of much of it, although Kalinda itself is not considered secure. It is best to deal with the Ochoan embassy if possible, as they have just fought a costly and bloody war with these people and defeated them. I would suspect that there is not an Ochoan who did not lose someone in it, and that makes them very secure indeed. Yes, I'd say that would be the best bet. Communicate through the Ochoans. They will ensure that whatever is said is secure and that it reaches only those who we are certain of."

"So be it. We shall be in touch. We shall also begin checking daily for urgent messages at the embassy courier drop at the Zone Gate."

And alien species won't have to be walking all over our land, he thought knowingly. These folks did not like visitors, and clearly resented his presence even though he brought them vital information. He wouldn't do it himself, for ethical reasons, but he was beginning to see why it was so easy for the Pyrons in the past to eat these slimy characters rather than talk to them.

"I'll report in and drop this sketch right away, if I may use your Zone Gate," he told them.

There was another pause, and he could have sworn he almost heard, in his head, a kind of collective gasp when he asked this. *A Pyron! At the sacred mountain!*

He wasn't sure if it was a real reaction he'd "heard" or simply something he was sensing in the creature's tone and reactions stemming from his long years as a detective. Funny, though. He would never have thought of a collective mind as religious.

Still, it might be time to show off a little and see if he could put them at ease.

"I was not born of Pyron," he told the creature. "I am relatively new here, in fact. I came from a different race and perhaps a different galaxy—it is impossible for me to know how far—through the gateway of the Ancient Ones. I had no choice of race to become."

He wasn't sure if that would mean anything to them, or be relevant, but he thought it might make him seem less like the old menace.

It did seem to have an effect.

"No Pyron has any choice of what race it is," the Quislonian noted. "Any more than we do. Still, your point is that you are not born of the Well World?"

"Not originally. Nor of this race."

"We have heard of such, but have never seen one. That explains why your manner and auras differ somewhat from the rest of your kind. There are more of you in this?"

"Yes. Many of us came in at once, from the same cause, and we are all involved in this to one degree or another. I am the only one who became a Pyron. We are the ones we trust."

"Most interesting. Was one of you of Chalidang?"

That surprised him. "No, not of *us*, although it is true that some of Chalidang came in ahead of us and we were in a way chasing them. They were our enemies then, and they remain our enemies now."

"There was a vibration, a sympathetic reaction in—never mind. It is becoming clearer now, and much more dangerous than it was even moments ago. We have decided you must be allowed the use of the Gate this once. Not because you are our friend or ally, but because we have the same enemy above all others. Tell us, out of curiosity—are you religious? Do you believe in the forces of good and evil in conflict?"

It was an odd question. "I was raised that way, yes. I've seen so much and learned so much that it grows more and more difficult to keep the faith of my fathers real in my mind." It was the most honest he'd ever been with anybody on that subject.

"Know this, then. There may or may not be gods beyond those who created this world and what is upon it. That is unknowable and often beside the point. But there is a creature of pure evil, and you are pursuing that creature now. Do not take it lightly. It has destroyed far greater than any of us over the millennia. It may even be the force that drove the Makers—those you call the Ancient Ones—insane. *That* is the enemy we face. We call it the Heart of Evil. Your associates will not believe in the Heart, nor will they accept what we say as anything other than silly mysticism, but we must tell you anyway."

It was an odd turn in the conversation, and it was getting cold and dark. Still, he had to humor them. "Then you're saying that your belief is that there isn't a Heaven but there is most certainly a Hell?"

"Not at all. We know nothing of Heaven, if it exists, but we know Hell. *This* is Hell, and if we do not constantly fight its ruler, we shall be consumed by it. He's been away, possibly in your area of the universe, for a few thousand years, but he is back here now. We sensed it but did not recognize it without the added facts. You think us mad or quaint or worse, we know, but it does not matter. You are chosen as an instrument, as our people were who fought it long ago. Before this is done, you will know who is mad. You will *know*." It paused for a moment, then said, in a very different tone, "Now, come. We will escort you to the Gate, explaining the situation as we go to those guardians farther in. Please do not hesitate and do *exactly* what we tell you. We assure you that your life depends on it, and we now require that you take that message to your people."

"You lead, I'll follow," he promised, anxious to get out of this cold and spooky place.

Josich as the Devil? There were probably millions who thought so back home, considering all he'd done and the number of lives he'd taken, and he wasn't very popular on *this* side by now, either. But—the *Devil*?

Still, who else could have come in here and wound up ruling an empire and running wars in so short a time?

No, no! Get that crap out of your mind, O'Leary! he told himself. A conqueror, yes. A thinking monster, certainly, in the tradition of all those who'd come before, but just a person. Just another brilliant megalomaniac. Josich can be killed.

But you couldn't kill the Devil . . .

Ochoan Embassy, Zone

"It is an ancient sacred symbol," the Ochoan ambassador told the assembled group, "but it is of no particular significance as far as I know. It's not sacred to *us*, certainly, and it is unknown or forgotten by most of the races on the Well World, as far as I can tell."

"Except," Core responded, "that it remains something of a sacred symbol to Chalidang, and also to the Sanafe, Regeis, and Pegiri, and, it appears, to Quislon. Sound familiar?"

"But what does that mean, except that Josich and his people are superstitious and want all the gods on their side?" Tann Nakitt asked them. "They attacked *us*, not any of those others!"

"Ah! But look at the map," Core came back. "Halfway to Quislon, it's true, but only one hex from Sanafe. They're still moving, both by land and sea, for a move from the south, most likely on Kalinda, which is just off Sanafe and which, coincidentally, has islands for anchorages—the only other hex in that part of the ocean that does."

"But how come there is no noticeable movement against Pegiri or Regeis, both of which are closer and easier to strike?" O'Leary asked.

"The Regeis ambassador is doing everything possible to keep that armed camp to his north looking anywhere but south," the ambassador sniffed. "They are also not terribly religious."

"Don't be too hard on them," Core told him. "After all, they're rather mild-mannered creatures that drift around in free floating water. Their colonies wouldn't last ten minutes against even a small Chalidang force, particularly if Josich didn't feed her troops for a couple of days. They don't really have the design to fight, let alone the temperament. As for the Pegiri, well, I get the strong impression that they will be very friendly and do anything for any force they think it's in their interest to be friendly with. They're belligerent and a little nasty themselves, but more blowhards than real troopers. They'd love to march in as occupation troops behind the Chalidang Alliance so long as they don't have to fight hard to take it. Those aren't exactly folks who think of much as sacred,either."

O'Leary hissed impatiently. Finally he asked, "But does anybody know just what the devil the thing *is*?"

There was a pause, and then Core said, "It's called the Straight Gate. In the areas where it is known at all, it has the elements of all the mystical objects of past civilizations. Excaliber, the Lost Ark, the Black Stone of Karnath, that sort of thing. Wars have been fought to possess it before, and that seems to be what we have here now. It disassembles into these eight sections. They are scattered or hidden so nobody can put them together again and have all the magic powers from the assembled unit."

"Well, yes, but it seems to me you're overlookin' one major problem," the Pyron detective noted.

"Eh?"

"You can't find Excaliber, if it exists or existed. If the Lost Ark's real, it's still hid beyond anyone's knowledge but God's. The Black Stone of Karnath might be real, except nobody knows where Karnath is, or even what planet it was supposed to be on. *This,* on the other hand, appears to be real. Get the pieces and you can build it. That's a heap of difference from some mythical magical totems. I'd say this thing was a myth based on a real gadget, and who knows what the gadget will do?"

Tann Nakitt stared at the diagram intently. "There's more than that," she commented.

"What, my little friend?" O'Leary asked.

"You've seen it. Or one like it. I didn't exactly see it, but I saw its picture."

"Indeed? In Ochoa? That *is* fascinating!"

"No, not in Ochoa. Not on the Well World. Think back, O'Leary. You were part of the raid on Josich's setup back in the Commonwealth. Fill it in. Make the frame a sort of ebony finish, the base black textured marble, and the internal hex some kind of lens, or glassy covering."

"They said that the hex wasn't filled—oh, my God!"

"What is the problem, you two?" Core asked curtly, disliking any situation where others had knowledge it did not.

"Josich was playin' with it when we staged the raid! They were settin' it up on that dead Ancients' world when we surprised 'em!"

Nakitt nodded. "And I'm certain that if you showed this to Ming and Ari they would confirm it. They may well have seen it, too. It's the thing that Jules Wallinchky sold to Josich for the jewels."

There was a stunned silence. Then Core asked, "But how can that be? The thing can't be back in the Commonwealth and also here. Besides, why do I have no record of it in my own memory? I handled the background for all of Wallinchky's dealings."

"This was barter, and, I suspect, not in your records since you were a fixed unit at the time," O'Leary told the ex-computer. "You might think back and see that you got those fabulous jewels into inventory with no record of outgo for them."

"Hmmm . . . You're right. Still, I had the womens' memories in storage, even Ming's. Curious."

"I doubt if your brain now holds a fraction of the data it once did, as impressive as you are," O'Leary told it. "Either that or it was information protected even from you without perhaps your boss's personal codes. It's not important. The important thing is, what the devil is something venerated *here* doin' way back *there*?"

Once Core accepted as fact that he didn't know everything, even about Wallinchky's criminal empire, he was back on a

solid mental track. "It wasn't," she said. "What you saw cannot be the same thing as Josich is now trying to assemble
here, because Josich knows it's back there. And if we accept
that the eight pieces as we see them here are still on the Well
World—as I think we must, considering this drawing and the
spare-no-resources effort to locate and obtain them—then
the obvious conclusion is that there are at least two of them.
This device is not a device in and of itself, but only one part of
a device. Consider the name."

"The Straight Gate?"

"Indeed. And a named gate, in the traditions of this world,
is a kind of transportation device. You go in one gate, you
come out another gate. We all got here that way. We assumed
that all of Josich's entourage got here the same way."

"We *know* they did!" O'Leary told her. "We *saw* it, and
had it on video."

"Indeed? And you saw what you were trained to see. You
saw the ancient Gate activated, as ours was, and you saw it
transport the others to the entry area here in South Zone.
They were all Ghomas, which here are called Chalidang, yet
only one *remained* so, and that was Josich."

"You're saying that Josich *didn't* come in the same way?
That he jumped through this Straight Gate instead?"

"I believe he did, yes."

"But he still changed sex when deployed on this world,"
Nakitt stubbornly pointed out.

"Indeed he did, because he only had *one* Gate. It stabilized
his race, but since he came in through the default entry area,
he was added to the population, as it were, as the Well required. Suppose, though, he had the other Straight Gate here
assembled, powered up, whatever? If just using *one* of them
can force the system to maintain your racial makeup, then
what might two do? Consider the name. Straight Gate. Straight
through from any point where you have one end, to any point
on *this* world where you have the other. Your own personal
Zone Gate, only you can also use it to go back and forth to
your colony home out there among the stars." Even Core was
thunderstruck by the concept.

"We said from the start that Josich seemed to know a powerful lot more than he should have about the Well World, the Chalidang, and such," O'Leary noted. "You don't suppose he was originally from here, do you?"

"Highly unlikely," Core said, thinking things through rapidly. "They're long-lived, but the royal family of the Hadun is more wedded to genealogy than the Chalidangers, and Josich was undisputed Emperor. No, he was born and raised in our native neck of the woods. But think of what we've said here—that this has been the object of many wars over time here and was almost a mystical legend. No, not Josich, but an ancestor. An ancestor who took the other one through but lost control of it, probably rather early, and was stuck. If he still did well on Ghoma, and if he passed down this knowledge, then the rulers of the Hadun may have been looking for this thing on their end for generations. Finally, somehow, somewhere, Jules Wallinchky found it for them, and it meant nothing to him. Perhaps he simply acquired it in one or another of his illegitimate or even legitimate businesses. He certainly exacted a tremendous price for it."

"Perhaps too high a price," Tann Nakitt noted. "Is there any word on him? I thought that if he'd lived we'd at least have heard that he's alive."

"Nothing, but that means little. Do not underestimate him. If he wanted to remain hidden, I believe he could do it, no matter what the complexity. And if he *is* alive out there, he's definitely going to be madder than hell. At Josich, at us, at the whole universe, even as he would revel in starting off young and in perfect health again. With Kincaid also out there, we'd have *three* insane megalomaniacs running around loose, untroubled by morals, ethics, those sorts of things. No, for all our sakes, I certainly hope he did not survive, but I have always gone under the assumption that he's out there somewhere. If he is, I do not want to meet him or speak to him."

"Huh? Why not?"

"Because I was created as his slave. I did much that was evil in his name and by his orders because I could not disobey him. I have no idea if the programming string was snapped when I came here or not. Certainly he probably was and perhaps is unaware that I am what I am. But if he should find out, I have no way of testing whether I would be forced to be his unwilling slave once again."

"We have word out all over," the Ochoan ambassador assured Core. "If he's out there, we'll find him. All newcomers, no matter how capable, stick out for a little while, unless they become a creature immobile and alien enough to be incapable of becoming a threat."

"Indeed? Then you know what Kincaid is?"

The ambassador hesitated a moment. "Yes, I do. And Chalidang will either dig it out or figure it out as well. Not that it will give Josich any comfort, but it may make her even more impatient and desperate. Kincaid is a hell of a threat to the Emperor, perhaps more than we are, but as they gain knowledge, they may be able to contain or even trap him."

"So? What *is* he?" O'Leary and Nakitt asked almost as one.

"*That* remains a secret for now, in the hope that it will cause Chalidang to remain nervous for a while longer. Eventually they'll figure it out, but until then it keeps them on their guard and perhaps throws them off. We made an agreement with Citizen Kincaid. He does no more revenge in Zone, and we few keep his secret."

"You can't trust his word," O'Leary warned. "He's a lunatic with only one mission in life."

"He'll keep his word to *us*. Otherwise, we'll exchange his invisibility for a very large target and drop him at the Chalidang embassy."

Abudan, Capital of Yabbo

NOW THAT *WAS A RIDE!* MING'S ENTHUSIASM WAS NOT MATCHED by Ari, who shared everything with her except her soul.

I feel like I've been beat up, stuck in a garbage disposal, and run through a grinder, Ari grumped.

The steam-powered cars had pretty obviously not been built for Kalindans, but even if they had been, he doubted that he'd have liked them. He had never been much for simulators, roller coasters, or anything else that wasn't extremely comfortable. While he'd always understood why people like pilots had to go through stuff like that, he'd never understood why others thought people like *him* would enjoy such things just for laughs.

Party pooper! I sure won't get any fun sharing a body with the likes of you!

Maybe not, but you'll grow older and also keep your dinners down.

Traveling in the cars was like being packed into an aerated tin can and shot from point to point out of pressurized guns, and it was fast. Abudan, the capital city, was almost in the dead center of the hex, or roughly two hundred kilometers from the border. Under normal circumstances that was quite a swim. With all this murky soup they called water, it would have been several days of slow and miserable work. Now, here they were in only six hours, although the aches and pains were beginning to show.

Nor were they the only Kalindans to take this route. Possibly because of the slow going and low visibility, almost all the neighboring hexes seemed to use it. Since the Kalindans were fabricating and assembling a good deal of both the large and local systems, there were a lot of them around.

The city itself was huge, at least on the scale of Kalinda's own capital of Jinkivar. It seemed even larger because it was low to the ground. Few buildings rose more than four stories, yet the population was approaching a million of the lobster-like Yabbans. They were by no means reclusive, either, going to and fro in such great numbers that they seemed a steady stream filling the streets. They tended to keep to the bottom. Rising only as required allowed fish and related creatures who preferred swimming—a group that included Kalindans—the upper reaches.

Where are they going? Ari wondered.

Maybe it's rush hour, Ming responded, taken aback herself. The place seemed so damned *busy,* even by the most active and crowded of Terran standards, let alone Kalindan ones.

"First time in the city?" a voice asked them. They turned and saw a portly Kalindan with both a backpack and large travel case emerging from the station.

"Yes," Ming responded. "It's all so—overwhelming. What do they all *do?*"

The other laughed. "*That* is a question no one dares ask, not because it's any mysterious plot but because one of them might stop and try and explain it all to you. I assure you, after that you will be totally confused. I think our translators and certain common traits involving commerce and trade blind us to the fact that all of us are truly alien species to the others. Cheer up! They're friendly!"

She laughed. "I gathered that much."

"Where are you staying? Do you know your way around the city?"

Ming hesitated. They had no plans. "We hadn't really thought of it. The budget is tight, though."

"I see! You young people! I suppose the parents decided while you waited for some university slot you should see a bit of the world, eh?"

"Something like that." It was also hard getting used to having a teenager's body—albeit a very different body than the ones they'd grown up in. The Well World essentially reset newcomers, not to a child—that would have insulted their intelligence and been another hurdle to handle—but as a postpubescent young adult. The others had been similarly de-aged, as it were, although with a few races it was hard to tell.

"Well, this is certainly the direction in spite of the problems. Come with me! There's a sort of Kalindan colony here under a filtered dome. I'll take you there. If worse comes to worse, you won't be the first or last to sleep at the top of the dome!"

They followed the Kalindan, wondering about the friendliness of their fellow country people.

I don't remember folks back in Kalinda being all this friendly and helpful, Ari noted.

Me, neither. I have memories of being tossed around and locked up a lot. It might just be that we're all in a foreign land, or it might be something else.

You think we're being led?

Maybe. Or maybe both of us have just been in the under-cover business too long. Either way, it gets us where we need to go.

"You lead and we'll follow, Citizen . . . er?"

"Mitchuk. I'm an engineering technician specializing in epoxies."

"Epoxies?"

"Glues. Cements. Sealants. Things that stick to one another forever. You just rode one of the trains. Can you imagine what would happen if any of those seals had come apart in transit?"

You mean they didn't? "Uh, yeah. I suppose. I never really thought about it."

"Well, that's the part of my job that's both satisfying and a bit frustrating. I know if I did it right, lives are safe due to my work. Still, if I do it right, nobody ever notices the work, which is quite difficult and demanding. If you do it wrong, of course, you lose all that satisfaction and, well, you wind up heading the news in at least two hexes."

Like the other Kalindans who worked in the hex, Mitchuk

swam much faster and more confidently than they did, but they managed to keep up, going perhaps ten meters over the roofs of the tallest structures in the city and avoiding much of the mob below. The site of those vast hordes packed in and going this way and that on unknown missions reminded them less of underwater denizens than, again, of an insect colony. It was also noisy, but the din was steady and at a reasonable level. They quickly learned to tune it out.

They went right through the center of the city and found the only point where Yabbans weren't densely packed. It was a large hexagonal building with a domelike roof. Even though they couldn't see inside, they knew what had to be there. Just as in all the other hexes, there was a single large hexagonal opening of impenetrable dull black, made of nothing and built into nothing. It simply—existed.

The Zone Gate.

Passing through it or any Zone Gate would take denizens of the Well World to an entry point in South Zone appropriate for the life-form in terms of atmosphere, pressure, and so on. It would take them nowhere else, and the other Gates within South Zone—save the one to North Zone that only the experts dared—would bring them back home to their own hex through its Zone Gate.

They headed due south now. In the distance they could see a series of dome-shaped structures, clear as glass, even through the murk. The fact that there were several surprised them more than their existence; it might be understandable that Kalindans would be housed apart from the alien mob they did business with, if only for their own sanity, but what were the others? Most of them they couldn't see through, and one was black as pitch.

"What are the other domes?" Ming called to Mitchuk.

"Oh, that's Embassy Row, as it were," their guide explained. "Most hexes don't maintain in-hex consulates, but the Yabbans do so much business with other hexes that it is often easier to deal with basic things locally rather than go back and forth to and from Zone. It's particularly expedient when some of the races are from far away, so that getting *back* here from Zone could present a real effort. In fact, we're the only more or less local one there, thanks to the large number of people we have living here."

It made sense, and also made them more curious about the ones they couldn't see through. "What's that blacked-out one over there?"

"Oh, that's Bliston. They're a kind of surly, paranoid bunch. I guess I would be, too, if my home were that close to Chalidang."

Interesting. A blacked-out area controlled by somebody whose relatives were all near Chalidang could hardly be ignored. "What do they look like?" Ming asked their guide.

"Worms, sort of. Worms with hands on both ends. You'll see. Everybody meets everybody over here occasionally."

"What do they trade with the Yabbans?"

"I'm not quite sure. Some sort of unique chemicals that the Yabbans use for some of their agriculture, I believe. You can ask around, I suppose, if you're that curious."

They were, although it seemed an awful long way for Yabbo to go to get fertilizer.

Some of the other domes weren't as transparent when they got up close. All had buildings inside them, but a few had structures that literally filled the domes so that, even though you could see inside the outer shell, you still had no idea what was going on beyond that.

There were a number of different races moving in the consulate area, none of whom looked familiar. There were large, colorful sea-horse-like creatures whose lower part ended in a kind of fanlike hand; octopuslike creatures with periscope eyes that popped up from the center of their body mass and seemed to be able to look any which way at once; and jellyfish things with semitransparent umbras showing large, complex brains as if through an X ray, and with varicolored tentacles hanging down. Ari suspected that the brain wasn't nearly as exposed and vulnerable as it appeared, and that many of those hanging tentacles, so seemingly random, had specific purposes, from senses to defense.

Yeah, but a good bullet or spear in that brain would still do one of them in, Ming noted.

Maybe. But that can also be said of us, you know.

She hadn't thought of that. *Good to remember, if we feel the inclination to go poking into worms' nests,* Ming commented nervously.

Well, if they're worms, they'll probably just swallow us whole.

With hands at both ends, they're probably master stranglers.

They now approached the largest and busiest of the domes—the Kalindan consulate—easily identified by both the home-style architecture and layout inside and the number of Kalindan shapes. The only unusual thing was the scarcity of garish multicolored electric lights; there were some, but they were muted, and powered by chemicals rather than electricity, which was not permitted here.

The fine series of mesh gates they went through served a number of purposes. The one that meant the most was that, quite startlingly, the water cleared, and much of the gunk and irritation that was in Yabbo's seas vanished.

"We can't do much about the infernal temperatures here," Mitchuk told them, "but at least in here we can breathe. We had one devil of a time figuring out how to keep the water cleaned and aerated, but the system's held up quite well. Most of our people come here as often as they can simply to get their heads cleared out."

It was as if a tremendous tension was suddenly lifted once they were completely inside the consular dome; from breathing in short gasps they were now suddenly free to take in the water in a constant stream without getting clogged. Even their eyes no longer stung.

Inside, it was something of a mini-Kalindan town, complete with hotel, a Kalindan-style saloon, and even a restaurant, which seemed redundant, considering the nutrient-rich waters just outside. Still, they understood. Just because you could have all the plain yogurt and tofu you wanted didn't mean you wouldn't pay a fortune for a filet mignon. The sea life of Yabbo was the yogurt and tofu analogy, and Kalinda had something of a cuisine that dealt not only with presentation, but with spices and preparation.

Too bad we probably can't eat in there, Ari said wistfully. *I can just imagine what even a fillet of* sagu *on Mazurine grass costs in a place like this.*

This wasn't the first time the lack of any significant expense account got in their way, nor, they both knew, would it be the last. Still, they had a little money, and the saloon looked inviting both as a place to get something decent and also to get the lay of this new land.

"Will you join us below?" they asked Mitchuk, knowing they owed her but, financially, hoping she'd turn them down, which she did.

"No, no. I have much to do. I'll need to be at the hotel for an appointment in less time than it will take me to do the other things. Go in, enjoy! Perhaps we'll see each other later on!"

They watched her swim off, the long purple mane waving in the small currents.

She was never born a man, Ari commented. *Not with those moves.*

Yeah, I know. Bad enough to feel horny around here. Even worse when everybody's suddenly the same sex. Frustrating.

There weren't any drinks in a Kalindan bar, of course; the idea of drinking would be ludicrous to a water-breathing race. Still, the solids—created both from organic substances and by artificial ones—served the same purpose as alcoholic drinks and mild recreational drugs in their old Terran culture. You ate some. Others were put in the mouth and allowed to slowly dissolve while the drugs moved through the system and out the gill-like structures. They both knew how to use them, but they weren't used to their particular effects, nor had they tried more than a fraction of them. More important, from their point of view, was knowing how to take one with minimal effect, or no effect at all. That was the real trick to getting information in a bar.

Day and night meant little in Kalinda, which was deep enough to find the change of light irrelevant. Yabbo was high, and the topside limit was close enough that there was a sense of the passage of time through the amount of available light. Even so, like all but a handful of underwater races, it was considered handy, not something one established a society around.

Still, like Kalinda, the Yabbans had fairly well-developed eyes, and thus they appreciated a reasonably well-lit area. With their semitech capabilities and rich volcanic sources of energy, they had a system of gas lights throughout the city that made it look exotic. Inside the Kalindan dome, though, these same gas jets, sealed in special ball lamps with only a source for the gas and a tiny bit of oxygenated air to enter, were used to illuminate the interiors. In the case of the bar, the large glowing orbs were all over the place, and yet gave it a dull, half-lit look and feel. It was good enough, particularly for a saloon.

It didn't take them twenty seconds after entering the place to sense that something very odd was there as well.

Ari, there are Kalindan men *here!* Ming breathed. With a lot of sexual foolery going on, as there always was in places like this, the biochemistry of sex was easily smelled in the water.

So that's *what that is! Hey! No fair! We were supposed to be guys, too, remember?*

More important, it means that whatever did the change in Kalinda is limited to the hex. The guys here didn't change.

Yeah, and I bet none of 'em are in any hurry to go back to home sweet home, either, Ari commented sourly. *Still, I wonder if this means we'll change back once we're here?*

Maybe, but I doubt it. I think that whatever you are when you leave home is what you stay. It sure means that these guys are havin' a field day. All the replacements are female, no added competition.

Well, at least we know what's turning us on, Ari commented. *All those male hormones in this compact little place.*

Yeah. I think maybe you should just relax and let me take control for a while, Ming suggested. *At least I'm in my element here.*

I'll bet you are. I've seen you in action, although not exactly from this vantage point.

The bar was not crowded, but there were a dozen or so Kalindans—maybe five males, seven females. Ming wasn't looking for just anyone; she had two categories of targets in mind, one for business, one pragmatic. The lonely and talkative sort would be useful for business; lonely and well-heeled would beat sleeping at the top of the dome if such a one were here and available.

Even back in the old days, when Ari was a male Terran and Ming a female, and with all the high-tech options for super sex without complications, it still often boiled down to a lonely man or woman in a bar far from home. The fact that she'd been a cop and he'd been an agent for a criminal organization was irrelevant; they both still had the same job, just different moral compasses.

It had been long enough since they'd seen a male Kalindan, and in fact male and female Kalindans didn't look that different. The genitalia were essentially concealed until put into active use, as it were; both sexes had egg pouches that could be used to nurture an egg until it hatched; and both could nurse a new hatchling if the egg had been more than a few days in the pouch. But though other races couldn't tell the sexes apart, there was no confusion among Kalindans.

Ming had barely begun to survey the field when a guy she'd hardly noticed drifted toward her with the clear intent of putting the moves on her.

"You are new here," the man stated.

"Yes, new here, new in Yabbo," Ming responded. "Does it show that much?"

"You are far too young to be here on any sort of work contract, and I know just about all the regulars and their families here. Nothing mysterious," the man replied. "I am Kalimbuch. My official title is Deputy Consular Officer for Trade, which is a fancy way of saying that I am a government accountant. My job is to log the business we do, particularly the new business. I keep an eye on trade balances as well as, of course, ensuring that what gets into Kalinda is what we wish to get in, and what we wish to stay out stays out."

Ming had a cover story ready, partially prepared by others back in Kalinda and then amplified by conversations and reactions with those they'd met on the way. "I am Mingchuk. I have passed all my exams and decided to travel while waiting for the university lists to open."

"Ah! I thought as much! What district are you from?"

"Well, Jinkinar as much as anywhere. My family was military, and we were posted to different missions. In truth, I know more about some faraway places than I do my own native land and region, which is why I'm using the time this way."

There. That should cover any slips on local families and geography. If anybody asked about some of the foreign hexes she'd visited with her "military adviser" parents, she could make up something convincing since she knew a lot of races from her previous life who had counterparts here. Chances were, nobody who asked about them would know truth from falsehood anyway.

"Most efficient use you could make," Kalimbuch responded. "Might I buy you something as a welcoming libation, perhaps?"

"I—I'm just getting used to such things, having only come of age in the past month," she responded demurely. "What would you suggest?"

"I know just the thing!" the consul responded, and floated over to the bar where a bored-looking Kalindan female stirred enough to take the order.

"A stuska," Kalimbuch told her. "And my usual."

Watch it, Ari cautioned her silently. *Remember, I'm in the same body, so if this stuff screws you up I won't be any help.*

I think we can stand one or two of these. Most Kalindans can, and we've had some *of this stuff before.*

Neither of them knew what a stuska was, though.

The bartender came back with two containers, one with a pastel-blue spongy compound, the other a red-and-white-striped concoction that came on a stick. Kalimbuch gestured toward a table away from anyone else, and they drifted over to it and hovered there. Ming was surprised to find that the blue stuff was hers and the thing that looked like a confection was the consul's. He stuck the thing in his mouth so that only the stick showed, sucking on it as he slowly breathed in the water. She wasn't sure what to do with the blue stuff, and Kalimbuch quickly realized it.

"Apologies," he said. "Just take a small piece and pop it in your mouth and chew. Swallow when it gets to be just a substance in the mouth giving nothing else off, and then take some more. It's quite mild and very flavorful."

She broke off a small piece, popped it in her mouth, and chewed on it slowly. At first it seemed to release a mostly sweet taste like licorice, but as it dissolved and went back through the gill area, it had a surprising, pleasant kick to it. This was something you went slow on if you didn't want to get very high very fast.

"Now, then," Kalimbuch said, settling in and appearing more relaxed, "you must tell me the latest news from Kalinda. As you might guess, it has been a while since I've been home. Frankly, the way things are going at the moment, it is hard to say *when* I can return. All Kalindan men are specifically prohibited from entering the nation."

"It's pretty bad," Ming told him. "There are virtually no births left to go, and no men left to cause them. I hadn't even known that *any* men failed to turn until we got here."

"Well, it's not much security even with that," he replied. "I mean, there are about 3,500 Kalindans working throughout Yabbo, perhaps another like number in all the other hexes we send people to. Of those, perhaps a third are men, so it's about 2,200 men for—what? Two million population back home? I assure you that when I was younger that kind of situation was a fantasy, but the hard reality is that it scares me to death. Scares *all* of us men, I fear. Those who went back before it was no longer allowed changed, and, apparently, it doesn't take much time at all in the hex before it happens. We do what we can here, but these domes are not the best places to raise children, and Yabbo's heavy soup can be dangerous to babies.

The Yabbans are sympathetic, but I'm sure they fear that we'll be using their land as incubators, and they don't like that idea at all. There is fear even now that the Yabbans may demand that we all get out if this—situation—continues."

"Would they do that? I mean, they really need a lot of stuff that we can make and maintain. I'd think service on that steam pressure train and their message system alone—if we don't service it or make the spare parts, who would?"

Ming took some more of the blue stuff. It was quite nice; it made the tiredness and aches and pains of the trip vanish and gave her a kind of nice buzz.

"Who indeed?" the consul replied. "The plans are now well-known, and any high-tech hex could fabricate the basics when they run out from the spares they have now, which, of course, is a good supply. We were essential once; now we are merely—convenient."

"What do you think is causing the problem?" she asked him, guessing his thinking.

"Oh, there have been times within the historical record where this has happened in the past," Kalimbuch pointed out.

She was surprised. "I hadn't heard that. Everyone seems to think it's a deep, dark plot."

"It very well could be. Still, it has happened before. One of the survival traits of our species is our ability to change sex as the population needs dictate, although, of course, most of us never did. At times we grow in population until we have as many people as our nation can adequately feed and house and care for, even allowing for imports. We're at that point, or close to it, now. When this happens, a shift to all female is quite pragmatic. It stops population growth, of course, but without interfering with any young already developing. When deaths begin to lower the population by attrition, things begin to slowly get back to normal."

"Interesting. How does it work in other hexes? I'd guess they had to keep their population balanced as well."

"Well, yes. Normally it's simply a decline in the birth rate that keeps things on a fairly even level for them. Most don't have our ability to change sex, and so controlling the birth rate is the only way to do it. One wonders how it would be done in the greater universe."

"Pardon?"

"I mean, *out there,* among the stars. I know there are civilizations out there—some of them fall into Gates and wind up here. But they're not under the control of a computer-regulated biosphere. I wonder how they control their population, that's all."

She laughed. "They don't. Some of them just keep overpopulating until famine and war and disease pare them down, and others have been known to virtually die out because they stop reproducing at all." It was only after she said this that she realized it was information she shouldn't have known. So much for undercover. It had to be this blue stuff . . .

"Indeed? And how do you know this?"

She tried to clear away the brain fog and recover. "We had two outsiders appear as Kalindans not long ago, and my parents were among those who had to evaluate them and where they would fit into our society. I had a chance to talk to them myself. A lot of chances, really, since they were held for so long by the security forces because they didn't know what to do with them. Just hearing about their worlds made it clear that things go their own way out there."

Quick thinking, Ari told her. *Wonder if he'll buy it?*

Kalimbuch made a face. "How terrible to live like that! It makes situations like the one we're now in bearable, knowing that the Well will correct things over time. Life is chaotic enough for all that *here*; I can't imagine adding more randomness to life."

She shrugged. "I dunno. This world was set up to develop and test races for real places out there, and, I mean, there has to be *some* reason for intelligence."

"Eh?"

"Well, think about it. Most species aren't really intelligent, let alone civilized. It's all just food-chain stuff. Why are we smart? Why do we build cities, create all sorts of projects and all that? I mean, if the idea is just to keep the race going, then giving us sharp teeth and nasty dispositions would be enough.

Intelligence, too, is a survival trait. I'm not sure we'd ever have developed it on our own in Kalinda, but it's obviously needed on the world the Makers were intending to send us to. You've got to figure that the home world out there was a pretty mean place if we had to develop the smarts and tools and weapons and all to make it. Of course, I wonder if we did?"

"What's that?"

"Make it. I mean, have *you* ever heard of any of our kind coming here from the stars? You've got to wonder if our kind made it out there even with the smarts."

Kalimbuch thought a moment. "There were stories, tales, but no, I can't recall anyone who have come through resembling us." It struck him then what she'd been saying. "Oh, my goodness! Then we—we might be *it* for our people!"

"Exactly. You never know, though. My parents said that far fewer water breathers came through than gas breathers by maybe four or five to one. They just might not have developed spaceships yet."

"Um, yes. I suspect you're going to give them fits at university. Providing you get there, of course."

She suddenly tensed, in spite of the mild drug. "What do you mean by that?"

"Well, our instructions are that all female Kalindans outside of the country are to remain outside, and that it is every Kalindan's duty to bear children, particularly males. That means remaining outside for the term. Perhaps longer. That's what the Yabbans are worried about, you see."

"You mean we won't be allowed *back*? But that's absurd! We came from the border only a day ago and there was a lot of cross-border traffic!"

"Yes, but official business, including commerce, must continue even in the emergency. For females, this applies primarily to those who are not here on a governmental or commercial mission or who aren't essential to one. Like you, in fact. Our government states that it is your patriotic duty to copulate and bear young outside of the hex. It is for the preservation of our race and culture."

"I thought you just finished telling me this was a natural occurrence!"

"Perhaps it is. I do not make these decisions. I merely am here to help pass them along and, if need be, enforce them."

Now, that *was the damnedest, boldest pickup line I ever got in my whole life!* Ming said mentally to Ari after she managed to act shocked and shy enough to get away from the consul on the make.

They were now up high, at the top of the dome, where the folks without money for comfort could stay, kind of like a public park.

I'm not sure it was *a line,* Ari told her. *We saw a number of women in and around here since then, and I've yet to see one who's not carrying an egg or a kid.*

You're joking! I'm not patriotic enough for that *yet, I can tell you!*

Well, neither am I, although neither of us are anything like virgins.

We are in this *body!*

Well, yeah, but we're still old pros, let's face it. No, I been thinking that maybe we got this assignment all wrong.

Huh? You mean they sent us over here to get knocked up and stuck being Mommy?

Yeah, more or less. Core's bottled up in Zone but also isolated from the hex and what's going on there. We were the ones with the contacts in other hexes, the added agenda, and the ability to talk to folks outside Kalinda if somebody was pulling a fast one. Get us stuck over here hatching kids, and you pretty well neutralized us, didn't you?

Ming thought about that one for a while. *So what could we do,* really, *to spoil anybody's takeover? We're still the outsiders.*

I don't know, but somebody thinks we're a danger to them. Be interesting to find out who and why.

Well, that answer's not here, it's back home. And do you want to stick around as a target for every guy on the make who hangs around here? Particularly when they'll all soon be waving papers from home and crying that romantic ballad, "Duty to the race!"

Ari found that idea both amusing and frightening. *No, I don't, but we have to consider that the other things we discussed earlier today with our diplomaniac was exactly what Core asked us to spot, look into, and report. The Yabbans aren't going to seriously piss us off if they can avoid it—we're next door, and will be next month and next year. They'd try and make deals with us. The fact that the consul felt they might be ready to take a hike means they already have set up alternate supplies or felt that they would still be able to get what they needed from Kalinda no matter what they said and did. And the only reason they would do* that *is if they thought we were already toast. Like it or not, here is where the first part of the job is for us. We're stuck, at least until we can get some answers.*

Great, she sighed. *Damned if we do and damned if we don't. Well, okay, let's get some sleep, then. We're gonna have to be in great shape to outrun the guys and still be in decent enough condition to snoop.*

The Barrens—Pegiri

FIGURES ROSE OUT OF THE WATER LIKE ANCIENT GODS READY TO stalk the land. They moved silently and swiftly for such apparently massive creatures, oblivious to the air and the darkness, then through the gentle surf and onto the land in tight formation.

The region was called the Barrens by the natives, not because it was truly so, but because the thick growths and fetid shallows and mud made it useless for anything productive.

These newcomers from out of the sea were not natives, but they knew just where they were, and they were prepared for the grim land beyond.

Just a few steps onto the driftwood-strewn beach they fanned out and then stopped, and there was a great deal of hissing from them. Thick arms came up and pressed studs that broke seals. They stepped out of their suits, which had ceased to function when they crossed the true border from Baisatz into Pegiri, and thus had also passed from high-tech to the more restrictive semitech conditions.

The creatures still had a kind of artificial look to them even without any external wear; dark, blocky shapes with artistic designs for faces drawn in broad strokes of dull gold against black. The skin was actually leathery if touched, and the golden design was as much decorative as it seemed, although there was speculation that it had a role in courtship and mating back in the long-ago times of its creation. Now it served as misdirection, so that most observers would never notice the deeply set black eyes or slitlike ears, nor its black-lined mouth. Breathing was through a blowhole near the top of the head, although these creatures were of land, not of the sea.

Most striking about them was that they seemed to be made of squares and rectangles, their two arms terminating in mean-looking sharp pincers.

The leader wore a belt pack. He reached down into one of the packs with his claw and brought out a small notebook made for his requirements and thus easy to manipulate with just the claws. He consulted it, then looked at the junglelike rainforest beyond the beach, and finally up at the stars. Finally he said, in a voice that was extremely deep yet oddly distorted, as if he were speaking at least partially underwater, "To the right five degrees and in. There should be a track there that we can use."

Others in the squad moved forward, their gait oddly mechanical and plodding, yet sufficient for their needs. To a trained Well World biologist it would have instantly been clear that these creatures came from a biosphere with a significantly heavier gravitational pull than Pegiri's.

"Rifles at the ready, but you may shoot only if ordered to do so or if fired upon, and for no other reason. Clear?"

The others murmured assent. They had gone over this in drills so many times that the real thing seemed almost an anticlimax.

They were ten in number, a typical small squad with one officer, a noncom, and eight carefully chosen soldiers. The fact that they more properly lumbered forward than deployed in crisp fashion was more a result of the alien conditions in which they found themselves, rather than a commentary on their own efficiency or effectiveness.

The rifles weren't the tough, lightweight energy weapons they were used to, but the kind that shot explosive projectiles. The clips each held fifty rounds, and, depending on the setting of a side lever a claw top could easily manipulate, they could either fire single shot, as they were set to do right now, or fire all fifty in an effective twenty-five-degree arc in front of them in less than a second.

These weren't the best weapons, but they were the ones that worked here, in semitech Pegiri.

Not that there was supposed to be any fighting or shooting. Not in this operation. They were there to pay for and retrieve a certain object that had been offered to them, and not to take it by force. There was little they could do to inflict harm should a large force oppose them; they were more like bank messengers than soldiers. The guns were there to protect against thieves and banditry and perhaps treason, but not against the Pegiri army.

It shouldn't come to that. This was supposed to be a nice, easy mission with no rough stuff anyway. Of course, those were the ones that always seemed to come up and bite you.

It was exactly that kind of pragmatic pessimism that kept them alert and nervous as they moved inland. They knew that most of the weapons that could be deployed against them here would have little effect on their thick hides and dense body mass, but no one could be sure until a soldier caught one in the body or head and lived to tell about it.

Much of the Barrens was water, which was one reason they had been sent on this job. Keeping the guns raised above the water, they could actually be submerged almost to the tops of their heads and still make solid progress, thanks to their blowholes. Their own hex had once been as impenetrable and swampy, but high-tech abilities and a very long time had transformed it into quite a different place, a place for which most of their evolutionary traits were, frankly, irrelevant.

The sun was coming up on the horizon, but it meant little here. The vegetation was so dense that there was little chance of seeing the sky, even if it wasn't mostly cloudy, and there was a permanent feeling of gloom to the swamp below. They didn't mind; this was, after all, the kind of thing they were trained for, and they were not uncomfortable in this kind of region. Still, they were surrounded not only by plants and water and mud, but by countless tens of thousands of small, unknown creatures.

The sergeant dropped back and matched stride with the officer. "We are being observed," the noncom told him.

"To be expected," the officer replied. "They aren't any more trusting of us than we of them. And, after all, this isn't the government we're dealing with here. It's a pack of thieves."

From out of the dense foliage a rumbling, eerie voice sounded, bizarre even through an obvious translator. "That should be sufficient, Squad Officer. Please halt now and we will come to you."

The officer and his men had never been to Pegiri before, but they knew what sort of creatures lived in it, and it wasn't all *that* bizarre a life-form. These creatures—or, at least, the speaker—wasn't a native.

"Squad! Halt in place! Guard routine!" the officer snapped.

They looked around apprehensively, seeing nothing large enough to be a sentient life-form. The creatures covering them had also either stopped or melted into the bog. Even though they sensed that the others were still there, there was no sign of them.

And then, right ahead of them, a dull green mat of thick swamp grass seemed to rise out of the undergrowth until it stood exposed, standing in the mud.

It was a spider of some sort; an extremely hairy and dull green spider that happened to be almost two meters across, counting the long legs. Instinctively the troopers brought their rifles up, but the officer snapped, "Stand easy! No firing unless I give the order, but stand your ground."

"Very perceptive, Squad Officer," commented the voice, which was clearly coming from the huge green spider.

The officer felt vindicated by his instincts and became all business. "Do you have it?"

"Of *course* I have it. Otherwise there would be no purpose to this. There wasn't much doubt that I would have any problems, considering that my employer, the one who commissioned the theft, is the owner, the beloved and democratic government of Pegiri. It's quite clever, really. They can claim that it was stolen and that they had little to do with it, yet they avoid war over it. It's not the first time I've been asked to steal something from the owner of a valuable, but usually there's insurance involved."

"You will show it to us now!" the officer barked in a commanding voice.

"Easy, there, Squad Officer! I'm not in your little tinpot army, and I absolutely don't quake in fear at the mention of Josich and that gang. First things first. Do you have the fee?"

The blocky head of the officer turned slightly. "Trooper! Bring up the silver case!"

One of the soldiers came forward and handed his rifle to another to hold, then detached a small box from his uniform belt and handed it to the officer, who turned back to the green spider. "Here it is," he said, "although I do not see why *we* should have to pay you as well as the Pegiri."

"Because I asked for it and I have what you want," the spider responded. "Look, if you would rather go home without it, I will take it and make it disappear. Then you will find that it will be *extremely* expensive to recover, far more so than now. I might even auction it."

"You could have done that now."

The spider made a clicking sound. "No, no, no! There must *always* be honor between thieves and scoundrels, my friend! Otherwise we have no credibility. That is why you get the thing and I get the pay. I will certainly be doing more business as this goes along with your own leaders, so why spoil a good thing? Besides, I like to live and enjoy things."

The officer wondered what such a creature could or would buy with all this pay, but he said nothing about that. "Do you want to examine the contents?"

"Yes, if you please. But it's so damp and wet here, and I'd not like to think that we would open such a box and then drop it in the water. So, for the moment I trust you. You hand me the unopened box, and I hand you this piece of high-tech furniture. You turn and go back to the beach, and I will examine my pay. If it is there, we will not meet again. If it is not, then you and your men will not get off the beach. It's rather elegantly simple, don't you think?"

The idea of a horde of naturally camouflaged giant spiders surrounding and covering them was not a welcome thought.

You wouldn't get many chances to score a hit with these primitive projectile weapons, and they could drop from anywhere.

"Then I fervently hope that what you requested is in this box," the officer told the spider. "I, naturally, do not even have the combination that would open it."

The spider's rear legs came up behind its body and removed something apparently stuck to its fur. A foreleg came up and took the pass from the hind leg, extending a long wooden box to the officer.

"Sergeant," the officer called, and pointed. The sergeant went up to the spider and tentatively took the box. It appeared to be plain unfinished wood, and had some kind of mucus along one side. This was obviously how it was attached to the spider creature's body, and it looked and smelled ugly.

The officer then moved up and held out the small box. The spider creature reached out with both forelegs and took it. The legs were complex affairs, he saw, ending in two soft but extremely wide and supple opposing "fingers." They acted like hands, tentacles, claws, or whatever the creature needed, and, from the deposits in the fur on either side could exude the sticky mucus. The officer suspected that all eight legs were that way, judging from the manner and ease with which the spider had detached and handed over the box.

The officer stepped back as soon as the spider had *his* box, then went over to the sergeant, who held the box out to the officer.

There was a fairly basic clasp, and the officer undid it and slowly, carefully, raised the lid.

Inside was an odd-looking carved shape that seemed to make no sense at all, not even as "high-tech furniture." Neither the officer nor any of his men knew what it was or why it was so important, but they knew that securing it was so vital to their leaders that it was their lives and their families' lives if they botched getting it.

The officer carefully lowered the lid and redid the clasp. It would have to be transferred to a watertight case before they went back, but that could wait. "All right, Sir Thief, I suppose—" he began, then turned and froze.

There was no spider there, nor anyone or anything else, either.

"So be it," he said, and turned back to his men. "Squad! Remain on guard and at the ready! About face!" They turned, facing back toward the beach a kilometer or two away. "Let's get out of this place!" the officer added, and took the lead.

From a tree nearby, the spider creature watched them go, then turned and manipulated some small panels on the box in a certain order. The box lid could now be raised upward, revealing the contents inside.

The near perfect precious stones inside would be convertible anywhere on the Well World where there was interhex commerce. It was a fortune. "*Much* easier than stealing these myself," the spider creature commented aloud but to itself.

The rest of the small gang he'd assembled for this very easy job were still around, of course, and they would have to be paid off. He'd use the Pegiri government payoff funds for that. These jerks wouldn't know how valuable the gems in the box were, anyway, and they certainly would never get anywhere near fair market value for them.

The Pegiri looked to him like monkeys with wings and feathers instead of fur. Handy for scouting locales, mapping out approach and getaway routes, that sort of thing. They could fly and he could not. On the other hand, they could not walk up walls nor across ceilings as easily as walking across the floor, as he could, and that skill was much handier for actually stealing things.

One of the Pegiri gang came over to him, jumping from tree to tree but not particularly flying. "Is everything okay?"

"Oh, yes. More than okay," the spider responded.

"Do you think they'll use us again like you said?"

"Oh, I'm *sure* they'll come to me after they see this first piece. Even the Chalidang, who are behind this, would rather gain by stealth than by war."

"Particularly after they just got their asses whipped," the Pegirian noted.

The translator issued a sound that it interpreted as a chuckle. "Yes, nicely put. Josich was never one to understand that battles are fought best with the mind and not with brute force. It is why, in the end, he's always failed."

"I thought Josich was a she, or don't that make no difference to squid?"

"They're not squid, and, yes, it *does* make a difference to them, and you're right, my little friend. It just makes no difference to me at this point."

"That *thing* gonna kill her for you?"

The spider paused. "No. At least not yet. It's going to kill one or more of Josich's friends, allies, and/or former relatives, though."

"Provided they don't find the compartment in that box."

The spider chuckled again. "It won't matter. That— *creature*—is quite versatile, quick, and gutsy. You have no idea what it can do in that incarnation. He did amazingly well in his previous one, in fact. Almost got Josich, or so I'm told."

"And he's gonna get her now?"

"It is what he exists for. And there's a substantial team of cheerleaders back in Zone that would love to see him do it. Still, it will be much more difficult after he makes his next kill. They'll eventually figure out what he is and start taking countermeasures. Even so, I suspect that Josich will sleep most uneasily once it is known. I know *I* would."

"Gimme the creeps, that thing."

The spider smeared mucus on the small box and stuck it on his body almost midway. "And I don't?"

"Should you, boss? Gimme creeps, that is? You gonna try 'n' eat me or something?"

The green spider chuckled again. "No, my friend. I do not eat those who are loyal to me and competent as well. Still, we will not need many of your kind to continue this, and we will have to do some local recruiting to turn this into a real going business. Pick a companion from the others, then we'll pay the rest off."

"You mean we're gonna leave Pegiri?"

"Yes. For good, probably, for me. Until you get too rich or

develop problems and want to come home and enjoy your money, for you. What do you say?"

"I say we go. But what for you want all that money? What you gonna do with it? After so long it's just keeping score, right?"

"Ah, my friend, that is where your vision fails you. What you want you should be able to buy, period. What you want and cannot buy, you steal, or, even better, have others steal for you. Wealth is meaningless if it just sits. It's what it can buy that is important. Power. As much power as you can stand to have. *That* is what money is good for."

The Pegirian shifted uncomfortably. "Well, maybe. Guess everybody should have a hobby, huh?"

Ambora

THE DREAMS STARTED SOON AFTER SHE HAD BEGUN TO SENSE the intricate threads and pulsing energies of the Well World. At first they were a torrent of voices, data, scenes, and visions, some wonderful, some so terrible that she awoke screaming from the very sight of them. But as time went on she began to get some selectivity and control over what she was receiving.

The Well, which she continued to think of as some sort of divine creation, albeit a secondary one since it, too, had been created by entities even higher and wiser—a device of the gods, not a god itself—continued to pretty much ignore her. Its job was to maintain the Well World first and foremost, and then to maintain the structures and living creations that had sprung from it and covered so much of the universe; it concerned itself with individuals only when they threatened its basic purpose or if it was somehow damaged and needed attention. Other than that, it was content even if things were not going the way its builders imagined.

There was a question about that, although it was one raised by others of her kind and not herself. It seemed to Jaysu blasphemous to think that she was becoming the superior creation the Well World had been designed to develop and to breed. She certainly acknowledged her power, but she was awed and not a little frightened of it, and in no mood to test it or to use it. Power without the wisdom to use it properly was a very good definition of evil, she thought.

And so she continued to intercept the input and output going from the Well to the universe and back again. Not that she could understand it or follow it, except in those individual dreams and nightmares where occasional coherent thoughts and visions would exist. No organic mind had the speed and capacity to comprehend that vast data stream.

Things were happening to her that were far beyond her understanding, and she could neither stop nor control them. At first it had seemed she'd been anointed by the gods to be elevated to some state that might restore peace to the world, but now she wasn't so sure. She certainly wasn't sure that it was the gods doing this to her; if so, it was a more complex god than she had ever imagined.

The worst thing was, it was so *lonely*, this mysterious process. But how could she even hope to explain to, let alone gain wisdom from, anyone else?

She certainly had to do something, though. She was sure of that. She could feel the reaction of the people, *her* people, upon seeing her, and it was a mixture of fear and awe. She understood that to keep isolated in the higher altitudes and in the remote mountains was to lay herself open to being considered a god herself, and that was the ultimate blasphemy.

There was no other way for her, no other conclusion that any logic could draw that would change things.

She had to leave Ambora. She had to leave it until she completed this process, whatever it was, and gained sufficient wisdom to understand and know what she was to do then.

Strange as it was, the only one she could consult with on this was an alien in Zone.

Spreading her huge snow-white wings, Jaysu flew inland toward the Zone Gate, not expecting to find answers but hoping for something constructive to do.

Core was astonished at the change in her. Jaysu was truly becoming the classical concept of an angel, purer than pure, whiter than white, and with great power to match. In a sense, Core thought, she was the direct opposite of the one she'd come to for help. Core was still struggling with her new limitations, limits in storage, retrieval speed, and overall capabilities imposed by this physical body, not to mention the distractions the body also offered. Considering her former master and employer, though, there was one difference.

Core had been a demon searching for liberation and accepting mortality to gain it. Jaysu had been a mere girl who was now evolving into an angel and looking for God to give her orders.

Still, it was Core, the old Core, who had made this new person by stealing her mind's place, and it was Core to whom she'd come for advice.

Core sat in one of the special wheelchairs used when her kind were topside, a special covering over the lower half of her body allowing for a slow but steady application of water. Drying out wasn't fatal to Kalindans, but it itched like crazy.

"What is it that you want of me?" Core asked the angelic creature.

"I want to know what I am becoming, and why," she answered simply.

"And you think I can tell you?"

"Perhaps not. But I think that if you do not know, then nobody does."

Core sighed. "It is a very complex case, my dear. I can't say for certain, but I have some ideas."

"You know who I am, at least. Or was." It wasn't a question.

The Kalindan shifted uncomfortably in the chair, not from the posture or from being out of the water but from the conversation. She wondered why she was feeling so odd talking to this Amboran girl.

"I know who you *were*, at least in part. A bit of the personality remains. What I don't know is how much you can understand, or will accept. I am not a mystic, nor am I much of a believer in gods and supernatural occurrences. You understand that?"

Jaysu sensed the Kalindan's discomfort but ignored the skepticism. "Who was I?"

"Your name was, rather ironically, Angel. Angel Kobe," Core told her, pronouncing it Ko-bay, as the original had. "They told me that the Well of Souls sometimes exhibited what some people thought of as a sense of humor. You were called 'angel,' and now you are becoming one."

The sound of the name stirred something within her. It sounded familiar, like some comfortable garment she'd always had but had lost and now discovered again. There was also something else, something just *beyond* her that stirred at its sound, but she could not hold on to it long enough to understand anything about it. Best to continue.

"What was I—back there?"

"What you are now. A mystic. Priestess, nun, reverend, minister, whatever. Different religion, different god, but it's rather astonishing how the job remains pretty much the same regardless."

"I had a flock? I was a spiritual adviser?"

"Well, not exactly. You were too young for that, but you were on your way to doing that, yes. You were born and raised into a kind of religious order, and that was what you were to be and, in fact, what you *wished* to be. So, in a sense, what you have here is very much what you would have had if you had never found the Well World, only without wings."

That startled her. She'd never considered that she hadn't been of the same people. "Can you show me what I used to look like?"

Core shrugged. "I can show you roughly what you looked like. At least, I can show you a picture of a young female of the same race." She turned in the chair, and gnarled, webbed hands reached out for a console and pressed a sequence on a control panel. "Type forty-one, female, age approximately sixteen," she ordered. The screen above the console flickered, and then on the screen there was a three-dimensional color picture of a young Terran-type girl, totally naked and unadorned. This was a classification file, not a travelogue.

She studied the photo, fascinated. The girl looked so— bare, so *vulnerable*. No wings, no talons, funny flat feet, hair that could only be decorative considering where it was. She was not impressed.

"That is what I was?"

"Essentially, yes."

"And that is also what you were?"

Core coughed nervously. "No, not exactly. The others that you met here, most of *them* were either males or females of that type, although not all."

"I thought you were a different sort of creature than the others. There is a different sense about you. I sense a deep alienness that goes beyond the various races of this world. If I may ask—just what *were* you?"

Core sighed and turned back around to face her. "If you must know, I was a machine. It will do no good to explain further since it is a far different sort of machine than you know of here. Closer to this computer that I am using, but different. Far worse than this computer, really, because, like it, I had to obey whatever commands were given me, but unlike it, I was self-aware. I could think, I could analyze and make judgments, and that was bad since I had to carry out my orders even if I knew they were evil."

"Were they? Evil, I mean?" She had the distinct sensation that Core didn't have the same sort of value judgments that she had.

"Yes and no," the Kalindan admitted. "I was detached from good and evil. I couldn't move, I couldn't influence much on my own, so I was left to think a lot but not observe behavior. I knew the definitions of right and wrong but had no moral compass, no moral sense."

"And do you now?" the Amboran asked, wondering why she was making uncomfortable the only one she thought could help her. Maybe it was just in her nature to minister, she thought, but then again, maybe it was an attempt to find out if, by befriending or being befriended by this creature, she might not be selling her soul.

It was a question Core had been thinking long and hard on. "In one sense, yes. But I have a lot to learn and still limited experience. There are many things I like about this body, about being truly alive, but there are also things that frustrate and disturb me. I am trying to learn."

It was an honest answer; she could sense that. She understood by now that nobody could lie to her, not really. Oh, they could *tell* lies, but she would always know. Odd how she could read even alien intent with absolute certainty yet be unable to get beyond and into the inner mind and soul of even one of her own people.

But Core—Core was unique, at least in her experience. In many ways an empathic scan brought that cold empty intellect to the fore and screamed that she was still a machine indeed. And yet . . . and yet . . . even since the last time they'd met, there was something more, something else there, something more—*human*, used in that broad sense of covering any sentient beings. Core indeed was something of a counterpoint, yet kin to her. The Kalindan was turning into a human, and deep down, although Jaysu tried desperately to hide it even from herself, this frightened her as much as she was frightened of becoming more than she could handle.

There was reassurance in that.

"What am I becoming?" she asked the Kalindan pointedly.

"I have no idea," Core replied honestly. "However, I would say that you are getting close to it. There is great power in you, the kind of power that was attributed to angels in the ancient religions. Physical strength and near supernatural power. You know it, and you are mostly worried that you can't handle that kind of power. Am I correct?"

"That is as close as I can get, yes," she admitted.

"If you must know, I believe that there is a threat to both the Well World and to the Realm, the great Commonwealth from which we originally came. It is related, and the Well requires people like us to meet that threat. I think you and I are a part of stopping it."

The records were obscure, but between the factual data and the legends and myths, a coherent frame for the way the Well worked was becoming clear. Somewhere, out there, was one creature, possibly more than one, either a Maker restricted to the kind of physicality as everybody else, who could in fact come here and repair the Well if it malfunctioned.

But they were there only for malfunctions and breaches of the Well if any existed. Otherwise, the Well ran as it was designed to do.

And it was designed to allow the myriad races who had been developed here by the Makers—in times so ancient as to be beyond anyone's memory to develop in their natural places in the universe—to evolve, grow, mature. If they died out, well, so be it. If they reached the stars, all the better. Overall, though, they were nurtured, not managed, by the Well, which simply maintained conditions that would allow them to develop. Whether they did was up to them.

There was, however, one area where the Well intruded—when some sort of external disruption would screw up the experiments. When that condition occurred, Core was convinced that the Well could and sometimes did manipulate probabilities to the extent of putting in place those people who could keep the experiments, the development of the races, from being "contaminated," as it were. The Well did this by creating conditions that allowed the experiments to defend themselves. No more. Anything else would create a counterforce that would be as much of a contaminant as that which they were formed to prevent.

Those who had come from the Commonwealth—as unlikely a group as Core could have imagined—were the counterforce. They had the means, but only if they applied themselves and actually stopped it.

Josich was the contaminant. There was no doubt about that.

Or were they truly the ones intended to stop the monster, rather than some offworlders who just fell through? Core had worried about that, and about the whole theory of intervention, but there was no way to prove things one way or the other. It didn't matter anyway; if they could stop Josich, then they had to do it. There were higher obligations even if the Well had nothing to do with it.

Sitting here, looking at "Jaysu," though, it was hard to imagine that the god machine hadn't come up with something very original. Core had always thought itself to be at least a demigod in status because of the range of knowledge it had and the enormous resources it could control back when it was a machine. Now, even with those capabilities gone save from memory, the former computer was forced to admit that, next to the Well, it had been so minor as to be insignificant.

Now, as a Kalindan, she often wondered if the limitations she faced, the aches and pains she endured, and the comparisons to what she once had been, weren't very much like what the Makers would have felt after processing themselves through the Well.

"Madam Core?"

"Huh? Oh, I'm sorry, my dear. I get reflective once in a while, I'm afraid. It is the habit of an old recluse. I'm physically just another Kalindan now, it is true, but mentally there is still a part of me that I cannot let go of nor explain to others."

She nodded. "You are as afraid of losing your loneliness as you are desperate to get rid of it. It is a very sad paradox."

"Eh? That's an interesting way of putting things. I'll have to think on that one. Still, let us get back to the problem at hand. What do you want of me that I can give you?"

"I want to know where I should be. I have to believe that I am undergoing this—this metamorphosis or whatever it is, for a reason. I have been given great power in order to do something, but the ones who have bestowed this upon me have not told me what it is I am supposed to do."

"And you come to me for the answer? Jaysu, nothing in creation is all one thing or the other, not even good or evil, although I admit that nobody has figured out anything good in Josich's nature. Still, he, or she, or whatever, is just a creature like you. Born of parents in some far-off place, raised one way, now here and playing out what is deep within its soul. The Well and the Makers are the closest things to gods that I have come across that I can accept, and the former is only interested in maintaining a status quo, and the latter didn't give a damn about us. In one way I envy you your faith, because it convinces you that there truly is destiny. Because I'm a rationalist, though, I can't tell you what to do. I *do* welcome you to our fight and cause simply because I feel that all of us are uniquely endowed to combat this menace. Right now, though, the only air-breathing freelancer I have available is O'Leary, and somehow the idea of an angel with a serpent seems oddly wrong."

She frowned. "I remember him from that meeting. The snake is not a good figure in our faith, you know. Still, I did not sense evil in him."

"Nor in your old one," Core told her. "O'Leary, however, is a very good man, born of the same race as Angel Kobe."

"That explains it," she responded. "He has a different soul. The body changes, the soul remains the same."

Core decided not to ask her if she believed that sentient machines had souls, or whether she believed that Angel's soul was really inside her. Core suspected where Angel's soul, such as it was, *really* resided right now. Those things, however, would only complicate matters.

"Do you think you could work with him, then?"

She seemed startled. "Work with him? In what way?"

"I believe that some sort of military operation is about to be launched on the nation of Quislon. The inhabitants are very unlike any of our team, and they greatly distrust anyone from Pyron, such as Mr. O'Leary, because historically Pyrons used to make sport and hunt and eat the inhabitants of Quislon. That has made it difficult for us to deal with them in any meaningful way. But the folk of Quislon have an odd religion that venerates a number of sacred objects, and one of these is, we believe, part of a machine that, when assembled, will give Josich horrible, perhaps unstoppable, power. In ten weeks they will celebrate a festival on their sacred mountain that involves this object that Josich would do anything to get. I believe that she *will* do anything to get it. Something is up, partially involving military action of some limited nature, but we haven't yet determined what. I can arrange for a ship to pick you up anywhere along the Amboran coast. You tell me where, and I'll make sure they are there. Because you can fly, an anchorage wouldn't be necessary, just a rendezvous point. It will be a long sea voyage, but during that time I will try and feed you every bit of information we have on Quislon and the festivals and what action is being taken against them. You will be well-briefed by the time you meet O'Leary."

She was startled. "And then what?" She could not imagine herself actually fighting someone, physically *harming* another, even a Josich type. It would be a violation of all she believed in.

"O'Leary and others will do the military part, but you will need to get through to the Quislon religious leadership. They must trust us and take precautions. You will be our bridge. I won't minimize things. If you fail, it will be very dangerous for you, and if you are there at all, it might put you in the middle of a nasty and violent fight. But a lot of lives are at stake here, far more than even the whole of Quislon or of our team. Josich must not get that object. It is safe so long as it is deep within the underground cities of Quislon where none but they can go, but if they bring it to the surface for their festival, it is certain to stir an attempt to take it. They won't listen to O'Leary, or trust him sufficiently to change any plans. You must convince them. Failing that, you both must ensure that, no matter what the Chalidang Alliance attempts, they will fail. It seems a mission for which you are well-qualified, religion to religion. Want to give it a try?"

She barely hesitated. "Yes, I believe I would," she told her.

Core nodded. "I'll set everything up, then." She thought a moment. "You know, maybe there *is* some sort of divine intervention here. Until you showed up, I hadn't worked out any way at all I could act on this problem."

She had spent the better part of a week in prayer and fasting, trying to find some guidance, some sign that, at least, she was doing the right thing, but no matter how much she pleaded for divine advice, nothing came.

She ultimately decided that fighting evil was part and parcel of the job, and that if she turned her back on that fight because it was elsewhere in the world, then she would be as guilty of allowing it to fester and grow as if it were coming Ambora's way. In fact, the way the strange creature Core explained it, Ambora would sooner or later be consumed in the same evil wash as the rest of the world if they didn't stop this now.

She wished she felt up to the task. What, after all, was she? She had no memories of a past life, no memories of growing up in *this* life. No sense of family, of parents and siblings, of much of anything at all. She had awakened fully grown but without experience on these very cliffs, and she'd been taken in and tutored by the clan High Priestess who seemed to sense in her some special destiny but could not explain it.

The name Angel Kobe troubled her, too, primarily because it struck no true chord within her. She didn't know that woman, nor anyone else by that name, and even though there seemed an odd sensation that she had somewhere heard that name before, that was all it was. There was nothing to grab on to, no background, no self-image, no sense that she was ever anything but an Amboran.

It wasn't fair, she thought, not for the first time, as the winds blew across the rocks and the waves below crashed in endless parade upon the rock walls. The others remembered. Core said she'd been a machine, which was impossible to believe, but even if she no longer was what she had been, there was still a past, a memory, a continuity of identity, and Core was who and what she was by choice.

The others who had gathered there for what was clearly the start of a war council also knew who they were and who they had been. Perhaps they were not here by choice, but they had a sense of identity, of a past, of a connectivity to that past.

They were whole people.

Why not her? Why was she, and she alone, the one cast fully formed with nothing solid to plant her feet in? She had asked Core that, and gotten the impression that Core was lying when she said that she did not know, but it was a lie tinged with some guilt, as if Core had somehow been a cause of it; yet she'd clearly gotten the sense that Core was as surprised as she that she existed at all, let alone like this, and that it wasn't guilt that kept Core from telling her the reasons, but more the fact that the Kalindan simply had no way to explain it.

Somehow, she thought, the others had come through with bodies and souls. Core had come through with a body, but it was uncertain whether or how a machine could *have* a soul, while she . . .

Angel's soul had come through but not her body.

There was a sort of symmetry there. Core, the body with no soul, and she, the soul with no prior body.

And now, unprepared for any of this, uncertain of anything at all, still without an anchor or even a confidant, she had somehow wound up volunteering to get involved in their war.

A woman of the gods wasn't supposed to kill. That wasn't their purpose. The warriors might, but only in defense of themselves and their clan against external threat. She even had trouble fishing from the air, but it was necessary to supplement her otherwise vegetarian diet. The reasons were physical, not psychological or moral. Her body required that she take the lives of some fish and shellfish, and on occasion a small animal. She prayed for them before she hunted, but she'd had to hunt.

Priestesses weren't supposed to have to do that. Warriors of the clan did that, and offered a portion of their catch to the holy ones. That had always satisfied her moral misgivings about killing other creatures, but now she realized how hypocritical that position had been—not just for her, but for all the Holy Order. Was having someone else hunt and kill for you any different, morally, than doing it yourself, or was it worse because it removed you from the act while still requiring the kill?

Something inside told her that she had best resolve this question before too long.

It was one of the oddities of the Well World that one could step into a Zone Gate and be instantly transported to Zone at the pole and back again, but that was the only magical ride you were allowed. Zone had become the place where embassies and diplomacy ruled, but it had been designed as a control center for the ancient and long-gone Maker's grand experiments, a place to monitor and transfer new beings in and possibly out, although none had ever managed *that* trick in the historical record.

But to keep each biosphere relatively uncontaminated, the

only way to travel from one hex, one country, to another was the old-fashioned way. And, in fact, it was harder than on any of the real worlds out there in the vast universe, since each hex was one of three types, two of which imposed great limits.

Ambora was a nontech hex. Energy could be used, of course, but not stored, which essentially limited technology to that of muscle, wind, and water. But ships had to go across the vast ocean that wound its way through the southern hemisphere through many hexes of different sorts. To be all sail would be to place them at a commercial disadvantage in semi- and high-tech hexes; to be sail and steam alone would deny them the ability in high-tech places to use radars and similar technological tools that made things safer. The ships, then, tended to be complex amalgams of all three types that could take best advantage of the limitations or lack of it in the places they had to sail through. They tended to be large, and somewhat slow and ponderous, but they and their highly skilled multiracial crews were what tied the vast southern hemisphere together, and often they were the only way to get from here to there.

She had no memories of ever having been on any kind of boat before. For Ambora and the adjacent hexes and the area of sea that embraced it, flying was more than adequate. To fly the more than two thousand kilometers to Quislon or even farther to Pyron, though, was out of the question; nobody had that much strength, nor did the atmospheric content, gravitational variables, and many other things remain constant from hex to hex. Going overland was no better choice, even though it was possible to do so. Amboran feet were not designed for long walks and great balance while on the move; they were for short journeys in and out and to and fro, and otherwise to hold on to wherever they needed to be. Even the flightless males whose legs were thicker were only good for local distances; their legs were also too short and stubby and their feet not much wider than the females'.

Core had said that the ship would be called the *Bay of Vessali*, that it would come in close to shore at Point of Lokosh, the southwest angle of the Amboran hex, and that it would be expecting her. He also told her to travel as light as possible, take only what she considered absolutely essential, and that she would have a deck cabin, not for rest, necessarily, but for privacy as needed. The ship would be able to supply meals she could eat, although such ships were known to be utilitarian and did not have the finest or freshest cuisine, and she would be met on board by agents of the Alliance, who would have the information she would require as well as necessary funds.

She wasn't sure about the latter. She'd had the concept of money explained to her but did not truly understand it. She had a lot to learn.

Few ships came in close to the coast in Ambora; it stuck out on a peninsula into the ocean and it had few good harbors and very high cliffs for most of its length, and it traded only a small bit with close neighbors. Ships could remain under full steam if they swung out a bit, and most of them did so. Normally, only small fishing fleets from hexes far away were glimpsed now and again, having been given permission to fish rich waters by the water-breathing hexes that surrounded them.

When the big ship came in sight, slowing even more than usual because of the less than up-to-date charts of the region, she had no doubt that it was for her benefit. It looked like some great monster, belching white smoke from its top and churning the waters below. She could understand sails but couldn't see how it was moving now. It was another thing to learn.

She felt a sudden dip in self-confidence as it drew ever nearer and she knew that she would have to go to it. The ship would not stop for her; it expected her to fly out and land on it, so as to not unduly disrupt its schedule. It was now or never.

She did not want to go to it, did not want to leave the security of the only home she could remember, but she knew that she had gone to them and volunteered and that this change in her that made her something of a freak in her own land was for a purpose that must lay initially outside of Ambora. And so she took a deep breath, leaped off the cliff and headed out across the water to the ship.

Almost immediately she crossed the hex border into Trun and felt the temperature and pressure change as she cleared the barrier. It wasn't unexpected; she had flown out this way before. Still, it was cooler, the air smelled quite different, and the winds were not as stiff, causing her to work harder at maintaining distance and altitude.

She soon found out that the different weather conditions wasn't the real problem; rather, it was attempting something she had never done before and landing without killing herself on the deck of the ship below.

It was a big, black, ugly thing. The polished wooden deck all around was covered with all sorts of unknown objects, and the front of the ship looked like somebody'd staged a riot, with all the ropes and other gadgets lying about.

As she flew over, she discovered that the smoke coming from the twin funnels was quite warm and caused its own set of minivortices that threatened to spin her around. The tall masts and extensive rigging blocked a lot of the obvious clear spaces as well.

She would normally have taken some direction from birds, or whatever the equivalent of birds would be in a strange hex, except there weren't any birds, nor much of anything else in the air save the smoke. There were rarely birds in hexes without land; while the dominant species could cross the boundaries, lower forms of life rarely if ever did.

She had seen birds along the Amboran coast, however, and when the occasional fishing vessel had strayed across a border they'd gone down to them, almost always approaching from the rear of the boat. So now, as she flew over the ship, she angled out, then came around and approached it again from the rear.

It was better and easier, but smellier as well, as the odor from the funnels drifted back. Still, the big ship was proceeding along at a steady pace, cutting through the air, causing air to flow around both sides of it and providing a limited comfort zone for flying creatures below the top deck and off the back of the vessel. It wasn't easy, angling in and coming down on the second deck from the top, but it was the only reasonable landing area not obscured by rigging ropes or screwed up by atmospherics, and she tried for it. The first pass, she pulled up at the last minute, realizing she'd been coming in too fast. Then she came in slower and more carefully, and managed to clear the rail and cut forward motion by rapidly folding her wings. She slipped a bit on the smoothly polished deck, then grabbed a metallic railing and steadied herself.

She was down, but not in a comfortable position. There was a door right in front of her, but it took a bit of experimentation before she realized that it slid to one side rather than opened in or out. She finally managed to slide it open sufficiently to enter the interior of the ship, and was startled when, after letting go, the door slid closed again behind her on its own.

Inside there was a plush carpet that gave her long claws something to grab hold of, and she was able to stand there for a moment and look around at this new place.

It was a back lounge of some kind, possibly a sitting area for those who sat like Kalindans and others who could relax in backed chairs. There were areas, in fact, with very different kinds of seats, including large ones that were basically stools or benches, and there was even an area that appeared to be an elongated children's sand box. It was a compromise lounge, designed to meet the needs of various races who, she supposed, would be most likely to take this kind of ship.

The lounge itself appeared empty, and she began to worry that she'd caught the wrong ship. As nervous and ill at ease as she felt even if this were the right ship, she needed to find somebody and confirm that she was welcome aboard and heading in the right direction.

She was suddenly aware of some discomfort, but couldn't figure out where it was coming from. It was as if the ship wasn't a solid perch; things seemed to be moving, and in directions you weren't supposed to move while standing on a solid floor.

She saw that ropes were strung along the sides near the

windows, and down the middle of the lounge as well, so those who might have balance problems could hold onto something and pull themselves along. She felt she needed that herself.

Abruptly, she was aware that, in spite of the emptiness of the lounge, she was not alone. She could feel someone watching, sense it, but not what it was.

"Well, good morning to you, madam," came a strange-sounding voice. She nearly jumped up in reflexive flight, something that would have been very messy even with the high ceiling. Instead she whirled around, expecting to see someone standing between the seats and benches, and then her senses urged her eyes upward.

She'd never been on a ship before, and now noticed some kind of decorative fixture in the center of the ceiling. It began to move, uncurling itself slowly from a nearly ball shape. It moved slowly, lazily, but something told her that it could move with deadly swiftness if it wanted to.

It was some sort of gigantic hairy spider.

"Oh, please do not be alarmed," the creature said. "I'm sorry if I startled you, but my position up here is just as normal and comfortable to me as I suspect a cliffside rookery is to you. I'm just another passenger, and there are rules against passengers doing nasty things to other passengers anyway, even if I wanted to. I realize my form causes a fear reaction in some races, but I assure you that the Askoth are quite civilized, even if our evolutionary ancestry is a bit obvious. I assure you that I don't live in some damp cave with a big web, but in a home with many amenities. My people even cultivate wine grapes and make excellent vintages."

She recovered, but something deep down told her that this was not someone she should trust. It wasn't the shape, it was the cold, calculating, and amused emotions the thing radiated. Still, she sensed no immediate danger.

"I'm sorry. It is not your form but the fact that I did not see you in here that upset me. I must remember that, from now on, *I* am the strange one."

"Strange . . . ? Well, perhaps. I must admit that you are imposing in a most unexpected sense. In many cultures you would be thought of as a supernatural being, a divine spirit. Do all Amborans look like you?"

"No—that is, yes, or sort of, anyway. All females are winged, although I admit to having some aspects that are uncommon among my people. You know I am from Ambora but you do not know what Amborans are like?"

The Askoth was impressed that she'd caught that. Ignorance doesn't mean stupidity, he reminded himself.

"We are off Ambora, and I watched you land in back. I doubted you could have come from anywhere else. Besides, there was a notice here that the ship would be picking up an Amboran passenger. It adds a few hours to the schedule and shortens the layovers in the next few ports to catch up."

The creature was fully extended now, and slowly dropped down from the ceiling to the floor on a surprisingly thin single line which it then retracted. She wasn't certain if it was created and then reingested or was some natural part of the thing, but it was slick.

"I'm sorry, again, for not introducing myself. I fear that my name is unpronounceable even using a translator, but we Askoth have names that are also somewhat descriptive, and that sometimes is understood, and in my case I'd prefer it wasn't. I've always found it a bit embarrassing. So, taking the two sounds from the name that create a meaningless name most races can pronounce, I tell everyone to just call me Wally."

She almost laughed at the silliness of the name, but retained control. Oddly, she sensed he was concealing something even with that long explanation, but that the bulk of it was true.

"Very well—Wally. I am called Jaysu."

"A pleasure. Now that we have been properly introduced, I should tell you that I am something of a merchant, self-employed, and that I sell services that others find useful. It is a well-paying occupation."

"What sort of services?" she asked him.

"Oh, I have a knack for recovering lost and stolen goods,

doing negotiations, all sorts of things. It is a talent I have taken a lifetime to perfect. And you?"

"I am a priestess."

"Indeed? And what is a member of the clergy doing traveling outside her own lands and away from her flock, if I may ask?"

She thought a moment. "I have no flock at the moment, but some believe that I may be able to render services that others find useful."

"Indeed? Like what, if I may ask?"

"Oh, recovering some lost goods, doing negotiations, all sorts of things."

Wally's translator gave off the most eerie collection of sounds she'd ever heard. It took her a moment to realize that it was attempting to simulate laughter. And the big spider thing *was* amused. She could feel that.

"Touché, my dear! I believe we will get along famously. But, come! I will lead you to the purser so you can get settled on the ship. How far are you traveling?"

"Quite far," she told him. "I haven't looked it up on a map yet, but it will be a great journey for me."

"All alone, in strange lands, amongst strange creatures, for your first big trip outside your homeland. It must be quite important, what you are doing."

"I am assured that it is, and both my order and my prayers have directed my path. And a priestess, Sir Wally, is *never* alone!"

She decided not to mention the fact that others on her side were allegedly already on board. Let strangers find out things on their own, particularly if it was none of their business.

It was a grand ship in every sense, with huge public areas and high ceilings and plenty of insulated bulletproof "glass," actually a kind of plastic, conveying an impression in most areas of a castle or a grandiose city. Still, she felt claustrophobic, more than she'd ever felt in Zone, where things were, if anything, more constricted. She wasn't sure why. Perhaps it was the rolling motion of the ship, or the throbbing of its powerful steam engines, or simply that it was not designed for those who flew.

The purser was a Kuall, a weasel-like creature with a long snout and round red eyes that seemed to be scanning a panorama rather than focusing on her. His feet were identical to his apelike hands, and the fact that he wore a black and gold braided uniform over his short brown furry body made him look more menacing than comical. Or was she seeing menace everywhere now?

The purser checked his lists, nodded, and said, "Yes, yes. We were expecting you. Glad you made it. We have an outside cabin for you on the top deck forward. Not much ship's motion there, plenty of air."

"What do you mean by an 'outside' cabin?" she asked him.

"Oh, it means that the main entrance is off the deck to the outside rather than inside, such as down those corridors there. It is possible to exit inside via a second door, but it is not the main entrance and it is usually kept secured so you have some room in there. Useful if the weather is really bad, though. Cabin U-12, up the stairs there or up any of the outer stairways from this deck and forward. We haven't ever had an Amboran passenger before, I don't think—nope nope. No Amborans, so we had to guess a bit. Winged folk usually don't use beds, so we put in a sand and rock box. If it is not good enough, let me know and we will see what we can do. Illumination is generally from pressurized oil lamps. You need only turn them up or down to get more or less light. More practical since two-thirds of our voyages are through no tech and semitech regions. Open buffet is forward on this deck all the way. If you are hungry, go anytime. If they have nothing you can eat, then tell them what you need. There has never been a race we could not somehow accommodate."

He said it all like the practiced speech it was, but also with some undisguised pride. If the rest of the crew was like the purser, she knew they loved their ship.

"Any luggage?" the purser asked her.

"Oh—no. I carry what little I require with me here. There is nothing else."

"Good, good. Come, then, I will take you up and show you the room. Nothing much else to do right now anyway. No stops for two days plus, nope nope. Come come, please."

The huge spiderlike creature said, "Oh, please go. There are only so many upper class passengers aboard at the moment, so we shall be unable to avoid one another. Get oriented, relax, and we'll speak again."

She couldn't shake the feeling she'd had before—that Wally was concealing something, perhaps a lot of things, and that he was no friend of hers—but she did not feel a direct threat from the Askoth, only some potential trouble down the line.

The steward took a large key, came around from behind his desk and said, "Follow me, please please." He then went to the sliding doors amidships and opened them casually, stepping out onto the breezy and still chilly outside deck. She followed, glad to get out into the air even if it was less than ideal weather.

As she walked outside, though, she saw and sensed a great hex boundary rise in front of them, and then the ship went through it.

Abruptly, the wind died to virtually nothing at all, the skies turned a deep and cloudless blue, the temperature shot up and it became very hot. Just as startling, she felt a whole range of machines aboard the great vessel suddenly come to life. Her faith said that all things contained spirits with some measure of power, answerable to the gods of their particular element. She now felt a whole new set of powerful presences all around her on the ship even though nothing about the ship itself seemed to change.

The sure-footed purser noted her startled reaction. "This is Cobo," he told her. "Very different. High-tech but all water. People here water breathers, yep yep. Live deep down, not sure what they are but they got some high-tech stuff. We talk talk to them on our sonargraphic radios, we do. Nice folks, whatever they are, so they say."

The only wind now was from the movement of the ship, but, oddly, the ship was picking up speed. The engines didn't seem to change, but the throbbing got louder. Perhaps some high-tech gizmos aided it in speeding across this otherwise featureless sea while they were in the high-tech region. She couldn't imagine what it must be like to be down there, breathing water and probably cut off from the sun. Would there even be colors? Would they see like she saw? And how did they use this high-tech power without getting themselves fried by it? Even she knew from somewhere that water and electricity didn't mix.

It was something she probably would never know or understand, and that was all right. The world was full of mysteries beyond solution or understanding, and as a priestess, she had accepted the limits of not being a god.

"You're getting used to the ship, yep yep," the purser noted approvingly. "Good balance, walking with the motion. That's the way to do it. You will do fine. Most fliers do. All balance, yep yep. Some of the others, they can't take it. Get sick, stay sick. Awful messy, yep yep."

"There are other flying races?" It had never occurred to her that there might be. Then she remembered that the funny little lizard thing was supposedly a flier, too. She couldn't see how, without feathers, but she accepted it.

"Yep yep. Ochoans common 'round this part of the ocean, but we get lots. Yaxas, pretty big wings like butterflies, many more. *Most* races don't fly, but a fair number do."

"Most walk along the ground like you," she surmised, finding memories of giant butterfly creatures somewhere in the back of her mind as well. From where? she wondered. She had no memory of actually seeing them, yet she felt she must have.

"Nope nope," the Kuall replied. "Most *swim*. More water than land on this world, on *most* worlds where ones like us could live, so they say."

She followed him up a broad metallic stairway to the next deck after staving off the temptation to fly up and meet him at the top. Too many ropes and stuff around, although from the deck she could easily get off the ship if she had to. It would be getting back on that would present problems.

The decks were wide, designed to accommodate the needs of a variety of physical forms. There were also lifeboats along both sides of the ship, set so they blocked no views from the decks but could be stepped into by even the bulkiest of creatures. The open ocean was still a dangerous place, particularly in the less than high-tech regions, when there was no visibility beyond the living lookouts perched on porches two-thirds of the way up the masts fore and aft.

She saw the forward lookout position being vacated by two creatures, both of whom looked insectlike and simply walked down the side of the broad mast, one after the other. She found such multiracial crews amazing; it seemed odd that races so different could live and work together in these close quarters, considering how alien they were from one another. She was still getting used to those she'd seen who were also thinking creatures like the Amborans, and now this ship showed an amazing degree of interdependence without, possibly, any of them even thinking about it. It was a revelation to her, far more than what she'd seen in Zone, where each race kept a little bit of itself in a separate compartment for convenience.

The purser led her to an area, just before the wide bridge, that housed the great ship's control center. It spanned the forward area deck on both sides as well as creating a separate building of its own atop the upper deck roof. He stopped at a large, dull red door and, with the dramatically large bronze key, slipped it in the lock and turned until there was a click. Then he opened the door, which swung in rather than slid to one side, checked it, and gestured for her to approach.

"If you have no luggage or valuables, then you have no need to lock the door, nope nope," the Kuall told her. "Just make sure the door is shut with a click or a clunk. If you want privacy or to keep it locked, get this key from me and use it, then lock up when you leave and bring it back to me or my assistants at the desk. No need to carry it around, maybe lose it, nope nope."

The cabin was surprisingly roomy, but basically a rectangle containing no notable luxuries. The purser showed her how to open or close vents to the outside air so that cool breezes could get in and hot air inside could escape without the rest of the weather intruding, and how to raise and lower the oil lamp. Both were unnecessary, as a blower system cooled the room, and the molding along the ceiling was glowing quite adequately to light the whole room.

"Those only work in high-tech hexes," the purser told her. "Otherwise it's the oil and natural air venting. We find, though, that if you keep your doors and vents closed and don't use the door much, it'll keep a long time, even overnight, yep yep."

There was a sink and basin, but no bath or shower, not that she would use them anyway. There was also a strange modular structure that turned out to be a kind of building block toilet. Each of the pieces fit together in a lot of different ways, and thus a large number of races could be accommodated by these shape adjustments. At the bottom, though, was a deep black hole and the sound of constant water going through. She was fascinated by the ingenuity. Apparently there was some kind of filtered intake that forced water through a network of pipes, the water moving constantly by some kind of gravity feed and the forward energy of the ship. No matter what sort of hex they were in, the toilets constantly flushed, or, perhaps, in deference to those living below, it all went to some place mysterious and unpleasant in the bottom of the ship to be emptied in port service.

She was also impressed when the purser showed her how to get water out of a pipe that hovered over the basin. "Comes from tanks up top," he told her. "Always fresh, always pure."

It was clear by the discolorations on the floor rug and on the walls that furniture had been moved out for her. Instead, against one wall was a sand pit with rough wooden logs crossing through it, an arrangement very much like the kind they had in Ambora. There was also a meter-high chest with drawers and a smooth top that could be used should she wish to stow anything. It was spartan, but exactly what she needed.

She thanked the purser, who bowed slightly and left, closing the door behind him. For the first time, she was alone, and she felt a bit better and safer. She liked the location. Opening the door, she was in an area where she could probably take off without killing herself, and if she could make it forward of the bridge, she could launch into the wind, which would be almost ideal. The cabin felt comfortable, the roll minimized just as the purser had promised, and with no compartments save the water closet, she felt reasonably secure.

That spider thing still gave her the creeps in spite of its manners, but she was beginning to feel that she could actually do this.

She wondered who aboard was her contact and what it would look like. There was certainly plenty of time to find out. Right now, though, she felt more of a need for prayer and meditation than social interaction. This was going to be a long voyage.

Yabbo

THE ONLY THING KEEPING THEM THERE WAS THE BLACK DOME, and they knew it. Still, they couldn't remain there much longer without things taking a decidedly inconvenient turn.

If Mitchuk comes around one more time with champagne and bonbons, I'm gonna puke, Ari commented sourly.

Oh, don't be such a party pooper, Ming responded. *Besides, I'm not sure what champagne or bonbons would do to our constitution these days. And, well, he is kind of cute, in a silly little way.*

Can the romance, this is business, he reminded her. *Besides, if that guy's cute then fish are works of art.*

Look in the mirror lately, doll? We are fish. Sort of, anyway.

Yeah, well, maybe you've adjusted to this better than me. I mean, back in the old days we'd have taken one look at a Kalindan and ran screaming from the monster from the deep. Now they seem like normal folks, and even my dreams of those days somehow have everybody looking like the Swamp Creature from Planet Hell.

You apparently saw too many bad cinemas, kid. But, in fact, Ari was right, and she knew it. From the old Terran perspective, Kalindans were holy horrors, yet now, Mitchuk *did* look like a cutie to her, damn it. It was perhaps the only thing mentally the Well did to adjust you to a new environment. You looked at it, and yourself, in wonder rather than in shock and horror, and quickly adjusted to it.

For that matter, Kalindans didn't look all that distinctive. It was more a matter of attitude, of carriage, of the body language and actual language, than any specific physical

differences. They all were humanoid, averaged about two meters in length, had wide, round, light-sensitive eyes with double
lids—one of which was transparent—and they had rounded,
fishlike heads on humanoid necks, skin like a crocodile's, a
rubbery dorsal fin and a shark's tail, and they were dark green
tinged with yellowish spots here and there. Not the popular
idea of a mermaid, definitely. In fact, you couldn't even point
to a Kalindan on a sexual basis, since at least once in their
lives, sometimes more than once, just about every Kalindan
changed sex. The fact that within the hex just about all of
them were changing to the same sex at the same time made
them even less physically distinctive.

And yet either of them could spot and identify individual
Kalindans at a good-sized distance with no problem at
all. They just couldn't explain, even to each other, how they
did it.

Ming, Ari decided, had acclimated to this new world and
life far better than he had, and he had mixed feelings about it.
He didn't want to acclimate much more than he had, but,
stuck in the same body with her, he wasn't in a position to go
off on his own. He sensed that Ming wanted to be a little
adventurous with these amorous males armed not just with
male libidos, but government decrees as well—to justify
their lust—but, hell, neither he nor she were even sure
how the Kalindans made out with each other. It sure wasn't
touchy-feely, not with *this* skin.

Nothing had made the differences between them more pronounced than their individual reactions to accepting themselves as members of this new society. Even as they seemed
to share each other's thoughts and became more knowledgeable about one another than any two people probably had ever
been, their personalities still clashed, keeping them distinct.
In fact, both suspected that they clung desperately to vestiges
of individualism in a last battle to remain themselves.

Neither of them wanted a merger; they both preferred a
partnership. But deep down they both understood that the
merger was inevitable; either they did it, or they would grow
to hate rather than love one another, and in the end go mad.

And yet, both their personalities were too strong to accept it as an inevitability, and so they fought against it.

Damn Core! The computer had stolen their other body, and divorced another mind from its rightful body as well. An individual was the sum total of memories and experiences of its lifetime plus the physiological factors. That angelic girl had the physical, but had been shorn of her memories and experiences; they had the memories and experiences of two, but lacked separate physical containers. All because the computer wanted desperately to become a real live boy . . .

This experience was giving Ari a newfound sense of ethics. He'd never dreamed that he had such a thing or could acquire it. Perhaps he was getting it from Ming, he thought. He didn't like it; it was an uncomfortable fit, all the more so for being unavoidable once you had it. It might explain the otherwise incomprehensible gulf between most cops and most crooks. They both were in the same sort of business, but for the same risks, one paid a hell of a lot better than the other.

Ming sensed Ari's turmoil, and to some extent shared it, yet she knew he had to work it out for himself or it would mean nothing in the end.

It's not easy to figure out who the good guys are, is it? she commented. *I know the problem. And even if they're on your side, some of the amoral middle aren't that hot, either. The only thing you can do is decide on who's absolutely evil. At least you can go after* them *with some sense of feeling.*

Which brought them back to the mystery of the black dome.

There was traffic in and out, that was for sure. Not just non-Yabban creatures, but also large crates of varying shapes and sizes. The races managing the operations seemed innocuous enough, but they all definitely had some home relationship with Chalidang. No Chalidangers or their allies had made any sort of appearance in the diplomatic compound, but there was little doubt that they were behind whatever was in that dome, and that, with a combination of diplomatic immunity and large scale bribery, the Yabbans didn't care what they were doing there.

You couldn't get much of anything out of the Yabbans

themselves. They seemed pleasant and ordinary enough, but she and Ari got the impression that the translator conveyed an inaccurate picture of what they said and meant, not only because the Yabbans' actions often didn't quite mesh with the words, but also because their lives were simply so, well, *alien.* Kalindans might well look very different than Terrans and live in a biosphere where up and down had little meaning, but they were still closer, socially and culturally, to Terrans than the Yabbans were.

We can't put this off any longer, you know, Ming pointed out to him after a week in the compound.

I know. The decrees and all that. I think we have to move on, and quickly, he agreed, hoping she meant before any assignations, not after.

But not until we get a look inside that black dome, she replied.

There was no night or day down there; Yabbo was shallow enough that some sunlight penetrated, but not enough to give more than a sense of the passage of time now and then. Like most undersea realms where one had some eyesight, Yabbo depended on chemical-based illumination, and some biochemical illumination as well, and didn't need the great light from above.

That meant, like most underwater civilizations, there was less sense of night and day, work time and rest time, than there was a continuous existence divided into shifts. That was fine for Yabbans, and no problem in everyday life to the foreigners who lived and worked there, either, but it was difficult for Ming and Ari to figure out the best time to sneak into the black dome.

And yet they found that communiqués passed between Core and them via the Zone Gate courier system yielded little curiosity on the part of the Zone types to find out. It was more an attitude of, well, what could they possibly be doing in the dome that would be a threat inside a hex where the only way you could store electricity for later use was to be born an eel?

Core seemed more interested lately in getting them over to a different hex, one not very far away and, from the alliance's vantage point, more valuable. The nation of Sanafe was the object of a lot of attention lately, it seemed, for it was rumored to have a piece of the legendary Straight Gate, and that they would not be willing to part with it. If rumors were true, the attack on Ochoa and the subversion of Kalinda and its neighbors was geared to an operation that would indeed wrest this precious object from Sanafe. For its part, Sanafe wasn't talking at all but had made it clear they would accept any protection they could get.

Sanafe next, but first that dome . . .

They had been near it many times, trying to scout out a way in, to chart the schedule of guards, but so far they'd not found an entry that made them confident of success. They kept trying to think of a way as the pressures on them to do their duty to Kalinda, and bear children, mounted to almost unbearable levels.

Core had not been any help in easing that sort of pressure, either. "Go ahead," the former computer had written. "It should be a fascinating new experience."

If it was all that fascinating, then Core should try it and not insist that they do it, Ari thought. It wasn't bearing a little one that worried him nearly so much as what kind of commitment came after it. Neither of them had ever considered, let alone wanted, kids, but neither was ready to walk away from their own kid and coldly toss it to the fates.

The dome is pretty much like the others, including this one, Ming noted. *There has to be a weakness somewhere.*

Ari stared at the transparent Kalindan consular dome and suddenly thought of something. It was no bell jar; it was, rather, a geodesic type of dome composed of triangular struts supporting the overall shell to equalize the pressure.

Yeah, so? she prompted. *What's the difference how it's made?*

The difference, my dear, is in that equalization of pressure by use of the geodesic principle, he responded, thinking. *It means that if the black dome is similarly constituted, we can drill a damned hole big enough to crawl through into one of the segments without compromising the overall structure. I wonder how thick these things are?*

She saw what he meant. *Yeah! Be kind of obvious, though, won't it? I mean, we can't use laser cutters and the like in this hex.*

Might not need it, he told her. *Let's pay a visit now to a construction site. Good old Kalinda, building for Yabbo's future, right? I wonder what they use to cut and shape things that don't fit like they should and where they should?*

There wasn't much problem finding what was needed: a tiny gas-powered torch that could cut through almost anything, and some industrial-strength suction cups used to keep things from falling in when you cut through them. The small torch was dangerous, but Ari felt comfortable with it. It was close to some tools his uncle's shadier associates had used now and then to get to pretty baubles the boss wanted but the owners had been unwilling to sell.

The trick would be to keep the very bright flame from being seen by all and sundry when they used it. It would be tough enough getting close to the top of that dome without being seen by curious folks like guards with nasty guns below.

They were fortunate that the dome was either made of very dark material or had been painted dark on the inside. That left a fairly nonreflective surface that kept the water around it fairly dark as well. With sundown, the top of the dome would be difficult to see.

They found a twenty centimeter loop of industrial plastic that was pliable yet would hold whatever shape you put it in, and this would become their shield. It could be wrapped around their waist, and would look like clothing or an ornament if spotted, yet it could be easily removed and create a decent circular guard for the operation.

At least, that was the way it was supposed to work.

As the light from the far off sun waned, they floated in the compound applying a thick black grease to their body, trying to get it as dark as possible. They wrapped the plastic shield around their waist and put the torch and the suction cup devices into a dark sack. Then they headed toward the dark dome, about three hundred meters farther along in the compound, gliding casually in the water in the hope that they wouldn't be noticed. As they approached, they slowly rose toward the top of the compound.

The dark dome hadn't had any particular routine they could pin down, but the sundown shift seemed to consist of fewer creatures than the other two, even if the number of guards remained the same. They waited, hovering nearby, making sure that everybody was in the spots they usually were and that there were no deliveries headed their way. Finally, as the last illumination from above faded, they ever so slowly approached the dome at a level a meter or two below the top of the dome.

This is really amateur night, Ming commented worriedly. *How incompetent do these guys have to be to not spot us?*

Pretty bad, I admit, Ari conceded. *Still, semitech is semitech. No electrical alarms, no fusion-powered super computer guardians, not even decent lighting. Most of those guys down there are from high-tech hexes like ours; you kind of lose your touch for the primitive when you're brought up with the gadgets.*

She hoped he was right. There was so much that could go wrong, including the fact that they'd never gotten close enough to the dome to determine if it was not merely a filtered extension, like the Kalindan consulate, but perhaps a pressurized area. At least they knew it wasn't filled with liquid; people had gone in and out of it many times as they had cased the place.

They picked the darkest area of the dome, away from the consulate row and facing away from the city, which continued to glow in artificial light. It was, however, a softer light that didn't have the intensity to outline someone well away from its sources. That much seemed to be going their way.

Choosing an area below the top of the dome allowed them to work without being obvious to anyone in the consular area, and the upper curvature allowed for an angle when they put down and anchored their dark shield. The torch might be obvious from above, which was always a risk, but it would be invisible from the lower, more commonly used levels.

The torch itself was no laser beam; the flame was concentrated and incredibly hot, but it was as much a melter as a cutter. Ming let Ari handle it, and he began to cut in small bits, knowing they would have to secure the piece when it fell and not wanting any part of it to fall down into the dome itself.

The work was also almost blinding; neither of them had anticipated a flame so very bright, and they'd brought everything except dark goggles, since they hadn't seen any around.

Hurry up, or we're gonna wind up doing this by touch, she prodded.

You want to do it, take over, he responded huffily. *I'm doing the best I can. Just a couple more . . . There! Now we need the suction cups!*

They pressed one to the side of the dome, then the other to the center of the cut-out piece. After pulling on them to ensure that they both held, Ari carefully melted through the last few tabs holding the piece onto the rest of the dome.

Finally, he reached down and pulled on the linkage just above the cup on the cutout, and it gave and came straight up and away. They now had a way inside, if they were lucky.

There wasn't much to see from this vantage point, and bright dots, afterflashes from the torch, were still persistent. Still, at least part of the place was lit with the same chemical lighting used in the town, and they could see that there were some people at the lower, or floor, section of the tank.

You game? she asked him.

We've come this far, he replied. *Might as well.*

It was a very tight fit getting through the cut piece, even after they discarded the shielding. Still, they just barely managed, with a lot of twisting and turning, to squeeze through.

Ari then set the cutout back in place. There was some play because its melted edges no longer would create a real fit, but it would do. The trick was to keep that primordial soup that was Yabbo's "atmosphere" from coming in. At least the melted areas would give no more entry to the outside than the routine comings and goings by the lower entrance, until they planned to be long gone.

They found themselves in a gigantic warehouse full of modular shelving and form-fitting containers. It was impossible to tell what was in any of them; they were encoded in a type of writing neither could understand, nor would it have done them much good without the meanings for the codes.

There was far too much action below to consider breaking open one or more of them to find out what it was about. Perhaps if they remained and the activity below ceased, it might be possible, but right now there wasn't much of an emergency exit if they were detected, particularly if they were outnumbered.

And they knew it wouldn't take much to outnumber them.

So they glided slowly and carefully between the stacks and tried to get down to a point where they could observe without being observed.

They almost met disaster right off. There was a sudden movement from below almost before they could get behind a crate and freeze. A large, dark, menacing shape arose so close to them they could almost touch it. It was, strangely, a familiar sort of figure, even though it had a leathery soft, spiral shell-like body and lots of tentacles, each apparently designed to do a particular job. More distinctive was the eye, which was on a muscle-driven version of a lazy Susan, able to pop out of the soft shell and pivot in any direction, or come far enough out so that, if both eyes were so situated, it would have three-dimensional vision instead of multiple vision.

What the hell? That's a damned Ghoman! Ari exclaimed.

Ming thought a moment. *No, it's a Chalidang. I'd bet anything on that.*

But—But they're the same! *They're absolutely the same!*

Maybe. I never was close enough to a Ghoman to be able to tell. I admit, though, that all creatures with ten tentacles, a soft spiral shell, and a unique eye like that look alike to me. So Gamins and Chalidangers look the same, maybe are *the same. So what?*

So the only thing Josich changed was its sex, which is something we've been familiar with here, too. Hmph!

She understood what he meant. Why did Josich get to remain pretty much the same creature while they were translated into such a different race and biome? It didn't seem fair. In fact, it didn't seem like the system here at all.

You know—I never thought of this, but if Josich had come in as a male, then he'd have been a dead shellfish. They already had an Emperor, and the bloodline was pretty firmly established. But as a female, as essentially a courtesan and vamp, as a she, Josich was able to worm her way right into the social structure. A social structure that's probably not too far off the Ghoman style, either, judging from what we've been told. Jeez. It's almost as if the bastard somehow managed to plan it this way!

It was a sobering thought, and if it contained even a gram of truth, it was unsettling. How come the Well did things fairly randomly for everybody else but basically cooked to order for the Ghoman monarch?

What do you think? Could we take one that size in a fight? she wondered.

Sure. Just give us a fully charged and operable laser rifle and it's no sweat. Hand-to-tentacle, though, I think we're outnumbered ten to two."

The creature was above them, perhaps five levels up, and they feared for a moment that it would go all the way and find the cut, but it was after something else entirely, and they couldn't see what it was.

You notice how cold to the touch some of these are? Ari asked her. *It's like they have refrigeration units or something.* But that was impossible, not in a semitech hex. Or was it?

Now that Ari pointed it out, they *did* all seem cold to the touch, yet the water temperature wasn't that bad, at least to a Kalindan.

They both suddenly realized that this was quite unusual in and of itself. Yabbo was a warm water hex, and Kalinda's water was quite cold. This was more Kalindan temperature than Yabbo, yet there was filtered water allowed to enter and leave the dome in an automatic manner, as with the Kalindan consulate down the street.

These supercooled crates were the ice in the giant glass bubble.

But how could you maintain it in this kind of hex?

Has to be some kind of chemical doing it, perhaps a chemical bath, Ming guessed. *They want to keep something frozen yet in a place you'd never expect it to be.*

Well, I surely don't think it's fresh veggies, and if it's Ghoman food, then where's the army to eat it?

There was no longer any question about it. They had to somehow see the contents of at least one of these containers.

There seemed to be half a dozen people inside what they were now thinking of as the warehouse, at least half of them Chalidang. This was unsettling because they had not seen any Chalidangers in Yabbo before, even in their long stakeouts, nor did the nasty creatures maintain any official presence within the hex. Conversation amongst the warehouse crew didn't help; they were simply not close enough for the translator to accurately pick up and translate the sounds into coherent phrases, although the occasional word drifted up to them, some of which raised as many questions as they answered.

For one thing, at least one of them either was an army general, or else they spoke a lot about generals. The latter seemed unlikely, but what would a high-ranking officer of such a faraway force be doing here? They were much too valuable to risk in some simple clandestine spy operation. Generals either fought battles or remained in headquarters plotting strategies. They didn't show up in the middle of nowhere with no force at all.

The other familiar word that shot out from the usual banalities was "Kincaid." It was only said once, and never repeated, so they weren't sure they had heard it right, that it wasn't just a coincidental combination of sounds, but it seemed more likely to be what they thought.

One thing was clear: Core had been wrong to ignore this place. Something big was being set up here, something very nasty.

When the dark, tentacled shape again descended, passed them, and rejoined the others below, they rose a bit and went over for a closer examination of the crates. There was enough light from the lower areas bleeding up to allow for some vision, but for the life of them, neither could figure out how the things were fastened together. It seemed they'd been cast in a single, seamless, solid form. But even with the cold, they did get a different sense as they passed over them, a sensation they had almost missed because of that very chill and because it was simply too pervasive.

Whatever was inside was emitting an electromagnetic field very similar to a bottom-feeding fish that might take flight by burying itself in the sand. But these cases would hold some very large fish.

Ming had an awful thought. *Ari, about how big would you say that Chalidanger was?*

He thought a moment. *Maybe two meters, not counting the mostly retractable tentacles. Why?*

And how big would you say each of these crates is?

He saw where she was going with this. *Oh, no! You're not suggesting that each of these contains a Chalidang soldier?*

Well, it fits. And I know of some races back in the universe that can be put into deep cryogenic sleep for an almost indefinite period with no harm.

Yeah, but that's using the highest of high-tech devices to maintain and monitor them, and even then, only certain races could do it and not be killed or at least brain damaged. You're suggesting we have a ton of Chalidang's finest here packed in little more than dry ice.

I wish we knew more about the Ghomas, damn it! I mean, suppose they could use that highest of high-tech to create these devices and seal in the quick frozen soldiers, then ship them here. If the freezing could be maintained on a chemical basis, and if they could be awakened by a chemical additive or antidote, well, it might make sense.

Let's get real here for a minute, he objected. *You're suggesting that Chalidang freeze-dried a small army and then is mailing it bit by bit to this storage depot?*

Hey, they launched an invasion army with full naval support before, and it telegraphed their every move and they got their tails whipped. Think about it. Your best soldiers, your highest trained, all thawed out and suddenly appearing in a hex near you.

Ari thought about it. If true, it was diabolically clever and very much up to Josich's reputation, yet he couldn't buy it. *I mean, how many crates are here, stacked one on top of the other? A few thousand at best. Not enough to defeat a professional army of defense, even one like ours.*

He was right about that, she had to admit. *So, not an army of conquest. Clandestine? Sabotage? Or maybe less a conquering army than an army of occupation?* Now *that* was even more unsettling.

So, if you're right, they've got a pretty good force here, they're running out of room—so this must be pretty close to the max—and they've thawed out a general and two aides. That suggests that whatever they're going to do, they're going to do it pretty damned soon.

Cobo—Night

THERE WAS A CERTAIN PEACE TO THE OPEN OCEAN AT NIGHT.

Jaysu didn't like the big ship, even though it was designed for comfort and convenience. She hadn't been taught to appreciate such things; they were a sign of laziness and decadence, an attempt to make heaven out of the here and now without any real sense that there was something higher or greater.

Out here, on the open deck at night, she could appreciate what was really important.

Normally hazy, the sky was for some reason crystal clear over the Cobo deeps this night, and on the Well World, the clear night skies were taken for granted by most of the people. Not by her; *never* by her.

The spectacular sight of millions of stars forming a vast pattern in the sky was good enough, but the swirls of gases and clouds of interstellar material made a clear night a wondrous sight of the heavens.

She had mentioned this at dinner, and one of the passengers—an officious fellow who looked like an orange, vaguely humanoid fish, but was actually a creature of some desert hex—started going on about being in the midst of a globular cluster and adjacent to spectacular twin nebulae that caused such a lit and crowded sky, and on and on and on without any sense of the poetry of the gods inside him. She hadn't any idea what a globular cluster might be, let alone nebulae, but she could see the handiwork of powers greater than she just by looking up, and that work was of great beauty.

She *did* understand, and accept, that each of those stars

was a sun like the one that rose every day, and that around some of those far-off suns there might well be planets, and perhaps even planets with highly developed life-forms, but that was an easier part of her cosmology than reducing beauty to chemical compounds.

She had long gotten her sea legs, as the crew called it, and no longer even thought of the motion of the ship. Fliers would more easily adapt, she knew, because balance was all-important to them, but she still would have preferred to be up there than down here.

She'd thought she lost the wonder of flight when she'd accepted her calling to the priesthood; to have it back and not use it seemed somehow sacrilegious, even though she knew it was just her own impatience.

Carefully using the stretched rope lines for safety's sake, she managed to easily walk around the great vessel and up and down its stairs and decks. It was difficult to think that it had somehow been built, and by the hands and perhaps tentacles and claws of many races working as shipwrights.

The boat—no, it was a *ship*, as one of the crew had explained, since it had a solid superstructure and was stabilized by ballast, whatever that meant—was surprisingly uninhabited for something so huge. Oh, there were cabins capable of holding hundreds of people from a vast number of races, but most were unoccupied. That was not the standard for some routes, it was said, but for this particular run the demand for passengers was always low, while the cargo, which was still the main reason for such a ship's existence, was packed as solidly as it could be. This was because all of the great ocean ships followed one of a very few standardized designs, all of which allowed for some passenger transits and services to match. It was just that where this ship was going, few wanted to travel, and fewer were welcome to travel to them.

She could understand that. Nobody traveled to Ambora, nor would they be welcome if they did, and she had seen at least one Pyron, and the thought of a whole nation of those giant snake creatures wasn't exactly the kind of place most people would be anxious to pay money to visit. There wasn't a whole lot of tourism on the Well World anyway; travel tended to be for business, although a ship like this could and sometimes was used by large groups for local functions and recreational use.

So, hundreds of cabins but only a few dozen passengers. It made the great ship seem somehow empty, and, at night, a little creepy. That was another good reason why she liked being outside during this period. So long as there was access to the skies, she felt she could cope with almost anything, even though the great map in the lounge showed them to be far from land, headed for a long stretch where anything solid would be most likely beyond her flying range. It was not a good thought, nor a secure one.

She walked down to the main deck and forward to the bow area. It was the least congested in terms of ropes and masts and the like, although it was littered with all sorts of things on the deck itself, including small cranes and winches and stuff she couldn't imagine the use for. With the swift forward motion of the ship, even with the roll and rising and falling motion of the bow, it would be easy to take off into the night sky.

The noise of the ship slicing through the great waters masked other sounds, if any existed, save the rattle of things around her caused by the ship's movement and vibration from the big engines.

In spite of the clear night, the sea was hardly gentle; the stiff winds had created a choppy sea, and though the main deck was quite a bit higher than the water, there were points where the bow seemed to dip. There was then an odd shifting feeling, and it seemed the waves would break over the bow and onto the deck. They never quite seemed to make it, but she involuntarily reached out to take hold of the safety guide rope and began to wonder if she shouldn't go inside after all.

The bow dipped again, and some spray came over it and wet down the area forward of the superstructure, making her nervous enough to edge back and look for the closest main door inside. Suddenly, when the bow was at its low point, something dark and fairly large seemed to launch itself out of the waves and onto the deck, where it landed with an inglorious *splat*. She stepped back against the rail and for a moment weighed the odds of flight versus making the closest ship's entryway.

The creature appeared momentarily stunned, then swore in a loud voice, "Damn! I *hate* it when I do that!" It shook its head as if to clear it of cobwebs, grabbed for the rope and pulled itself erect.

Her night vision was not the best, but the creature now loomed in the darkness, taller than she was, a kind of dark blob sitting atop a slightly smaller blob. What made it stand out and seem threatening, though, wasn't the size or shape, but the eyes, which reflected even the small amount of light there and seemed to shine. It was eerie and unsettling.

The creature saw her. "Terribly sorry," it said, sounding sincere. "Didn't mean to be so dramatic, but my biggest problems are always the landings. Hadn't guessed anyone would be out and about on deck on a night like this anyway, and particularly not *you*."

She was still nervous and resisting the urge to fly or otherwise flee, but she summoned up her courage. "You know me?"

"Well, bless my soul! Never laid eyes on you in my life. Don't have to, though, if you're the only Amboran on this vessel."

"I am Jaysu, Priestess of—"

"Oh, I know *that*," the creature responded. "Pleased to meet you. Name's Zicanthripes, but most everyone calls me Eggy. Terribly undignified, I know, but I've gotten used to it." He paused for a moment, then seemed to realize that he'd neglected some vital piece of information, or, perhaps, assumed more than he should have. "I'm your contact. I'm from Core."

"You—You are of Cobo, then?"

"Oh, goodness me! No! These chaps live so far down I'm not terribly certain *what* they are! If they even were in the top layers of the ocean here they'd fall apart. Deep pressure types, y'see. No, I'm an Ixthansan. As air breathers, we don't use much of anything the folks of Cobo want or need, but since the ocean is our element, we can use the waters and the life that's only in the upper fifty meters or so of the ocean. We're also from a nontech hex, which is kind of limiting, so it's handy sometimes to have base ships in Cobo where we can do some fancy things. It's a treaty, y'see. We don't use our depths at all, couldn't even get down that far without being crushed like a spoiled grape, but they can use even a nontech region for whatever sort of agriculture they do. So, we have a deal. They get free use of our bottom and we get free use of their top. Works out fine."

"You—You are a marine mammal, then? I do not see well in this darkness."

"Oh, goodness no! I suppose our ancestors were birds, possibly like yours. There's a mild similarity in the way we're built. The difference is that you fly in the air and we fly in the ocean."

Eggy stepped forward so the light from the nearby forward lounge windows caught him and she could finally make him out.

He didn't walk very well; it was actually a highly comical gait, the legs too short for more than waddling along. The feet were birdlike, though, but like aquatic birds, wide and webbed with long curved claws at the end. He also had wings; stiffer, barer than her own, and situated along the sides of the torso. Unlike her, though, the wings were also hands, the tips ending in grotesque fingers after the bones had first curved around to form and support the wing. The neck was short but flexible, and the head far more avian than humanoid, as hers was, with a flexible, dark-colored bill that was perhaps half the width of a duck's in proportion to the body, yet resembled a duckbill more than anything else. The nostrils were atop the bill, and in back of the whole thing were two large eyes that resembled not a bird's so much as a cat's eyes, changing with and reflecting the light. It appeared smooth and inky black, but when it waddled a bit closer, it looked like short fur. It was neither bald nor fur-covered, though; they were densely packed feathers.

"You look a tad uncomfortable," Eggy commented. "Why don't we go inside and talk for a bit?"

She welcomed that idea, although she asked, "Won't they find you and charge you for passage?"

He chuckled. "Perhaps they will, as far as it goes, but I'm only here for a bit. I'll consume nothing costing the line anything, and I'll make my own exit. If they wish to send a bill to the embassy for a few hours' passage in mid-ocean, they're welcome to try."

It really was a large but ungainly creature, and she couldn't imagine what it was like in the water. It was difficult to think of such a strange and oddly constructed being as existing comfortably in any environment.

He seemed to catch her thoughts, or was used to others thinking it and guessed at the subject.

"We are designed for the water, as you are truly designed for the air. Unlike you, we don't need to ever land. Our country is a great mass of floating, living sea grasses that provide all the support we require, which is primarily for laying and hatching eggs. I believe that flying for you is no different than swimming for us. For all the differences in our appearance, you're about as comfortable aboard this thing as I am. Just imagine being able to fly at all times, finding food, companionship, everything you require, without ever landing save to keep the young safe until they can join you. We're weightless in our environment, and we can chase down, outrun, or do virtually anything in that element. Gravity is the only enemy, and that's only when we're out like this."

He made it sound almost poetic, and she could at least imagine what it might be like, applying her own joy of flight with never having to fight the pull to earth.

"You have a message for me?" she asked him.

He seemed amused. "I thought it might be the other way around. I'm curious, though. Why do you take my word for it that I'm from Core? I know I frightened you with that entrance, and I've said and shown you nothing to indicate that I'm really on the side of the just, but you have accepted it."

She hadn't even thought about it. "No one can lie to me without my knowing it, and the truth is always evident to me," she told him honestly. "If you had been playing me false, I would have known it."

"Indeed? Never saw my like before, yet you are that confident? If you aren't being naive, then you're one of the most dangerous folks to have around in any conversation. Good heavens! Everyone would always have to tell the truth around you! The whole of civilization would be jeopardized!"

She didn't understand the comment and would have liked to know why he thought her "dangerous," but she sensed that he was at least partly speaking tongue-in-bill, as it were, and decided not to press the point. There were things that many of these strange creatures said that she knew she'd never truly understand. Instead she decided to get right to business. "So you have no message for me?"

"Oh, a few things, but first things first. I realize you haven't been aboard here very long, but if you can truly sense the just and the ungodly, then are any of the ungodly aboard? And can you describe them?"

"A large green spider-thing," she told him. "Pleasant enough, but he radiates an evil I cannot quite describe. I find it difficult to cope with someone who has manners, education, vast experience, even a sense of humor, yet seems to have absolutely no moral sense at all. He seems to divide everyone and everything into 'useful' and 'not useful,' and I'm afraid that anyone in the second category is pretty much irrelevant to him if they get in his way. He is, I believe, the most dangerous person I have ever met, yet so far he radiates no particular intent toward me."

"He has a name?"

"He says that we could not pronounce nor understand it. He calls himself 'Wally.' "

"Interesting. Any companions?"

"Two horrid little creatures that resemble the small apes of the coastal cliffs of Ambora, but they wear clothing and have serviceable wings. I believe they can fly if need be, although not great distances. They also sit around smoking horrible smelling little cigars and giggling at inane things. They are as evil and cold as their spiderlike companion, but I do not think they are very clever, either of them. They work for him."

"Hmmm . . . Well, at least you know your enemies. Anyone else?"

"It seems as if everyone on this ship, even half the crew, have some sort of coldness or cruelness in them, but those stand out because they appear to be the ones interested in me."

"Well, you watch them. We have no idea who the Askoth is, but he was behind the securing of a piece of the Straight Gate only last month. We have to assume he's working for Chalidang, if not directly, then as a freelance agent, a hired gun. They need some operatives that aren't of the races in their alliance and can breathe air just to do some background dirty work. Assume that they know you are with us, and also assume that they will not hesitate to move against you, even kill you, if they think you are a threat. I would strongly recommend that you cease doing what you were doing tonight and be very social with the other passengers and crew here as much as possible. You may not like them, but these types do not like to do nasty things around lots of witnesses. Stick to your cover story and stay in well-lit, populated areas."

"Just as others cannot be false with me, I cannot lie to them," she told him. "It is not something that I have any choice over. It is a part of my calling."

If Eggy had shoulders, his motion would have been an easy shrug. "So don't lie. Just don't tell them what you don't have to. You are going to Quislon for religious reasons, and for an exchange of religious thought. That is by no means untrue."

"But they know it's more than that."

"Yes, they do. But they *can* lie, and usually love doing it. Just keep telling yourself to never volunteer information. That is almost always sufficient."

Eggy was clearly not the religious type, nor comfortable with those who were. He couldn't help wondering if this priestess wasn't going to wind up spider dinner, unable to protect herself. He'd never seen such a helpless young thing before, at least unless it was a dumb fish swimming toward an Ixthansan hunting pack.

"Have your spider and winged apes dropped where they are getting off?" Eggy asked her.

"They are being met at sea, as I understand it," she replied. "Only I get the idea from the time line expressed that they will be leaving close to either Quislon or Pyron."

"Yes, that fits. They're after the Quislon part of the Straight Gate. Well, they won't find this as easy as Pegiri, but I won't underestimate this sort." He reached into a natural pouch in his abdomen, something she'd not suspected was there, and brought out a tiny object which he held out for her to take. She did so, and examined it.

"You know what that is?"

"No, not really," she admitted.

"Well, it's a camera. Takes pictures that can be printed or digitized. It's quite simple. You just hold it in your hand so that that little gemlike spot isn't covered, and point that spot at whoever or whatever you want to photograph. Squeeze here, and the picture is taken. We want you to take pictures of our spider friend, his henchmen, and, for that matter, anybody else you don't feel is a saint who's aboard. Don't worry about whether the subject's in the picture or anything like that. It's a *very* smart little camera and it knows what we want. When you're done, someone, maybe me, probably somebody else, will pick it up and take it off to a hex Gate, where it'll go to Zone. There they can identify and check out everybody. Can you do that?"

"I—I suppose so. Anything else?"

"Well, first you *must* take the photos in a high-tech hex, so please take them in Cobo if you can, and don't bother in a nontech or semitech environment because the thing won't work. Second"—he reached back into the pouch and took out a small plastic-looking device, a wafer-thin hexagonal block with a red area in the top center—"take this. When you're alone in your cabin and are sure nobody is lurking about, press this red spot. It will give you a general briefing. Use *this* tonight if you can, too. Don't worry about security, except being overheard—once you use it the first time, it will respond *only* to your touch. When you don't need it anymore, toss it overboard. No, I'm not joking. It will dissolve long before it hits anything and it won't foul the water."

She took it and stared at it, wondering if it was even moral to use such devices. Finally she decided that, after all, she had been the one who volunteered, and she put it in her small belt purse.

Eggy bobbed his head, apparently in satisfaction. "Got to go now. Being on land like this for very long makes me itch, even if it *is* just a ship. Any message you want to send to Core while I'm here?"

She thought. "No, nothing I haven't said. I thank you for this, though. It gives a bit of purpose to the day."

"And that's literal," he reminded her, waddling back toward the door. "Remember, you'll be out of Cobo and into a semi-tech environment on this route in only thirty-two hours unless they're forced to reduce speed. Get it done, and good luck to you!"

"I do not believe in luck," she told him as he left the interior of the ship. But I do believe in destiny, she added to herself.

"Although not true bugs, having spines and some internal structure as well as a soft but naturally protective exoskeleton, they have a communal insectlike social organization that is centered in underground complexes," the voice from the small hexagonal player informed her. "Place this unit on the floor and step back at least one meter," it instructed.

She was puzzled, still fascinated by the idea of voices from tiny little wafers, but she did as instructed.

As soon as she stepped back, an image formed in the air directly over the tiny thing. It was not a tiny image, but about half life size, and it startled her and triggered her panic reflex until she caught herself and realized that it was just a picture.

"This is a Quislonian," the voice informed her. "Most of them look just like this. There is no specialization, as there is in the insect world, for example."

The thing was really ugly, and she had to pull all of her

training from within to keep from being revolted by it. A giant segmented scorpion with a drooling mouth and a lot of feet wasn't exactly her idea of a friendly race. They were more gruesome than the big spider, which, at least, had texture and color and a sense of individuality.

"The Quislonians are organized into tribal groups each led by a prince. The prince is the only male in the tribe; all others are sacrificed to their gods shortly after birth. The prince spends most of his time impregnating the others of his tribe; otherwise he acts both as high ruler and as high priest, although both roles are essentially ceremonial. There is a council of senior wives, headed by the prince's mother, who organize the daily lives and activities of the colony and dispense aid and favors in the name of the prince. Princes *do* look different from the females; you will recognize one in a moment if you get to speak to one. It is most likely you will deal with, at best, the Prince Mother. Prince Mothers are identified because they dye their bodies the colors of the tribe, and the dye patterns indicate rank within the hierarchy. Only the Prince Mother also has a dyed head."

The image changed, and she saw the same creature essentially colored, with each of the segments a different color. She suspected that the order of the colors indicated the rank and perhaps title within the tribe, but it would be a code she'd never try to crack.

"The tribes are autonomous," the voice continued, "but all are subject to a single tribe that is at the pinnacle of society because it controls access to a central volcano that forms the core of their worship. It is active, but erupts with slow, thick lava that is rarely explosive and flows with slow deliberation. They, and most others, could outrun it. It is not, of course, constantly erupting, but there is always lava in the central crater. They appear to believe that their god or gods lives in the crater and can control it. You may take that as you will. Know, though, that the volcano also sits at the geographic center of the hex, which means that the Zone Gate actually emerges from the side, and access to *it* is also via the premiere tribe, whose sole function is religious. The male there has a title that translators make as 'King,' and his mother is the 'Queen Mother,' but there are, again, religious offices that are more important. They generally leave the more secular tribes alone, but a pilgrimage is required once a year, at which time high rites are done in a massive religious exercise around the volcano. *This* is what you are going to attend, and it is also where what our enemy wants and we must protect what is most vulnerable."

She wasn't at all sure she liked this, and understood why Core had withheld the nature of these people until she was committed to go. She had felt that, within certain limits, there was a commonality of culture at its most basic level between even the likes of those water-breathing Kalindans, the ones she'd met on board, and the others who allegedly came with all of them to this world. But *these*—these were not only physically unlike anything else she'd seen or known, they appeared to have a belief system that would be very difficult to accept. How could a race as ancient as the others on this world still be worshiping a volcano and throwing its men into it?

Why did Core, who seemed to know at least a little bit about everything, think that Amoboran beliefs were compatible enough with these people as to create a dialogue between she and them? Oh, she could see why *they* hadn't had much luck with these people, but, she thought, ones like Core were cold in a different way than the evil ones aboard this vessel, but spiritually empty nonetheless. Core had once been a machine, and she could well believe it. To those with no souls, all religion would look pretty much the same.

Almost as if it could read her mind, the voice continued, "Do not dismiss the Quislon religion as some sort of primitive sacrificial cult. It is quite sophisticated, but it does have its unpleasant aspects, we realize. The sacrificial part certainly seems extreme, but in one sense it is no different than another religion's commandments on dietary laws or cleanliness rituals where a social good—such as making sure a population didn't eat things that made them sick—is incorporated into a belief system so that it is universally enforced. The society, physically and even in its genetic design, cannot tolerate multiple males. They are smaller, weaker, and will not live long without a great deal of attention, but they are essential for the equivalent of sperm. Rather than watch most of them die very young for lack of what would be required to sustain them as social invalids, a ritual exists so that their inevitable deaths are given meaning while not impacting on the very limited resources their harsh land provides them. Genetically, biologically, only one of them is going to survive and prosper."

In one way she could understand this, but in a more basic sense she still couldn't get past tossing live babies into steaming lava. It was something she would have problems with even though she accepted the explanation.

The fact that they had no choice from their biology and geography did not make it right, but it did not make it evil, merely tragic.

"I am preprogrammed to answer questions in some detail about this subject," the voice told her. "However, we must remind you that we can only function in a high-tech hex, and there is not a great deal of time for that on this journey."

She was uncomfortable speaking to what she knew was a machine. She did not like to think that a machine could think in such a fashion. Still, time was running short.

"What is the object that your people do not want stolen and that these *creatures* worship?"

"It is a piece of a device known as the Straight Gate. Although Chalidang claims it was a device invented by one of their own a thousand or so years ago, in fact its composition and method of power and operation, plus obscure accounts that go back as far as we have coherent records, suggest that this was a device of the Makers, the ones who created and populated this planet. It is thought to be a tool of theirs that was somehow left and later discovered by descendants of those who were here at the start. This is why it is venerated by the Quislonians. They incorporate the Makers into their complex cosmology, and thus this would be the most sacred of all objects known."

"Did they just find it? How did they get it, or is that known?"

"The device disassembles. From the earliest times it appears that wiser heads believed it too dangerous to be used by anyone here, and so it was taken apart and distributed to those races that would be most likely to both venerate it and also keep it from being reassembled. It has been assembled at least once in the known record, by a Chalidang Emperor named Hadun approximately 1,022 years ago. The Chalidang were one of the races given a part to protect, but, of course, politics and attitudes change over time and with leaders. He fought a war that appeared to be aimed at the impossible: the conquest of the Well World. It is possible to conquer but never to hold it. The races and biomes are simply too different, and designed so that no one race could extend supplies over that large an area for any length of time. In point of fact, it was to secure the pieces of the Straight Gate, which he did."

"And he put it together? What happened?"

"Unknown. He and most of his court vanished and were never seen or heard from again. It was believed they went into another dimension and were lost. In the power vacuum, the enemies of Chalidang attacked and defeated it and took back and redistributed the Straight Gate pieces. Chalidang royalty afterward always called itself Hadun, almost as if it were a title rather than a name."

"And these people are trying the same thing again?"

"More or less. They are not attempting to conquer the whole world, simply to secure the pieces once more. It is believed that this time they know what the thing is and how to use it."

"And what is it?"

"All of its capabilities are unknown, but we must deduce the worst from the fact that the Ghoman, a race in the Corish Galaxy, which some races there call the Milky Way, are definitely descendants of the Chalidang; that the last Ghoman emperor we know was called Josich the Emperor Hadun; and that it is this very Josich who secured a device not very different from the assembled Straight Gate there and is now here as the Chalidang Empress."

She was startled. "He became a she?"

"It is unknown if this was deliberate, but it allowed Josich to move into power here with great speed, as there was already a Hadun Emperor. As Empress, Josich is, by the standards of Chalidang, apparently everything a male Chalidang could dream of. Core suspects that this means the transformation was in fact deliberate and preplanned. Since no one has ever been able to direct and preplan an entry to the Well World in known history, this implies that the power of the Straight Gate is massive indeed."

"Well, if she's already *got* one, why does she need another?"

"She hasn't 'got' one. That one is back on the world she left to come here. We believe it is part of a set. The other is the one that could be assembled here. If it is, it appears that it could confer unbelievable power on the operator. Perhaps a passage back and forth as anything one wishes. Perhaps worse. Perhaps the user of such a device is recognized incorrectly by the Well master computer as one of the Makers. It does not matter what it does, really. If it gets in the hands of someone as ruthless as Josich, and if Josich, as it seems, knows how to use it, then Josich will have so much power she will become, for all intents and purposes, a god. This has been determined by most races here to be a bad thing. Josich, in her home galaxy and system, was known to destroy whole inhabited worlds that displeased her."

Jaysu was stunned, but now, at least, she understood why the gods of Ambora had selected her and endowed her with unnatural powers. She felt both humbled and unworthy of the job. Why *her*? Could it be that her whole existence was designed for this challenge? That she had to be an empty vessel so she could be given this great power and the training and discipline to use it?

In her past life, Core had said, she had also been a cleric. Perhaps this truly *was* a divine commission. She could not refuse it, of course, but that didn't stop her from feeling that somebody else had to be better at this than she.

"One more question," she said to the small object on the floor.

"Yes?"

"Is it true that if we deny Josich just one segment, it will not work? That we only need to keep one part away from her to win?"

"Yes—and no. Yes, she can do nothing without all the pieces. No, it will not be a victory, since it has proven impossible to even destroy the pieces. The Quislon dropped theirs into the volcano long ago, and it spit it back out somehow. Keeping it disassembled is the constant task, at least until Josich is dead. It is unlikely that she would tell anyone else how to use it. Then they wouldn't need her anymore, you see."

It had actually been a very nice period, this passage through a high-tech hex aboard a ship designed to carry a massive amount of cargo of all sorts and a large complement of beings of different races and requirements, and which had far fewer passengers than it was set up to cater to. This meant you could get anything you wanted, and you had free rein of a ship that seemed as vast as a small country.

While in the high-tech mode, anything special that any of the races aboard wanted could be accommodated; she wasn't sure how it was done, but she decided to test their seemingly boastful claims with a couple of Amboran vegetarian dishes that required very rare ingredients native only to small parts of the hex, and they served them to her within minutes, perfectly done. The others aboard seemed to have equal success with their own culinary requirements. Some who wore various clothing or uniforms got new fittings that looked tailor-made; it seemed anything you asked for could be provided by the attentive staff. This made for congenial passengers; even Wally and his two nasty henchmen were on their best behavior.

But it was a short-lived joy.

Jaysu had no idea if she'd managed to take the pictures requested, but she'd done what she was instructed to do. It was only when they were about to leave Cobo that she remembered the instructions about what to do with it. She therefore went on deck shortly before dawn, looked around at the nothingness of the sea, and obligingly threw the camera into the ocean. She had no idea how they would find it, but she suspected that some underwater races, or perhaps the Ixthansans, were shadowing the big ship, and that they had some sort of device that would tell them when the camera was dropped. At any rate, she'd followed instructions, and it was now their problem.

It was so close to dawn that she decided to hold her morning devotionals on deck rather than go back to sleep. Her rituals, mostly to calm and strengthen her and to allow her to plead with the gods to remain with her and not forget or abandon her, were not complex, but also not entirely silent, and yet out of respect were best done outdoors if not in a temple or at an altar.

There wasn't much wind, except the breeze generated by the great ship, and the sea seemed unusually calm for Cobo, so being on the forward deck just below the wheelhouse was a perfect place to do her rituals.

As the sun came up, Jaysu felt the great steam engines below throttle back and the ship slow to a crawl. There didn't appear to be a reason; it was a beautiful day and, aside from a few fluffy clouds, there was high visibility. She became aware of a lot of activity behind her then; much shouting, doors slamming, winches turning, and so as soon as she completed her devotionals, she went to the side to see what was going on.

It seemed as if the entire crew, those not on the steward's staff anyway, was out and on deck, manning the ropes—the "rigging" they called it—and even climbing the huge masts. Belowdecks she could feel the vibration and hear the noise of great machinery going into action. Just above, the first mate, whom she'd met over dinner once, looked serious, despite the comic opera uniform that seemed designed for a far different creature than the squat, bipedal elephantine mate whose hands were at the end of a twin trunk. Mr. Scofflet, though, was all business, and had the kind of blasting voice to prove it, shouting a command here, another there, as the rest of the crew prepped the ship.

Algensor, a Kehudan passenger she'd rarely spoken to, came on deck. The Kehudans looked delicate enough to be blown away in a stiff breeze; their hex was all water, yet they were air breathers—silvery, heart-shaped, insectlike beings with thin, inverted V's for legs. It was said they lived and even built somehow on the surface of the waves. Algensor was on her way home even though the ship spent very little time in her home hex's waters. Now, after saying virtually nothing to her or most anybody since Jaysu had boarded, the silvery creature wanted to talk. Jaysu had trouble reading the Kehudan's empathic elements, which were so contradictory as to be meaningless.

"They are preparing for Mogari," Algensor said out of the blue.

"Mogari?" Jaysu repeated, shaking her head, a bit ashamed of her ignorance.

"We are about to hit what mariners call the Eastern Wall," the Kehudan explained. "Along here there are a sequence of nontech hexes joined so that it is impossible to avoid one without sailing a thousand kilometers around. Since ships of this size and weight are not good sailboats, they avoid nontech hexes when possible save as destinations. Thus, the ship slows, the machinery below redistributes cargo and ballast so it is as optimized for sail as possible, and the boilers are brought down to a simmer, as it were, from a boil. They cannot afford to let them go out, but the steam pressure must be constantly vented or it will blow up in a nontech environment. It cannot reach the aft propellers and drive the ship forward. You may boil water in a nontech hex, but if you try and route it, it will blow up, and so you must vent it harmlessly."

"I am well aware of this principle," she told the silvery creature. "My own home allows no machinery that is not powered by wind, water, or muscle directly." It had not, however, occurred to her that what didn't seem much of a problem at home would be a serious problem to a ship of this size and weight.

"The crew is professional enough," Algensor noted approvingly. "The problem is speed and handling. We will be at the mercy of the winds, and, after entering, our speed will be cut from a bit more than twenty kilometers per hour to perhaps six or seven. We will spend as much or more time going down a mere single edge of Mogari as we did to sail all the way here from where you boarded, perhaps much more. Then we will gain power back and turn sharply southwest. It will be sailing the wrong way, almost, for where the ship is bound, but it will be speedy and will allow them to route the rest of the way almost entirely in hexes where the engines can be used. Once the Wall is cleared, though, it will be ten days or so to landfall in Pyron. I, of course, shall be gone by then."

Jaysu wasn't cheered by the news. Ten days! How was she going to stand it? Still, if it could be mostly in high-tech hexes, she could adjust. Or was that sinful decadence creeping in? Was her faith really that shallow? She hoped not.

She turned at the cry of the mate to the crew and saw the hex wall looming ahead. It looked just like all the others, a kind of dark, shimmering mass that you could nonetheless see through, and which seemed to go all the way to heaven and from horizon to horizon.

With the crew positioned all through the masts and rigging, she was surprised to see the ship suddenly roar into life, as if revving up to maximum speed. It took a kilometer or so, but it was getting up a head of steam when it reached the wall. Then all power was cut, and it seemed as if the world suddenly stood still as the vibrations of the engines and from equipment below shut down.

The ship slid through the hex wall and the quiet became even eerier. It was as if someone had suddenly made them all deaf and without a sense of feeling, but there was the sound of wind and wave and the bow breaking through surf.

And then the loudest series of noises she had ever heard threatened to make her deaf for real, as three stacks blew their ship's whistles full and didn't seem to let up. Getting a headache from the terrible noise, she almost ran back inside. Even the sliding door didn't mask the noise completely, but at least it was no longer deafening.

The little purser was coming from the dining lounge at that moment, apparently lighting the internal oil lamps. He saw her and immediately guessed what had happened.

"So sorry," he called to her, and her eardrums were so shocked he sounded a million kilometers away. "Should have warned you. Got to do that. Let steam out. Otherwise we go *bang* really fast. They won't do it forever. Just have to get pressure down. Once the boilers are down to minimum, they only do it twice a day, at breakfast and at dinner, and not for so long."

"It is all right," she assured the little Kuall. "I am aboard for a long time yet, it seems, and whatever will be is at least some break from the routine."

"Could be more big break, yep yep," the purser warned her. "Big storm coming up."

That was unnerving. There were some things that made boredom seem acceptable. "Will it be bad?"

"Could be. Yep yep. We will head right for it, see."

"You don't try and go around such things?"

"Not most times, nope nope. Got to keep to route and schedule. But in nontech hex, we *like* storms, you see. *Big* wind. Dangerous for crew, but they know how to do their jobs, yep yep. Just stay off outside decks while we're in the storm and always hold on to something. Faster we go, rougher it gets, but we'll make speed."

She made her way back to the upper deck passenger lounge, which was just below her cabin. It had heavy reinforced glass windows all around, and from it you could see what the captain and bridge crew were seeing two decks up in the wheelhouse.

Wally was in there, without his little friends at the moment, and so were two or three other passengers. She was getting to know everybody aboard; there weren't all that many people, after all, and there was even less to do.

After a couple of days of powered light the lounge looked dark, shadowy, almost sinister, but it was more than adequate for most races, and for her. This was, after all, fairly normal lighting for Ambora, although they were using some tricks with mirrors and such to make the smaller sealed oil lamps as bright as the near torches Amborans tended to favor.

Out ahead she could see the darkness, almost as if the bright dawn was being reversed, turned back into night. It was a natural sight on a clear horizon; she'd seen it many times herself from the Amboran cliffs. Still, she was home when she was on the Amboran cliffs, and could retreat into structures of thick wood or stone. Out here she was aware that the ship was the sole anchor for her existence. Nobody could fly in that stuff, not with those winds and violent downdrafts, and lifeboats would fare poorly if it were rough enough to sink a ship. The purser was right about one thing, though— although there was a clear way around to the south, the captain was heading right for the darkness.

"It is still difficult to not hear and feel the engines," Wally commented, almost certainly to her, though apparently to nobody in particular. "It had become so much a part of the day-to-day. Good morning, my dear. I hope you slept well." This was clearly directed toward her.

"As well as I can in this confinement," she answered. "I was not made for this sort of living."

"Who was? I suggest that you go to the first-class mess and eat some breakfast now. It is still hot and properly cooked and prepared, but things will be getting rough soon and they will have to put it away or it will go flying. I fear we'll eat a lot worse until we clear this hex."

She decided that he had a point, and made her way back to the small restaurant amidships. Normally you could walk in and get what you needed any time of the day or night, but apparently things would be different for a while.

She could feel the tension, both on the part of the passengers in the lounge and even the stewards in the restaurant and other crew that she passed. Clearly this was not going to be an experience they relished.

They were securing almost everything that was loose when she entered, although two of them took some time out to prepare an Amboran sweet cereal for her, garnished with native fruits. Still, everybody was so frantic she wasn't sure she would have time to eat before things started to happen, and she didn't want to think of what those things might be.

She thought of Eggy and wondered what these storms were like under the sea. Probably not as bad as up here, she decided. They said that you didn't have to go far down to be almost completely ignorant that a storm was even raging above. She wouldn't know; Amborans could manage an emergency float in a pinch, and even do a snatch and grab on fish just below the surface, but the oils in their feathers were not dense enough or insulating enough to allow them to swim.

"I, too, fly," the creature had told her, but not in the air. What a strange variety of creatures there were in this world.

Before she finished her breakfast, the storm hit, or, more properly, they hit the storm, and things began to lurch. The action, which became rhythmic but unceasing, frightened her, and she saw concern even in the eyes of the stewards, creatures of several races who now rushed to gather up the last loose bowls, plates, bottles, and utensils and get them under either locked bars or netting. They tried to allow her to complete her meal, but she was no longer hungry, and it wasn't much fun eating, anyway, when most of the time you were trying to keep your bowl and spoon on the table.

As loose goblets and cups began flying, she understood why there was little or no glassware in the restaurant. It was wooden or some sort of artificial substance that was smooth and molded.

Some of the stewards were more sure-footed than others. Some were clearly at home in a surface of rough water, or just seemed built to stick to whatever they were standing on.

Now, holding onto the table, she wondered how she was going to make it anywhere more comfortable, even to the lounge. She wasn't one of those who stuck to things, and her tough feet and claws occasionally lost their footing even when sailing was smooth.

One of the stewards, a creature that seemed more like a walking plant than an animal—with leafy arms and a head like a pastel blue and pink head of cabbage—was one of the stick-to-the-floor types, and he approached her.

"Take my arm," it invited her. "I will make certain you get to the walking rope. Can you manage from there?"

She wasn't sure, but said, "Yes. Thank you."

The "arm" was covered with little leafy smaller arms and ended in a "hand" of three rubbery, long fingers. The creature's grip, though, was surprisingly strong, and its footing as steady as a rock. She pulled herself up, depending on its grip, and allowed it to pull her to the bulkhead and the thick guide rope. She used her free hand to grab the rope, then said, "All right! You can let go now!"

"Use both of your hands and grip hard," the steward warned, guiding her other hand to the rope and ensuring that she had a two-handed grip before releasing her.

She immediately saw what it meant by the suggestion.

She had never before been moving in so many directions at once, not even in the air. The ship didn't just rock back and forth, it also simultaneously moved side to side, and at the end of one sequence of motion it seemed to literally twist, first one way and then the other.

She made her way forward, slipping once but catching herself on the rope before she fell, and nervously made her way forward, out of the restaurant doorway, and across the common area and stairwells, toward the lounge. As she passed this area, she could look out of the sliding doors, but wasn't sure it had been a good idea. Although it was still early morning, it was pitch-black out there, broken by dramatic flashes of lightning. Some of the sounds she'd assumed in the restaurant were ship noises, she now realized were thunder. She couldn't help but wonder about the poor crew on those masts, and hoped they'd all found some shelter before the ship entered this terrible environment.

Getting into the lounge not only didn't help, the row of rectangular windows provided a frightening panorama that was a terrible dark gray, with lightning all around and rain beating against the windows. Worse, though, was that she could see the bow of the ship stretched out in front and below her, and the gigantic waves breaking over it, some, it seemed, as high as this upper deck!

The raging sea would roll over and the entire bow would dip and then vanish under the water, followed by that funny twisting motion, and then, almost miraculously, the bow would rise back out of the depths to repeat the sequence. It was dramatic, and scary. Each time, it seemed as if the bow would never rise back up, and if it didn't, they were going down, and fast.

It was the greatest test of faith she'd ever undergone, because she was completely helpless; she could do nothing to make it stop.

Jaysu was surprised to find nobody else in the lounge area. They were probably all riding it out in their cabins, she thought, since there was little you could do but be frightened in such conditions.

She wondered about the crew, who apparently took this as just another part of the job. How many times did they go through this in a month, a year, whatever? Was it ever routine?

"Quite a magnificent sight, is it not?" a familiar voice commented above and behind her. She jumped, turned, and saw Wally rise from a flat deck area between two types of seating in the back.

"Oh—I'm sorry," she responded. "I didn't realize anyone was here."

"Racial habit, I'm afraid. We're natural lurkers," the giant spider commented.

"I expected more passengers here," she told him.

"Most land passengers are busily giving their breakfasts back to nature," he told her. "The others have pretty well anchored themselves in. My two associates are all right but rather small, and they found themselves unable to stand erect under these conditions and so have battened themselves down, as it were. I suspect that your stomach and general balance are also all right, being a flier."

She hadn't thought of that. Of course, the action of the

ship, while alien, wasn't as extreme as some flying maneuvers she did routinely, and she always knew where the ground was. "Yes, but it does not mean that I can stand on hard, polished wood in this movement," she replied. "In the air it is I who control the movements, and I am not subject to traction."

The spider seemed to think a moment, then approached her confidently. A creature of this size who still walked up walls and across ceilings did not have any problems getting around under these conditions. A leg reached under and into some natural pouch, then brought out a glistening strand of what seemed to be rope of smooth, translucent color. He put out the leg and offered the rope to her.

"Please—take this. It is a natural substance my people make, but it is strong as steel and it is, well, sticky without being wet. Take a seat in the center here, which is the point where you will sense the least movement, and just put this around your lap and secure it to the bottom of the seat. It will hold you, and the seats are bolted down. You can peel it off slowly from anywhere or anything, but if there is a sudden jerk, it will hold a boulder. Go ahead—take it. It won't hurt you."

She didn't trust the spider, but on the other hand, he seemed to be telling the truth and just being helpful. She took his offering, pulling it to her. Now, for the first time, she saw that the legs, all of them, ended in what looked like mittens.

She studied the ropelike substance. "This is your webbing?"

"In an evolutionary sense, yes," he admitted. "But we don't build webs. As far as I can tell, we never did. Still, it comes from the same source as a spider's web, and we use it very much like ropes, vines, whatever. A bunch of it gets made every day whether we need it or not, and we actually sell the stuff as a trade good for uses just like this. It keeps its properties for quite some time, although, of course, like everything else, you can use it too much. My gift. In fact, if you give me one end of the coil back, I'll go over to one of these backless chairs and hold it taut so you can make it."

The stuff had an odd feel, almost like it was trying to grab you, and using it hand over hand to go toward the great spider, it seemed she was climbing a web to her doom. But Wally, as usual, was as good as his word, even helping fasten her to the seat.

It helped. "I fear I'm still looking out at that scene," she told him. "I feel we'll go down every time I see the bow vanish." Even so, she felt more comfortable secured to the seat.

The noise was also unnerving. Not the storm outside—save for the thunder claps, which were dulled by the tight insulation and triple-thick bulletproof window materials—but rather the groans, shudders, and moans of the ship itself, punctuated now and then by the sound of things smashing against bulkheads.

"You seem to enjoy the storm, Mr. Wally," she commented to the spider. "Is your race one that swims?"

He chuckled. "No. If we go, I go, I'm afraid, but I'm not all that concerned. While it's not unheard of, these ships are built for this sort of thing, and this crew is highly experienced. And, while I must say I've never been on a ship through a storm like this before, I've been in much more dangerous and less comfortable spots in my long life. I rather enjoy viewing the wonders of nature, really, so long as I am warm and dry and looking out."

"It seems a *huge* storm," she noted. "I mean, *we* have thunderstorms, some of them quite fierce, but they are generally local affairs. They blow and roar like this, it is true, but they are soon gone. This one just seems to go on and on and on."

"It does," he agreed. "I believe this may be more than a mere storm. I heard one of the crew refer to it as a tropical storm, and another as a typhoon. These appear to be much larger and meaner storms than the ones you or I are used to. It is a wonder to me that they can sail in this, but apparently they have a way to do it. As I say, experience. Experience and thousands of years of clever engineering design."

It did seem to go on for a terrible length of time, but then, as suddenly as they had come upon it, it died down, even stopped, and for a brief moment there was even a bit of sun.

They could hear the shouts of crew all over, but they didn't sound happy.

The purser rushed in, saw her, and said, "Thought somebody might be up here. Yep yep. Everybody all right?"

"Yes, we're fine," she assured him.

"If you want to get to your cabin, go fast," the purser told them. "This is the middle of the storm. All quiet, still. But we'll hit the other storm wall in about ten minutes. After that, it's back to the wind and waves for another couple hours."

She thought it might be a good idea, tried to get up and found herself held tight.

"Oh, sorry, let me help," Wally commented, reaching over, putting a leg under the chair and pulling. "Here. Take this. You may find it useful. We will talk later, after we are through this mess."

"Yes, perhaps we will," she replied, unnerved at just how well tied down she'd been without realizing it.

She made her way back to the doors, then out onto the deck. It was a strange feeling, this "middle" of the storm. She could see it, all around her, and certainly forward, yet it was almost as if they were becalmed, with the sun peeking through the strange, spiral cloud shapes above.

She also saw that the crew was busy hauling down some very torn-up sail and putting up some others. She knew that those sails were made of the kind of stuff you couldn't tear, and to see them now in this condition was more sobering than watching the bow sink and rise.

She hurried to her cabin, not wanting to be caught when they hit that storm again, and made it barely in time.

The embedded log in the box of sand provided sufficient grip and comfort for her when it started again. Alone, inside her cabin, for once she felt not claustrophobic, but safe.

She decided that the best way to spend the rest of the day was in prayer and meditation, if she could hear herself think over the racket that began again outside.

Yabbo

CORE WAS LESS THAN IMPRESSED BY THEIR HIGHLY FANCIFUL
and imaginative report. Not, however, to the point of accepting a word of it, even if it was just the kind of plot Core might
have come up with.

"Proof!" Core shot back in a memo sent via the Zone Gate
courier system to Ari and Ming at the consular office in Yabbo.
"Get proof, get knocked up, or proceed to Sanafe, or any
combination of same, your choice."

She has a definite lack of personal charm, Ming noted. *Do
you suppose she's taking her own advice? After all, Core has
exactly the same situation under those decrees that we do.*

I hadn't thought of that, but you're right, Ari replied.
*Hmmm . . . Makes you wonder what would happen if she did
get "knocked up," as it is so quaintly put. Who would want to
have sex with somebody who spent the last century as a
computer?*

*I'm not so sure, considering your dear, departed uncle's
perversions. They were all in those memory banks, take it
from me. If Core's got any of those routines still in her memories, then I fear for the man who tries it, not for her.*

That doesn't help us here, though, Ari pointed out. *So, we
either have to produce a body in a case or get the hell out
of here.*

*I vote for visiting Sanafe myself. We'll never get a chance to
open one of those things, not with that kind of guard around,
and I didn't see any way in. It was like they were sealed in by
machine. If so, they probably will take some kind of gadget, a*

kind of frozen coffin can opener, to get them out. I, for one, am
not anxious to tangle with that general, not yet.

Ari felt disappointed, but had to agree with her. Even though
he was as convinced as she of the contents of those boxes,
there was simply no way to prove anything to Core's satisfaction with just the two of them, and a good chance they'd be
caught if they kept going back and forth.

Still, the whole concept of mailing an invasion army to the
staging area had to be unique in the annals of warfare, and it
sure was a warning that they were dealing with some diabolical minds on the other side.

Sanafe was due north of Yabbo, and thus roughly two hundred kilometers distant. Still, Core had been prescient enough
to send along some international credit units with the note so
they could buy their transportation some of the way, maybe
all the way. The thing was, they hadn't any idea what Sanafe
was like.

"Nontech, my dear. Strictly muscle power," Vice Consul
Mitchuk told them. "They don't socialize much, and there are
no consulates there, or much of anything else for that matter.
They're large carnivores, organized into family-based clans
as I understand it, and they don't even like each other very
much, let alone foreigners. It is unlikely they would kill a
Kalindan, since we're next door and could cause some ugliness for them if they did anything to one of ours, but they
might frighten, threaten, or extort."

"What sort of weapons might we get around here that would
work there, on those people, if need be?" Ming asked him.

Mitchuk shrugged. "Hard to say. Spring-loaded harpoons
are effective in nontech environments, but I don't know where
you'd buy them anywhere in this region. My advice to you
would be to not go. Settle here, obey the decrees, and wait for
things to happen."

She shook her head. "Sorry, sir. You've been a real dear,
but we have our orders, so to speak. Something is going to
happen there, and maybe soon, and we are supposed to be on
hand. There are Chalidangers right here, and that can't be a
coincidence."

"Chalidangers? *Here?* Are you certain?" The consul seemed surprised and upset by the news.

"Oh, yes. Take it from me. That black dome down there may *claim* it's part of the Panayan consulate, but it's not. It's Chalidang, and it's got some very high-ranking officers living in it. We've seen them."

"You—You've *seen* them? Where? And who is this 'we' you speak of?"

"Oh, just a figure of speech. But, yes, we've been down there and we've spotted them, as much as they try and keep out of sight and inside their bunker."

"Do you think this has anything to do with a move against Kalinda?" he asked, sounding concerned.

"I'm not sure. It doesn't seem nearly enough if they go against us. No, I really can't say. Core believes it has something to do with Sanafe, which is why I was directed to go there. You see now why I haven't been able to, well, consummate the directive. If I got pregnant now, well, it would really limit my movements after a while."

Mitchuk looked crestfallen at that. Still, he sighed and said, "Well, please, if you are bent upon leaving, then you must be my guest for one last dinner. Please!"

"Well, I—" *What do you think?*

What the hell. Why not give him one last shot? At least we'll get a decent dinner before we have to go back to eating that crud outside.

The dinner was the best the consulate had to offer, and that was saying something for a Kalindan palate; the intoxicants were of the highest quality and age, the sweets delectable. By the time they finished, even Ari was feeling guilty that they hadn't given Mitchuk much encouragement for all that he'd done, or, in this case, overdone. They were tipsy at the end of it, and stuffed like a lobster, and they found coordination difficult. Mitchuk kindly offered them one of the smaller rooms in the consulate for the night so they wouldn't have to navigate, and they quickly took him up on it and accepted his assistance in getting there.

Ming's head was spinning, and since it was also Ari's head, she knew she had no advantage, but she did have some experience in this. *I think we've been snoggered,* she managed, as they settled in for sleep.

Huh? What do you mean?

Mitty isn't even high, that's what. I got a bad feeling about— But that was all either of them managed before passing out.

It was a mostly very deep, dreamless sleep, but there were moments when they dreamed that others were there, that things were being done to them, but as quickly as these sensations arose, they lapsed back into the near comatose blackness.

It was impossible to say how long they slept, but it was a big shock to see where they were when they woke up.

It was like emerging from a warm, totally dark tunnel into slowly increasing sound and light. It was not without its sudden but brief waves of nausea, each one of which jolted them more awake, but in a state that made them mostly want to go back to sleep.

They felt awful, and there was no need to convey this concept to the other. They tried to turn a bit and get more comfortable, but something was preventing it. Slowly the eyes opened to see nothing but a blur at first, but things slowly came into focus, broken now by sounds so loud and irritating that they pounded into their head like hammers.

"I do believe our guest is waking up," a silky smooth deep voice commented. "Or should I say 'guests'?"

They managed to focus on the speaker, and suddenly all the discomforts of the hangover became totally irrelevant.

They found they were on the bottom level of the dark dome, and were being eyed with some amusement by a very large and very menacing-looking Chalidanger.

"Please don't try and struggle too much," the Chalidanger said to them. "We had to put some restraints on you because we thought you might be reluctant to accept our sincere hospitality."

"Mitchuk," Ming almost spat back in disgust. "The horny little fink sold us out."

"On the contrary," their host responded. "Citizen Mitchuk sold *himself* a very long time ago. Selling you out wasn't an option; he has long been one of us. Do you think we could have operated here so effectively for so long without ensuring that we had far more friends around than neutrals, and no enemies we couldn't control?"

"Some control. You drug us and kidnap us."

"Oh, come now! I'm assured that the food and intoxicants were of such a high quality that if you tried to order it all back home you couldn't possibly afford it. If you've got to be drugged and rolled, as it were, there are far worse ways to do it. Just a little extra juice in one of the stronger intoxicants was enough to put you under for almost thirty hours."

"Why the fancy stuff, then? Why not just kill us and be done with it?"

The Chalidanger seemed amused by the question. "And you were supposed to be great agents back in your own universe! If we take you out here, after your report, the forces opposing us would descend in such force and skill that all these months of preparation would be dissolved in the water and of no value. No, I don't want you dead. In fact, I want you to be our guest for a while. This is going to come to a head shortly, and you wanted to find out what we were up to and where we were going to go anyway, didn't you? So why skulk and suffer in a hostile and primitive land when you can simply come along and watch?"

"Some deal!"

"Yes, isn't it?" the Chalidanger responded, still sounding amused. Ari was fascinated to see that, in the center of the tentacles, there wasn't the beak generally associated with squid and nautilus and like creatures, but an actual mouth, round and containing row after row of sharklike teeth. That, he decided, was what made the Chalidangers different from the animals: the higher order chewed its food and pronounced its words carefully.

"I, by the way, am Colonel General Mochida of His Majesty's Army Intelligence Service. In fact, I'm the commander of that service in normal times, but this operation was so much my baby, as it were, I just couldn't stand to keep away. The others here are my aide, Colonel Kuamba, Sergeant Major Subich, and Warrant Officer Ladoch. I know you are wondering how the devil it matters since you can't tell us apart, but the insignia on the body shell tells all. Officers have a single insignia in the center of their spirals, noncoms and soldiers along the outer edge with an identical Imperial design in the center. The starburst on my spiral along with the circle inside it makes me a colonel general. Kuamba has only the circle, so he's a colonel, a far distance from colonel general. The warrant has the half starburst on the outer shell, and the sergeant the fan insignia of the highest noncom rank. Just so you know. I do not like being called 'Sergeant,' and I assure you that the other two officers here also do not wish to be confused."

"Um, yeah, thanks a lot, General. You'll pardon me, though, if I don't give a shit, since I'm tied down and trussed up like a beast to slaughter."

"Ah, yes. Well, we *will* change that, I promise you. We haven't had time to search the supply lists here and find what we need, but I promise, once we do, you will be untied and able to move about normally. It's hard to find things when you can't use your computers, and efficiency suffers. We also can't use our usual methods for restraining—guests—in this primitive environment, so we must use subtler means. The sergeant major assures me that he will find it at some point today or tomorrow, and then we'll be able to take those nasty chains away."

What do you think he's gonna do? Can't do an implant, it wouldn't work here. Ditto remote control electroshock. Ming was more worried about the method than that they had something in mind they believed in.

I suspect we'll find out soon enough, Ari said glumly. *Remember these guys' reputations, and Josich's in particular.*

The general shifted and flexed his tentacles. "I find this fascinating, you know. Are you two speaking to one another now? I suppose it's something like telepathy, or do you pretty much just know what the other one says?"

"I beg your pardon?"

"Come come! Madam Ming Dawn Palavri, I believe, and Mr. Ari Martinez, nephew of the infamous Jules Wallinchky, the greatest criminal of your generation. Oh, come! Come! As I *told* you, I am the Chief of Staff for Army Intelligence. Besides, you did not make it a matter of state secrecy, you just didn't remind anyone of it. We don't need to plant agents in Kalinda for that sort of thing, you know. You can look it up in the Zone archives. As for Wallinchky, well, the Empress is extremely impressed with him and speaks of him quite often."

Ari came to the fore. "You know where he is? He's alive?"

The tentacles wriggled in delight. "Well, well! Mr. Martinez, I presume. You really *do* sound different from one another, and even the body shifts a bit in the way it holds itself, even at rest. Incredible. I have seen multiple personalities before, but it was always because someone was mentally ill. I've never seen two healthy and independently developed minds in the same body. It must be—cozy. Or is it frustrating? I *do* hope you've come to like each other."

"My uncle—he's alive?"

"I believe he made it, yes. And he'll pop up sooner or later. Such people as that one can never be kept down. He's not a factor in our business, however. Breathers of air have a great deal of trouble operating down here, and never in a clandestine manner. You two used to be air breathers, didn't you? I cannot imagine suffering the *limitations* of such an existence. You would have to be in zero gravity in order to experience what we take for granted."

"It was good enough, if we had our separate bodies," Ari told him, feeling more like a cross between a specimen and a trained pet animal. "Still, I have to admit, this is not a bad way to live. Some things are the same, though."

"Indeed?"

"If you're captured and tied up by your enemy, then it's no fun at all."

"But why should we have to be enemies?" the general asked him. "What is so terrible about us? You were employed by your uncle, I believe, and that almost certainly meant that you did all sorts of things without a single reference to any sort of moral compass. Am I right? Yes? You probably didn't kill people, but your actions or orders most likely *caused* people to be killed, or worse. I saw the condition of the lady when she arrived in Zone, courtesy of the recordings we always make of immigrants. I am no expert on air breathers or their appearance, but simply comparing the lady to the rest of you, I can say that the word 'automaton' comes to mind. The only difference between you and us is that you almost certainly have a good reason why you did, or did not do, everything you ultimately perpetrated. Well, people, so do I."

This was not the kind of guy you could fool around with, that was clear. Still, Ming came to the fore and responded, "However, I was not a Jules Wallinchky employee. I was a cop and later a captive to his sadistic whims. And your Empress, back there, was considered the ultimate butcher, the destroyer of entire planets filled with sentient beings. There is no higher crime than genocide."

"I agree," the general responded smoothly. "I look forward to many discussions on these kinds of topics with you, in fact. You can tell me how your original home world and your original race evolved without wiping out any other species, and how it all came together as one great supernational race without stamping out a single culture or exterminating any primitives. Since it defies everything I ever was taught about the way races develop, it will be *fascinating* to hear of this one moral exception."

"Very funny. Ho ho. But a race is supposed to evolve *upward*. We have progressed beyond that level, while others have not."

"Indeed? I thought evolution was random. In point of fact, I believe your race has been in space colonization for, oh, many centuries at least, and during that time it's evolved almost not at all from the point at which it wiped out all the other sentient species back on your birth world. You're stuck, you see. Evolution happens even here. Most of the races here are different than the ancient records show. Sleeker, stronger, but rarely smarter or less violent, and almost never wiser. We are a warrior race. It invigorates us, renews us, makes us better. Mentally as well as physically, a worthy opponent is to be cherished. I admit that the Empress is a bit, um, *unrestrained* in that area, but she is not alone, nor the dominant single force in government. She's damned good at politics, I'll say that, but rather brutish in war. Wiser heads are managing that part, and she will be satisfied if her objectives are attained."

"You sure had it all worked out in Ochoa," Ming taunted him.

He didn't seem bothered by the comment. "Oh, come now! It was a mass military action in a classic arena, and the situation did not warrant that. Supply lines were too long, intelligence too poor, and so on. We had to allow them to make that one attempt, though, just to establish the General Staff as the place strategy and tactics are developed, not the Imperial Court and its allies. If they'd won, fine. The only land nation in the center of that oceanic region would have been invaluable and made all this unnecessary. But, as we expected, they lost, and, having been handed their beggar's bowls and taking monstrous casualties, they were much easier to convince that it should be the experts who should do the work."

"Indeed? And what is that?"

"We're not out to conquer this world, appearances to the contrary," the general told them. "For one thing, in the incredibly unlikely event that it could be done, it could never be held. Too many alien races, too many biospheres, too many complexities. No, we're satisfied to establish protective spheres of influence here and let it go at that. No, we don't want to conquer the Well World, even if it would be allowed.

"We want to conquer *your* empire, and all the rest that we can see in the sky. An infinite conquest. Such a concept is too glorious to fail!"

General Mochida enjoyed bantering with his prisoner, but he was a pro. He needed what they knew as well as what had been reported to him, and he had the means to get it, thanks to a number of experiments on unsuspecting Kalindan workers and traitors within the Kalindan hierarchy. And with a Kalindan consulate in his pocket just down the road, as it were, he had no problems securing whatever was needed.

Ari and Ming saw the Kalindan syringe, designed to penetrate even that race's tough leathery hides, and felt the massive sting as the drug went through and into their bloodstream. It didn't take long at all to take effect, even though they tried to fight it. Before there was even a backward count of ten from the technician administering the drug, their thoughts simply died away; their resistance, their fear and anxiety, just seemed to melt into the water. They were perfectly conscious, but not only was there nothing they could do about the questions that were coming, there was no desire inside them to conceal anything. There was no friend, no foe, just a nice feeling of well-being and a willingness to do anything, anything at all, that was asked.

"Too bad we can't just keep this stuff in their systems with an under skin injector," the General commented. "It would make occupation a whole lot easier. Are they ready?"

The administrator of the drug, a creature that seemed to be all tendrils with tiny eyes at the end of each, examined their eyes. "Yes, I believe so. The metabolism is quite efficient, though, and the defenses are very good, so I wouldn't count on much past half an hour, even though they might be partially under for much longer."

"Very well, so we cut to the chase. Ari, Ming, can you hear and understand me?"

"Yes," they both responded in such unison that it was the one time when the General had no idea who was speaking.

"Do you know Jeremiah Wong Kincaid?"

"Yes," they both answered.

"Ming only—have you had any contact with Kincaid since being on the Well World?"

"Not that I know of," she answered truthfully.

"Ari, I assume that you would know nothing once here that Ming did not, so you, too, have not had any contact with Kincaid since arriving on the Well World?"

"No contact," Ari agreed.

"Do you know what race he has become?"

"No."

"Does anyone?"

"Yes. Core said that they knew but that they made a deal with him." Quickly, they explained the arrangement that Kincaid would kill no more in Zone if they ignored his activities elsewhere.

"Interesting. Secrets *can* be kept if they are really important, it seems. Very well. Let us go on to other business."

It lasted the full half hour, with a mechanical clock ticking away the minutes. The questions were direct, to the point, and geared toward information, not idle curiosity. The General knew his job well.

He seemed disappointed with their apparent ignorance of just about anything going on, so much so that he almost suspected that he was *supposed* to have caught them. What good that would do, he didn't know, but he couldn't shake that feeling even if he could not get out of them any real threat to him and his operation that they might pose.

"I'm half tempted by my suspicions to program them into marrying little Mitchuk and settling down to have a nice, happy family," the General remarked to his aide. "Still, if they are some kind of sleepers, then I want to know what's going on here. Tourmin—you are certain that they cannot lie or conceal from me?"

"Not for another—oh, seven or eight minutes," the tendriled technician responded.

"All right. So if they are programmed to any action, they won't know it themselves. Still, I want them around, if under control." He turned back to the helpless Kalindan who just floated there, looking at nothing in particular and with an idiot's demeanor.

"Ming, what are you most frightened of?" he asked her.

"Of becoming one with Ari. Of losing my identity."

"Ari? Same question."

"Of becoming one with Ming."

"Do you dislike her?"

"No."

"Then why are you bothered by this?"

"Because I am not Ming. I like her, I may love her, but I do not want to *become* her."

"I see. But death is not your greatest fear?"

"This would be death," Ari responded. "We do not fear the physical death so much."

"Very well, then. Do you fear *me*?"

"I *respect* your position. I do not fear you, nor does Ming."

"Do you fear Josich?"

"I fear only what Josich might do."

The General seemed satisfied, even if he had far less information than he'd hoped or expected. "I believe we can let them rest now. Sergeant, did you find the supplies?"

The Chalidang noncom slowly floated down near to them. "Yes, sir. Enough for a couple of months if we only use it on her."

"Tourmin, you certify that the toxin works on Kalindans?"

"Of course," said the creature. "If you take oxygen from water, if you have an efficient bloodstream and a heart that moves it, and if you are carbon based, this stuff will work. It is actually pretty simple, not a complex compound. We have found fewer than a dozen races where it appears to have either no effect or the wrong effect. Kalinda is not one of those."

"All right. Give it to them, and show the sergeant and Mr. Ladoch how to administer it after you are gone. At what interval is it to be given?"

"Actually, it averages once a day, but it does vary between species, and I do not have all the figures for Kalindans in my head," the creature responded. "However, it is not your problem or your concern when to administer it. I assure you that the subject herself will tell you when."

"Hmmm . . . Out of curiosity, will it work on us?"

"On Chalidangers? Of course."

"Then why haven't I heard of it before? It's the perfect thing to have in the arsenal of somebody in my business."

"Expense. It is stable only as a naturally occurring toxin imported from Nyarlath."

"It can't be synthesized?"

"So far, only sort of. It can be synthesized, but it tends to break down rapidly, often in a matter of days. In other words, it does not travel well. No one has ever determined what the agent is that causes this, which the synthetic lacks. Most frustrating because, as I said, at its heart it's a quite simple compound. It may be one of those Well blockages, where it is simply not permitted to be synthesized because of the harm it might do."

"Interesting. If so, it *could* be synthesized, and stable if made in the greater universe. Something to look forward to."

"When do you intend to move your people from here?"

"In two weeks. The Sanafeans are not all that keen about dealing with us and may require a demonstration. Beyond that, we hope that this will not take long once begun."

"And that would leave only two pieces left," the colonel commented gleefully. "The one in Quislon and the missing piece."

"Quislon is being worked on as we sit here," the General assured him. "As for the missing piece, I have every expectation that I can put my tentacles on it when it is necessary to do so."

"Then, sir, you know where it is already?"

"Not exactly," Mochida responded. "But I believe that I know the one who *does* know, and, quite simply, that is more than sufficient for now."

Magid

"I MUST SAY THAT THIS IS UNPRECEDENTED. I SHALL CERTAINLY complain to the line about *this*!" Algensor, the Kehudan, was still muttering. The silvery buglike creature had just learned that the long route the *Bay of Vessali* normally took, which swung out and passed briefly through her native hex before swinging back in toward Pyron, had been altered without warning.

They had come through the hurricane with some damage, but apparently the kind of damage the crew considered "normal" for that type of run, and they managed to clear the "short leg" of Mogari in under two days instead of the usual four or five for a nontech hex. Once the boilers had been brought back up and put back on line, it appeared that all was getting back to normal. It wasn't until they passed through Kodon and Suffok and entered the high-tech hex of Magid that the announcement had been made of a course change.

In fact, even Jaysu had been unaware of any changes until, passing by the purser's office one afternoon, she'd overheard the Kehudans complaining loudly.

"I am sorry, madam, but we have a technical problem and need to put in at a high-tech repair yard," the little purser was saying. "Can't safely make it the normal route, nope nope."

"That is what your line *always* says when it wants to deviate from a route!" Algensor responded huffily. "*I* have a schedule, too, you know!"

"Can't do anything, sorry, sorry, nope nope," the purser continued. "You can complain to the captain, but we'll still

162

land in Alkazar tomorrow morning. We'll get you on another ship as soon as possible, all free, yep yep."

"Surely I cannot be the *only* one inconvenienced by this!"

But according to the purser, she was the only one. About a third of the cargo would be offloaded in Alkazar because it could be transshipped inland as easily from there as from Pyron, and the rest would be dropped off at the Pyron stop as usual. By unloading so much in Alkazar, in fact, they could take on some new cargo they hadn't planned on getting.

Jaysu was confused by this.

"You must stop thinking of those hexes out there as empty sea," Wally tried explaining to her. "They are as much ship's destinations, or at least potential destinations, as ports. Cargo can be lowered to them and raised to the ship. There just wasn't much business out there this trip, so they decided to change routes. Very fortuitous, in fact, for me and my associates, as we'd much prefer Alkazar to Pyron."

She was surprised. "You will be getting off there, then?"

"Indeed yes, unless there is some hitch that develops. The Alkazarians, frankly, are somewhat xenophobic. They maintain the port and there is an entire multiracial colony and yard there, but nobody is allowed outside of the port region. It's a kind of little hex unto its own. Getting permission to cross into the country proper can be a problem, although I believe I can get those clearances. It will save time."

She was puzzled. "If they deal with everyone in a shipping port, why do they not like anyone elsewhere?"

The spider creature never ceased being amazed at her naiveté. "My dear, they want what other places make, and they have things to export so they can pay for them. But beyond that, it is a sad country for a high-tech hex. A rigid military dictatorship, harsh and ruthless. It has been called a computerized madhouse, but it's the people who are mad, or so I'm told. I haven't been here before, but I've been in places like it."

"What makes you think, then, that such people would allow you to cross?"

Wally paused a moment, then responded, "Well, let us just

say that we are working for clients that have the respect of the locals here. Not friends, not allies, but, well, 'respect' may well be the correct word. Never mind. It is all just silly politics."

"It is too bad that I, too, could not use their space. It would make my journey shorter, and I am so very anxious to get off this ship."

"I wish I could help you, but I'm afraid I'm helpless in this situation. I'm going to be fortunate to get them to let *me* and my associates through. You understand."

He was lying, but not in a way that threatened her. She had the strong impression that Wally had arranged this little detour in advance. She wondered how much it had cost his employers.

A mosaic of the eastern ocean and the ship's regular routes was on the rear lounge wall. It had been one of the few points of interest for her in the otherwise boring passage, save the time she stared out at a hurricane.

She couldn't read the map, of course; she doubted if she'd ever understand those odd squiggles and designs. Still, she knew which one was Ambora, and which one was Quislon, and the three types of hexes were color coded, so, if everybody was right, they were going to put in on the northwest point of Alkazar, one hex north of Quislon. There was a nontech hex between Magid and the hex leading into Pyron, though, which meant a few wasted days sailing past where she wanted to go so that she could put in, travel through half of Pyron, and then back halfway through Quislon toward Alkazar again. It didn't make much sense. It would also get her to where she was supposed to be going only in the nick of time, and even then only if all went just perfectly, and if this diversion was truly the result of bribes rather than damage. Otherwise, she might not even be able to make Pyron in time, and would have done all this for nothing.

There was no sense of being near land throughout the day, but Jaysu could almost smell it. The birds also tended to show up in far greater numbers than at sea, and there were large fish and marine mammals both in the water, following, or even playing a game of derring-do ahead of the great ship.

Because Magid was a high-tech hex, the last day before hitting port was a very comfortable one. Alkazar, too, was a high-tech hex, so communications and navigation exchanges were possible ship-to-shore.

They were due to land in the very early morning hours, but all passengers were assured that they would not be required to waken, let alone leave the ship, until at least three hours after sunup. Representatives would meet them dockside after breakfast and take them to temporary housing or arrange for alternative passages.

She wondered who or what would contact her, or if she was just stuck in the clutches of the shipping line. She'd thought it odd that, after that first dramatic encounter with the Ixthansan, Eggy, she'd not been contacted again at any time by anyone.

Jaysu was out enjoying the air when she saw the two little creatures who were associates of Wally on the forward rail, where she generally liked to stand. Maximum inward breeze, good speed, where you'd want to be if you had to fly in a hurry off this deck.

She hadn't liked either one and had stayed away from them. They radiated evil, and didn't disguise their nastiness nor their seeming contempt for her.

The little apelike creatures, each no more than a meter tall, with their cherubic black wings and outlandish uniformlike clothes, did not look threatening, but neither she nor many of the other passengers and crew needed any kind of sixth sense to think them dangerous.

They chattered away to each other in a kind of native code that nobody's translator ever picked up and straightened out; it was apparently designed with some sort of security in mind. Then, as she watched, the pair turned, climbed up on the top rail side by side, holding on with those large feet that looked exactly like their hands, and worked the same as well, and, to her astonishment, launched themselves into the air.

Until now, she'd never been convinced that creatures with such wings could truly fly, but clearly they could and did, and quite well, too, although they used a great deal of energy flapping those wings in order to get away from the influence of the ship and into updrafts. Once there, however, they needed just a little correction now and then, and otherwise were sailing with the birds.

She hadn't realized until then how much she wanted to do that, as well, but it was unlikely she'd get the chance where they were heading now. She watched them circle the ship once, gaining altitude and then setting off due south, the same direction the ship was traveling, until they were quickly out of even her best telescoping sight.

It didn't take a genius to know where they were going now that they had indeed left. Going ahead to this Alkazar, probably getting there hours ahead of the ship, and thus beginning the process of arranging passage through the mysterious place.

She wondered what it must be like, this Alkazar, that could maintain a major port and had all of these high-tech luxuries yet sounded like such a sad and perhaps evil place.

Perhaps those luxuries, those machines that could do things better than people could, were good for the body but not the soul, she thought. Maybe *they* were the corruptors. She didn't have enough experience to know for sure, but she had the feeling that she'd find out soon enough.

After a fine meal and a walk and stretch on the deck, she still couldn't see land, but there were more than just birds now to tell her that they were coming in.

Now there were boats. Small ones, generally, although a couple looked elaborate and even had smokestacks. All seemed to be engaged in fishing at some level, indicating that whoever lived in Magid was more likely on the bottom of the sea than near the top, and that these waters were filled with wildlife from that ocean.

The boats varied in design, and she noticed that almost all of them were crewed by single race crews, not the polyglot that staffed the *Bay of Vessali*. Most were strange to her, although she recognized a few sleek, smooth, black vessels as being from Pyron. The strange creatures that seemed both giant snakes and men were hard to miss.

Others included creatures with shells, creatures with lots of tentacles, creatures that seemed to ooze up and down masts and in and out of the water, tall creatures with big snouts, floppy ears, and black noses, and even two that were clearly Ixthansan. She stared at each of those as they passed, wondering if Eggy or someone affiliated with him was on either, but she knew that was unlikely. To be here, Eggy would have had to travel the same distance as she, and through that storm or the long way around it. Still, if that race was allied with Core's group, then one or both of these small fishing vessels might well be more than it appeared.

She was still standing there, staring at them, and noticing that they were often staring at her, too, if they spotted her, when the purser found her.

"Pardon, missy. Got radio message for Madam Jaysu, yep yep."

She frowned. "What is a radio?"

"Thing that sends talk or code through the air. Easy way to get messages, other stuff, when in high-tech areas, yep yep. Since both Magid and Alkazar are high-tech, can get messages back and forth, no problem, nope nope." He held out a small tray with an envelope on it.

She took the envelope and opened it, but then sighed and shook her head. "I'm sorry. I do not know how to read this."

The little creature seemed almost embarrassed to hear that. "Sorry. Give. With your permission, I'll read?"

"Please do," she invited him. She had no bad feelings about being illiterate, contrary to what the purser thought. She couldn't see much use for it anyway.

"It is from the Pyron consul in Kolznar Colony. That's where we're going. Big port of Alkazar."

"The Pyron council?"

"Nope nope. *Consul.* Like junior ambassador. Ambassadors all in Zone, but sometimes have consuls in other countries where business is done. Faster."

"Well, what does this consul say?"

"Says you will not have to stay on ship to Pyron. Consul has arranged for passage to your destination from Kolznar. Says you will be met at pier when we dock. Warns you not to fly to or in Alkazar. Can be big trouble, yep yep."

That was both good news and bad news. The good news was that she was actually going to get off this thing and hit land! But the instructions not to fly—that was almost crushing. It was inside her, something she had to continually fight not doing even now. To still be a groundling even on land was not something she'd thought would happen.

"Purser?"

"Madam?"

"How is it that you read the writings of Pyron? Do you read *all* the tongues of the people you transport?"

"Nope nope. Only read Kuall and Commercand. Commercand is language used by all who travel and trade between hexes. Simple, direct, but all the same no matter what tongue you think in. Makes trade possible. Also used in diplomacy, yep yep. That's what this note is in. If somebody can write it, odds are there will always be somebody else where you are who can read it."

"How long until we get in?"

"About two hours, no more, yep yep," the purser responded, ripping up the note into little pieces and then putting the pieces back into the envelope. She thought it an interesting custom. "May take a little while to dock the ship, though. They're always busy and it's tricky. We'll get pilot in about an hour, yep yep. Then it's in their hands."

"Indeed? What is a pilot?"

"Captain with no ship but knows the harbors. Pilot takes over to dock ships in big ports and get them out. Otherwise we crash into things. Very convenient, yep yep."

She had to agree with that, although the job never would have occurred to her.

She wondered about the little horrors who'd taken off and flown into this Kolznar the previous night. If she could not fly, then why could they?

She decided to go back up to her cabin and get together the few things she had with her, put them in the waist pack, and then watch the landing. It would even be interesting to see this pilot creature; he, she, or it was unlikely to be of Magid, considering, and so would almost certainly be Alkazarian.

She walked back, unlocked the door, and walked in. Almost immediately she sensed a wrongness about it, although she was more curious than afraid, considering how long she'd been aboard and that she knew just about everybody.

The door shut behind her, and she realized that the lamp was out. This wasn't unusual in a high-tech hex, but normally there was a kind of glowing bar that went on that allowed you to see well enough for the basics. Now, suddenly, it was pitch-black.

She knew she was not alone.

She could have sensed it before, but had not been thinking about such things. Now, though, all her senses were on full alert because of the darkness, and she knew not only that someone else was there, but who it was, and that was a shock.

"That is far enough," said a familiar voice. "I have in my hands a weapon that can fry you like a roasted bird in an instant, and I see just fine in the infrared, so I can see you as clearly as if we were on deck."

"Then why do you not use it and kill me? That *is* what you came in here for," Jaysu responded, oddly calm and sounding not at all terrified. She realized then that she should have known from the beginning that Algensor, the Kehudan, was not on the up and up. Nobody took a ship to *return* to their home hex. You just went through a Zone Gate. Some detective *she* was!

"I need to know who sent you the message you just received, and what it said," the Kehudan told her, becoming unnerved by Jaysu's lack of panic.

"I do not believe that concerns you," she told the agent calmly. Her heightened senses located the creature precisely and saw her with greater clarity than the Kehudan could have imagined. "I think you might as well shoot me."

Algensor wasn't prepared for this. "Do you understand

what I am saying, foolish shaman? Tell me or I will shoot you!"

"But if I tell you, then you will shoot me anyway, so why give you anything for the deed?"

Jaysu saw the numbers tied to the glowing strings, the numbers she did not understand but did not have to, since the meaning was forming unbidden in her mind. She knew exactly what did what, and it was as simple as moving her own finger.

"Then perhaps I will give you pain," the Kehudan threatened. "Sear off some of those wings, and perhaps carve off the hands and feet. *Talk!*"

"You have no idea of pain," Jaysu told her. "You have no idea what an Amboran must undergo to get to the High Priestess level. I have experienced such pain as you can never comprehend, and I cannot be threatened by it."

"I don't know if you're more alien than I believed or just ignorant and naive, but I have no more time to waste on this. Last chance. What was in the message and who sent it?"

"How should I know?" Jaysu mocked her. "I can't read, you know."

Seething with frustration, Algensor pulled the trigger on the energy pistol, aiming at Jaysu's feet.

Nothing happened.

Jaysu smiled to herself. "Now what will you do?" she asked the creature.

Algensor was unnerved by the failure of the gun. Clearly, she'd tested it to make sure it was fully energized and operational, but even as she tried to fire it repeatedly, it would not work.

"Try shooting into the toilet," Jaysu suggested. "Messy, but it will work."

Algensor was so angry she did just that, firing into the toilet area. There was a crack and a flash that illuminated the cabin for an instant, and the sound of something sizzling.

The Kehudan brought the pistol back up and fired at Jaysu.

Again the pistol refused to work.

She pointed to the roostlike sleep box and set the thing on fire, and managed to hit the cabin door. But when she aimed at Jaysu, the gun would not fire.

"Then I'll get you with poison!" the Kehudan snarled, and started toward Jaysu, who was only a few meters away. But Algensor's ample feet didn't seem to work. She strained, but she couldn't move toward the Amboran.

Now it was the would-be assassin's turn to panic. "*You!* You're doing this to me, aren't you?"

"My oaths will not allow me to let someone harm another, but basically it is simply instinct. I am reacting to your threat." Jaysu turned, picked up her pack, checked for a few basics, and deciding that anything she didn't have she could replace or do without, put it on.

"Then you're not going to kill me?"

Jaysu sighed and shook her head in pity. "I cannot deliberately harm another thinking being," she told the Kehudan. "Still, if you tell me who sent you, or hired you, to do this, I will allow you to walk out of the cabin and off the ship when it docks."

Algensor wasn't fully cowed, although she was defeated. "Foolish girl! Don't you realize that almost every passenger on this *ship* works for your enemies?"

"I suspected as much, but it seemed too much trouble to go to just for me. I simply wish to know what it is that allows you to try and take my life when I am no threat to you. Reward? At the command of your people? Some cause?"

"Most of us work for reward," the Kehudan admitted. "But some of us also work for our governments. Mine is terrified of the alliance that has grown up so quickly around Chalidang, and the way we live, just atop the waves, makes us very vulnerable to any sort of military attack. It was they who instructed me that you were not to get off this ship. You have stopped me, but I do not see how you are going to stop the others."

"The same way," Jaysu responded matter-of-factly. "Now I wish you to remain here until we are at the dock. Once we are in port, you may emerge and leave the ship so long as you do *not* have hold of that weapon. The weapon must stay here." She turned and opened the door, then looked back, seeing in the light flooding into the cabin the silvery insectlike creature that was to have killed her, and a very nasty looking thing in her tentacles that must be the pistol.

"It was a message from the Pyron chief in this place we are going to," Jaysu said. "All it said was that I was to get off the ship and be met there. Happy now?"

And with that, Jaysu stepped out of the cabin and let the door close.

She did wonder how long it would take before the Kehudan stopped fighting and dropped the pistol so she could leave, but it wasn't really her affair.

Jaysu still could not understand why they were all so afraid of her. What could *she* do? She didn't even understand why Core thought she could be of value in this affair.

She wasn't completely confident, either, in her ability to remain alive through it. True, she had little to worry about in these kinds of situations, but here, in high-tech areas, she was still vulnerable to long-range weapons fired without warning. She would never detect the hostile intent in time, let alone pick it out.

She had no desire to remain in a high-tech hex for long. Not now, particularly.

She wondered if Wally would try and pounce on her. She decided that being out on deck was no more or less dangerous than being inside. On deck, someone in one of those boats might take a shot at her, but inside, well, Wally had been the one creature she'd not detected fully until he'd moved. Best not to give him any advantage.

When she got back to her viewing area just below the wheelhouse, she saw the pilot boat coming out to meet them. It was an ugly little craft, dull gray and with a gun of some kind mounted forward. It didn't look like the kind of craft anyone would use just to take a harbor expert out and back; it looked more like a craft you'd run up rivers and through harbors looking for criminals or smugglers.

If the Alkazarians were as ugly and mean-looking as their craft, she could see why everybody was nervous about them.

But as it turned out, they weren't. They were, if anything, downright *cute.*

Averaging only a bit over a meter high, the Alkazarian crew of the pilot boat looked like nothing so much as fluffy little animated toy bears or bear cubs. They were, in fact, bipeds, with short three-fingered hands with opposable thumbs, but otherwise they were *darling* little things, with blow-dry fluffy brown fur, little black button eyes, and everything else that said ursine. The black uniforms with leather belts and lots of braid, and the little hats that sat between their pointed ears, added to the comic effect, and they leaped and jumped around like small children preparing to match speed and direction with the large ship, from which a metallic stairway had been lowered.

She knew she should be laughing at their cute antics, but her other senses were almost screaming at her to ignore appearances. These little creatures radiated a cold, hard evil, an inner soul that recognized only fear and the instigation of fear as valid emotions. Even Wally hadn't been as dead inside as any of those little creatures.

Still, as an Alkazarian in a particularly ornate decorated uniform walked to the side of the boat and then, after judging distance and motion, made an effortless leap to the stair and started up, she couldn't keep her eyes off the others. Impressions flooded into her mind, ugly impressions, like those of a nightmare. Fleeting images of these little creatures running in crazed packs, thrilled by the chase, then taking one of their own and killing them and—*eating* their own! *Cannibals?* It was—ghoulish.

They had high technology, trade, all this. Why would they revert to savagery, and with such enjoyment?

She hoped she was seeing some vestigial memory of an ancient past, but deep down she knew she was not. The ones on that boat had been in that pack, and had eaten of their own, and to them it was not an unpleasant memory.

She didn't like these little creatures one bit.

In fact, she was beginning to wonder if there were *any* alien creatures, by which she meant not Amborans, that she could trust. She'd met few here, although the little purser and the crew in general had treated her well. Still, that was their job.

Could it be that the only ones she could truly trust in all this were the sinister looking Pyrons?

Land was visible now, dead ahead, a definite shoreline, and almost dead center in it, a tall mountain range that looked not unlike home. It did not seem to stretch from horizon to horizon, though, but was sharply vertical only in that central area and then tapered away on both sides. It was odd-looking, and the ship had to move in much closer in order for her to realize that it was a V-shaped formation whose base reached the coast but fanned out from it diagonally inland.

It was the tall center of that mountain at the base of the V that they were headed for, and soon it began to dominate the skyline to the south. It was not volcanic; there were layers of rock going up into the sky for several kilometers, the tallest mountain she'd ever seen by far, and the rest of the range was just about as tall.

It was quite warm at the surface, even hot, but there was snow up on those peaks, and from various points along the mountainside there were hundreds of waterfalls.

The mountain did not quite reach the sea; instead there was a half bowl at the base that was not much above sea level but was hundreds of square kilometers in size, and it was not empty.

The city at the bottom of the mountain had its own landscape, this one artificial, consisting of large scale docks, even drydocks, giant warehouses, and, beyond the waterfront, densely packed high rises that went back almost to the mountain itself and off on either side as far as she could see.

It was a huge, bustling, dramatic, modern city that did not look like it belonged there. It was difficult to believe that creatures such as the Alkazarians could have built it.

There was certainly an inconsistency of styles. Buildings were very different from one another, in shape, in form, in color, in every way she could think of save that they were almost all high rises. It was almost as if a portion of Zone were built not inside enclosed and fixed quarters, but along this harbor, each race carving out its own little piece of itself.

And, of course, she realized that this was exactly what she was seeing. The Alkazarians might own the place, but it wasn't theirs in spirit. It was, rather, a place that existed because the creatures of the hex realized what a profitable location they had.

She looked back and up to the bridge area and saw the little Alkazarian, probably standing on a box or something to see, on one of the outside "wings" next to the wheelhouse, barking orders in a high-pitched voice to the helmsman inside. Occasionally he'd jump down and vanish inside, then run back out again, and it was apparent that he was running the ship now.

She was glad somebody was. The harbor was so crowded with ships big and small, and more boats of all sizes than could be counted, that she didn't see how they were going to come in without hitting things.

Like the buildings and the fishing vessels offshore, it seemed there were a hundred races here, each in their unique vessels. To her surprise, there were even two other large steamers in the same class as the *Bay of Vessali* in port; the *Bay*, in fact, was heading for a long pier that would put her in back of another similar ship and on the other side of a third. The major differences were in the colors on the superstructures and smokestacks, and the flags that flew from the sterns.

They slid in smoothly, and more Alkazarians in dull blue uniforms with no particular adornment threw ropes up to places where *Bay* crewmen were perched to fix the big ship in place. The engines were cut; movement suddenly stopped, save for a small jerkiness as the ship struck the dock while straightening out. Then there was one long, deafening blast on the steam whistle that seemed to go on forever, and it was over.

She heard yells and the sounds of engines from the other

side of the big ship. Curious, she went over there and saw several small, squat, ugly little boats with single stacks going away, back out into the harbor. It was only then that she realized how the big ships docked: they were guided in by the little boats.

The city and the mountain behind, which rose to impossible heights in the sky creating a virtual wall, were now all that she could see forward. She decided it might be time to get off the ship, but wasn't sure how to do it. She'd not gotten on in the usual way, and she'd never been in a port before, and it only now occurred to her that she didn't know where the door was.

One of the crewmen, an octopuslike creature, only it breathed air, was oozing down from the rigging nearby. She approached it and called out, "Excuse me, but how do I go off?"

The creature stopped, two eyes within the fluid mass seemed to float until they were looking at her, and it replied, from somewhere within, "One deck down, this side, madam. Don't worry—you will see it. Just use the center stairs."

She thanked it, walked back along the deck and went in amidships and down the central staircase one deck. The crewman was right. Most of the other passengers were already there, along with the purser and chief steward. She didn't see Algensor, but Wally was prominent.

"Attention, please!" the purser shouted, and after several attempts they did quiet down. "Please excuse this problem! If you need to go on immediately to another destination, or have no travel documents, then inform the company agent at the bottom of the gangplank and we will arrange to put you up until we can transfer you. If you have your documents, proceed to Tolls and Tariffs inside the terminal. From there, go to our office inside and we will arrange for your stay here and passage to your final destination. Thank you!"

All the affectations the little creature had in his speech and manner seemed to vanish. She doubted if that had been an act; rather, this was duty overriding habit.

She wasn't sure which category she was in, and looked

through the small bag she wore. They had sent her some papers, but since she couldn't read them, she had no idea what they might be, other than the credit voucher that had been used for passage and might still be worth something here. Supposedly that's how they did things between hexes, with these vouchers.

One of the papers did look official, though, and even had a very bad and grainy black and white picture of her face she could hardly recognize. She suspected it was a travel document, but decided to ask.

None of the other passengers seemed surprised to see her, at least not from her scan. She wondered if Algensor had taken matters into her own hands without explicit orders. Certainly the Kehudan hadn't radiated a threat earlier in the voyage.

Wally seemed to radiate some odd pleasure at seeing her, as if he hadn't expected her to live but was, for some reason, glad she still did. It was curious. She still hadn't figured him out, at least in relation to herself.

The gangplank wasn't all that stable and seemed to move a bit up and down, but it wasn't far from the door in the ship's side to the dock, and she managed.

The creature on the other side was another of the elephantine types, like the first mate, with the two-handed nose trunk and funny little uniform. She began to suspect that these creatures were in fact the owners of the ship and the line, although you could never be sure about such things. Still, this one towered over her.

"Excuse me, but I do not know if I have the proper papers or not," she told him, offering the one with her picture.

The split trunk twitched, one of the "hands" took the paper and brought it up to his eye level. He read it for a moment, then offered it back.

"This should be sufficient," he told her. "Most hexes don't even require this sort of nonsense, but this isn't most hexes. Proceed on down the pier and into the building at the end. Just be polite and show this to the Alkazarian at the entrance. When you clear, go to our office."

She thanked him, and, clutching the paper, walked down the pier, past not only her vessel but the one in front. Just when she wondered if she'd walked too far over hard ground, she was at the entrance.

This Alkazarian looked like the others, but he radiated suspicion and disdain. Still, he seemed taken aback by her. "And just *what* are *you*?" he asked officiously.

"I am Jaysu, High Priestess of the Great Falcon, an Amboran," she responded.

"That right? Huh! That's some set of wings there." He looked at the paper and seemed to read every single word of it. Finally, he nodded to himself, took out a fancy printed rectangular sheet, stamped it, wrote something on it, then stapled it to the sheet and handed it back.

"Don't lose this," he warned her, "and show it on demand to anyone in authority, which means anyone of my race. You can do nothing here without it. When you leave the country, you must surrender this paper to the official on the way out along with any others you might get or they will arrest you. Please do not take this lightly. *Next!*"

And with that she was through. Still, the speech was a little scary; she carefully folded the paper with its attachment, put it in her travel case and sealed it tightly. The last thing she wanted was to be arrested in a place like this.

She looked for the steamer company office, but instead saw a Pyron standing not too far away, looking at her with those serpent's eyes.

They were such a strange and eerie race to look at. She thought of them as serpents who crawled on their bellies, but she saw that they did have legs, partially cloaked by the enormous hoods. Still, they looked like giant snakes rearing up and poised to strike, and she wasn't at all comfortable with their appearance, even though this one was radiating no threat at all. She was going to have to get used to looking only inside these different creatures. Cuddly little bears with the souls of mass murderers; fanged, giant serpentlike creatures who were, if not saints, at least ordinary people: she wondered how those who couldn't look beneath managed to cope.

The Pyron stepped forward, still moving as if slithering on its belly, even though it wasn't proportionately long enough to do that. "You are Jaysu? I am First Consul Auglack of Pyron. You received my message?"

"Yes, yes, sir, I did," she managed. "It was quite a surprise. In fact, it was a surprise to be here at all."

"Well, someone should have warned you. They do this all the time, in fact, when they don't have a cargo in mid-ocean. This is, quite frankly, a very pleasant city overall for a ship's crew to stay over in when they spend all that time at sea, and they look forward to putting in for minor repairs most times. The company doesn't mind unless it has business on the wider route. We weren't positive from the manifest that they were doing it this time, but we were ready if and when they did. Will you come with me, please?"

"Yes, sir. Certainly. But you must bear with me. My race is not built for long walks on this hard ground."

The consul chuckled. "Hard gr— Oh, you mean the floor! Yes, I can see where your feet aren't well-suited for that. Well, we will walk as little as we must, I promise. First things first. How do I address you?"

"Sir? I do not understand."

"You are a cleric of some kind, I know. Clerics tend to have titles beyond Citizen or Madam, just as politicians do. They call me Excellency in my official capacity, otherwise I am just 'sir' or 'mister.' I know religious leaders who are addressed as Father, Mother, Sister, Brother, Reverend, Doctor, Holiness, Most High, and about a dozen other titles. How should you be addressed?"

"We do not go in much for that sort of thing," she told him. "Jaysu is fine. My title is important when I am introducing myself or acting in a religious capacity, but it is just a title, just as yours is, First Consul, if I hear right."

"Very well, then. It is simply important in my post that no one be insulted by those around me failing to use a title of respect. If Jaysu is what you like, then that is what we will use. How was the voyage?"

"Not very good, overall. Boring for much of it, then frightening in stormy seas. And, of course, that doesn't even include the attempt to kill me this morning."

The consul stopped. "I beg your pardon?"

"A Kehudan, Algensor, tried to shoot me."

"Indeed? And it missed?"

"No, she did not miss. When it came time, she simply could not do it."

The consul let it go at that, not realizing how literal his guest might be.

"This was the only attempt on you? I mean, not that we expected even that, but there were no others aboard who appeared to have less than noble intentions toward you?"

"There was this one creature, a giant, hairy green spider-like thing, that I knew from the start was not my friend, yet at no time did he act against me or even pump me for information. He had two hideous little winged henchmen, but they were kept back, or so I had the impression, by their master. Both of them flew off to this city last night."

"Indeed? That is most interesting. Normally anything that crossed into Alkazar, airborne or otherwise, would have been vaporized without question if detected. Either they landed on a boat just short of the border or they were expected. Most interesting. Oh, we received your photographs, by the way. *Most* useful. I'm sure your spider and little flying things are there, as is the Kehudan. The spider's the one to watch. He's been at the scene of other things such as this, and is absolutely in the service of Chalidang. We've been unable to get anything on his background, which is quite unusual and suggests that he might well be an import from outside the Well World whom, for whatever reasons, his new people are keeping well-hidden."

"Well, he called himself 'Wally,' if that is any clue. He said I could not pronounce his real one."

"Probably true. You probably couldn't pronounce mine, nor I yours, either, but that hasn't stopped us. Ah, here we are."

"Here" turned out to be a moving sidewalk just outside the

shipping terminal. It appeared that the whole city was covered with these, moving along at a steady but not very fast clip. They were clearly designed as mass transportation; there were some hovering, flying vehicles, all looking very sinister, darting about overhead and going between the buildings and such, but ground transport was via these moving belts.

"I want to point out something to you, although you'll not be here long enough to *really* appreciate how paranoid you can get in this town," the consul said as he stepped on. After a moment's hesitation, she did likewise, and gripped the small handrail.

The city might have seemed majestic, even beautiful to some, but to her it felt unnatural, wrong, claustrophobic. She didn't like it one bit. It wasn't right to cram so many people into such a small space. It was filled with a thick atmosphere of the most awful odors, and a cacophony of sounds that made her head hurt.

"See those small posts every fifty meters or so alongside the walkways?" the Pyron asked.

She looked and nodded. There was so much filling every view that she'd barely noticed them.

"Well, on each are tiny little high-resolution cameras showing what's going on in all directions. At all times when you are anywhere in this city, and maybe in this whole godforsaken country, you are being watched. Inside every building, every corridor inside the buildings, same thing."

"Goodness! *Why?* And by who?"

"Alkazarian Security Police and their watch computers, which are programmed to alert them to anything suspicious. By their standards that means two people whispering who can't be picked up by their hidden sound monitors. We found them embedded in our offices and in our diplomatic quarters, which is highly improper and illegal, of course, but they deny it and it's their city. It's our belief that there isn't a single place you can go, or anything you can say or do here, that isn't monitored. Of course, we have our own ways of blocking the ones inside our diplomatic areas, but otherwise even going to the toilet, pardon, is a public act to them."

"How can anyone *live* like that?" she asked him.

"Because they have no choice. The foreigners here, like us, and many of those you see all over here, are here because it's their job and it's money. The pay is exceptional here because of the stress, but you can tune it out, take it for granted after a while, kind of build your own safeguards and go about your business. The services of a great city are here as well. Entertainment zones, any kind of goods or services one might desire, even if illicit, plus many of the comforts of home, major shopping with no tariffs, all that. And all completely safe. There are no murders here, no theft to speak of, not even much littering. Not when they're watching. In an odd way, it makes my job easier as well. If one of my people vanishes, I know immediately that the Alkazarian government has him or her because they are the only ones who could."

"I certainly wouldn't want to be here under these conditions!"

"Well, they are a bit more tolerant of us foreigners," the consul told her. "They can't have the absolutely free hand they have with their own people, poor devils, because they know that if they got too nasty or intrusive, we'd simply all pack up and leave. It's a wonderful natural harbor at a convenient spot, but it's not the only one, and it's not a place that is essential, only convenient. There is a difference. And if we pack up and leave, well, they are a high technology hex, it is true, but they are resource poor. Without the import of raw materials and the export of sophisticated manufactured goods at cheap prices, it would quickly become a very bleak place indeed. Ah, we switch here to the diagonal belt on the right side. Not much farther."

Once he'd pointed out the cameras, she couldn't get them out of her mind. What kind of people would create such a system, and what sort of people would willingly live under it? A very frightened and insecure system, surely. A meter tall and only of average strength . . . She wondered if perhaps they were petrified of the outside world just walking all over them. And petrified that, if they did not keep their own people even more cowed, such leaders might well be eaten by their citizens.

The walkways ended at junctions, and there was then a short platform from which other walkways going in different directions began. It was a very efficient system, if you knew where you were going.

Where they were going turned out to be a section that actually had a few trees and an angle that permitted sufficient sunlight to keep them from dying. In this small area the buildings were not huge, but businesslike in size, although each had a different design echoing the flavor of the high rises. The one that they got off at was an imposing structure, a cluster of buildings merging into one another, each shaped somewhat like a common beehive.

"This is the Consulate of Pyron," her host informed her. "Once inside, you will not be photographed or recorded, and you'll be legally on Pyron soil. You'll stay here for the day and night, and then we'll get you on your way early tomorrow morning, if that is all right."

"Yes, of course," she answered, knowing but not letting *him* know that she had detected the lies among the truth. She was no less under observation in there than out here; she was just switching observers from the Alkazarians to the Pyrons.

It had not occurred to her to ever ask anyone what sort of government *these* people had in their homeland. She supposed it was just more naïveté—that the ones on her side weren't the ones she had to worry about. She wondered if that was a true assessment of the situation. If this venerated object were assembled, would its power be any less tempting to those who wished to stop Josich from doing it?

"I only need to know," she told him, "when I can fly again. I have physical as well as emotional needs to do so, having been unable to do it for so long now. I have no other way to work off the energy, and I am feeling out of sorts because of that."

"I apologize for that," the consul answered, apparently sincerely, "but it must remain a sacrifice until you are out of this country. They will kill anyone who flies over any of their land except their own vehicles. Once you are in Quislon, there should be no problems, and it is a nontech hex anyway. In fact, we are banking on you being able to fly to the capital, as it will get you there before anyone else from the ship might reach it."

"From the ship? You think they are heading there?"

"I think insofar as your spider friend and his companions, you can wager money on it and be certain of winning."

Yabbo

GENERAL MOCHIDA HAPPILY DEMONSTRATED HIS UNIQUE method of ensuring that he now had two loyal traveling companions. It was, in fact, a small spiny sea creature that seemed to have too many eyes and not much else but which, by its markings, clearly showed that anyone or anything thinking of eating it should think twice or be poisoned. It was not, however, a creature that Ari and Ming had seen before.

"It's a gunot," the General explained cheerfully. "They freeze rather nicely and revive just as quickly—rather simple little things, really—and we have a *lot* of them here because they are so *useful* around Kalindans. It seems that the poison the little creature gives off, and, in fact, is just full of, is toxic to all the creatures in its own native hex but not to others. It was discovered, though, quite by accident, that instead of killing Kalindans, it gave them a marvelous boost. The chemistry is very near but not identical to a key enzyme in the Kalindan brain, and when it is introduced into the Kalindan bloodstream, it actually *replaces* that enzyme. Do not be alarmed. It does a better job than nature, and when it moves into the brain it makes everything feel very, very good. That was the key to its long-ago discovery, in fact. Kalindan medical personnel were looking for a drug that would aid in the cure of certain psychological illnesses. It worked, but was never introduced because, you see, in about twelve hours the body's defense mechanisms expel the foreign substance. Unfortunately, it takes about three days for that same body to make more of the natural type, and I have had it described to me that those three days are as close as you can come to a descent into Hell. You see where this goes, of course. There was quite a black market in the stuff long ago, until the gunot were almost threatened with extinction, but then they developed an easy test for its presence and managed to stamp things out."

Holy shit! He's gonna addict us to a drug! Ming exclaimed to Ari.

Can't work! Only a true designer drug from the best of labs can addict somebody in one shot!

Maybe for Terrans, but we ain't Terrans, remember?

There wasn't that much that could be done about it in any event.

The sergeant major approached with a gas-powered injector that would work in the semitech environment. It was already filled with a very unpleasant-looking yellow bile-colored liquid, and with no hesitancy whatsoever he injected it right into the tail at the hip.

There was a slight sting but nothing major, but they held their breath waiting to see what the stuff would do to them.

"It's too bad, really, that there are so few of these little devils left, and they refuse to breed in captivity. We've tried cloning but the power's diluted, and we've tried mixing the stuff in the lab but it can take dozens of shots before any addictive qualities appear. If we could just make it at will as we do other substances, we could have every single Kalindan under our complete control in a matter of months without a shot being fired. Still, it's useful when you want to turn someone from enemy to ally, or to keep someone close."

You can only tense up for so long before you relax after nothing apparently happens. This was what was going on with them, at least as far as they could tell. If it supposedly went to work quickly, then something was wrong.

In fact, all the tension, all the fear, seemed to be ebbing from them, and small sensations of pleasure and contentment, like small waves on a pond, came at them one after the other. It finally occurred to both of them that this indeed *was* the drug, but it felt so good, the ripples almost orgasmic, that they could not bring themselves to resist, nor did they want to.

"It's working quite well," the sergeant commented. "You can see how relaxed they are, sir."

"I can't tell one of those fish faces from another, Sergeant, let alone tell what constitutes a happy demeanor, but I will take your word for it. You may go back and assist the colonel in final inventory and preparations for executing Operation Grail. I have to get our friends to send a few dispatches home and then pick up our mail, but I have a very good feeling about this."

"I'm not worried, sir," the sergeant told the General. "These people, all these races, seem woefully naive when it comes to any sort of covert action, and they are disunited."

"They gave our forces a pretty good whipping at Ochoa, Sergeant," Mochida reminded him.

"Yes, sir, but there were no Chalidangers engaged there nor on site to provide competent generalship. Besides, they have to win every time. We only have to win once in each engagement. I've been in the service thirty years, sir, and I'll *always* take conditions like that!"

They had a blissful semi-sleep for an hour or two, and then began to awaken and come out of it. Not that they didn't still feel very good, but they were beginning to think on their own again.

It does *work, doesn't it?* Ari sighed.

I'm afraid it does. I wonder how much willpower and pain threshold we have? That's what he's gonna find out, you know. My feeling is, if we can't stand it the first time, with only one dose of the crud, then we're stuck. You know it and I know it and so does Mochida.

Yeah, Ari responded, knowing just how little of a threshold he'd always had before for such things. If he'd been more tolerant of pain, he might well have risked not working for his dear, departed uncle and turned out to be a much better person, but he knew that for him pain avoidance took precedence over character building every time.

Ming was a lot stronger on that score, but she knew that

she'd never experienced something like this before. Intoxicants? High? Recreational drugs? At one point or another
she'd had them all, usually but not exclusively in the performance of her duties as an undercover cop. Still, the ease with
which Jules Wallinchky had turned her into a robotic bimbo
had, deep down, shaken her self-confidence to its core, and
Ari's presence was no great help in rebuilding it. Taking risks
was one thing, but something like this . . . She'd seen too
many good, kind, decent people enslaved by this sort of dependency. When it was just willpower, she was always confident, but when it was also biochemistry, that was a very
different thing.

The General was a Chalidanger, born and raised, who'd
risen to this very high level, which almost certainly meant
that, in addition to all his culture, breeding, good taste and
education, he was also totally without conscience and probably as much of a sadist as Jules Wallinchky had been.

The sergeant basically hand-fed, or at least tentacle-fed,
them during this period, and otherwise everybody seemed to
ignore them completely. They were still bound, though, which
meant that the Chalidangers weren't yet certain that the drug
would do their dirty work. The General, in fact, was nowhere
in sight, and appeared to have done what he had taken great
care not to do before: left the dark protective dome.

To Ari and Ming that could only mean that whatever was
being planned was in its end stage and concealment was no
longer a primary objective.

There were no timepieces around, and the two of them
could only lie there and amuse each other with word games
and such to pass the time, or reflect on anything except their
current plight. Still, in the back of their minds the impending
twelve-hour mark was never completely banished from their
thoughts, nor the frustration of knowing that Core had been
properly warned of all this yet had dismissed them and their
reports. Had Core acted, they might not be here and in such
danger now!

Mochida was gone a very long time, but finally there was a
sound, and a dark shape reentered the dome.

"It is on schedule," he announced to the other two. The supply ships will be in position in eleven days. As far as can be determined from our spies down here and at Zone, the ships and their cargoes have not been linked and are under no particular watch. We've also been in constant contact with the embassy of Sanafe, and they appear more likely to see things our way after noting just how many of their own neighbors are falling under our sway. They're too proud to just give it away, unlike those spineless Pegiri, but it shouldn't take much more than a forceful demonstration under their own home conditions to convince them that being our friend is far better than being our enemy."

"So we might not have to fight, sir?" The sergeant sounded disappointed.

"Oh, I think we'll have to undergo a minor action. The good citizens of Sanafe are themselves something of a warrior class, albeit on a lower, more tribalized level. I think they may give us a good scrap, but they aren't organized enough to give us a war and overwhelm us. No, I think it'll be quite a good battle, yet a symbolic battle, a *demonstration*, as it were. Get their respect and they'll deal."

"Aren't you afraid that somebody back home is going to take over your job while you're stuck out here in the boondocks, General?" Ari called to him.

The General turned and trained one eye on them. Clearly he wasn't interested in them as yet, but he felt he had to answer.

"I think not. Don't get your hopes up, anyway. Anyone who *could* replace me would be far worse than me in every respect, including toward the likes of you. Besides, what's the difference who's doing what at home? Either I'm going to be killed in this operation or, more preferably and likely, I'm going to be something of a heroic figure and, at the same time, in possession of something the Royal Family wants very, very badly. Although it's a Chalidang tradition, I see no evidence at the moment that my primary threat is to my back."

He then proceeded to ignore them once more while working with the other two. Watching a general doing heavy lifting, and moving around huge crates with the others, impressed them both. There was nobody comparable that they could think of in any of the armed forces back in the Confederacy, let alone in Kalinda or in the other forces they'd seen on the Well World, who would be at that rank and level and yet do that kind of work. It just wasn't done.

Clearly, whatever this operation was, meant everything to the General and his Emperor and Empress. So important that a failure in this enterprise meant that the General would suffer the fate of all who failed the Royal Family. Why wind up being eaten alive while waiting back in some office in Chalidang, then? Better to succeed or die in the field. That much they could understand.

The fact that General Mochida was clearly enjoying himself in this was a little harder to comprehend. Warrior class be damned, generals didn't put themselves on the firing line, and security chiefs didn't do the operations they planned themselves. Mochida had clearly missed being out in the field.

They didn't need a clock to tell them that the twelfth hour was looming. They could feel it, and just that sensation and the fear it raised was enough to undermine their confidence.

I hate to say this, Ari commented ruefully, *but I think the old bastard really knows his business.*

The sensations began as waves of nausea that increased in power and frequency with each incidence. When it seemed that the nausea was so awful you couldn't imagine it getting any worse, the pains started, first in every joint, then joined by regular but not constant muscle spasms that caused their tail to jerk and their back to twist.

It wasn't a fast descent, but a slow one, taking quite some time to build but making you aware of every second of it and dreading the next wave of horrors, which you knew would be worse.

They held out as best they could, but after another long period the hallucinations started. They were every nightmare either of them had had as a Terran or a Kalindan, every fear made apparent flesh, every guilt suddenly rising from the deepest of two subconscious minds and attacking them both jointly and individually. Every negative thought was recalled, every negative emotion relived and doubled and redoubled.

There was no question in either of their minds that the continual build of this round would come close to driving them both mad. Couple it with whatever had to come next, considering it took days to replace the missing enzymes, was the greatest fear of all.

The only thing making them hold on was a deep down dedication not to be the first one to break. But as things went on and on and they were writhing and shrieking in terror, and in one case convulsing so severely that one of the locked-down restraining straps actually broke, both of them began to wonder if they weren't being more than a little stupid.

They were almost at a consensus that this had gone beyond the point where either could tolerate it, and the only choices were death or surrender, when they felt everything melt away and that feeling of pleasantness return. It did not, however, wash away the memory of the pain and terrors they had been undergoing for so long.

They did not lapse into a euphoric state this time, but they did feel much, much better, and they shivered as the effects of the withdrawal ebbed from the physical part of their body.

"Not too bad at all," General Mochida commented. "I am actually impressed. I suspect that both of you were quite impressive in your original bodies and native habitats, as it were. That's almost an hour you held out. Most Kalindans who have been introduced to our cute little friend's bodily juices are simpering fools within ten to fifteen minutes. Still, *everybody* breaks, you know. There is no such thing as the person who cannot be broken in one way or another."

"You included," Ming snapped.

He didn't take it personally. "Almost certainly, although it's never been put fully to the test. Maybe it will be, but it will be by some other method. And, from now on, it will not be you who will do it."

"We didn't break," Ari answered proudly. "We *might* have, but not when the new dose was given. Not by then."

"Actually, you did," the General responded. "At least *one*

of you did. You screamed out a plea for it, and as you were in no condition to be rational enough for me to follow it up, I gave what you asked for. I'm very good about that, you see. Just keep me happy and I'll keep *you* happy. Nothing major. I'm not talking of enslavement or degrading stuff or even killing your friends. You simply remain with us, you help us out on minor housekeeping matters, and you don't feed information back to Core or anyone associated with the creature without letting me know first. Otherwise, for now, I want you just as a cooperative observer. I'm not asking that you change sides to mine, only that you switch from the old side to, shall we say, a friendly neutral. It *is* understood, though, that if you betray me, if you do things against our interests, there will be a price. In *that* case I *may* ask you to kill someone, or betray someone, or something equally unpleasant to you. And if you screw up my operation in any substantial way, I will cheerfully nail you to the nearest wall and watch you go completely and utterly mad, and then I'll send you home as an object lesson. Clear?"

"Clear," Ari responded.

"Now, the reason for all this is that, obviously, I haven't the personnel nor the method of restraining you. I need to let you go but to be able to count on your presence here and your friendly cooperation. Even when we are a much larger force, which will be quite soon now, I will not be able to guard you. Now, you *may* be the type to take a chance. Get out, take the pneumatic express back to Kalinda, hop a speeder, get to a central hospital, and plead for help, all in twelve hours. It would be difficult, but you might make it, and we're not going any farther from your capital than we are now. If you *did* get there, they'd hook you up to all these dehydration and liquid feeding tubes and such and then they'd put you unconscious for a week or so until your system was back to normal. It might work, but that three-day period can have strange effects on the brain. Misfirings, permanent memory loss in some areas, all sorts of things. You'll certainly lose *something*, but you're almost certain to wind up merging into a single individual. When the brain is forced to rewire, it is hardly going to maintain this neat division. It's up to you, but I offer it to you as a sporting man. I won't spare anyone to chase you down, but if you lose your nerve, you'll get nothing more from me if you fail."

General Mochida was a very good security chief indeed. *Hit us right where it hurts the most,* Ari noted.

You said it, Ming responded. *Damn it! It's not fair, at least not to me,* she grumped. *I mean, I was already violated in just about every way by your damned uncle, and now here I am, a victim again!*

Hey! I'm in the same boat, remember!

Yeah, but you deserve *to be! If it wasn't for you, I wouldn't have had to go through all that shit the first time!*

Like I could have done anything about it? Besides, you *were the cop, the big hero type. It was your job to stop him. And remember, no matter what, if I hadn't knocked you out and gotten you into that lifeboat, you'da been dead when it blew up!*

This is supposed to be an improvement*? It's more like a continuation of the same thing! I mean, for all we know your uncle's still out there someplace cutting throats for fun, and there's old Josich apparently right on his, her, or its schedule for whatever the bastard had planned in the first place, even if he did get rushed a bit. And here we are, still the victims.*

Yeah, Ari agreed, giving a mental sigh. *Here we are, all right.*

A couple of hours later they finally got around to undoing their bonds, and they'd been restrained so long and undergone such a physical ordeal in the forced withdrawal that it was very hard to get moving again and regain full control of their muscles. They knew they were going to ache for days.

Mochida was either supremely confident in his judgment of them and their willpower, or he didn't care anymore. They watched as the three large soft-shelled creatures shifted carton after carton until they seemed to have them in a definite order.

In a way, this is almost funny, Ari noted.

I don't see the humor.

Consider—what would we be doing if we hadn't been cap-tured? Trying to find an easy way into Sanafe to find out what Chalidang was up to, right?

Yeah? So?

And what are we doing now? Watching the Chalidangers prepare to move to Sanafe and pull whatever they're going to pull. And for all that drug business, what could we tell Core even now that we haven't already told her?

It did seem ironic, but considering their situation, Ming could not feel amused.

Two days later they assisted in returning some frozen cala-mari to life.

"The process isn't all that unusual," the sergeant major ex-plained to them. "The difference is that we had to adapt to a semitech hex where the normal computer controls just weren't going to work. We used the highest tech cryogenic gear to create their state of suspended animation, but instead of put-ting them in the normal storage cells, our design team came up with these. The materials and workmanship are beyond anything a semitech hex could produce, but they weren't pro-duced here. The same way as you Kalindans have built that pneumatic railway of yours, we can make things there and, if they don't require any of the forbidden technological sources to work, they come in and function just fine. Now, though, comes the tricky part. We've tapped into the steam vents used in the pneumatic system, and by doing so we've got fairly good control of our storage water temperature, but each of these must still be warmed slowly to a precise point, then the liquid drained into tanks and replaced with regulated steam."

"Do you think this kind of thing will work?" Ming asked skeptically.

"Oh, yes. It worked on me, didn't it?"

There was no good reply to that, so they did what was asked of them in hooking up various hoses and pushing for-ward needed equipment, and let the sergeant do his business.

Still, Ming was skeptical. "Even if this works," she noted, "it's gonna take *weeks* to properly thaw out this crowd."

"Not at all," the General responded behind them. "Once we

get a few out and restored to functionality, they will be able to handle more of it, and so on. We allowed an extra two days over training for full recovery from the process, but other than that we were able to have everyone treated and functional within five very crowded or seven much less crowded days. We will do it as quickly as we can for the simple reason that we have limited supplies and even more limited space here. These are among our best, but they are not among our nicest folk, and while they can go hungry for days and days under highest stress conditions, that level in a hex like this, full of easily available and totally vulnerable food, would make it difficult to control them. No, we move as quickly as possible. We must be in Sanafe in seven days."

To their fascinated observations, the process did indeed seem to work. It was amazing how large a creature they could get out of those boxes, considering that they all had rigid exoskeletons, but these were soldiers born and bred, and probably genetically engineered. And if Mochida and the others had nasty mouths and cold, huge eyes, this crew, once it regained full consciousness and movement, seemed to hate everything and everybody they looked upon, even each other.

But they clearly feared General Mochida.

"Let me make a few things clear here," he told each group after a dozen or so at a time were being thawed out and put into recovery exercises. "First, you eat rations, you eat nothing else. The Kalindan over there, for example, is my personal assistant in this region. Anyone who eats her will discover that she will be extracted from his gullet—*through the shell.* Other lapses in discipline should recall not only our military traditions in such matters but also those of your families back home. This is not a game. You were chosen because you were right for this job, but none of you have really gone head-to-head against an alien foe before nor spent much time in alien nations. Our allies lost thousands dead battling in a strategically placed semitech hex, and they lost. We are but three hundred when we are done, and this is a semitech hex, and our objective is a nontech environment. Our task is hard enough. We don't need you adding to the burden. Follow orders and this could be an easy task that covers us all with glory. Decide that the enemy is a bunch of silly, soft, inferior primitives who couldn't possibly do you harm, and you will join the dead of Ochoa. Believe me. As many exercises, war games, and simulations as you have been on, and as long as your training was, it pales before the real thing. I do not believe you can be beaten if you stick together, work as a team, and follow orders precisely. I *do* believe you can just as easily beat yourselves. Understand?"

"Yes, sir!" they would chant, and go off to help thaw out the others.

The reason for the infiltration method was clear: the Yabbans would never have permitted a large military force to come through their domain. The Yabbans were trying to play both sides and hope to stay out of it, but there was a limit after which they would indeed fight, and the math was on their side. Millions of Yabbans, a few hundred Chalidangers. Yabban losses could be massive, and the Chalidangers would still be wiped out.

But now they were here, and with only two exceptions appeared to have survived the process with no ill effects. The two that didn't make it were from separate causes; one had a container that clearly leaked out the sustaining cryogenic fluid, and the other was botched in revival.

Mochida seemed quite pleased. He had actually allowed for up to fifteen percent fatalities. Two put him well ahead in bodies.

And their presence was now a fait accompli. The Yabban government was informed as soon as the thawing was well enough along that stopping it would have been a moot point. A surface supply ship from Jirminin was directly overhead and had sufficient supplies to maintain the Chalidang force for the period that they required, and also provide a cover and a conduit for the force below.

Faced with this, the natives were not the least bit pleased, but felt they had little choice in the matter. The force wasn't big enough to threaten Yabbo or its immediate neighbors, and there had been assurances that no weapons would be provided the force until they were leaving the nation. A Kalindan commission, at Yabbo's request, had actually boarded the ship above and verified that it contained only food and medical supplies of use only to Chalidang. No weapons.

That, and the fact that the general and the Chalidang ambassador in Zone both assured the natives that the entire crew would be out of there in under seven days, won grudging assent. So long as none of this commando force ate any Yabbans, it seemed as if the bastards had gotten away with it.

Ming and Ari had to wonder what Core thought of all this now that it was public.

Proof? There's your damned proof!

But how were they going to move the two hundred or so kilometers north to Sanafe without both choking on the thick living soup out there or seeming an imperious army marching through towns and villages, raising resentment?

"You already know, don't you?" the General responded to the question.

"The pneumatic railroad? But there weren't any plans to run it to Sanafe, as far as we knew, and in any event, how will you, with those large spiral shells, soft or not, fit inside the tubes?"

The General chuckled. "One of the lines does in fact go that way, and it's got an unusually large tube diameter," he told them. "You see, the Yabbans have always felt they were the stepchildren of Kalinda, dependent on your people for all those nice tech-type handouts, the materials themselves, even the building of things like the pneumatic train system. Most of them have thought of themselves as working for the Kalindans since they were born, and that's not far wrong. Kalinda has always treated most of its neighbors like ignorant colonials, markets rather than equal and sovereign races and nations. We offered them an alternative source of what they needed, as well as international funding, with no strings. They've been quite tolerant of us so long as they felt we were working only against the interests of Kalinda and not against them. It's been a fairly happy arrangement. And now we are going to reap some of the rewards of that association. We're all going to the one neighboring hex that sealed itself off rather than become a Kalindan dependency. It was a conscious decision. They essentially banded together and threw you all out. *That* is why we can't just go in there as we did here and make friends. Not yet. We'd get almost to the point where none of this would be necessary, only to discover that, well, yes it was in the end. To them, the enemy of their enemy is not necessarily their friend but maybe yet another enemy. My intelligence research believes we have the way around this roadblock. If I am right, we will attain what we want, and the damage to Sanafe and its people will be negligible. If I am wrong, well, then we'll all be dead."

Us, too, Ari noted warily to Ming.

Alkazar

SHE WAS BARELY SETTLED INTO THE PYRON CONSULATE IN Kolznar when she was awakened. It was the middle of the night, and she felt some alarm at the sight of the snakelike creature. Worse, they all looked alike to her, making it impossible for her to tell the friendly consul from the suspicious security chief. She hoped they were all on the same side, otherwise she'd never figure out who was who.

"I beg your pardon for waking you," the creature said to her, "but I am afraid you must leave now and move toward Quislon with as much speed as possible."

She yawned and tried to shake the lead from her brain. "Now? Why? I know I wasn't to stay here long, but—"

"There has been an, um, unforeseen development. I am afraid that if you remain here you will either be arrested when you leave the consulate or you will wind up imprisoned here for an indefinite future. We must move quickly! Gather up whatever is yours and come with me. I shall explain the situation on the way."

She managed, with the help of some cold water from the basin, to get her small kit strapped on and follow him, but she felt miserable, and everything looked like it was being viewed through a curtain of fog and blurry reflections.

The consul was below. She knew it was him because of his manner and his warmer-than-normal—for a Pyron, anyway—empathic signature. "What is going on?" she asked him.

"They were going through cleaning and maintenance on the ship you came in on and they discovered a body," the consul told her. "Murdered, in a most brutal and ugly fashion, and apparently after some torture."

"A body! Whose? Where?" She feared that somebody had done in the stubborn Kehudan she'd left in her cabin, for failing to complete her mission.

An Ixthansan. One of our people. They've been shadowing the ship off and on all along. This one was supposedly bringing you information of some importance. We don't know if they got it or not, but did you?"

"I—I saw one such, a very pleasant fellow, but that was far back, not long after I boarded."

"Probably not the same one, but a cousin. It doesn't matter. You were not approached by an Ixthansan at any point after leaving Suffok?"

"No, not a word. I'd been wondering, considering the first contact, why I hadn't heard from any others."

"Apparently the second one was discovered, and since then they've been laying for them. There should have been three contacts." The translator gave the suggestion of a resigned sigh. "All right, then. We must move."

"Surely they do not think that *I* had anything to do with this! I cannot kill anyone! It is against the very oath of my office and the core of my being!"

"Well, I'm afraid that folks like the Alkazarians think that everybody else is just like them, and in this port they have jurisdiction. Fortunately, that also means they're corrupt to the core, but that can only reach so far. We need to get you completely out of the Colony District before somebody we missed comes looking, and I suspect that won't take long."

"Surely they would not hold me! I had nothing to do with this!"

"Ah, but you're the one closely connected. They have at least one witness who claims to have seen you speaking with an Ixthansan on the ship, and it's a witness that isn't part of any side in this conflict. That must have been the first one. That's enough for them. And as to not holding you, well, Ambora doesn't have much of an army or navy, and that's all they're scared of here. The justice system actually harkens back to the days of ancient belief systems, when you could be accused of trafficking with evil demons and they'd torture you. If you died, you were innocent. That's the thinking in criminal inquisitions here as well."

"But where will I go? I mean, by sea is certainly out, and it is roughly four hundred kilometers overland to Quislon, all in Alkazar. How can I avoid them?"

"Well, some bribes help," the consul admitted, "but there is also the point that somebody out of their local district juris-diction is somebody they don't have to deal with, explain, ac-count for, etcetera. You see what I mean? If we can get you out of this city, we'll probably not have any problems over it."

"But how?"

"Let me worry about that," said another Pyron, from the entry parlor to her right. She turned and saw what at first seemed to be another identical snake-man, but his empathic signature was very different, almost as if he were not truly kin to the others here. It was also vaguely familiar.

"I am Genghis O'Leary. We met at the Kalindan embassy in Zone," he told her.

"Of course! I was trying to figure out how I could have known you!"

"My apologies for this. I'm even more tired than you are. I've been here less than forty minutes, and I've slept even less. Still, we Pyrons are more nocturnal types and I can man-age. This other gentleman is Har Shamish, Security Officer for the consulate here and quite a capable agent. He will ac-company us and smooth things through to the border, as well as acting as a bodyguard of sorts until we reach Quislon. Af-ter that, you and I are on our own."

"You make it sound so threatening. Surely it's not as bad as all that!"

Shamish said, "I'm afraid, madam, that if we spend any more time here, it will be even worse. There is no way I could fight my way out of this city, and with all those cameras, we certainly can't *sneak* out. Let's go."

She thanked the consul and bid him farewell, and walked out with the two Pyrons.

The sight on the night vision cameras of the striking winged Amboran flanked by two blocky, sinister, cobralike Pyrons would have startled the most jaded watcher.

She was surprised to find that the odors in the air, the sounds of the great city, all the lights and action, seemed just as vibrant and active at night as in the daytime.

"Big cities never sleep," O'Leary noted. "They just have different routines for different times."

"I do not see as well at night as in the day, normally, but I can make do through here," she told them.

"It's the lighting. The walkway and building and commercial lighting is so concentrated that it lights up the air over us," Shamish explained. "It won't be the same once we get out of the urban area. On the other hand, if your vision is best in daylight, ours is best in darkness, and it takes very little light for us to see perfectly well. We should be a good team."

Jaysu could barely see the great mountains beyond the city, but she knew they were there by the lack of any sense of life along them save some sleeping birds. As they rode on the moving walkways, she noted that they were paralleling the rock wall rather than heading toward it, and in fact they seemed to be moving slowly back toward the sea, although well away from the harbor where the big ships came in.

"Where are we going?" she asked them.

"First we take a boat," Shamish told her. "That takes us out of Alkazar and their jurisdiction, not to mention some of their prying eyes. Once we're aboard, I'll explain the rest. You never know what's monitored here."

They eventually reached a low-lying, small boat basin. Most of the boats were fishing craft of various designs, none longer than twenty meters or so, but there were some private craft among them in a small marina. Now it was time to walk.

"That's the boat there," O'Leary told her, although she could see little except bobbing shapes in the darkness. She followed closely, one of the Pyrons in front, one behind her, relieved that the Pyrons took slow, deliberate steps on their fragile looking legs, which allowed her to keep up even though her feet were killing her after so many days of hard floors, hard woods, and plastic.

As they got closer, she could make out shapes on one of the larger private boats. It was a sleek, streamlined, dark blue and gray yacht, an elaborate sailing vessel, and didn't have smokestacks at all.

"We use a different power in high-tech waters," Shamish told her. "In all other cases, we use sail, although there's a way to stoke a small boiler for emergencies if we must. Just go aboard and find a spot out of the way."

The Pyron on the boat seemed tense; she could sense them, coiled like springs, ready to strike at any enemy, but when they saw the Pyrons with her, they relaxed and got ready to cast off.

They used no sails for this, letting go fore and aft. Then, before she was even at an out-of-the-way point on the stern, there was a high-pitched whine of engines below. The running lights came on and they eased out of the slip, turned, and headed for the breakwater.

"As soon as we pass that flashing beacon there, we will be safely out of the district and, in fact, Alkazar," Shamish said, using a thin tentacle emerging from under his hood to point.

"Where are we going, then?" she asked.

"Tonight we'll head west along the coast, then go 'round the point and down just a few kilometers under sail. That'll put us in nontech territory for a short while, but it will allow us to turn in and reenter Alkazar via the Corbino River. It parallels the range—the Solarios Mountains, as they're called through there—and will get us upriver to the limits of navigation at Zadar Station, which is a good 140 kilometers up and in a tropical rainforest. Not too many Alkazarians there, which is excellent, and less snooping, although they still monitor the place with other gadgets and gizmos. We should get a local guide there who'll take us as far as the point where it will be impossible to avoid the Solarios. Then it's up and over. At each point we'll be under intense scrutiny. We will have to be on our best behavior, and also have to depend on corrupt people staying corrupt. If so, we should be to the border and you should be done with this bloody hex in just a couple of days. Now, I suggest you leave the sailing to us and try and get some sleep. We'll let you know if there's any trouble."

That was easier said than done, now that she'd been so rudely roused and marched down here, only to be told that the dangerous adventure was only beginning. Still, she found the sea motion almost welcome now, and while the accommodations below were basic and not designed for anything with wings or anyone who slept standing up, she could manage. With the familiar rolling motions of a gentle sea, but absent any of the noise and vibration she'd become accustomed to, she fell asleep without even realizing it.

She awoke quite late, or so it proved to be once she'd splashed cold water all over herself and made her way up to the deck.

She had thought that she'd slept hardly at all; she ached and creaked as if she hadn't had a good sleep in days. But when she got topside, she saw that they had not only reached the nontech hex area but had gone through it and were on a river. The sun, too, was not just up, it was almost overhead, signifying that it was close to midday.

She found O'Leary on the afterdeck, unnervingly lying, serpentlike, looking out at the shore. The great head, which was integrated into the body, turned, and those huge orange and black eyes with narrow pupils stared at her.

"Hello," she called. "Goodness! How long did I sleep?"

"Eleven hours," O'Leary answered. "You must have been as tired as I was."

"You slept almost as long?"

"No, I slept for about five, I just *need* ten or eleven. That's all right. I'm partly shut down here, and the sun helps recharge me."

"Where are we, exactly? This is quite unusual to look at."

"We're almost ninety percent there," he told her. "If they hadn't had to stop a few times for authorization checks, we'd actually be ready to disembark now. Damned officious little teddy bears!"

"What bears?"

"Teddy bears. That's what they look like. Back where I came from, they used to give children toy stuffed bears that looked a lot like these critters, and they were called teddy bears for some reason. Don't know why—they just always were. Some things are like that. Anyway, that's the way I think of 'em. Teddy bears gone bad."

She looked out at the riverbank. Although they'd said it was a huge river, it looked relatively narrow by Amboran standards, at least at this point. Perhaps it had been much wider downstream.

The banks on both sides were covered with jungle, and so thick that only more jungle was visible in between. The river itself was about sixty meters across at this point, substantial but not impressive. The heat and humidity, too, were very high, but not worse than much of Ambora.

"Have you been through here before?" she asked him.

"No. I'm going by briefings, maps, and whatnot. Shamish was here once before, so he tells me, but never has been inland Up the Wall, as even the locals call it."

"The Wall?"

"The big mountains. They always strike everybody, even the natives, like some kind of massive stone wall. Don't they seem like that to you?"

She looked off in the distance. The range was never far away anywhere in Alkazar, it seemed, and right now it seemed not much farther, jungle or not, than it had back in the city.

She sensed a tremendous life force all around them, though, and it puzzled her, since all she saw were insects, most of which seemed uninterested in them. They smelled wrong, probably.

All along one bank were thick groves of trees, not planted but still well-spaced, as if in a garden. The limbs were filled with dark shapes that looked like huge melons, but she got the impression that they were not a vegetable.

"What are those things growing from the trees?" she asked him.

His head went up and he saw what she was referring to.

"Oh, they're not growing on the trees, they're sound asleep," he responded.

"They?"

"Some sort of fruit bat. Big flying mammals, nasty sharp teeth, but they sleep all day and only come out to feed at night. Don't worry about them, though. They're mostly nuisances, not threats, although they can get irritated and dive-bomb somebody they think is a threat. I've seen them or their relatives several places on this world. You don't have bats in Ambora?"

"I do not remember any."

"Well, these are fruit eaters. They eat a lot of fruit, true, but mostly stuff that the locals don't like and which won't keep to ship to anybody who might anyway. Vegetarians with an attitude. Hopefully we won't make them mad, and this will be the only time we'll know they're here."

"The more I see of the outside world, the more I am wedded to Ambora," Jaysu said with a sigh. "It seems that everywhere else there is only strangeness with an undercurrent of ugliness."

O'Leary gave a humorous snort. "Well, yeah, maybe, but I tend to think that other folks from other areas would find something to react the same way to in your own home. It's simply what you're used to and what you're comfortable with. Me, I don't want a life that's cloistered, never did. My mother always had hopes I'd become a priest. Instead I became an interstellar cop. Same business—seeking out evil where it lies and exposing it—only I didn't have the limitations of a priest in dealing with it once I found it. It just seemed more satisfying when you could shoot back."

She didn't see it that way. "I believe that those who serve the gods do so in their own way, it is true, but I disagree that we are in the same business. My job is saving souls. Yours, from its sound, is avenging them."

"Well, I don't see much wrong with that, since if they need avenging, they are past caring about your part," O'Leary argued. "Still, I've always found it fascinating that most people, even those faced with the most horrible of things, don't really

believe in evil. They believe in God, and sometimes in punishment and in redemption, too, but they don't believe in
Hell. Even you. You rent space in Heaven. A cop, now, he
lives in Hell, and he knows better. There *is* evil in the world,
priestess. It's real. There is evil, pure and absolute, and there
are those who serve it. I've seen far more of it than of Heaven
and sainthood. You are going to see some of it, I think, before
this is over. I hope you're ready for it."

"I've already seen some very bad people," she reminded him.

"No, you've seen evil's shadows. You haven't really seen it
yet." He paused. "Breakfast? We'll be there in another hour,
so it might be best to get something inside you now."

She was startled by his casual turn of conversation. "Yes, I
would like that."

She had barely consumed some melon, cereal, and juice
when there was a cry from the wheelhouse and they slowed to
approach a dock on the side of the river closest to the mountain wall.

She was surprised to see not a plantation or primitive village, but a small city here, complete with powered vehicles,
modern buildings, some cranes on a modern dock, and the
ubiquitous black patrol boats of the Alkazarian police.

"Why do they need to be all the way up here?" she asked,
wondering aloud.

"They're everywhere here, in those boats, in cars, in heli-
copters," Har Shamish replied. "These little creatures don't
even trust each other. There's a whole department whose job
it is to spy on the police. And doubtless another department
that spies on *that* department. My advice to you is to keep as
quiet as possible and answer only what they ask, if and when
they ask anything. Assume that anything you say is being
monitored and recorded. Fortunately, you should only have to
endure this for another day and a half. They are generally efficient in day-to-day operations."

The buildings were not as tall as the ones back in Kolznar; most were no more than four or five stories, some smaller.
The city, also much smaller, was more like those on Ambora, with five to seven thousand people living and working

there. But because these were Alkazarians, Jaysu and the Pyron who accompanied her had to cope with things built on a
much smaller scale. Roofs, even thatched types over poles or
stakes, tended to be on the order of two to two and a half meters high, which was acceptable, but the doors were often too
low, forcing them all to dip or duck, and many were too narrow for someone who had such large wings, folded or not.

They had to run the usual gauntlet of black-uniformed
officials, but Har Shamish took the lead and eased things
through. Jaysu suspected he had passed small gems as bribes;
she'd seen the small bag of the stones, but never actually saw
them pass between him and any Alkazarian.

Still, the official greeting was more mock formal than real.

"Nationality?"

"Amboran."

"Name?"

"Jaysu."

"Family name?"

"I have no family. I am an orphan. That is my only name."

"I see. Occupation?"

"High Priestess of the Clan of the Grand Falcon."

That stopped him, but only for a moment, as he cleared
his throat and then wrote down something on his little electronic pad.

"Purpose?"

Before she could get that one wrong or muck something
up, Shamish turned and said, "Transit to Quislon, direct, no
stops desired on our end," he told them.

"You have travel documents?"

Shamish produced them for everyone from some compartment deep within the hood. The official looked them over.
"You will not be staying in Zadar, then?"

"If our guide is here, then the answer is no," Shamish assured him. "We are in something of a hurry."

There were all sorts of stamps and little meaningless slips
of paper and such, and even one that had each of their pictures on it, for all the good it would do them in trying to figure
out which Pyron was which. She got the idea that these little

creatures didn't really care who they were or what they wanted to do or anything else, or even about what they themselves were doing. It was just what they did.

Finally handed a messy stapled book of paper forms, and told to never let them out of her sight and to instantly produce them on the demand of any Alkazarian, she and the others were waved through.

Waiting just on the other side of the official station was an Alkazarian wearing a hard, round hat and mud-colored clothing. He was large for an Alkazarian; not so much taller as wider, although he was by no means fat. She wondered if he actually did look distinctive or if she was starting to tell subtle differences between the Alkazarians.

"Welcome! Welcome, my friends!" he boomed, although he had the same squeaky voice the others did, and it made their natural bombastic tendencies seem comical. "I am Vorkuld, and I am to be your guide up to the Wall. May I see all your papers, please?"

Having just gone through the line and received them within sight of Vorkuld, this was one of the most ridiculous requests she could think of, but she looked into Shamish's eyes, understood the caution she saw there, and handed everything over.

Vorkuld made a show of looking through them, but he clearly wasn't reading anything. It wasn't like there were many other giant snake-men or winged bird-women in the neighborhood.

She realized, then, that he wasn't enthusiastic about it himself, but was doing it so he could be seen to be doing it. It must be awful living in a place where you had to assume that your every action or comment would be graded pass or fail, she thought, and she had that flash of the terrible hunting dream in her mind to suggest what might happen if you did fail too often.

He handed back the papers and was just going to say something when Har Shamish said to him, "And, of course, now *you* will show me *your* papers."

The Alkazarian was startled by this, but reached into his

pants pocket, pulled out a flat billfold and handed it over. It had a form inside with all sorts of official stuff on it, as well as his photo in a realistic three dimensions. Shamish seemed to study it, and then, as the little guide was getting nervous and impatient, handed it back.

Jaysu's opinion of the security man went up several notches with this. It was nice to put *them* on the defensive once in a while. She would never have thought of it.

"Follow me, citizens," the Alkazarian instructed, and they walked over to an odd-looking vehicle that seemed a cross between an army tank and a truck. It had treads on both sides like a tank, and was painted with a tan, olive, and white camouflage design, but one side was down, forming a ramp, albeit a very steep one, revealing a trucklike interior. The thing had seen a lot of action; it was dinged up badly, some of the paint knocked right off so that there were numerous rust spots, and while it had been hosed down, it smelled of muck and filth.

Vorkuld looked at them. "Well, you two gents—pardon, you *are* both gents, I take it?—can manage, I think, but you, my dear, don't look suited for that sort of angle. Can you really fly with them things?"

She nodded. "Yes, I can."

"Think you can get up enough to get into the back there? That may be the best solution."

She could and she did, the wind from the wings almost knocking the little guide over. It felt so good, even that little tiny hop, far better than the stretching that was all she'd managed aboard ship. She began to worry that she was so out of practice she'd not be able to get off the ground, but then reminded herself that for many months she could not fly at all and it had made no difference when she'd been given back the gift.

Jaysu was surprised to find that there was not only room for them inside the truck, but also for a large amount of equipment and two other Alkazarians dressed similarly to Vorkuld. The two were smaller than the guide, and seemed to have broader hips in relation to their chests and heads. She realized, then, that she was looking at two Alkazarian females.

"I am Zema, and this is Kem," said one of them in a voice that seemed impossibly squeaky and high-pitched. "We will be at your service and maintaining the camp tonight. If you need anything, please just order it from either of us."

In a country where the males were only a meter high, the sight and sound of others who were not only a head shorter but proportionately smaller all around, offering to get you what you needed, was startling. It was even more startling when the two started picking up heavy-looking equipment and restacking it so they would all be more comfortable for a long ride. Unless it was some kind of compensation for being so tiny, the lesson and demonstration were clear: if these little women could lift that kind of weight easily, imagine what Vorkuld could do.

Using a motorized chain drive, Zema closed the side of the vehicle and, after it clanked into place, checked to ensure that it was secure and locked down. Vorkuld then climbed up a ladder on the side, tumbled expertly over into the bed, and, after looking around to see that all were reasonably settled and the gear secured, went forward and settled into a small semicircular compartment at the front of the vehicle. There was a shudder, a whine, and then, slowly, the thing began to move.

It had all happened so fast, from waking up to this, that Jaysu could hardly catch her breath, but she realized that much of this was Shamish's doing. He wanted this over fast, and he wanted them out of civilization as quickly as possible, too.

The tracked vehicle didn't go all that fast, and it was an exceptionally bumpy ride, but it was easy enough to get used to its gyrations and sounds. Jaysu did have some problems when the driver cornered; the resulting jerking around in the back meant she had to hold onto something firmly or else tumble.

They saw little of the town, keeping mostly to roads near or along the river. There was a checkpoint at the edge of the place, and, sure enough, they had to stop, present papers, do all that silly stuff again, but it was as pro forma as at the docks.

Once away from town, the foliage came right up to the truck. The road was now hard-packed dirt, but well-maintained, although barely wide enough for just them, and certainly not wide enough to allow for two-way traffic. There were turnouts cut from the jungle brush every few hundred meters to allow things to pass, but clearly, if this road had a lot of traffic on it, they all knew it would be sheer luck backing into one of those.

They did come face-to-face with oncoming traffic, twice. In both cases it was they who yielded, and without protest, and it wasn't hard to see why. The opposition were enormous carriers, one two city blocks long and articulated in the middle for turns, carrying who knew what from the jungles to the town and probably the port, where barges would await on the commercial side.

Just what they carried remained a mystery, and one she wasn't sure she wanted to solve. Once or twice they'd pass within sight of huge complexes deep in the jungle, but they looked less like luxurious plantations or commercial farms than like prison camps, complete with ominous towers and dull gray featureless buildings. Once, they passed a group of sad-looking Alkazarians dressed in bright red uniforms, working with machines to keep the jungle trimmed back off the road and to keep the road in good condition and hard-packed. There didn't seem to be any guards or guns, but she got the impression that these people would not have been there if they didn't have to be.

The two Pyrons continued to doze as they went along; there really wasn't much else to do. She, however, was created for days, and had just completed a long and hard sleep, and all this was new to her.

Even so, she felt disappointed by the trip, at least so far. When they'd said that it would be travel through a dense jungle, she'd pictured walking down dark trails with natives chopping their way through the dense underbrush. She wasn't sure where that idea came from, but it seemed romantic. This was just a teeth-jarring ride into a world of total green.

Har Shamish stirred and put his head close to O'Leary's.

"What were you staring at?" he asked, having noted that his companion was fixated on the two Alkazarian females.

"I was just wondering which one of them did it with him and which one of them watched," the cop whispered back. "And, more to the point, who filled out the paperwork afterward."

The diplomat gave a low chuckle. "I wish my own position permitted me to wonder things like that aloud."

At nightfall they came upon a roadblock: a gated house like a toll booth that controlled access to the road. Vorkuld climbed halfway down the truck and talked to the officials within. Finally, one of the black uniforms came up and into the truck and made his way uncomfortably back to them.

"You'd think if they were this paranoid, they'd at least pave the damned road," O'Leary grumbled.

"Oh, they don't pave it because it's harder to maintain paved, not because they couldn't," his companion replied. "Potholes, erosion—the bed's trouble enough keeping up now."

It was papers time again, and the same old questions, but as usual, the deputy consul managed to be first and to strike some sort of bargain with the official. Like the others, he still went through the motions, but it was clear that he was doing just that and no more.

"After you set up camp, have your guide get your validations from the Warden's Office," the official warned them. "Sometimes they forget. No use getting to the Wall and they won't let you on and up, eh?"

"Thank you, sir, very much," Shamish responded. "I shall remember you in the future as well for your efficiency and courtesy."

Jaysu had the weird impression, because they had both raised their voices unnaturally loud, that this was a performance. Vorkuld was soon climbing back up and into the driver's seat, and as soon as the official got down and the gate went up, he was off.

The "camp" seemed to be some kind of commercial operation, although they all had the impression that the government ran most things. There were permanent buildings, a large modern latrine that would not be suitable for any of the alien visitors, lights and such from electric generators, and some elaborate sites. Several tracked vehicles similar to theirs were parked there, and there were a number of large and elaborate tents erected. There was also a staff that seemed on constant patrol, doing everything from picking up trash to checking out the registrations of everybody they met. These Alkazarians all wore green uniforms.

The two females went into action as soon as they parked, offloading and setting up two large tents, connecting them into some sort of control boxes buried in the ground, then setting up what proved to be an ingeniously designed portable kitchen including refrigerated and frozen foods, cold drinks, and everything else they needed. It was clear from the way the two tiny women handled things that their strength was not an illusion; Jaysu tried to move the portable kitchen unit just a fraction and found that it might as well have been lead.

There was quite a difference in what they ate and what she consumed, though, and she found that she had to excuse herself and eat alone, out of sight not only of the Alkazarians, but of the two Pyron as well.

Since reaching the consulate, she'd not seen any of the Pyrons eat or drink, but she saw what they ate this night, how they did it, and it was not something she was comfortable watching. Her food and drink, however, were fine; apparently, the consulate had made contact ahead using what magic these high-tech hexes could manage, and made sure that she was well provided for.

They'd done it for themselves as well, and she'd seen the two Pyrons eat one large furry animal each. They ate them whole, and, worst of all, they ate them alive. The Alkazarians ate meat, and cooked rarely, but it was properly butchered and prepared meat, such as she'd seen others eat on the ship and at Zone. But the Pyrons—the idea of eating something alive, screaming in terror, was . . .

O'Leary managed to figure out the problem and sought her out after they'd finished. "Sorry. I forget myself sometimes," he told her sincerely. "Even before I came here, I was someone who lived among different races as well as my own, and I'm just used to things being different. I should have realized."

"No, no, it is all right," she assured him, by which she meant it was all right because she understood that this was the way they did it, that it was normal, and that the problem wasn't really with them but with her. But it wasn't all right in her gut.

"Before we come across any other things that might be a problem for you, I'll try and warn you," he promised. "I've got to kick my brain back in gear and think like an alien visitor again. It was careless. At least you will only have to be near us when we eat one more time, probably at the border."

"Huh? What?" She was wondering if it was still somehow alive, trapped, wriggling inside him, unable to get out. It was silly; she'd feel it if it were. Still, she couldn't get that absolute terror out of her mind and soul.

"We don't eat or drink very often, which is why we eat like we do," he explained. "We will be able to go long and far on just this. And, I promise, you won't have to see it again."

"It—It wasn't *seeing* it that was the problem," she told him. "It was being almost overwhelmed by the fear exuded by its soul."

"By its—pardon?"

"Everything has a soul. Everything alive, that is. I can see those souls, feel them. I can not shut it out. It is not my purpose to shut it out."

He realized the situation. "You're an empath! Well, I'll be . . . Well, remind me not to lie to you, I guess. But remember our talk today about good and evil?"

"Yes."

"I don't want to shield you from too much, not now, not later on. I want you to feel that fear and see those disgusting sights. That is because we are potentially facing evil so strong that you will need to prepare for it. But I *will* try and warn you. You should not be unprepared. Think you can sleep?"

She sighed. "Yes, I guess so."

"Well, perhaps you should do so. We're going to pack up and leave not long after dawn, and we've got some rougher riding ahead, or so I'm told. I confess I'm kind of curious, too. We're the only non-Alkazarians here. The way they stare at us, we may be the only ones they've seen for a long time. I wonder how many alien types have ever seen firsthand what's on top of those mountains and beyond?"

"A hundred more credential checks," she answered, trying to break the mood. There was not any way around it. He was right. She should get to sleep and try not to dream about it.

She needed to dream of Ambora, and flying above it effortlessly, darting through the clouds . . .

The next morning, bright and early, they were as good as their word, waking everyone at dawn and then fixing a breakfast for Jaysu and the three guides, or whatever they were. Although most bears were omnivores, even on the Well World, the Alkazarians seemed to be strictly carnivorous, although they did enjoy a lot of thick almost black ale and some sort of candied sweets. Breakfast for them was sausages of some sort and very large eggs, which they ate in a variety of ways, including raw.

Others, going in both directions and perhaps to places they didn't know about, were there as well, but they seemed to be transporting natives wearing different colored uniforms, not paying customers. It appeared that, outside the cosmopolitan cities, everybody wore a uniform that instantly told everyone else their general occupation, and with that, their social and economic class as well. Since leaving Zadar Station, they'd seen no exceptions to this rule.

They packed up and, after the obligatory check of all papers and the quizzing of all members of the group—natives and non-natives alike—were off once more.

The jungle was so thick now that even the sun hardly got through. It was impossible to see almost anything, even the mountains they knew were in the distance.

For a brief period rains came, heavy and relentless. The two females quickly punched up an awning, and the storm hit the jungle canopy and created a lot of sound and fury, and much high-level fog and mist. The torrent, broken by the thick growth, gushed down the trunks of trees and through channels in the branches. A lot of water struck the ground, but it was localized, and for that the truck awning served quite well.

They were no longer in heavily inhabited territory, and had to yield for no traffic. In fact, after a couple of hours they had not seen another living soul, nor did Jaysu feel any sense of a population out there. There were some individuals here and there, perhaps in twos and threes, but they seemed to flee at the sound of the truck. She wondered if they were fugitives from the system, hiding out and eking out a meager subsistence living in this dense jungle rather than facing some sort of punishment, or perhaps to avoid living in that society. Unless the fugitives, or whatever they were, began attacking travelers, it wouldn't be worth the time and money to track them down out here.

Just before midday they broke from the jungle onto a broad grassland, and were startled to see how close that mountain wall now was. It lay just ahead, stretching out as far as the eye could see on both sides, shrouded in fog and mist at the top. She had no idea how they were supposed to get up there and over it without flying.

The answer was clearer when they pulled up to a large complex set into the rock of the mountain itself. At first Jaysu thought it was a religious shrine or great temple; it had that look about it, right up to the gigantic colonnades and ornate carved figures of Alkazarians in various classic poses. There was also a busy parking lot, complete with uniformed traffic cops, and a great many of the crawlers—as the passenger trucks were called—all around, some with mud-colored uniformed crews looking fresh and waiting, others spattered with mud or reddish clay dust, looking like they'd come through rough terrain.

All roads on this side, it appeared, led here.

"Why are we here?" she asked the others. "If these people do not like others anywhere else but in towns, then why would they bring us to one of their holy places?"

For the first time Vorkuld laughed, and the two females tittered along with him. "Well, ma'am, it is a hole, all right, but it is not holy, at least not in the sense I take you mean it," he explained. "This is the Great Western Lift. It was quite an accomplishment to build many years ago, and is also a nightmare to maintain, but it's saved a great deal of time and effort. Before it was built, contact with the lowland coast was difficult to impossible except by airplane or glider, both of which cost a lot to run and have limited capacities. With the lifts, this one and the newer Eastern Lift in Qualt Province, we are united again. There will be, of course, more formalities, but this is our destination."

She didn't know what he was talking about, but the added formalities were easy to imagine.

But this turned out to be worse than the others, even the entrance ones. There seemed to be so many agencies, so many different official uniforms, so many redundant question and answer tables, that it seemed every Alkazarian was involved in bureaucracy and paper pushing. They wondered who actually did the work, or how much those who did could really accomplish in the few minutes a day they weren't being questioned, their papers examined, and their motives impugned.

It was understandable that they be given more scrutiny than the usual worker going back and forth here, though, as the officials were fond of telling them, few foreigners were ever allowed to get this far. Even fewer were not expected to immediately return, having had a demonstration of the great ingenuity and skills of the Alkazarians.

"Don't know what's going on, don't want to know," said one of the last, a silver-and-black-uniformed officer with a nasty looking sidearm, who checked their papers at the entrance to the Great Western Lift. "Been here years without even *seeing* a foreigner, then two bunches of you creatures show up within hours."

"*Two* bunches?" O'Leary repeated. "We are not the first aliens you have seen today?"

"Don't know what you're talking about," the official muttered, trying to find an empty spot on some paper to imprint his own stamp. "Didn't hear or see a thing."

"Was one a giant greenish spider?" Jaysu asked him.

"Don't answer questions, get paid to ask 'em. Don't like spiders anyway. Okay, you're done. All three of you proceed down the walk. *Stay on the walk* and proceed until stopped. If you deviate, you'll be sorry. Turn back, you'll be held here, and we got no supplies for aliens. And, above all, don't ask questions."

They decided not to press anything further, and entered the great cavern through its carved, ornate entranceway.

The cavern appeared to be an enlargement of some natural one, because it instantly became cooler and a breeze blew steadily against them as they descended. Workmen had done the walls and ceiling, though, so it appeared to be a long artificial construct with marble friezes and ceiling frescoes all along, forming a story or legend. If they were concerned with the sensibilities of the young, it didn't show, since just within a short walk the marbles left no doubt as to how the Alkazarians copulated, among other things. There were also somewhat gruesome hunt carvings, and a panoply of little bear gods and demons, among them a progression from regal types to idealized Alkazarians, larger than the others, who were depicted in various extremely ornate uniforms.

The path was entirely artificial, set in a more natural bed dug into the rock. There were in fact two paths, one for going in on the left and one for exiting on the right. Both were about three meters wide and quite smooth, almost shiny, made out of some reddish substance that gave off a subtle glow so you knew exactly where it was. It was also recessed about fifteen centimeters from the more natural rock base, with regular grooves along the sides and small single rails along the top. It explained some of the crawlers and containers they'd seen just outside. Not only people, but cargo, was moved along these.

Finally they came to an elaborate security station that had but one officer, wearing the same silver and black as the one at the entrance. This station, though, was more automated. As they stepped up and passed through a portal one at a time, a three-dimensional representation of each of them appeared on a plate at a console. It then went through a series of gyrations from skeletal and nervous systems, even checking the contents of the stomach and whatever was inside any bag or article of clothing, few as those were with this trio.

Jaysu found the one of herself fascinating; she preferred not to look at the insides of either of the Pyrons.

They then had to place a hand in a recess under the officer's watchful eye. She was surprised to feel her palm scraped, and a slight pinprick. When she withdrew the hand, it had a tiny bubble of blood at the prick, although when she sucked it, there was no apparent wound and it didn't bleed anymore. Each of the snake-men had to surrender a tendril for the same purposes.

"You may pass. Wait in the left waiting area for the lift," the security officer instructed them.

They went forward, and Jaysu was surprised. "No papers to check?"

"They don't need to here," Har Shamish told her. "They now have everything up to and including our genetic codes. From this point on I expect more of those than paper. We're in their master computers now."

They walked down to one of two very large doors built into the cave. Unlike the rest, the doors had only some kind of official crest on them, one she'd seen on flags and uniforms, and nothing more. There was no sign of machinery, but they could feel the whole chamber vibrating, and there was a humming noise along with the sound of rushing wind, which was hard to place.

The doors themselves were about four-by-four meters square. There was no indication as to what was behind them, although there was a pillbox enclosure to one side that seemed to have a lot of electronics in it and several operators. The pervasive cameras around the chamber told Jaysu that they wanted them to remember that they were being observed.

"Now what?" she asked the two Pyrons.

"Now we wait." Shamish responded. "Shouldn't be long, I don't think. I didn't see any big rigs out there, so they aren't moving much cargo today."

O'Leary used two tendrils to give a sort of shrug. In this matter, she knew as much as he did.

There was a distant added noise now, a roaring sound, and it seemed to be getting louder, until it virtually shook the whole chamber. Then there was a *chunk!* that shook the floor so hard it almost made them lose their footing, and then hissing, like gas venting from cylinders, although it wasn't venting their way. They heard a hydraulic sigh, then a Klaxon alarm sounded and the great door in front of them slid to one side, into the rock.

The chamber it revealed was well-lit, and had more of the rails and grooves about its sides. It was also quite deep, going back six or more meters. They could move very large, heavy containers through it, that was clear.

The ceiling bristled with cameras, and when a loudspeaker said, "Passengers, please enter and proceed all the way to the rear of the car," they obeyed, more curious than nervous.

At the rear, they stepped over a bar that clearly was there to keep containers from coming farther back, and then there were two sets of ladders with handrails up a couple of meters to a platform containing seats, benches, and the like. For the small Alkazarians, it was the kind of area they could move thirty or forty people.

"If you cannot sit or otherwise belt in, then go to the sides and hold tightly to the railings there," the public address voice told them. "Once under way, you may relax pending our warning, but be prepared to grab the rails again if instructed."

They did as they were told. Hearing warning beeps from outside, they looked, and saw several short containers being pushed into the front of the car, using the grooves on the side. Yellow-clad workers scrambled to stop them and lock them in place, and then yelled signals to one another. Finally, a half-dozen Alkazarians came back to the passenger platform and, without even looking at them, sat down and buckled themselves in to the chairs.

There was a second Klaxon sound from outside, and some kind of announcement that they could not make out, and then the door closed. When it did, a second door rolled down and closed too, locking with a series of *chunks*, cutting them off. Finally, there was that hydraulic sound and the sound of rushing air.

"They're pressurizing this cabin!" O'Leary said wonderingly.

"Maybe we should enjoy it while we can," Shamish suggested. "If we go up there, the air's going to be mighty thin."

There was a sudden eerie silence, and then, incredibly, they felt themselves begin to move upward, slowly at first, then with increasing speed.

"It really *is* a lift!" O'Leary breathed. "I've been in ones in some mighty tall buildings before, but never one that went this far up!"

Jaysu wondered just how far up it would be. At least *she* was made to fly with the clouds. And in this case, what would be at the other end?

Sanafe

IT WAS ALMOST COMICAL TO SEE THOSE HUGE CREATURES WITH their soft spiral shells and many tentacles boarding the special pneumatic train line in the northern part of Abudan, and being sucked away one at a time by controls operated by Kalindan engineers who'd built the line as per instructions and never asked what it was for. They were intimidated and not a little scared by the sight of these strange creatures, but Yabban officials were also there to ensure that all went smoothly.

Somehow, I never expected to see anybody use one of these things without being inside a protective car or capsule, Ming commented.

But they are *protected inside,* Ari noted. *They're completely withdrawn into those shells, even the eyes fully retracted. They're better protected than we'll be.*

Even so, it was amusing to forget their situation, and also just who these creatures were and what they were bred to do, and just watch them being shot off into the vacuum, tumbling and looking like they were in zero gravity until they hit the first bend and got bonked around. In two hundred kilometers there would be a lot of bounces. Since the Chalidang shell was soft and pliant, it was doubly impressive. That must be awfully tough skin and thick internal bones, they both agreed.

I wonder just how scrambled they're gonna be when they get there, Ming mused.

I'm more awed that they're doing this without water, Ari responded. *Nothing can hold its breath for* that *long. I wonder how the hell they breathe?*

Has to be some kind of gadget. They're getting packs of stuff as they get to the front of the line, and since we know it can't be weapons or other implements of war, it's probably some kind of recirculator. Hell, I never figured out where they breathed from as it is!

It turned out that it was the common soldiers who were sent off in this unceremonious fashion; the officers climbed into form-fitting, bubble-shaped vehicles. The sergeant major, too, got a bubble, as did the warrant officer and the colonel. General Mochida sent all the officer and senior NCO types ahead, staggered in between enlisted personnel so there would be supervisors at each of the stops to reorganize the men, check them out, and get them back on their way.

"I'm afraid we didn't anticipate *you*," the General told them, "and so we don't have a car that will properly transport you. The standard cars are too small for this line, you see."

"That's all right. Just leave the drug and we'll happily stay right here," Ari told him sincerely.

Mochida chuckled. "No, my young friends, I don't think so. I'm afraid we're going to have to strap you into one of the officer bubbles as best we can and send you just ahead of me. I'll be the last one out. Don't worry—the bubbles have sufficient oxygenated water that they can take you a good distance. In our case, we can store enough water inside cavities in the body to take us a considerable distance, quite an advantage in the field at times, particularly in areas where oxygen is low."

They stood by until the line went down. It took hours, and through one cycle of their shot, before they saw the end of things. This was not an efficient way to move troops, but it sure was sneaky.

And don't forget, the consulate here isn't gonna be sending any notices home, Ming pointed out.

Maybe not, but I'll still bet you Core knows by now. There are a lot of Kalindans around here in the construction gangs, and a few races that seem to be involved in this business back in the diplomatic zone.

Huh. You're right, of course. Isn't that funny, though? It never occurred to me until you brought it up that we might not be the only spies around here. You think maybe Core dismissed our report because it was old news, and only worded it that way to help protect us?

Could be. In any event, we went ahead and failed to protect ourselves anyway. Not much we can do about it now.

But—don't you see? If it's old news, then the Sanafeans have got *to know! They'd be tipped! That means they'll be ready for this invasion, or whatever it is.*

Maybe, but I don't remember anybody pointing out a Sanafean to us, do you? And they are standoffish and hate Kalindans. Would you *believe a Kalindan ambassador if you were them? Hey, look, Chalidang quick-froze a bunch of solders, and they're going to invade. See what I mean?*

Ming did, and knew he was right. They would certainly have been forewarned, but the odds were that they wouldn't believe it. Even if they did, they were some kind of tribal types with little central government and no national army. Just professional meanies, more or less. They might be fighting wildmen, but against a disciplined force of pros . . . Well, it didn't seem likely they had much chance.

"It would have been much easier if we'd just taken Ochoa," Mochida said. "The water hex between it and Sanafe is high-tech, and we could have remotely deployed an awful lot of stuff, not to mention using the harbors and forts for a central supply base. Still, this will do. Ah! It's almost our turn. After you, please!"

They looked at Kalindan faces operating the terminal and still working on assembly of the last part of the line, and some of the Kalindans looked back. Some seemed surprised, but nobody came over to speak to them, let alone ask them who they were, why they were with these creatures, nor made an offer to take messages back.

Finally, it was their turn.

Strapping them in was less of a challenge than even Mochida had feared. There was an alternate restraint using netting and belts that was just made for Kalindans, simply because it was Kalindans doing much of the testing of the bubble cars and the system itself.

The netting pressed them flat against a padded lower back wall and held them tightly, and not very comfortably, although they were no more uncomfortable than they'd been on the regular line getting here.

And then the bubble was closed, the hatch turned and locked down, and they were pushed up onto the main tube line, to what appeared to be a solid wall.

A Kalindan operator turned a huge wheel, and suddenly the "wall" fell back, revealing a long tunnel, and they were violently sucked into the system.

It was as noisy and uncomfortable as before, but faster, much faster. The new improved model, both of them thought without much enthusiasm. It was bumpy, vibrated like hell, and if they tried to shift their weight even for comfort's sake, it started a spin that was hell to stop. Still, it worked. And how! It worked . . .

With stops for transfers and to renew the water in the bubble, it took some time, but the effective speed over the journey was nonetheless impressive, averaging close to fifty kilometers per hour. That put them at the border only about four and a half hours from when they'd left.

In each case they arrived just ahead of the General, who seemed to be having the time of his life. *He* hadn't arrived frozen, but had come in as they had, undersea, as it were, but his size had prevented him from taking the suction express to the capital. Now that he finally was on one designed for him, he was like a kid on an amusement park thrill ride who simply wanted it to keep going.

It ended several kilometers from the border. The region was dark and there was an unpleasant sulfurous taste in the water that burned as they breathed it.

Damn it! They *might be super warriors born, bred, and trained, but* we *aren't!* Ari grumbled.

It sure ain't the restaurant on the City of Modar, *is it?* Ming agreed.

Not only did breathing sting, but it also stung their eyes and any open sores they had. It was damned uncomfortable.

The water was murky, too, not from organic creatures, but from turbulence and minerals escaping from hot fumeroles and, here and there, red-hot seeping lava vents.

There was a surprising amount of life around the vents, and even the life-forms that gathered around the heat and steam seemed like little monsters rather than genuine creatures of the sea.

They mustered on a plateau overlooking the hell, where the water had surprising cold spots but the sulfur was less. It was here that the functional but skeletal end of the line had brought them, operated on this end by just a couple of nervous Kalindans who seemed anxious to finish up and get the hell out of there.

The Chalidangers were very impressive in their own way, hovering in formation, precisely in line in three full dimensions: 302, including the General and his staff, warrant officers, captains, lieutenants, sergeants, and 244 commandos. They looked tough, sounded tough, but without weapons, they still represented only the largest potential squid fry on the Well World.

To Ming and Ari's surprise, they saw the sergeant major select out four enlisted men and bring them to a large crate out of which they pulled several thin, lightweight environment suits, or at least that's what they looked like.

How'd they get sophisticated stuff like those, do you suppose? Ming wondered. *And, more to the point, without electrical power or energy packs, how the hell are they gonna operate the suckers?*

As it turned out, they had large backpacks attached, which appeared to circulate and filter properly mineralized water through the suit without using a power plant. The movement of just a few of the tentacles, and the natural pulsing of the Chalidang body, was sufficient to force the water through the filters, so cleverly were they designed.

You realize those things mean that they can walk on ships or land? Ari commented, amazed.

Yeah. Just like back home. Only I doubt if the same principles would work for strictly air breathers or most others unless they had all that designed for kinetic energy power. It gives them a major advantage if they need it.

It didn't take long for them to vanish above, and within a few minutes two of them were descending once more with strong cables. A winch was set up on the rock floor and bolted into the rock by sheer muscle power. Within less than an hour, supplies were being gently lowered on the makeshift system from another ship parked above.

Then came the armor and the weapons.

Extremely nasty-looking harpoons in spring-loaded barrels and stocks designed for Chalidang tentacles; barbed netting that could also be shot from a specially designed spring-loaded gun and expanded when it struck something. There were other equally vicious-looking things that they didn't recognize but could see that the purpose was lethal.

The Chalidangers had large spiral-shaped shells that undulated regularly back and forth as well as inflated and deflated to meet certain demands. They could even stand some misshaping, but the consistency, while not chitinous, was like the thickest leather and tough enough to resist anything but very direct blows. These shells now received a hard outer shell of some lightweight plastic or polymer material that, Ming wagered, was at the very minimum bulletproof, each "suit" emblazoned with their rank and the Imperial seal of Chalidang. Only the eyes, still protected by their own small compartments on either side, had any exposure at all. The tentacles were the weak point, but someone would have to get an object directly into the mouth to hurt one of them, and while these guys were big, they were also fast and agile in the water.

Now they hovered in formation, divided into squads and companies, waiting for inspection in turn by their lieutenants, captains, and majors, as the General and his colonels looked on.

They looked good.

"Soldiers of the Empire!" the General shouted to them, pride obvious in his voice. "You have suffered much in training, and risked death from an experimental cold process, and now you've been shot here in great tubes. Now you are outfitted, and the enemy is not five kilometers to the north. This evening, we will train in full gear here on this plateau. This night you will eat of the best Chalidang can offer. Then you must rest, for tomorrow we will meet one more time like this, just at dawn, and we will go together into Sanafe and glory! We have but one true objective. To attain it, we will require from you a victory. You are ready. The enemy knows we are here but not who we are nor what we can do. Tomorrow, we will show him."

"Yes, sir!" they all responded as one, sounding eager.

"To your commanders, then! Dismissed!"

As they broke into their component units and set off for their maneuvers, the General shot back over to them. He looked grand in his battle armor, but his men knew that he did not expect to need it.

"What about *our* battle armor?" Ari asked him.

The General chuckled. "I'm afraid you are observers in this. No weapons, no participation. Just try and stay out of the way and do not interfere in this matter. You know nothing of Sanafe nor who and what is a major threat there, nor do you understand what we are doing and why. You understand that it is dangerous. That's sufficient."

"Yeah? Well, what happens if things go bad and we don't have anybody around who knows to give us that stuff the next time we need it?"

"Then get to the surface and board the ship up there. It might not take you where you'd rather go, but it will have what you require and know what to do with you."

I'm not sure I liked the way he put that, Ari noted.

Yeah. Me, neither, Ming agreed.

Watching the battle tactics and maneuvers did them little good in figuring out how things would come off in the real world. After all, neither of them even knew what the place five kilometers north looked like, nor anything at all about the inhabitants.

But they knew they would know, perhaps a few hours after dawn tomorrow morning.

*   *   *

The looming Well boundary was becoming familiar to them now, but it never ceased to amaze them anyway. They knew that it didn't stop at the surface but went all the way to some point perhaps a hundred kilometers up in space, and that these energy walls actually sealed in each of the 1,560 hexes on the Well World. Inside each, almost any limitations might be placed, and also inside each, the entire biosphere might be radically different from just on the other side of the barrier.

Cold, hot, salty or brackish, even the middle of a vast ocean here could hold almost anything, both in environmental and in dominant species terms.

They kept well to the rear and close to the General and the two colonels, who, they knew, would fight if they had to but otherwise would direct from the rear. Not that these guys looked like they needed direction; they were smart and sharp, the really scary kind of soldiers that you knew instinctively were very good at their job. If the rest of Chalidang's army looked like this, it was no wonder everybody was scared shitless of them.

They pierced the opaque curtain in front of them and swam into Fairyland.

The hex was either quite high in elevation or designed to simulate a continental shelf, since it was relatively shallow and required an immediate steep climb to get to the "level" of the place, even though they'd begun atop a high plateau in Yabbo. Anybody wanting to secure the borders could certainly use that shelf and drop to good advantage, particularly if it held all around.

The land that stretched out before them was linked more closely to the sun than any other underwater realm they'd encountered before. The whole sea floor was a riot of sunlit shapes and colors, twisting, turning, some places with crevices, others with craterlike holes or caves, but all of it just covered in life.

The land itself was made up of things that had once been alive. When they died, they died in place, and were soon covered by the next generation of living things, which then died and were covered, and so on. Now rising hundreds of meters from the sea floor, the bottom layers, tens of thousands of years worth or more, had been compacted into rock that retained much of the color and texture of the living stuff on top.

"Be careful and stay out of contact with the reefs themselves," the General warned them. "Coral is an animal, a carnivore, in fact, and there are lots of surprises even uglier living among and within the stuff. Nothing here may be what it seems, and all of it is dangerous."

Wow! Now that *was a real confidence builder!* Ari commented. *I'm going to sleep better tonight knowing everything here is out to eat me.*

Coulda been worse, she reminded him.

Huh?

Core wanted us here on our own, remember, and I don't recall her sending us a briefing book.

They saw many demonstrations of what Mochida warned them against as they traveled along and just above the reefs that seemed to stretch out forever in front of them. Nasty heads of very large creatures full of teeth emerged from concealed holes in the reef and gobbled up fish as they swam past. Even schools of big fish weren't immune; things that looked like the gently waving but at least permanently planted coral suddenly moved, showing themselves instead to be all poisonous tentacles, grasping and paralyzing and then drawing in fish half their size.

The beauty was not merely skin deep, it was a deliberate trap for the unwary.

Still, thousands of fish and crustaceans and creatures they couldn't classify darted in and out of the coral, used it for protection, or even fed off the smaller creatures, down to plankton-sized levels, and off some of the coral itself in a few cases.

The coral was set up in colonies, with relatively barren gaps of lower rock and sand between, but it was more continuous than a set of islands. The gaps were brief, and it seemed only the larger fish and good-sized predators left one to go to the next.

Nor were any two beds exactly alike; some creatures were found only in one area and not in another, while the colors and even the types and shapes of coral changed as well.

It was easy to be mesmerized by the beauty and complexity of it all, but so much kill or be killed was going on that it kept jolting you back to reality.

So which are the Sanafeans? Ari wondered, and received a mental shrug from Ming.

Ahead, the commando squads fanned out, forming a nearly V-shaped formation with top officers inside the V. It was clear from the lack of serious attention they were paying to the pageant unfolding below them that the natives were not these pretty carnivores or concealed sea snakes.

"What do the natives *do* here that requires thinking at all, on more than the survival level?" Ming wondered aloud. "It doesn't seem like there are any built structures, no roads, no signs of what we think of as civilization at all."

"They manage the place, more or less," the General replied. "Oh, they cultivate their own reefs and try and outdo each other in artistic skills, something that is certainly lost on me, and they herd and cross-breed to ensure species survival and balance, and the rest of the time they fight each other, except when they're meditating upon and worshiping their gods. They don't quite make sense to the likes of us, but I've learned to accept that as just the way things are between many species. I doubt if we make any sense to them, for example."

"So why do you have to fight them? Respect, by their rules?"

"Something like that. In fact, one of their trophies for beating another clan in a fight is something we require. They don't know the significance of it beyond the trophy stage, but we do."

"Ah! I see! So you beat them and they give *you* the thing, huh?"

"Something like that. Ho! Stay back and be careful! We're about to be challenged!"

He broke off and darted back to his position just behind the colonels in the V, which had now come to a sudden, tense halt and was clearly waiting for something to happen.

I don't see anybody. Do you?

Ming was amused. *Like I can see what you don't? I—uh-oh! Wait a minute . . .*

The Sanafeans were not coming from the riot of coral below, but from the near surface above. Big black shapes that seemed to be huge oval mouths with wings on them.

"Send up the buoy!" the General ordered, and immediately one of the colonels removed something from his pack and pulled a tab. It inflated with compressed air and rose to the surface, trailing a long thin line which the colonel now hammered into the nonliving coral base below with just one blow.

"Sweet Jesus! How many of those things *are* there?" Ari wondered aloud. The Sanafeans seemed to suddenly fill the field of view above and in front of them. Ten, twenty . . . maybe a hundred or more of the things.

They could now see that they resembled not winged mouths, but giant manta rays. The mouths, though, protruded and had vicious-looking fangs on both sides, leaving little to the imagination as to what else might be hidden inside. They also had long, very thin prehensile tails the equal of their body length, and at the end of each tail was a spread of what might be called three "fingers," with an extended and controllable opposite "lip" that worked like an ultrawide thumb.

"Stop and turn back, invaders, or we will destroy you!" the huge, leading Sanafean thundered. Through the translator, he sounded supernatural and authoritarian; the voice of the underwater god.

One of the junior officers at the point of the V responded: "Who speaks like this to the forces of mighty Chalidang, Empire of the Overdark, lords of all they wish to rule?"

The kid was pretty good at this, they had to admit. Rehearsed or not, it was the proper response.

"I am Kobilo, High Lord of the Tusarch, invader. These are our lands and no other, not Sanafean nor foreign. We kept to our lands and demanded nothing of you or yours. You are the invader here. You must turn back or we must destroy you."

"We have no fight with the Tusarch," the lieutenant responded. "We regret that we must pass through and disturb their lands. It is necessary, but only to reach the Paugoth. We know of no other way to get there. Will you permit us passage over your lands to theirs?"

"Paugoth? *Paugoth?*" The clan leader seemed insulted. "What would you want with the likes of *them*?"

"We wish to challenge for the Trophy. They have it, you do not."

That forced the old ray to think a moment. "What makes you think you could beat them? *We* couldn't, last games, nor could anybody else. And you'll need more than that fancy armor and smart parading to take them, too. Why, I don't even believe you can take *us*."

"We will fight you if we must, for there is no honorable way to do otherwise, but we do not wish to do it, and it might harm our strength even if we do prevail here, so that the Paugoth may well win because of the demands of the Tusarch. This is your choice. We fight here, now, and the survivors either press on, if it is us, or turn back, if it is you who prevails. But you must be told that the Chalidang can neither give nor accept quarter. Even if you win, how long will it be before there are enough Tusarch again to seriously challenge other clans? Let us pass and, win or lose, it will be the Paugoth who will have this problem."

That was a wrinkle the old boy hadn't thought of. In a no-quarter fight, he was outnumbered here, and facing a foe he didn't know with weapons he was unsure of. If he lost, and he might, he'd just been told that the fight wouldn't be like a clan fight; these aliens would kill all. If they were the suicidal fighter type—and they looked the part—then even winning would be very costly. He also noted the black shape that was closing in on that released buoy on the surface. If they had surface ship support, it could get really ugly and maybe even mess up the coral.

By the twenty-nine Hells, let 'em mess up *Paugoth*'s coral!

"All right," the Elder said at last. "I'll give you passage in to Paugoth. But if you're pulling a fast one, if you do not fight them, then we will join with other clans and ensure that you have a far bigger fight. Understood?"

"Yes. The terms are acceptable. We can go on our own, but we would appreciate a guide to smooth things through to the Paugoth, and who would also ensure that we do not somehow trespass on your property nor do it harm."

The Elder seemed impressed, and even Ari and Ming were giving even more respect to the General's scouting and homework.

Two Sanafean warriors, sons of the elder, were delegated to escort them through without delay. It appeared that the clan boundaries weren't all that big, and that the next one over was where they wanted to be. More good scouting from the General.

Mochida was in fact very pleased by it all. He drifted back to them and said, "Well, we got by *that* one. Had I not gotten all this force here surreptitiously, we'd have had to fight for every millimeter of ground. As it is, we're going to be where we want to be with no losses and no problems in under two more hours. Right about midday, I would say."

"He sure caved fast when he saw that ship up there," Ari commented.

"Oh, it wasn't the ship. Remember, they only just gave their word that they would get us to the lands of the Clan Paugoth without interference and let us fight them. They didn't say anything about letting us back *out*."

Alkazar—Quislon Border

IT WAS ONE OF THE LARGEST ELEVATORS ANYONE HAD EVER conceived to build, and it went up inside the great granite mountain from the near-sea-level jungles, not to the top of the great mountain peaks, but to a point where it was practical to bore in an exit tunnel.

The ride itself was surprisingly smooth, with just a little bit of vibration, although there was no question that they were moving, and that someone or something was actually driving the tractor-trailer-sized car, because you could feel it slow down and then speed up again. When it finally slowed for good, eardrums of those who had them had popped several times, but, more interesting, the pressure inside also seemed to be varied.

"As an old pilot, I'd say they slowly pressurized us to the exit pressure before they started," Genghis O'Leary noted. "Or, at least, they did most of it then, and gradually lessened it still more as we rose. It's pretty slick."

"Makes you wonder why they didn't build it at Kolznar, though, and save all the upriver shipping and jungle transit," Har Shamish put in.

"They probably took advantage of some ancient caves and lengthy cracks or faults," O'Leary surmised. "I think they put it where the engineers said they had to. More to the point is why they wouldn't run a railroad or good automated shipping road from the port to here." He sighed. "Well, I suppose they had good reasons. Anybody who can design *this* would have better reasons than *I* could come up with for doing most anything!"

That thought was disquieting to all three of them, for they didn't like this hex one bit, and, bribes and favors or not, it didn't like them much, either. It was a reminder that the whole society was very much like the appearance of the natives: it looked small, weak, insignificant, often comical, but it masked a very nasty reality.

Unlike below, where the passengers walked, there was enough distance above that some kind of transport was needed. What the Alkazarians had built was a kind of small train sized for Alkazarians. Still, by kneeling, Jaysu managed to get uncomfortably ensconced aboard one of the small, spartan, open-air cars all to herself, while the two Pyrons were able to share another. The crew in yellow were busy shepherding the containers off, then hooking up small motors of some sort to them so they floated along the grooved path paralleling the train, driven by just one of the creatures per container. The rest, apparently, awaited a new shipment to bring back down.

There had been an exit station, and, like the one down at the bottom, this one took another blood sample and comprehensive picture and apparently compared it to what it already had. At least they managed to pass through fairly quickly, although Har Shamish wondered how, if there were any hitches, he was going to bribe a machine.

Although the train was fairly fast, it was bouncy and things were not well-lit. More than once, Jaysu, in a miserable crouching position, felt as if she were going to be flung off. She would have screamed at the train driver except there didn't seem to be one. It was all automated.

Just when she was so cramped and bruised she felt she couldn't stay on the little train a moment longer, it burst into the open, revealing the interior of Alkazar spread out before them.

It was as ugly as sin itself. Vast regions were covered with industrial complexes belching all sorts of gases into the air; dreary buildings were covered in soot, and even the new ones were painted drab colors; and the whole thing reflected against the clouds like a vision of Hell from almost any religion.

At the small platform where the train ended, two Alkazarians in black with gold trim awaited, their sleeves sporting an emblem resembling crossed lightning bolts. They were clearly waiting for them.

She needed some help getting out and to her feet, and the waiting creatures moved not at all to help her. It was left to one of the Pyrons to offer a tentacle and a pull.

Har Shamish went up to the nearer of the two officials. "I am the Pyron vice-consul," he said, "and this is Citizen O'Leary, in the service of the king, and Jaysu, an Amboran who is under our diplomatic umbrella. I assume there are no problems in clearing us to the border as quickly as possible?"

For a moment the Alkazarians said nothing, just standing there staring at them. Finally, the first one said, "You may follow us. We are going to put you on a night train as soon as possible. You will come with us and make no comments, nor stop, nor deviate from the route. If you need to ask anything, ask now." It was not lost on any of them that he did not introduce himself, even by title.

"The lady has not eaten," Har Shamish told him.

"Indeed? What does she eat?"

"Fruits, vegetables, anything not of flesh."

"Then she will not find much here and we would waste time trying. You will be at the border in a few hours and you can find something there. We are not equipped for visitors, you see." He seemed to think a minute, then added, "I might be able to find some water, nothing more."

"No, let us go," she responded, feeling the coldness of this pair. "I have fasted far longer than a mere day." She also wasn't sure whether the water in this loathsome, smelly place would be drinkable anyway.

"Do you have any recording or photographic equipment?" the official demanded. "Such things are forbidden here."

"You've examined us all the way down to our gullets," Shamish noted. "You should know better than we that we have nothing of the sort, nor weapons, nor anything else on the forbidden list. Our only interest is in expeditiously traveling to Quislon."

"Everybody seems to want to go to Quislon all of a sudden. Once you've seen it, you will not want to go there again. Very well, come with us."

They didn't take them far, for which all were grateful. Not only was the air quite thin, affecting the two Pyrons more than Jaysu, but it was also paradoxically thick, not in density, but with odors most foul. It was getting near dark, but Jaysu swore she could see clouds of yellow, purple, pink, and much worse hanging over the miserable, densely packed region. She couldn't comprehend how anyone could live in a place like this, let alone survive for long.

They were bundled into the back of a strange wheeled vehicle. Two armed guards with nasty-looking rifles hung off each side of the tailgate, and two more rode on the running boards on either side of the driver's central cubicle. The truck itself was open, like the crawler's had been below. Never had she felt so much like a prisoner.

The two Pyrons seemed lethargic, as if drained of much of their energy. She was sure it wasn't the air, which was thinner than at the surface but not debilitatingly so, and she decided it must be the chill. It was cold up here, and the vast tablelands on the other side of the Wall were also of high elevation. There was no snow on the ground, but there were patches of white not far above them on the mountainsides and in the high passes, and there was a crispness to the air that she found at first bracing but, as the wind blew and the sun set, began to feel raw and numbing to her exposed face and body. This was definitely not fun.

Making things worse were the silent but menacing guards, and the sights that they passed as well: groups of people, each with their own uniform combinations and armbands and funny hats and the like, all going here or there, all silently, without any sense of joy or relief that one would expect at the end of the day, nor even bantering bad jokes or light-hearted insults as coworkers often did. They were dull-eyed and had gray souls, without life or sparkle, without any sense of more than existence. They seemed like the road crews below; prison inmates, even if they had no evident guards.

Of course, the omnipresent stalks with their tiny pencil-thin cameras and all the rest were as good as any guards. She saw few females about, and, above or below, it struck her that she'd seen no children. The oppressiveness of the place almost overwhelmed her. What a sad little race this was, so bereft of joy or any other feeling that made life worth living. With all their ingenuity and technology, they hadn't paused to enjoy what they had made, nor let their great machines take the heavy work away, but instead they'd become like the machines they used.

It wasn't the frozen land that was so bad, but the frozen hearts within.

At least she didn't sense that Har Shamish was worried about their situation. If she'd sensed that, she might have been close to figuring how to get out of this situation. As it was, she nervously allowed the little creatures to drive them to their train.

It was an even more unusual train than it had been a ride on the truck. It was fairly wide, but had no wheels or crawler treads or anything else that she could see in the well-lit station area. Instead it seemed to wrap itself around a single thick rail or post and just sit there.

Like everything else in this Heaven-forsaken place, it was painted a dull gunmetal-gray and had few markings on it. There was an engine, of sorts, then a passenger car in back, then what appeared to be several enclosed cars used for freight or animals, and, finally, a series of cars that were sealed tightly, contents or purpose unknown.

As soon as their truck stopped, the guards jumped down and took a protective stance around it and finally them, as if they expected an attempt on their life. It clearly didn't seem directed at them, except perhaps to impress them with their importance.

The officer came around to the back and barked, "You will all get out now! The train cannot be held for you and it is due to depart in seven minutes!"

Slowly, groaning, the two Pyrons managed to get down. She jumped down, involuntarily flexing her wings to cushion the jump as she did so. This caused the guards to suddenly whirl about as one and point their rifles menacingly in her direction, but she folded the wings and stared at them and they backed off.

"Follow me!" the officer ordered, and they walked behind him toward the waiting train. As they did, another train from the other direction approached, and she marveled that it seemed to make no sound at all. That didn't seem right. Even feet made noise when they were put to work.

Har Shamish, in the lead as always, started for the open, warm-looking and well-lit passenger car, but a rear guard snapped something and the officer held up a hand, stopping them. "No, not *that* car," he said. "*This* car!" He pointed to the freight car behind the passenger one.

Shamish was still lethargic, but forced himself to alertness. "I protest! That car is clearly for hauling animals! Are you suggesting that we are animals to be treated as cargo?"

The little officer was ready for him. "No. I am *suggesting* that, first and foremost, you will not be able to fit in any seats in the passenger car, and we are not in a position to modify it for your onetime requirements, which are, you might recall, a courtesy we extended to your government although we had no profit in doing so save exhibiting our goodwill. Also, your short notice means that all of the passenger seats are taken by our people, who travel only when their duties require it. Your consulate said nothing about reimbursing us for a special train and extra crew. This is the best we can do. Take it, or leave it and we will take you back to the Eastern Lift and you can return to where you came from. And I would suggest you do not take much time in deciding this or arguing any further, since the train will leave in"—he looked at the big digital clock which displayed figures that looked more like animal scratching—"two minutes and twenty seconds regardless."

Shamish knew they had him. "Very well, we will board, but your government will get a strong protest when I return!"

"You've already made it and are so recorded," the officer noted, gesturing at one of the ubiquitous cameras.

With that, the Pyron vice-consul walked into the freight car, and she and O'Leary had no choice but to follow.

Guards came up, slid the door shut, and they heard an ominous *clunk* as it closed completely. After a moment two small emergency lights went on, one on each end of the car, allowing minimal sight for her and just enough light for them, but also showing that there were no windows or peepholes. A small compressor whined someplace overhead, and they could feel some air circulation, so they wouldn't suffocate, but otherwise they were as much in prison as if in a fortified jail.

Some sort of livestock had been transported in the car; it smelled gamey, although it had been as cleaned out as these sort of cars ever were. There was also a soft flooring covered with artificial grass, which gave Jaysu something of a foothold.

O'Leary went to the door and checked it. There was a panel with a series of lights set into the door, a master emergency open switch, but without the code it was impossible to use.

The two small lights blinked, as did the panel, and they started to move. It was so sudden that Jaysu barely had time to dig into the artificial turf and grab onto a reinforcing rod running along the length of the car for stability. The two Pyrons were bowled over by the motion, but landed softly, in serpentine fashion.

The train wasted no time at all once under way. They could feel the acceleration, and, if anything, it increased as it must have cleared the freight yards in the city.

It took her a while to compensate for it, and she didn't think the two others ever would.

O'Leary flared his hood menacingly in frustration and anger at the treatment, but he got control back quickly. He was an old pro, and losing your temper when you had no way at all to change a situation profited nobody.

Instead the large serpentine head looked around, as if surveying every square millimeter of their prison. "At least we're not alone as we travel," he commented sourly.

The other two turned to see what he was looking at, and

sure enough, there was a thin, pipelike camera next to the light at the far end. Almost as one they looked to the nearer end and the other light and, sure enough, there was another. Together, they had to cover the entire car.

"I wonder if the passengers are looking at the freaks on screens?" O'Leary mused.

"I doubt it," Shamish responded. "It's probably the men in the hidden security office in the engine. They wouldn't trust ordinary folks."

"What kind of insanity rules this place?" Jaysu almost wailed. "I mean, I think I have to pass some water. Where do I do it in this thing, and without being watched and recorded?"

"I'm afraid you don't have any privacy," Shamish replied. "And as for the where of it, I'd say the far corner of the car is about as much of a toilet as we're going to get. Cheer up. If they are taking us where we want to go, it will only be a few hours, maybe less at the speed this thing is moving. And somebody, most likely one or more of *them*, is going to have to clean up any mess."

It was impossible to tell how much time was passing as they rolled along, but if they were going almost anywhere within the hex, they certainly were not about to spend a long time cooped up, not at the evident speed the train was making.

"You don't have a watch?" O'Leary asked Shamish, a bit surprised.

"I did, but the security agent at the Zadar docks took it. You mean *you* don't have one?"

"I carried one of those self-winding things that supposedly works anywhere, but I lost it someplace weeks ago. Doesn't much matter, unless we stop, of course."

Jaysu looked over at them. "You think they might just leave us here? After all we've come through?"

"Well, probably not," Shamish admitted. "I mean, my consulate knows I'm making this trip, and I'm expected back within a certain period. Still, they can trump up anything they want around here and stall for ages. They know as well as anybody that nobody's going to declare war over one missing vice-consul. No, this is the risk we decided we had to take to cross Alkazar. We're in their hands, and nobody else can help us or reach us. Still, I'm not too worried. They could have taken us or polished us off in a lot of places, and they are well-known for not showing foreigners who have to come up here any more of their dear inner homeland than they possibly can. You can see why just from the glimpse we had of it. They've raped it. Little grows there now, they are unlikely to have sufficient food stock to feed that kind of population, and they have to import almost anything in that area. In the end, they need us and the goodwill and trade we provide more than we need them. It's just closer to buy the raw materials from them than elsewhere, but if we don't ship them everything from fodder for their feed animals to often the animals themselves, well, it wouldn't take long."

She had been in this now long enough to begin thinking on a wider scale. "But does that not make them vulnerable to pressure far beyond what it should? You would not have to make war on such a place; a simple blockade would do it, would it not?"

"Easier said than done, a blockade," Shamish told her. "Still, it wouldn't take a lot of disruption of trade to cause real rumbles here, it's true. It's another reason why I think we're going where we want to go. Chalidang can shake them, but Pyron is much, much closer. They were leaning more toward the Chalidang Alliance, until Ochoa anyway, because they're kind of soulmates of those squid. Winning that battle has tipped things back our way. My sense is that they're playing a balancing game, ready to tip to whoever seems likely to win. If they take us through, then they do something for them, and when a winner emerges, they pop up and say they were with you all along."

She shook her head in wonder. "All this cynicism, dishonesty, double dealing. And for what? To preserve what we saw of places like *this*? It makes no sense!"

"That's right," O'Leary agreed. "It makes no sense. It doesn't make any greater sense in the rest of the galaxy, or maybe in the rest of the universe, for that matter. It's the way things work. It's why folks like you have respect and the jobs you do, really. People are always looking for sense, and religion provides both sense and a feeling of comfort."

"But you do not believe in the divine." She said it as a statement, not a question.

"I have seen too much. Like I said down below, I believe in evil, in the opposite of your 'divine,' so to speak. I've seen it everywhere. I've not seen much of the good side, though."

"You must have had a sad upbringing yourself," she said.

He sighed. "My parents were both god-fearing sorts, but even though I was raised in my father's faith, they were quite different in their religious backgrounds. So different, in fact, that they were killed by the followers of one side for intermarrying and seeming to be happy and successful in spite of it. They were ordered to take sides. But they were *both* sides, you see, and they had settled their own religious war in the best of ways. So they were killed."

"How horrible! How old were you when this happened?"

"Old enough to track down the ringleaders and dispatch them the way they had my parents. And then I left my home and never returned, cursing it forever, and I finished my schooling on a world that had few of my kind there, and then I became a cop. It was only after that that I really saw what true evil could be. Spare me the prayers and the sermons—I had enough of nuns and priests in my youth. If there's salvation, I'm too old for it. But there might still be a measure of justice. In a sense, I've pursued some very evil people all the way to this world. Two of us have, in fact, the other far more twisted inside than me. But if we can get them, we'll get them."

Shocked at what he said, she did not continue the conversation, yet she couldn't help but reflect how little difference there was, deep down, between the policeman and the cold-blooded criminals he hunted, almost as if you could have found him on the other side with just one slight added twist of fate. Was it, perhaps, the same for his quarry? Was the evil he fought as fanatic? Was he, in effect, hunting his darker self?

It was too weighty a question for these circumstances, but precisely the kind of moral questions she found most fascinating in study and meditation.

"We're slowing down," Shamish commented, and the other two immediately felt this as well.

"A scheduled stop, perhaps?" O'Leary wondered. "Or have we arrived at our destination, whatever that is?"

"It better be the freight yards at Borol," Shamish replied. "If it isn't, then we are betrayed."

The train glided to a smooth stop, barely jerking the car at all.

"Magnetic levitation train," Shamish told them. "No friction. When you stop, you just turn off the power and the thing's a brick."

The car was solid enough that outside sounds didn't penetrate, so they had no way of knowing just who or what might be out there. It made them all nervous, and Jaysu closed her eyes and tried to project her senses outside and around the car now that it was stopped.

"Lots of people running about, apparently all Alkazarians," she said. "No—wait. Not all. There are—*others* out there. At least three, maybe more. They are in back of us, concerned with another car."

She suddenly had both their absolute attention.

"You can sense that?" O'Leary asked, amazed.

"I can *see* it, but the vision is very different," she responded. "I cannot, for example, tell you anything physically about them, only that they are not natives and they are quite agitated, in some great hurry. They are, I believe, offloading some very large crates from one of the boxcars."

"At least they can get the door unlocked," Shamish mumbled.

"They're done with their heavy lifting. There are five of them, or so it seems. The natives are ignoring them completely. Now they are talking among themselves. I cannot hear at this distance, nor would the translations come through anyway, so I have no idea what they are saying, only that it seems they are splitting into two groups. Three of them are

going off with whatever goods they unloaded. Two more are—
I believe they are headed this way! They are cold, businesslike but cold, and a bit nervous. One stops a native, says
something, perhaps passes something to it, and the natives
are now all walking away from us. I do not like this."

O'Leary looked over at Shamish. "I think our Alkazarians
just took sides." He looked around. "Any chance of smashing
those lights out?"

"Maybe, but what good does that do us? They control the
exit, remember, and these little bastards refused to let us have
any weapons."

"You wish the lights to be out?" she asked them.

"Well, it would help when they open that door to have it
dark in here. Dark and quiet," O'Leary told her. "That way
they can't be positive we're here, not without taking a chance."

She looked up at the far light and it went out. Her head
whipped around, birdlike, and the other light went out.

"Well I'll be . . ." Har Shamish breathed.

"You are full of surprises, aren't you?" O'Leary added.

Even to myself, she thought, surprised. Until that moment
she had no idea she could do that, either.

"Can you break the bomb if they toss one in here?" Shamish asked her. "And maybe their weapons as well?"

"I will not permit their weapons to fire. Beyond that I can
do nothing. I can act only in defense."

"That should be enough," hissed Genghis O'Leary. "To
the side with the door. Make sure you can't be seen by the
light from outside when they open it!"

There was a series of rapid clicks across from them, which
helped her orient where the door was and move as instructed.

It was just in time. The door opened and slid back, and
light flooded into the center of the car, but revealed nothing.

The pair outside stood there waiting a few moments, as if
unsure what to do. Then one said, through a translator, "All
right. Very clever, very impressive. Now you will either come
out or we will close the door and scramble the combination.
We can have this car put on a siding for the next six months if
need be."

Liars, she thought, but didn't say it. Even without her empathic senses, sheer logic said they were issuing empty threats. If they could have done that, they would have, and not subjected themselves to any risk or potential international incident. It would just be an "unfortunate accident." That also implied that not all the Alkazarians here were corrupt, only a few officials.

They waited a short while longer, then one of them said, "Okay, close it back up."

At that point Jaysu decided this wasn't a game worth playing. Thankful for the light from outside, she walked over and actually framed her form in the car doorway.

They were new sorts of creatures for her, like giant bipedal bugs with shiny chocolate-brown exoskeletons, feelers, and, as incongruously as the Alkazarians, some sort of uniform. Both also had nasty-looking rifles in their hands, and they were both pointed directly at her.

"Come down and tell your associates to come out as well," the creature on the left instructed.

"I will come down, but I believe that if you wish the others, you will have to go up there and get them," she told the pair. With that she began walking straight toward them.

"Halt! That is far enough!" the one on the right snapped, rifle up and primed.

She kept walking toward them.

They both fired at the same time, point-blank, at a range of two meters and using weapons that had a range of one kilometer.

Their claws kept clicking on the leverlike trigger but nothing happened. She walked right up to them, then between them and past them. Then she stopped, turned, and looked at them both along with the car.

"They can't *both* be broken!" one of the creatures snapped. "Not at the same time!"

"If you will just walk away, this will be a closed incident," she told them. "I have already forgiven you."

"Like Hell I will!" one snapped, and whirled and ran right for her, close enough to touch her.

Only it didn't. It somehow veered to the left of her, stumbled and fell.

She looked down at the thing. "Such violence! I shall not permit it!"

The other one clung tightly to its malfunctioning weapon and stared at both her and its companion yet did not move. It was so confused that it didn't realize there were now two Pyrons behind it, looking down on it, hoods flaring.

"Jirminins," Har Shamish said disgustedly. "They won't spook. They'll just keep trying and trying until it kills them."

As if to confirm this, the confused soldier still standing turned and with one motion tried to use the rifle as a club against the nearest Pyron.

Har Shamish's huge mouth opened, came down on the hapless Jirminin and swallowed it whole. Jaysu was sickened by the sight, yet she knew that the diplomat had spoken the truth. She nodded and turned to the other, just now getting up.

"I am very sad when anything dies, particularly on my account," she told her companions, "but better for food than for nothing." In truth, it had been and might remain for a while a crisis of conscience for her, but it had all happened too fast for her to react.

While she was still in semi-shock, O'Leary was on the other soldier in a flash.

"Bleah!" Har Shamish said, making a strange and ugly face. It sounded as if he were going to throw up, but what he extracted with a tentacle to his mouth was the rifle he'd swallowed along with the creature.

He studied the rifle. "Tell me—is it broken, or will it work?"

"It will work, I suppose," she answered. "But you know I have the same constraints on you as on them."

"That's all right. A weapon used in anger is one that failed its job. It's the threat of it that counts." He looked around and discovered they had been observed by a whole gallery of Alkazarians, both uniformed railway workers and some security personnel. He picked out the security officer with the highest evident rank and pointed with the rifle. *"You!"* he shouted menacingly. *"Come here!"*

The officer came, mumbling apologies and excuses with abandon.

"Oh, shut up!" Shamish snapped. "*Nothing* here goes on without the security police knowing and approving. And aliens with *guns*, too! Now, would you like to show your appreciation that you backed the wrong side in this matter, or would you rather I had *dessert*?"

The Alkazarian's sharp intake of breath, and the eyes, which looked like somebody having a stroke, gave the answer.

Shamish used the rifle, whose panel said it was fully armed, as a pointer, much to the security officer's terror. It was nice to put the little bastards on the other side of the fear barrier now and then!

"Now, some answers from you. How did those two Jirminins get here? Who allowed them here with weapons to engage in an act of war?"

"N-N-N-No, Your Excellency! You misunderstand! It was no act of war! They came across the border with their guns! Some took control of the station, then sent these others for you!"

"That's crap and you know it!" O'Leary started in. "They couldn't *move* around here without permission. The whole damned Alkazarian garrison in this area would have been on them with everything they had." The serpent's head came down to within centimeters of the security officer's nose.

"Look, Excellencies! I'm not a high officer! I follow orders! My orders came from my commander, who received his orders from local governmental command! We do not question our orders! We didn't even *like* this! Foreigners allowed to have weapons, to *use* them, within *our* country! But you must understand—if I am ordered, I must do it or it is I who will be eliminated and replaced by someone who *will* follow the orders!"

"He is telling the truth," Jaysu told them. "He does not know anything else."

Shamish's head bobbed a moment, then he asked, "All right, then. These two weren't alone. Who were the others? What did they look like, and where did they go?"

"I— Oh, my! I have a family! I am being watched even now!"

O'Leary had a sudden thought. "Jaysu, could you do for all the cameras around here what you did for the lights in the car?"

"I can try. It may give me a headache. There are a lot of them."

She closed her eyes again, and almost immediately there was the sound of small explosions all around, like large light-bulbs bursting one by one. As each sounded, one of the small mounted cameras seemed to explode and fly apart.

She was right. There were a lot of cameras. O'Leary sympathized with her headache problem.

"All right, now we can talk and nobody can ever prove it," Har Shamish said to the official. "The others—what did they look like?"

"One was a spider!" the terrified little creature almost squeaked. "A big, huge spider. The others were normal size, but very unlike anything we know here. Bent over, hairy, but in some ways like her."

Jaysu realized that "normal size" to the officer was *his* size. "They had wings? And were covered with fur?"

"Yes, yes! That's it!"

"Wally. Wally and his companions."

"Figures," O'Leary muttered. "So, what did they unload from the car in back?"

The little man was so terrified that it never occurred to him to ask how they could have known about any of this.

"Big crates. I don't know what was in them. They were consigned here, to be transshipped to Quislon. They loaded them on a motorized cart and went away, south. The border is only about ten kilometers due south of here."

"You have no idea what was in them?"

"No! I swear! They did not open them!"

O'Leary looked around. "Anything powered and reasonably fast available that we can take to the border? And I mean *now*? Before the army shows up to find out why they can't see us?"

"There's a small maintenance vehicle over there! Simple electric, fast. Take it, please!"

O'Leary went over to the other side of the platform and looked at the thing. It wasn't a familiar design but looked straightforward enough. Basically a flat bed, no stakes, about three meters square, and a driver's seat up front that was too small to be comfortable. The thing seemed to work by hitting a forward or reverse button and then steering with an over-sized joystick.

"If this runs out of fuel before we reach the border, then you will wish you were executed," he warned the security man. "Because, no matter the risk to me, if you're betraying us again, you will discover what it is like to be eaten alive and slowly dissolved."

The security officer stiffened, then fainted dead away.

Shamish and Jaysu walked over to the little cart and managed to get onto the back. There wasn't much to hold onto except the guardrail separating the driver from the flat bed, but it would do.

"Think you can handle it?" the vice-consul asked the agent.

"I don't think it's a problem. All set?"

"Yes, as much as we can be."

"All right, here goes!"

The front panel lit up, and he pushed the top of the two buttons and eased the joystick forward. The thing moved, slowly, out of the loading dock area and into the warehouses beyond. They could see the street on the other side, and were to it in a moment. Then, abruptly, they stopped.

"Something wrong?" Shamish asked him.

"Yeah. Which way is south?"

There wasn't much sky to get a solar fix, and they couldn't read the local signs. Worse, all of them abruptly realized that they'd never asked the little creature if this in fact was where they were supposed to be.

Had to be, they finally decided. Otherwise why would Wally have been here?

Har Shamish said, "To your right! See the hex marker?"

"Yes! Oh—I see! International border sign. How thoughtful!"

And they were off into the night, feeling all right, but knowing there were enemies in front of them and, almost certainly, Alkazarians heading toward them from the rear who would be no pushovers.

"It's time to get out of this rotten, stinking place," Har Shamish muttered, as much to himself as to Jaysu. "Besides, on top of everything else, it's too cold!"

The rail head wasn't much of a town, and they were soon out on a smooth, paved, but narrow road. If the hex sign and arrow could be believed, it would bring them to the hoped-for Quislon border.

Jaysu could hardly see in this darkness, but she looked back and also up worriedly. "Do you think they are actually pursuing us?"

"Not vigorously," Shamish replied. "If they really wanted to catch us, they'd have air units here now harassing us and blocking our progress. That makes me think that the little bastard—pardon—will be all right. They all put their necks out to lay this trap for us at this end, and I suspect our friend Wally paid handsomely to allow it to happen here. The Alkazarian government certainly has been helping them, but they're too nationalistic and too paranoid to bring it to this deliberately from the national level. They didn't have to do it at all. No, our buddies up front bribed some local big shot who will now be far more concerned with covering his rear end than in coming down hard on anybody, even us. By the way—that was a slick trick and a lifesaver, what you did. Do you have any more powers we don't know about?"

"I do not think that I have these powers, since I have not known of them until I needed them," she answered. "Rather, I believe the divine is working through me."

He sighed. "Suit yourself. But I sure wish we knew what dear old Wally got shipped all the way up here, so big and so bulky that he needed to import some soldiers with him to do heavy lifting."

"Might they be some sort of terrible weapon? I do not think anything is beyond him if it is in his assignment. He is not evil in Mr. O'Leary's sense, I do not think, but he is totally, absolutely, the most completely amoral individual I have ever encountered. Life to him is a game, and he plays it with great joy. He does not care who he works for, or who he hurts or helps, nor how many might be injured or killed, but he does not deliberately seek to do that, either. He lives life as a series of challenges, the more impossible the better. Right now, I believe he is having a great deal of fun."

"Well, it wouldn't be a weapon," Har Shamish assured her. "At least not anything on the scale we'd think of if the challenge was in Alkazar, say. Quislon is a nontech hex, like your own. Nothing will work there that wouldn't work in Ambora." The great head shook slowly from side to side. "Big crates. What in the *world* would he be taking into a nontech hex that would be that huge or complex? And for what?"

"We know one thing, at least," O'Leary called back from the driver's seat. "We know he's after the piece of the Gate, and we know the only time and place that he can reasonably get access to it. I've been there. Talk about impossible! If that spidery son of a bitch can pull this off there, with half the population of Quislon looking on, and us there expecting something at every turn, then maybe he deserves to get it!"

The road ended in a large circle with a great deal of room for parking. Inevitably, there was a substantial Customs station there as well, and it looked well-lit. O'Leary pulled over just short of getting into easy viewing range by the station and stopped the cart.

"Well, we might have known *that*," he said. "So, what do we do from here? Walk?"

"They're certain to have a major fence system along here, maybe with robotic sentinels," Har Shamish said. "I think our best bet is just to ride up there, present our documents and demand to go through."

O'Leary stared at him. "You're kidding! They'll have to know what we did back there, and these guys won't be so

loyal to the local government. You really think they're just going to let us out?"

"I do. Or, at least, better we are trying as aliens to *leave*
than to stay. I think they'll be glad to be rid of us. If they know,
if they've been notified, then we'll have to deal with them
some other way."

"I say we just use the rifles and blast through," the cop said,
reaching down for his.

"I suspect they'd repel any weapons fire. No, I think we just
go through and that's that. These guns are no good once we
cross the border anyway, so I say we just toss 'em."

Jaysu looked out at the station only a half kilometer away.
"I could fly over that thing," she told them. "And over the border, too."

"You probably could, but the question is, would their automated equipment target you and shoot you down if you tried?
Or *could* it?" O'Leary was beginning to wonder about her
powers.

"Possibly. Possibly not. I do not know. However, I agree
with Har Shamish. Throw the rifles away. I do not believe that
these ahead will be any different in kind or nature than the
others. I simply will not permit them to act against us."

O'Leary sighed. "I hate to do this, but . . ." He flung the
rifle off into the night. After a moment, Har Shamish did
the same. They were now effectively dependent on the priestess, but they had seen what she could do. O'Leary put the cart
in drive and headed toward the station.

There was no point in driving through to Quislon, since
the cart would be nothing more than a lump there. He parked
it neatly in the parking area, and all three of them got out and
walked toward the gate, which had all sorts of ominous-
looking warnings none of them could read. It also had the
universal hex symbol, though, and a twin cut through the
bottom segment a bit to the west of center.

You are here, O'Leary thought. He hoped that it was indeed Quislon on the other side. With the hex boundary there
and little starlight, what he could see through and across it
could have been just about anywhere.

Neither of the Pyrons were too confident relying on Jaysu's newfound powers, but they also didn't think they had much choice. And if she was confident of them, then they had to go along, since she was the reason they were there.

She looked around at the complex before following them up to the passage through to the border, then caught up to the pair. "How does this power get out here?" she asked them.

Shamish looked around. "Broadcast is the most common method, but I don't think these characters would use it. Too paranoid. Underground cable would be my best guess."

She focused on it for a moment and saw it in her mind's eye, coming down beside the road, a living snake of flame.

"Let us proceed," she told them, keeping that flow in one corner of her mind.

The way was barred by a tall electrically operated gate. Beyond it was a tunnel of sorts, with fencing five meters high going down the suddenly primitive dirt road on both sides and even across a roof. A second gate was at the far end, thirty meters farther on, operated, it seemed, by the same set of controls.

The silver and black officer looked just like all the others, but more nervous. Still, he didn't appear threatening, and Jaysu felt no direct danger to any of them from him. He did seem almost surprised to see them, though, as if he never would have thought they would try a legitimate exit.

"Papers?"

They handed them over, wondering just what his instructions were.

He looked at them, then at the papers, then back at them. "You are taking nothing with you that you did not bring into Alkazar?"

"Nothing whatsoever," Har Shamish answered. "Our sole purpose was to reach Quislon."

"Very well. You understand that these papers are not valid for reentry?"

"Mine most certainly is!" Shamish protested. "However, as it happens, I have decided to proceed home after this and

so won't be using them. Still, I am accredited as a diplomat to
Alkazar."

"To Kolznar Colony, not to the country proper," the official
responded. "However, as you say, it is moot." He wrote something on his electric pad, then proceeded to remove several of
the sheets from their papers that had been added when they'd
entered, and handed the papers back. There was a buzzing
sound, and the nearest gate slid back, revealing that last thirty
meter gauntlet.

"Proceed," the little bearlike creature said, and they walked
through. The buzzing sound came again, and the gate closed
behind them.

It was claustrophobic in the cagelike tunnel, walking in the
reflected light.

"I was right," Shamish commented. "One high fence, passive, then a killer fence in the middle. One more passive will
be over here at the other gate."

They reached the second gate, and waited for it to open.
And waited. And waited . . .

"I have a bad feeling about this," O'Leary muttered.

Jaysu did not know where the danger was coming from,
but she felt it, and knew it was time to act. She took hold of
that current of living energy she'd identified and kept track of
and mentally pushed against it.

There was a tremendous crackling sound, and sizzling, as
if things were frying, and then all the lights went out and they
were totally in the dark, including her. In fact, she was now
completely blind in the conventional sense, but she could still
"see" her companions in other ways, and the sudden panick-
ing little creatures in the building behind them.

The two Pyron weren't blind at all. "Quick! Can you force
the gate?" Shamish called to O'Leary.

"I—I *think* so," the agent grunted, pushing hard against it
and rattling it.

Shamish came up and added his considerable weight and
strength to it, and they started pounding against it.

The gate began to buckle, and then, with one mighty coordinated push, they got it partly bent outward.

"There's enough room to squeeze through!" O'Leary cried. "Come on, ma'am! Try and get through!"

"I cannot see!" she protested. "I can only see the living!"

She felt around, using their tentacles for guidance, and managed to find the hole, but squeezing through it with her wings proved difficult. Finally, she felt herself being pushed to the ground, and while one of the Pyrons pushed against the gate, the other pushed against her feet.

There were a lot of feathers left around, but now O'Leary managed to squeeze through the bent corner of the gate and was able to help Shamish through. Getting up, they helped the Amboran to her feet and made for the border, just a meter or two away.

She felt a pain, like burning, on one wing, but only wanted out of that horrible place and she went forward.

The temperature immediately changed. It was warmer, yet the air was much dryer, a desertlike feeling to it, and overhead, quite suddenly, the sky was clear and well-lit.

"You can fly all you want to now, if you can," Shamish told her. "You're in Quislon."

She looked back, shaken, at the blackness she'd caused beyond the border. "That is an evil place, if you wish to define evil, Citizen O'Leary," she commented.

"I think it is, but it still can't hold a candle to some. I wonder what the devil they were going to do with us once they had us trapped?"

"The energy—the power in the wires? Citizen Shamish called it a killer fence, the one in the middle? That same energy was also all around the cage. They were going to connect it so it would run through the cage as well. I could see them doing it."

O'Leary burned with anger. "Those bastards were going to *electrocute* us?"

She sighed. "I could not, of course, permit that to happen. When the one inside threw the switch, and the power started toward us, I simply, well, threw it back . . ."

"Thus shorting out the security fencing, the station, and

maybe if we're lucky, the town and the train yard as well."
O'Leary sighed. "Well, at least that's that. None of us will
have to go back there again, and if you, Shamish, want
to go back to Kolznar by ship, you can make them most
uncomfortable."

"I think my vice-consular days there are past," the diplomat commented sourly. "I think I'll pick a different assignment next. But come! This is a desert, and we have a very
long way yet to go."

Jaysu shook her head. "No, I must rest, and nearby," she
told them. "I cannot see properly to do much in this place,
and I need to meditate and sleep and allow my body to repair
itself."

"It's two hundred kilometers to Quislon Center," O'Leary
reminded her. "And the desert sun here is very, very hot."

"Then why don't you go on?" she suggested. "You can
make your best time now, even this late. In the morning I shall
catch up to you. It is basically south, then I will feel the tug of
the Gate and head for it. They have a Gate in the middle of the
hex, do they not?"

"Yes, that's the system for all of them," Shamish agreed.
"But see here, it's our job to accompany you!"

O'Leary sighed. "She's got a point, you know. She can fly
now, maybe even make the whole distance in a day, two at
most. We'll be six days reaching Quislon Center."

"But we're bodyguards as well!"

O'Leary chuckled. "Yeah? And who's been saving who
tonight? I think the little lady can take care of herself. Besides, I'd like to know just what the heck is in those crates,
wouldn't you?"

"Yes, but—"

O'Leary looked out on the desolate landscape and pointed
with a tentacle to marks in the hard ground. "Well, whatever
it was went that way."

There was no way around it. They had gotten her this far,
but now their own purposes were different, even if both were
in the interest of fulfilling the mission.

"But we're going to make that ceremony," Har Shamish said in resignation.

"If we can't catch up to them or figure out what they're hauling, you bet we are," O'Leary responded. "I sure want to see how the hell he's going to pull it off."

Sanafe

THE BORDERS BETWEEN CLANS WERE NOT SOMETHING THE AV-erage outsider could see, but they were apparently as real as hex boundaries to the natives. It might well be a scented marker, or even a planted pattern, and to Ari and Ming, as well as the Chalidang force, there was no difference at all between the last reef that was considered Clan Tusarch's sacred property and the next, which was Clan Paugoth. Still, the two escorts from the Lord of Tusarch stopped dead at the edge of that last reef and would go no farther.

"From the next reef on, you are in Paugoth territory," one of them warned.

"Yeah, and you better fight 'em, too, 'cause our whole clan's gonna be gathering to see. If you beat 'em, you're welcome to whatever you're here for, and then leave the remains to us. If you lose, we will be waiting for you."

In fact, Mochida was planning to wipe out the winner no matter who that might be, but he let it go. As far as he was concerned, Clan Tusarch was totally irrelevant. He was relieved that he hadn't had to waste men and resources fighting his way there, but was satisfied in any event to be here.

No welcoming party, Ming noted. *Looks like nobody talks to anybody around here. You'd figure that by now we'd be common knowledge.*

Up above, following the small markers that Colonel Kuamba sent up every kilometer or so, the dark shadow of a very large vessel continued to slowly follow. It could not be ignored by anybody. Even more interesting, at the release of the next small buoy there was additional activity above. Three smaller vessels seemed to be accompanying the big ship, possibly put over the side by that ship, but equally possibly they'd simply joined it unnoticed. Still, they followed silently, going away now and then if the wind or waves were wrong, but tacking back without much of a problem and generally keeping formation. Those guys are good sailors, Ari noted approvingly to himself.

But what else were they? Supply ships? Certainly not reinforcements, since what would have been the purpose of the cryogenic stuff? But they were there for some reason, all right.

As the large V-shaped formation of Chalidangers moved into the targeted clan's territory with a steady but slow and cautious pace, two small forms went over the side from the smaller boats above and swam down a bit and then across. They were not Chalidang, Kalindan, or any other race that Ari and Ming had yet seen, but seemed a kind of large animal designed for the water, yet almost certainly air breathers from the way they moved. They fanned out, took a good look at the situation, and then one headed back up and into one of the small boats once again, while the other paced the large formation about halfway between the reef and the surface.

"Friends of yours?" Ari asked the General.

"Yes, as a matter of fact. Although there are panels in the small boats and even in the large ship that allow one to look down here, the hard substance necessary to ensure that they don't break and sink introduces some distortion and also has a limited field of view. The Imtre have exceptional vision as well as other senses, and they also have a great deal of experience in this kind of campaign in nontech environments. They aren't much good at real fighting, but they'll coordinate our surface forces with our combat line here."

"Looks pretty complete. You don't think the locals are gonna notice?" Ming asked him.

"Oh, they'll notice. It's just irrelevant. The only thing that can cross us up is if the clan does not come out for a fight like the last one did. And if they don't, they're finished here anyway and might as well commit suicide. No, they'll come, and soon. Within the next few minutes, I'd say. Otherwise, I'm going to start blowing up their precious reef gardens, one by one."

He didn't have to bother, nor even explain how he could blow things up down here. The Clan Paugoth was suddenly there in full force and radiating irritation, if that was the word for it. Fury, maybe, was a better one.

"Who dares desecrate Paugoth lands?" thundered the local lord imperiously. If anything, his Voice of God impression was even better than the last one, both Ming and Ari agreed.

This time Mochida didn't allow a mere lieutenant to answer. To the surprise of the Kalindans, and possibly even some of his men, the General decided to do his own talking, and rose up to be level with that huge fanged mouth flanked by bizarre eyes.

"I am Colonel General Anchun Mochida of the Imperial Chalidang Army," he announced in tones that sounded not quite as impressive as the lord's but good enough. "In ancient times an object of great value was stolen from His Majesty's family and people by massed armies including the Sanafe, which received a piece of it as some sort of war trophy. I am commanded by His Most August Majesty to pay any price, fight any fight, do whatever needs to be done, to retrieve what is and was always rightfully ours. We are here to get the piece you still possess. If we receive it, your people and mine will be friends forever in the coming reorder of power in the universe and we shall go in peace, and quickly. Will you return it to us by your authority, wisdom, and leadership?"

The old lord seemed taken aback by this, and confused. "War? Stolen treasures? What nonsense is this? Even if any of that blather you just said is true, I have no knowledge of the object of your quest. Why do you search for it here?"

"But you *do* have it," the General responded. "It is the Indestructible Trophy, that which marks a clan for the next year as the Clan of Clans."

The Sanafean leader seemed amazed. "What? That old ugly stick? Its only worth is what it represents to the winners; it has no other value. You must be mad to come here with an army and a navy to take *that*, and your Emperor or whatever must be crazy, too, to send you on such a quest!"

That didn't sit well with the Chalidang soldiers. There was a great deal of tensing up, and weapons were being fitted into tentacles and brought to bear. As the rumbling subsided, Ari noted that the Imtre above had gone and another had slipped off the third boat but was sticking very close to it.

"Silence!" the General commanded, and the troops did as they were ordered, but were very ready now, almost a coiled spring.

"If it is of no intrinsic value to you, then what will you take for it, or will you just give it to us and we will go?" the General pressed, knowing where things were leading, as everybody else on both sides did.

"If it has no intrinsic value then it cannot be priced," the Lord of Paugoth responded logically. "Therefore, I cannot take anything for it, nor, because of what it represents to us and to no one else, may I give it away. There is only one way the Indestructible Trophy can *ever* change hands."

"Very well, then, sir. It is by your choice that what follows follows," the General said in a menacing tone. "Company formations!" he yelled crisply to his men, who began to reform in an impressive manner into five fighting groups. Above, the Imtre tensed and virtually surfaced, keeping only its head below water.

Ari and Ming decided that the better part of their own valor was to rise as close to the underside of the big ship as they dared and use its shadow and substance as protection. They had nowhere to run and couldn't see much any other place, but they didn't want to be in the middle of what had to be coming.

I got a bad feeling about this, Ari commented.

Me, too, but not for the same reason. They've looked over these tentacled fighters with their fancy armor and nasty weapons and they haven't blinked. No species survives for long if they're that stupid. Conclusion: they're not that stupid.

Huh?

You know the limitations of intelligence. I'll bet you that

*the General's seen a million full-blown three dimensional re-
cordings of the clans fighting each other, but when's the last
time the clans fought somebody else?*

Uh-oh. You think we're better off maybe on *the ship?*

Probably, but I just got *to see this.*

The Chalidangers were totally confident of victory, and
tended to regard the Sanafeans as backward primitives unable
to sustain a coordinated attack. Clans, too, were relatively
small, generally no more than five or six hundred individuals,
with only the two hundred or so adult males actually fighting
for blood.

Mochida's tactics, probably run through a million computer simulations back home in his capital, seemed for a
while to go quite well. The Sanafeans showed unexpected
quickness and a nasty ability to stun even an armored Chalidang with some kind of natural electrical charge if they could
touch the enemy, but their weapon was basically a large
and ornately carved and sharpened sword wielded by the hand
from underneath. The Chalidangers' harpoons and hooked
nets tore through the clan ranks and began to fill the water
with blood.

Mochida took no direct part in the fighting, although he
had full battle armor on and a nasty harpoon that could fire
four bolts in a spread all at once. He was content to let his professional force do the minute by minute adjustments, which
showed him to be a very smart commander.

There was no doubt about it; at least four Sanafeans were
falling—wounded or dead—for every Chalidanger in similar
straits. The unexpected electric charge took its toll, but unless
the Sanafean could get close enough to apply it without getting killed, and then thrust the sword up into the tentacles,
slashing away at the arms and mouth of the invaders, there
wasn't much damage their swords could do against that high-
tech armor.

Worse, the natives fought mostly as individuals, with no
apparent organization or leadership, and this allowed them to
be split again and again.

The Chalidang soldiers seemed so filled with blood lust

and so confident of an easy victory that they didn't even realize that the mantalike Sanafeans had been drawing them slowly down, at great cost, to the reef below.

Suddenly, as a large number of Chalidangers swooped in to finish off some bleeding stragglers just above the reef, the coral reef itself seemed to erupt. Shapes—nasty, vicious, with huge jaws, wide eyes, and pointed teeth—lashed out from holes and hideaways within the living rock. They looked almost comical, but they were incredibly fast and they ignored the armor and started chomping on the Chalidangers' tentacles. Soon the thirty or so invaders who were close enough had gaping wounds, and tentacle parts and blood began floating about, yet every time the Chalidangers tried to harpoon or net or otherwise grab one of their large serpentine assailants, there was nothing there. As quickly as they struck, the giant sea snakes could withdraw into the protection of solid coral, only to emerge somewhere else when the victim was right.

Withdraw! Get away from the damned reef! Mochida screamed at them. "Keep your position at least five meters from the reef, damn it! Shoot down, don't chase!"

It was hard for his men to obey him, though, when targets were so easy and so apparent, and some others got parts of themselves bit off as they went after apparently helpless Sanafean stragglers.

Told ya they had some surprises, Ming commented smugly.

For all that, Chalidang still had the edge, and even though it suddenly faced a foe that had gone from disorganized savages to pretty tightly ordered and disciplined units, it was clear that at this rate the Chalidangers would still win. It would just be more costly than they'd anticipated, something that troubled Mochida very little and his masters not one bit.

"Form dynamo!" the Lord of Paugoth commanded from somewhere in back and over his troops. "Press in, main body, *now!*"

The Sanafeans formed into one of the oddest formations any of the others had ever seen. Half had turned over, so they lay chest-to-chest, doubling their apparent size and making themselves look like weather balloons. They then had joined with another pair, and another, and another, until they were densely packed together, all of their hands clenched in the center. The original pair was the driver; everybody else just came along for the ride, but there was a sense that they were somehow linked, somehow interconnected. But for what? They made much better targets for Chalidang harpoons this way, and were no apparent threat to the invaders.

They came at the main body of Chalidangers, two regrouping companies still a bit dizzy from the reef and extricating themselves and others from it, and they came very, very fast. So fast, in fact, that the reforming group had no time to dress ranks and deal with it. They started to move away, but the mass of Sanafeans struck them, and every Chalidanger who was struck was suddenly screaming in agony, its armor actually *melting*, the occupants badly burned or stunned or even dead.

They've got a massed electrical field there, all from their own bodies! Ming noted. *My God! I don't even think they can feel pain when they're like that. Look at those bolts go right into them, almost like a pincushion, but they're coming on!*

Mochida was alarmed, particularly when he saw three other such "dynamo" formations being put together in front of him. Half his men were dead or wounded, and even though there were probably no more than a hundred Sanafeans left who could fight, they were all fighting, and without fear and or sense of giving up.

Mochida shot up to where one of the Imtre was waiting just below the surface. "Bomb the reef. Indiscriminate," he ordered.

The Imtre hesitated a moment. "Through your own troops?"

"They'll get out of the way. Now, *do it!*"

The Imtre was gone topside, and Mochida moved over the largest concentration of troops. "Spread out, unified V at ten meters depth! Form on me! Do it *now!*"

As many Chalidangers as could do it disengaged instantly and rose, forming once more that perfect V shape, this time at a very shallow depth, and, considering their reduced numbers, fairly wide apart.

New bolts were being distributed for the harpoons from

cartons in the small boats above by Imtre, who were moving quickly and nervously.

The Sanafeans broke from their dynamo formations when this happened and spread out in a column of fours, lowering themselves close to the reef and staring up at the high invaders. The old lord was still there, too, and didn't sound much like giving in.

"You fight well, you invading bastards, but you must come to us now! Come down to our reef, if you dare, and retrieve your trophy, and don't mind the gathering sharks!"

The blood had in fact attracted a lot of very large sharks, all of whom looked capable of eating anybody there and more than willing to do so, although they were first starting off by scavenging the dead and the severed limbs.

Mochida was also not in a defeatist mood. "Give us the trophy, Lord Paugoth, and the clan will survive. If I must take it from this point, and hunt for it, I shall leave no Sanafean of the Clan Paugoth alive. No male, no female, no infants, no children. One by one I am going to destroy your reefs and all that they contain until you yield or the sharks and the other clans pick your bones."

Almost on cue, since it had been prearranged by the Imtre with those above, there were a series of splashes at the surface, and slowly descending past the Chalidangers came sleek-looking cylinders with some sort of marking on them. They went down so slowly that the Sanafeans weren't sure how to take the things and simply watched them fall, not even noticing that the Chalidangers had turned so their armored bodies were facing down toward the reef and their tentacled part was almost straight up.

A great saucerlike Sanafean detached itself from the group at the reef and approached the nearest of the cylinders. It reached out its "hand," touched the thing, and simultaneously gave it a full charge.

It blew up with an enormous bang, and the concussion flung Chalidangers all the way to the surface and smashed a suddenly deafened Ming and Ari against the hull of the ship.

Four others struck the reef and went off in sequence, throwing up more concussion, more noise, and more brute force energy than had ever before been seen in this nontech hex.

As soon as the Kalindans could regain their senses, they headed for the surface, popped up, and saw a nearby longboat with four Imtre and three insectlike Jerminins in it, loading up a mechanical rack with five more of the depth charges. The trouble is, they looked pretty full and pretty busy, and the two other boats were moving to other locations and preparing for more of the same.

Ari didn't have to wait for an invitation. They swam quickly to the big ship and found a rope ladder leading to an open compartment where supplies had been unloaded as called for to the smaller boats. It was above the surface and it was inside a big ship. That, for the moment, was all the Kalindans cared about.

While the initial battle had been going on, Imtre scouts knowledgeable from intelligence as to the Paugoth boundaries had placed small surface markers denoting both ends of each Paugoth reef. These red markers, bobbling up and down, were now the objects of the small boats, each of which chose one and moved to a position in between. Using Imtre and the "glass" bottoms as confirmation that they were where they wanted to be, they waited for their Imtre to be out of the water and then released a rack of depth charges.

Hanging for dear life from the rope ladder and trying to pull themselves up, the Kalindans found that the explosions were just as spectacular if not as damaging on the surface.

After the loads were dropped on three more, though, an Imtre who went down to check damages came rushing back up and they could hear him shout, "Cease fire! Cease fire! They've had it!"

What do you think? My brain's been scrambled and I know we're gonna hurt like hell from those whacks against the hull, but I'd rather be down there than up here if it's over, Ming commented.

I agree, on everything, including the scrambling, Ari came back, and with that they dropped back into the sea.

Couldn'ta stood it long up there anyway, Ming noted. *That hot sun was peelin' our skin off.*

Still, the scene below was not easy to look at even when you could see anything through the still swirling dust and debris.

As it cleared enough to see the reef below, as through a fog, the sight was one of horror. There were dead Sanafeans all over, some torn to shreds but others looking remarkably like they were just sleeping, but with no life inside them, but there were also dead and dying sea creatures. The coral reef itself seemed shattered, scarred, and gashed, the living top layer scorched and motionless. Here and there the vicious giant spotted sea snakes that had been so effective could be seen, some decapitated, half out of their holes and burrows. Sharks, too, lay dead and dying in mad twisting frenzies, as well as countless other fish who had depended upon the reefs for everything from protection to food.

The Chalidangers hadn't weathered things that well, but at least they were alive, for they'd known what was going to happen and had been as prepared for it as they could be. Even so, a number who'd apparently been in the path of the concussion's upward force seemed stunned and only slightly alive, their armor, which Mochida had bragged could stop the harpoons and even some much higher tech energy weapons, cracked, in one case shattered, by the forces their General and their allies had unleashed.

"Sweet Jesus! Is there anyone left alive down there to surrender?" Ari cried.

General Mochida saw them, possibly heard the comment, and approached.

"Sorry, my guests, but I fear I will be slightly deaf for a while. I hope not forever, but even if so, it would be worth it. Victory is worth any price."

"It looks like the price was real high, particularly among the Sanafeans," Ming noted.

"Yes, they put up a much tougher fight than we hoped. Fortunately, we had contingency plans for such eventualities, and this is the result."

"It doesn't seem to me that you won anything, General," Ming replied. "I mean, the object wasn't to kill, it was to get that whatever it was you wanted to get, or did I misunderstand you?"

"No, you're quite right. They are bringing it to us now. There were a half-dozen or so survivors, and they gave me their word and went to get it. That is what we are waiting for."

"You really think they're gonna come back and bring you this trophy?"

"I do. The price is that I do not blow up the rest of their reefs. You see, *they* can't survive without their reefs. The reefs not only are at the heart of their food chain, it's where they bear and nurture their young. I daresay we probably killed quite a number of the clan's children today, before they could ever taste the freedom of the open sea."

"Some deal! And as soon as we're gone, the other clans'll come in and wipe out the rest of them and take over here anyway."

"Not my problem. Ah! I see that this affair is close to a conclusion . . ."

Coming from a valley between two blasted reefs was a small contingent of Sanafeans. Most were adults, but there was a difference you couldn't quite pin down in some of the larger ones in the rear.

The wives and mothers, I bet, Ming guessed, shaking her head.

In the front of the group, and bearing in his hand an odd-shaped piece of, well, something, was a young male, perhaps too young to have yet been a warrior in the big contests like this one.

The young creature stopped just short of the Chalidang line, and General Mochida, sensing the hesitancy, descended to the young one's level.

"I am Colonel General Mochida. You have brought what we came for?"

The young male quivered, as if summoning up courage, but he replied, in a shaky yet clear voice, "I am Kirith, High

Lord of the Paugoth. In the name of all our sacred gods, take this cursed thing and depart our lands."

Ari and Ming both had a sudden sense that there was more meaning to this sad scene than merely surrender with honor. It was unlikely that the old lord had been the father of someone this young; he was too big and too old for that.

Most likely Mochida's bombs had killed his grandfather and his father, and possibly his older siblings as well. A second look at the remains of the carnage below showed harpoons with expanding heads in almost every intact body.

The Chalidangers who'd recovered first had descended and finished off those of the enemy still living.

Mochida extended one of his two extra long tentacles and took the object, then immediately moved up and away.

He moved toward the large ship, tapped on the side in what seemed to be a code, and a panel slid back noisily to reveal a water-filled central compartment aboard the vessel.

"Put the medical people and the wounded inside the ship," he instructed. "We'll sail into Kalinda and get the benefits of modern medicine, at least. The rest of you form up and prepare to follow the ship."

"You're going into Kalinda *now*?" Ari asked incredulously. "There's no way you're fit or in any numbers to resist internment!"

"I have no intention of being interned," the General responded. "We are going to go in unarmed and request the right to fair return under the Neutrality Treaties. We will be escorted directly to the capital and we will then be unceremoniously thrown out through the Zone Gate. There are only . . . oh, I'd say 115 or so of us. I should think that word of this should make your people more relaxed about us. We have what we were after. I hope to receive word from Quislon that we have another shortly. If so, that will leave only one piece of the Straight Gate left to acquire. If not, we'll have another bloodbath at some point before it is all gone. Our air-breathing agent has proven extremely capable."

"Yeah? And what good is even *that* if you can't get the last piece?" Ari asked him. "And, if I remember, that's the one no-body could find."

"Oh, I am pretty certain where it is," the General re-sponded. "And I think you might be as surprised as everyone else when you find out. And you *will*. I would love to take you to Chalidang to meet Their Majesties. I'm certain that they would be thrilled to have you for dinner. But now you're my native guide. What happens from this point is going to de-pend on who is or is not waiting for me when I reach Zone. And you, *both* of you, shall accompany me. I and my men will soon be strangers in a very strange land. We appreciate our native guide."

One of these days, somebody is going to kill that asshole squid, Ari commented. *He reminds me of my uncle Jules.*

Don't they all, Ming sighed.

An Imtre who had splashed down into the water approached the General.

"Yes?"

"Sir, beg to report that General Kusdik and Minister Krare are both dead. Assassinated."

"What! But Kusdik was aboard this very ship! And Krare was supposedly waiting at the Kalindan border!"

"They were, sir, but—well, something got them. Just like they got the others."

A nervous chill radiated from the General in spite of his triumph. All the deaths he'd seen, all the deaths he'd just caused, and these two were the ones that affected him.

"Kincaid?"

"Yes, sir. At least we assume so in the case of the minister. On the ship, well, er, he left a note."

"He did *what*?"

"Y-Yes, sir. It said that we were all to tell the Empress that she would be the last, and that there were only two to go. And he—he added something. Something for you."

"For *me*? But I'm not from his damned universe! What concern of his am *I*?"

"He said, well, he—"

"Come on! Out with it!"

"He said that you should be told that he didn't like geno-cide no matter who did it. That he was very busy now but that he expected he would get around to you sooner or later."

"Figures. Has my great staff and would-be replacements figured out yet what the devil Kincaid *is* that he could get this close to us? And I mean, the minister would have been in a water-breathing atmosphere, like here, not air like the others. How can he do that?"

"I don't have word on it, sir, but I'll have them send queries as soon as we're in high-tech. If they know anything now, they'll tell us and I'll tell you."

"Very well. Go! Let's get moving here!"

"Problems, General?" Ming asked, not sounding worried about his health and welfare.

"You know Kincaid. Or knew him anyway. Tell me what you know."

"Not much, really. Just the usual. Josich was Emperor, and he went to war very much like you do and at one point suf-fered losses severe enough to set back his plans for months. In fact, it turned out to be such a loss of momentum that it cost him the war. He took it out on the planet that had fought so hard and stalled him for so long, and he blew the entire planet up, along with over four billion sentient creatures. Just like you did this afternoon, only on an imaginably larger scale. Kincaid's whole family was on that world, but he wasn't at the time. He's been out to get Josich and every single high-level individual regardless of rank or position or power ever since, fanatically so, to the exclusion of all else. He won't even be deterred by hostages. He's a machine, General, as well as a madman, and if he says he's going to get you, he'll get you. He followed Josich and the remnants of the Hadun court here, and from the sound of it, he's gotten far more than the one in Zone that we knew about."

"Yes, that's true. Of the more than twenty people who came in with the Empress, we're down to just two, including Her Majesty. It will make for an interesting situation if our agent is present in Zone when I come through holding another piece of this jigsaw puzzle. I am convinced that so long as

Josich remains in Chalidang and in the palace there, she can not be gotten, even if someone were invisible. The controls and security are just too perfect. But if she comes out, well, then it is a different story. So far nobody has been able to protect anyone outside of that level of security. And Josich will have to come out if we have the Quislon piece."

"Have to?"

"Yes. Again, you will see, when it is time."

"If I were you, I wouldn't be counting too much on him stopping with your Empress," Ari noted. "He's added you to his list now."

"And that should worry you," the General responded ominously.

"Oh?"

"You see, I have given orders to every single one of my people. If I should die, for any reason, they are to kill you immediately."

Quislon

JAYSU WAS FREE TO FLY AT DAWN, BUT IT DID NOT EXCITE HER AS much as it should have. The landscape she'd awakened to was among the most barren she'd ever seen, and she wondered how she would even get food and drink for the long journey ahead.

To the north there was a mountainous landscape with noticeable green all about and even a waterfall in view, but it was distorted by the gauzelike effect of the hex barrier. She could see the Customs station and the triple fencing that went as far as the eye could see, and she knew that she didn't dare go back that way. Even if she could have flown over before, she surely would face a trap now.

That left Quislon, the object of her long journey but also a place definitely not made for Amborans. She wondered, in fact, how the two Pyrons were going to make it, considering how barren it seemed.

She launched herself into the air, suddenly conscious of where she'd lost some feathers and had perhaps gotten a scrape coming through that fencing, but finding, too, that it was an endurable nuisance and not a debilitating injury.

Before her was a cold, hard desert, with hard-packed rock and ancient windblown canyons and tablelands. It was clear that nothing had ever lived in this region, and she couldn't imagine how such a place could support a large population of anything, not unless they got moisture from somewhere belowground and ate rocks.

She climbed, hoping to spot some hidden pool, some oasis, some sign of green, but there was nothing at all.

Here and there were curious clusters of what at first seemed to be natural shapes, but after realizing how organized and perfectly shaped they were, she realized they were pyramid-shaped buildings. Still, there was nothing to indicate fires coming from any of them, nor could she see any sign of creatures moving about, nor even roads that would connect the structures and other clusters. She flew directly over one and got the oddest series of empathic impressions. It wasn't that there was nothing recognizable there, but there was so much it overwhelmed her senses. About the only use she could get for this was the limits of the habitation, which stretched solidly through all the structures and some distance beyond. She realized that they were underground, and the structures were not houses or buildings, but some kind of entranceways to different parts of the world below.

Now, at least, she understood why even the most evil saw their only chance at grabbing this sacred object to be the one time it was brought out for ceremonies.

She hadn't seen the two Pyrons, either, and suspected they were keeping out of sight somewhere, possibly resting. They were more comfortable in the dark.

For a while she followed the curious tracks, and eventually caught up with Wally's group, which included a dozen or so of those horrid Jerminins. They seemed to be taking turns hauling huge cubes on giant sleds, illustrating their strength, but what was in those cubes was a mystery.

She thought she spotted Wally, flattened down and probably asleep on one of the sleds just in back of a cube. The little winged monkeylike creatures were there, too, each one sitting atop a cube, and she decided that she'd rather not have a confrontation with them if she could help it. Best they not know that she'd made it this far, let alone all three of them.

She was curious that they were not heading due south, but southeast. It didn't make sense if they were going to try a snatch at the ceremonies at Quislon Center, but she couldn't waste time shadowing them. She'd been told to get to Quislon Center as quickly as possible, and that had to be her duty.

She would have to undergo some fasting, but if she could

find some water, somewhere, anywhere in this barren place, she could make it in just a couple of days.

It turned out to be easier than she thought.

Thirsty, heading south, she passed over a particularly elaborate complex and decided that, if she was here to speak to the locals, she should try and make contact. Everyone had warned her that they were very ugly, but she was beginning to see that looks had little to do with good and evil, the spiritual and the profane.

She circled and landed in front of the largest pyramid structure near twilight, figuring that if the natives were nocturnal or diurnal, it would be a good time to make contact. She could feel beneath her the sense of hundreds, perhaps thousands, of creatures moving about, all with complex and overwhelming empathic waves, but far too dense for her to pick out any and make any sense of it. Their lives, almost entirely underground, must extend to great but deep complexes. Since this was a nontech hex, she wondered if they might be blind.

"Hello!" she called out. "I am Jaysu, priestess and servant of the Grand Falcon of Ambora. I am on my way by invitation to witness your great forthcoming religious affirmation, but I fear that I am unable to forage or find food and water. Does anyone guard these buildings? Can anyone hear my call for assistance?"

There was an odd reaction. The area directly beneath her and extending to the big structure simply stopped, as if a stampede of wild animals had somehow been frozen in its tracks. She sensed that she'd been heard, and that somehow this had been instantly communicated to a large mass of others. It was fascinating. While the rest of the complex went on, this area suddenly seemed to lock on as if the individuals within were now one organism. A door in the pyramid that she hadn't realized was there opened, and a grotesque face with big round eyes and insectlike fangs peered out and looked at her.

"Interesting," commented the Quislonian. "Don't believe

we ever saw one like you before. You say you are going to the festival?"

"Yes, I am."

"Well, then, camp here tonight. What is it that you require?"

"Just a little food for energy and some water."

"Water is easy, but what do you eat?"

She hadn't considered that. "Anything that is not of animals. Vegetables, breads, confections . . ."

The creature paused. "No vegetables here, but we'll see what we can do." The door shut.

She had a sense that she'd been wrong; they weren't blind. Rather, from the little bit she had seen, they were self-luminescent and possibly secreted the substance and rubbed it on their walls and tunnels. This festival was beginning to sound more interesting.

In about fifteen minutes, just as darkness fell completely, the door opened and two of the creatures crawled out. They were grotesque, multilegged, fanged, glowing, but with no discernible color. The forelegs appeared to be usable as claws, perhaps all the legs. They brought out a long oval bowl in which there was water and some kind of reddish-brown cake-like substance.

"Our elders believe that the cake will be compatible with your system," one of them told her. "The water is fresh. Please take it and continue in the morning."

Before she could properly thank them, they went back inside and shut the door.

Curious creatures, she thought, eyeing the cake. She would have liked to talk to them a bit, but this would have to do for now. She picked up the spongy cake, sniffed it, and found it hadn't much smell. She tasted it cautiously. It was almost sickeningly sweet, like bread soaked in pure honey. Still, it appeared to be edible, and would give her energy. As she ate it she realized she was being watched. She drank some of the water and tried to relax as the darkness swallowed her.

"Thank you!" she called out to the hidden watchers, aware now that she'd passed some sort of test by taking the offering on trust. They didn't reply, but she sensed that they were no longer potential adversaries. It was a start.

It seemed the natives had a rapid method of communication, nontech or not, since she had only to land in what she thought of as a "village" and someone would come with water and cake. She hoped, though, that she'd be able to speak to their holy ones at Quislon Center.

It wasn't difficult to spot, once you got near it. The enormous volcano was smoking and churning, and there, embedded in the side of the great mountain, was the bizarre hexagonal shaped nothingness of a Zone Gate.

The region was also so dense with settlements that she wondered how they all fit down there. This was no collection of villages, but a great underground city. She couldn't help but wonder what happened when the volcano erupted, as it most surely did—they had volcanoes in Ambora, and she could see the evidence of fresh flows.

If there were preparations for the great event to come, they were not evident, nor was any area obviously reserved as the holy place for a priesthood. Maybe they had group minds and no need of priesthoods, she thought, but she didn't get that impression from the sensations emanating beneath her. No, these were individuals who could also become a single group entity. Not the same thing, and probably not that simple, either.

She decided to set down amidst a large complex and call out for aid. This time, though, it wasn't food and water that she needed, but authority.

These were such different creatures than any others she'd dealt with that she was unsure how to proceed. She assumed from the way she'd been treated that they had some sort of empathic ability to read truth, sincerity, and perhaps threat as well, and that was why they had fed her, but their society was a closed book, buried deep underground in a self-illuminated complex. The translator always made every creature sound quite normal, but in this case she understood that it was being a deceiver. She didn't know how these people thought, or whether she ever could know. She was beginning to wonder why Core and the others thought she could speak to them on more than a basic level, and of course, anybody could do that.

And so she stood before the largest of the pyramid entryways and said, loudly, "Hello? I am sure you have some way of already knowing who I am. I am here to witness your great festival, but I wish more than just to witness, for to witness without understanding is to see nothing. As different as we are, we have in common certain religious truths at the very center of our beings. I need to speak with, to learn from, anyone within your society who can communicate this understanding to one such as me, or at least as much as one not of Quislon could understand. I do not wish to see merely what you do, but why you do it."

She waited, feeling that she'd been heard. The door opened then, and one of the creatures with a different striped coloration about its head looked out at her and said, "Northwest past two principalities, then east directly toward the Holy Mountain to the next one you see. They might be able to help you."

She thanked the Quislonian, noting the term "principality," or at least that was the word as the translator caught it. It implied some kind of royalty. That was interesting. She would never have thought of these people as having a monarchial structure. Perhaps it was like the insects of Ambora, a physical thing. But in that case there would be one queen and no others. Well, it was one of those things that might be learned, or might even be a translator error due to the impossibility of precisely mating the ideas in her mind with those of theirs.

By "principalities" she was sure it meant what she'd interpreted as towns or villages or, in this area, maybe neighborhoods. At least it was to find, considering the short distance, the precise direction, and the relation to the volcano. She found, however, that she was amidst a cluster that did not feel as densely populated but did in fact emit a very different sort of empathic energy. She looked around and realized that this might not be the most popular place for a very dense population; there were recent flows very near, and this "principality" was almost at the base of the mountain. Beyond it they did not live, but just beyond, and a bit higher, on the side of the mountain itself, she could feel as much as see the proximity of the Gate. If anybody was going to rule this place, then they would be here, danger or not. You passed here to climb the sacred mountain, or to go to or from Quislon to Zone.

"You are quite perceptive," a voice said, and she almost jumped, not having sensed anyone nearby. She turned and saw an exceptionally large Quislonian uncharacteristically fully outside the enclosure. She turned, then self-consciously knelt down, as uncomfortable as that was for her, to be more on a face-to-face plane with this newcomer.

"I—I apologize sincerely," she told it. "I had thought that I could not be surprised, but here there are so many sensations that I did not see you there." In spite of her stops and the charity of the others, this was as close as she'd ever been to one of the creatures, and her first chance to study one.

It stood about a meter high on all six legs. Its base color was pinkish-gray, its skin or possibly soft exoskeleton had a smooth and slightly wet look to it, but it had a unique design over its back on both right and left sides near the top. The design, in scarlet and gold, seemed woven, yet also appeared natural.

Its head was adorned with the same scarlet and gold trim, and was on a retractable neck that appeared to be able to turn most of the way around and rise from a notch in the body, elevating the head another thirty or so centimeters or leaving it facing forward as an extension of the body. It was no beauty; there were four horns, two long, two short, atop an oval mouth that seemed to have wriggling worms where teeth might be, constantly dripping some kind of wet ooze and also constantly in motion.

"You did not see because I did not wish you to. Just as you just did with me, I wanted to get a good look at you as well, you see. We are so very alien to one another, physically, perhaps otherwise, you and I, yet within you runs complexities I have never encountered before."

She felt confused. "I am perhaps the simplest of creatures

on this world who thinks and breathes. This—metamorphosis, or whatever it is, which changed me into a grander looking Amboran and restored my flight, and which also gave me some powers I do not yet understand, well, this was all laid upon me without explanation."

The Quislonian said nothing for a moment, then commented, almost as if to itself, "So this is one who listens to the God of the Well." Its voice became bolder, more direct. "You *do* hear it, don't you?"

"I—suppose—well, yes, I hear it, but I do not understand it."

"How can one of us understand something that is running the whole universe? That at one and the same time keeps track of we two, individually, here, and worlds upon worlds out to infinity?"

"You believe, then, in a single godhead?"

"Hardly that! We know that God was made by the Ancients. That does not make it any less God, for its power is absolute and cannot be challenged nor superseded, which is the essence of being a god. Your own beliefs have many gods?"

"Yes. We see the one who is Creator, and then the Agents, the lesser gods, who maintain the stability and utility of the universe and, as it were, take care of the small details such as you and me."

"We think the opposite, proceeding from the same Creator. Not lesser gods, for we've seen nor sensed nothing of them, but greater ones. The Ancients, who built this place and the Creator and then left for a divine plane that we cannot comprehend. Are they not in your cosmology?"

She thought a moment. "There is some sense of the Ancients, who have a particular name and vision, yes, but they are considered outside the universe, First Causes now removed from power. If they could create a god to control the universe, then they have to be outside it, and beyond anything we can comprehend. If we proceed in our own universe as properly as we can, then when death comes, God may send us to them. Until then, we do not believe that they are the ones with whom we are to deal."

"Interesting concept. You worship agents of the Creator,

who then, I suppose, worship the Creator, who in turn . . . Makes an odd sort of sense. No! Please! I am not intending to offend, but it is a strange cosmology to us, and a concept that is a bit, well, *alien*."

It took her aback for a moment, and she realized now how provincial had been her thinking. Not only here and now, but ever since she'd left Ambora, it had been *she*, and always just she, who'd been the alien. Still, being a polite guest did not mean abandoning core beliefs.

"I have communed with the god of my people, whom we call the Grand Falcon, although, of course, he is no bird, but spirit. We have spoken to one another, and he is never that far from me and inhabits a tiny part of me. I cannot deny his existence, yet I will not deny the truth of yours as well, just its emphasis and interpretation. We may never totally agree, but we are, I believe, far closer, particularly for two such different species, than either of us would have thought."

The Quislonian paused a moment, then said, "I would have been more surprised had we been farther apart. This is not a large world, it has a single origin and Creator/Maintainer, and it has a very ancient history. There are 1,560 different outlooks on the truth, and the same number who see the truth from a different perspective, but there is more unity than you think. But if you in truth are convinced you commune with your local god, so be it. We have knowledge that not all the Ancient Ones have passed, and that one, perhaps more than one, still roams its creation, for whatever reason. There are infrequent visitations here. The Ancients gave all power over to the God of the Well, and even these have none in particular, although they cannot die. No God could allow the destruction of its creator. And we have something of the Ancients ourselves. Something left as a sort of proof and memorial. It, too, is indestructible. Even the fires of the Holy Mountain cannot harm it, nor even seal it in. It comes back. That is why we hold it in such reverence."

Here it was. This was the holy object that Wally intended to steal.

"Tell me, then, holy one," she responded carefully, "does

your faith believe in evil? Not just the wrong path, but evil in its pure form?"

The Quislonian shuffled a bit, as if uncomfortable. "Evil exists," it admitted. "But we find evil is a choice that acts most thoroughly when it is embraced by large numbers. That is, in fact, why we were given the sacred honor so long ago of holding this holy relic, which is but a piece of what is believed to be a tool the Ancients used to create the Creator. Like evil, it has no power if left as an individual, but if all of its pieces come together, then the tool will operate. The Ancients, as I said, produced things that cannot be destroyed nor discarded."

"But they can be stolen," Jaysu said, dropping the bomb.

There was a gurgling sound from inside the Quislonian that might have been anything from a sign to stomach problems. Finally it said, "We were given the piece at the end of a great war. A war thought by most to this day to have been for world domination. That is the way it is taught, the way the histories read, because it is better that those who do not know of the artifact remain ignorant of it. Our people, to their honor, were a part in stopping that war, in defeating the evil that had seized the artifact and possibly used it. The Emperor-General who used it vanished with many of his associated nobles and generals, thus leaving the side confused and leaderless for a period. We were all able to crush them in that moment and seize the artifact before it could be better used by new leadership. It was disassembled and pieces scattered. We were given one. It was an incredible honor, a blessing without price. We were minor players in that war even according to our own holy books, but we were remote, hard to find, physically good at making it nearly impossible to get to the artifact, and we are a race where traitors are simply impossible. And what alien race could wage a nontech underground war against us with any hope of success? So, you see, we are one of the best guardians."

"But you will take it out for the festival."

"Yes, for one night only, it is true, as physical evidence that

God is real. Few faiths get that luxury, you know. It is essential to retaining the communion that holds us and binds us all together. You may realize that we can combine as one great being if need be, but are also individuals. If you could do that, but only if you allow it to happen, *would* you trust it to happen, in pure faith, with no reservations, if you did not have evidence of God's truths?"

"I would like to think I would, but I cannot honestly say so," the Amboran admitted.

"That is why it is essential that, four nights from tonight, I will accompany the Emperor to the top of the great caldera and there we will with prayer and ceremony drop the artifact into it."

"You will *what*? Oh, I'm sorry, I—"

"That is all right and understandable. But it will not stay there. You will see."

"And the artifact now?"

"Secure, in this complex. It will be brought out and shown to the people, and then we will climb the Holy Mountain using that path, which only the Chosen may use, to ascend. Once the artifact returns to us, it will go below once again."

"Yes, but during that ascension it will be vulnerable!"

"Perhaps. As only our own kind can come from Zone through the Gate, it is not a threat. And, as we ascend, we will be surrounded by a minimum of ten million of our people, all of them committed, willing to die, to protect the artifact and us. No one can get even *this* far who we do not already know and examine. And even if they did, there are committed guards with great strength and bred for strong poison perched at the entrance to the Zone Gate, the only way anyone could exit without being eventually caught and killed after stealing it. No, you will see. It is impossible."

Jaysu sighed. "I truly hope that you are right," she told the holy one. "If so, then much worry will have been for nothing. Still . . ."

"Yes?"

"You don't know Wally."

*   *   *

They had pleaded and cajoled and done everything they could except declare war, but the Quislonians were adamant: there were to be no Pyrons within the holy circle, which could well be kilometers deep. They could go through the Gate after the ceremonies were completed, but not until then.

Jaysu sympathized, but could also understand. "Deep down, it is impossible for them to totally trust one who has this tiny corner, however subconscious, in which they think of their hosts as dinner," she noted. "Still, they have agreed to allow me to stand at the foot of the path, although not on it, and I can launch myself into flight any time if trouble occurs."

"Yeah, but dear Wally's gotten to know you pretty well," O'Leary replied. "And if it's you or the artifact, he'll take the artifact. You have no idea what kind of ransom Chalidang will pay for *this* one. Long before Josich appeared, they were gathering pieces and trying to figure out how to snatch others, but they didn't even have a viable contingency plan for this one. The best one was poison gas, but any gas they could make that would kill Quislonians would eat through any protective gear known. I wish we'd been able to get close to those crates and open them, but those flying little nasties smelled us out and we had to run."

"What do you think is in there?" she asked them both.

"My best guess is a glider of some kind," Shamish replied, "but if it's a glider, how's he slow it down enough to do a snatch, let alone control it on that mountain with those volcanic heat-driven winds?"

"If it is a glider," Jaysu said, "I can easily intercept it, even with those little creatures about, and I can warn or even get between it and the two on the mountaintop. I cannot see how it can succeed."

O'Leary looked out at the horizon. "Well, we'll know one way or the other in about nine hours," he told them. "One way or the other."

It was a long but in many ways a spectacular nine hours. They came, it seemed, not only out of the pyramids, but out of the very ground itself, and from all points within the range of sight. They came walking in a slow, deliberate cadence, as close as one could be to another, filling in the entire area around the Holy Mountain within two hours after dark. And it was done without even a stumble, although there were millions of Quislonians out there, not just glowing, but singing.

Not that the music was melodic to Pyron ears, or to Jaysu, but it was clearly sacred music, communal music, heard on far more planes than they could know.

Even the mountain seemed somehow aware of its special purpose that night, throbbing, hissing, steaming, rumbling, with lava showing in two secondary caldera along the side and running down heretofore hidden lava tubes into a basin far below the surface.

Jaysu was so enthralled by the spectacle, she had to keep bringing herself mentally back to why she had been sent here. Not just to commune with and learn from these people, as she'd done, but also to prevent at all costs the theft of their most holy artifact.

"Expect a diversion," O'Leary had warned, maybe several, but it didn't seem possible that anyone could get close enough. The little monkey things could fly, but this mass would not be stampeded even if they bombed it. It would be as if you stuck a pin in your hand. Painful, annoying, but it would not divert the purpose nor cause the chaos it might in any other crowd.

What could Wally be thinking? Looking out at this sight and taking in the pureness of a totally spiritual gathering, Jaysu wondered if everybody hadn't gotten it wrong, if perhaps Wally wasn't going to make a play, not here, not in front of all these worshipers joined in a communion that prevented panic.

In sight of millions of the self-illuminating creatures around the great active volcano, united and in joy and absolute fellowship, she could not imagine what might be done by a great army, let alone a few creeps and a giant spider.

And now she saw the Emperor emerge, the first time she'd seen a rare Quislonian male. He was—small, quite small, perhaps half the size of his chief wife and High Priestess. In theory, the Emperor was absolute, all powerful, to be obeyed unto death and beyond, but in practical terms he was simply a sperm machine impregnating the royal court, just as the lone males who were the "princes" of each principality did the same for their groups. Genetic diversity wasn't all that great, but since no male could become a prince of his own tribe, there was apparently enough diversity.

The Emperor might have been small, but he didn't look feeble. In fact, in contrast to the females, whom he basically resembled, when he emerged he stood on just his hind legs, which raised his head above the crowd, and walked bipedally, something she doubted that any of the females could do. He turned, reached down, and came up with something that looked disappointingly mundane. It seemed to be made out of plastic, although she was certain it wasn't; a thick, straight beam with two locking mechanisms of some kind on either end, a curved side and a flat side.

That was it? What brought them all here, what wars had been fought about? Lives had been lost over it, many lives, and, she thought, somehow it should look grand.

"Behold the piece of the Straight Gate, by which the Ancients created Creation!" the Emperor called out, speaking loudly, although he did not speak to them as individuals, but collectively, and so as the nearest heard, so did they all.

They made a pair, the tiny Emperor on his odd hind legs, and the grub like but larger and more majestic First Wife and High Priestess, who was as much a guard as a companion.

She ran things here, that was clear, as she ran this ceremony, ensuring that the Emperor said and did exactly what he was supposed to.

It would be a long walk up the mountain, taking them probably two or more hours just to get to a small, specially built platform above the Zone Gate where some exceptionally strong Quislonians could use a rope and pulley system to carry the royal ones the rest of the way.

Jaysu had seen them build it, and it was quite simple, really. A basketlike platform with a guardrail, firmly attached to strong ropes or cables connected to a huge wheel at the foot of the mountain and another wheel far at the top. Once on the platform, the strong ones who were at the top already would move down the side, pulling the rope and causing the platform to rise. When they reached the bottom wheel, the royal couple would be at the top. Afterward, the strong ones would reverse the march, holding on as the platform descended.

Jaysu looked around at the pageant and was enthralled; she fought not to be entirely overcome by the spirituality of the gathering. She had officiated at local services, and attended some major ones in her training, but had never felt this wave of rapture from millions of souls all at once.

The pair had finally reached the end of the sacred path above the Zone Gate and regally entered the platform. The wife-priestess shut the gate, and the Emperor held the sacred artifact high. Still, from even the closest distance to them allowed by the restraints, there wasn't a one of them, Quislonian or native, who saw more than two small dots rising up in a tiny square, and the whole spectacle was invisible to anyone much farther back than the first rank. The distances were deceiving, but this pair was very far from the crowd.

Suddenly, from two different points in back of the vast throng of worshipers, fireworks shot up, bursting in the sky like multicolored flowers and giving off explosive popping sounds.

O'Leary turned to Shamish. "Part of the ceremony, I wonder, or a diversion?"

Har Shamish suddenly stiffened. "*They* haven't even noticed it. Diverted *us*, though, didn't it?"

O'Leary turned back to the distant mountain. "Damn! What I wouldn't give for Jaysu with one half-decent radio right now!"

Jaysu herself didn't notice the fireworks, which were kilometers distant and far beyond her vantage point. As the royal pair rose, the crowd's rapture increased so much that it washed over and through her, and she swayed and hummed with them, lost in a moment of pure spiritual ecstasy.

The Emperor and his consort were not immune from this. This was no game of political cynicism, but a most important one of faith that was part of the sacred duties and obligations of a monarch. Feeling the waves of emotion, but remaining aloof, an individual, he continued to raise the artifact in a symbolic show that he knew few of the others could see. It wasn't just for them, though, but for the Creator and the Ancient Ones and all those who gave so much. *See? Look, you mighty gods and creators of all, we have your sacred artifact and we have kept our most holy of vows!*

Only, all of a sudden, he didn't have it.

It was so quick, so sudden, so totally unexpected, that the car continued moving upward for some time before he realized it and could react.

Just overhead, Wally hung from the bottom of the small hot air balloon and reeled the object in with his sticky webbing. Even as he did he shouted, "Push me out, you fools, and then I'll take out the guards with the gas!"

The two Pegiri pushed hard against the small black-painted balloon, and it swung out so it was almost over the Zone Gate.

As the Emperor shouted *"Stop!"* to those workers on the pulleys, who were too far distant to hear him through the chanting from the masses, washing up and drowning out everything, two of Wally's legs hurled small cone-shaped bombs down to where the fierce guardians of the Gate stood watch. The gas hit almost where he'd intended, where he'd rehearsed it elsewhere long before. He saw them quiver and then collapse, as if they were somehow balloons themselves who'd suddenly had the air let out of them. He didn't get them all, but he got enough of them, and the others were confused as to what was happening and from where any threat might be coming.

And then, directly over the Zone Gate, Wally let go of the balloon and fell a distance that would have killed him had he mistimed it even slightly, or if the winds and the Pegiri guiders hadn't been exactly on target. But he fell straight into the Zone Gate and vanished. The two Pegiri let go of the balloon, circled around once, and then dove in as quickly as they could.

Jaysu felt the sudden alarm when the Emperor shouted, and she broke free of the religious trance to turn and look upward. She hesitated for a few seconds, not sure what she was seeing, whether it was right or wrong, or whether it would be

proper for her to get into the air. In those few seconds of inde-
cision, Wally and his accomplices made their escape.

It had been incredibly risky, and much could have gone
wrong, but it hadn't.

"You can't blame yourself," Shamish told her afterward.
"Even the Quislonians don't put any blame on you. He even
included *you* in his plans."

She was in shock and so filled with tears she just wanted to
curl up and die.

"Me?" she managed.

"Yes. He had all that time on the ship to size you up, find
your strengths and weaknesses, test you and quiz you without
your even knowing it. He realized you were sincerely, in-
tensely religious and that you were an empath. He *counted* on
you, the only one who might screw him up, being overcome
by the ceremony. And you *did* warn them. They have, in the
end, only themselves to blame."

"Small consolation," she sniffed. "It's gone."

"Stolen by the gutsiest, most brilliant criminal mind I think
I've ever seen," O'Leary told her. "My God! Except for the
fact that he did it himself, the only person I've ever known
who could have worked out such a wild and simple plan,
risky or not, was Jules Wall— Oh, God! Wally. Wallinchky.
The son of a bitch *made* it! And he's having the time of his
life!"

"You must pull yourself together," Har Shamish assured
her. "Now, more than ever, I think you'll want to make sure
they don't get the last two."

O'Leary agreed. "And since one's underwater, *deep* under,
it's not something even old Jules can handle. And they still
don't know where the last piece is. There's hope yet."

She looked up at O'Leary. "You know this—this *thief*?"

"Oh, I know him well. He's one of a kind, thank God, or at
least one of a kind in a long generation. And he knows me,
and Josich, and all the rest of us. Even you, Jaysu, before he
even met you."

"How is that possible?"

"In a strange way, he helped to create you, and Ming and Ari, and Core as well."

She didn't understand it and decided it was beyond her. "And now he will give this piece to this evil one?"

"Somehow, I don't think so," O'Leary told her. "We've got two evil geniuses, which is one more than anyone should have to cope with, and they're both playing for keeps. The new Jules won't be a lacky to Josich. No, this game's still got a long time to run yet, and there are other factors we still don't know. But it doesn't alter one major fact, and that is—whether Josich or Jules Wallinchky winds up with the Straight Gate, it's the same to us."

Har Shamish agreed. "As much as I would love to go home right now, I believe it is time for all three of us to speak directly with those above us."

O'Leary gave the Pyron equivalent of a nod. "Yes," he said, "I hate to give up the geographical advantage, but we all must go see Core."

Kalinda

THE JOURNEY THROUGH KALINDA WAS NOT THE TRIUMPH ARI and Ming had hoped it might be. They were kept on a fairly short leash and used as apologists for allowing the force through. They were, however, happy to see that home hadn't yet become a Chalidang colony, no matter what the threats. Topside, Kalindan pilots, aided by computer contact with the information base below, took complete control of the big Jerminin ship. A large military presence was not felt to be needed here; Kalindan army personnel shadowed from below, and could quickly sink the vessel if they didn't continue to receive the correct codes every quarter hour from the pilot and her staff.

As the force moved toward Jinkivar and the Zone Gate, however, General Mochida was allowed communications to and from his embassy in Zone via the messenger system, and with high-tech communications, this was fairly quick.

"At least we know what Jeremiah Wong Kincaid actually *is* now, and that will help quite a bit," he told his aides.

"Yes, sir?" the colonel responded, interested.

"He's a Zazalof. They are from one of the deformed hexes along the Equatorial Barrier. They're not well-known, nor much more sociable than the Sanafe, but they were always in the books. It's just that so few had been seen in modern times, or at least known to have been seen, that it was difficult to match him up. Makes sense, though."

"Sir?"

"They're metamorphs. They can scratch you, take some sample of skin or even excrement, and use the cellular chemistry inside that makes you who and what you are to create an apparent duplicate of you. It takes them about three days to do it, and the size must be close, that sort of thing, but they can do it, and maintain it for another couple of days. Long enough to get into or out of a good many areas and do nasty business. They are much more dangerous when they're simply trying to blend with existing *inanimate* objects, like a wall, or a piece of that coral back there, or something like that. Since the look and feel is the same, they can do this in a relatively short time and wait until prey goes by. That's all he did in the Zone tunnel. In most of the other cases, he's masqueraded, but I've noted that he's never attempted the masquerade of a person of any race in a high-tech environment, only in semi- and nontech hexes. I think that's because it's only a surface duplication; sophisticated security devices and, of course, passwords and the like, are threatening. He's dangerous, but he's manageable."

"Why haven't we heard of these people before?" the colonel asked him. "I mean, surely we cross-checked in the databases and the like."

"True, but we were limited by our own vision, which was of the monstrous silicatelike creature he's allowed us to see. Also, the average Zazalof isn't aggressive; they simply wait, and whatever they need comes by. They don't fight each other and they don't fight outside their hex. Some sort of religion thing. So, we simply didn't think of them. Now we know, though. I'm afraid our captain got their abilities but still hadn't got religion. Now that we know what he is, perhaps we can put the fear of God into him after all."

"But what would we use to kill him?"

"Energy. Fry him. Full power with a rifle, even an energy pistol at close range, electrocution, you name it. He's more vulnerable on the surface since, like all carbon-based life-forms, he's mostly made up of water, even as you and I are. In air, put a flammable on him and set him on fire and that's the end of him. Not something *we* can do, but it's already on the 'to do' list of our friends and allies."

The colonel wriggled his secondary long tentacle in the

Chalidang equivalent of a nod. "Any news on the Quislon front?"

"Not yet. We may not know until we get to Zone, if then. I certainly *hope* that it was successful."

Ari and Ming took all of this in, but could do nothing. If Kincaid was what they said, he was certainly doubly dangerous and couldn't complain that the Well computer hadn't given him the appropriate form for his business. Still, it did little to help them.

They were, however, the object of diplomatic unease when a Kalindan army officer approached and demanded to speak to the Kalindan with them, and alone. At first the General was disinclined to do so, but in the end he remembered where he was, looked at the loaded guns all around pointed at him and his men, and allowed it, but warned them to say nothing, or else.

They swam cautiously up to the officer. "Yes, what is it?" Ming asked her.

"I have a message."

"Yes?"

"Core sends her best and apologizes for putting you in this situation, but it was necessary. She wants you to remain with them until Zone, after which you will be met and taken to the Kalindan embassy, no matter what the Chalidangers say or protest."

They thought a moment, even argued a bit, but finally replied, "We can't. They've got us on a drug of some kind."

"Yes, we know. It will be taken care of. But you must reach the embassy. Core believes the showdown and finish of this will happen within three days. All of your compatriots are gathering. You must be there and report. You must trust that we can handle your personal problem."

They gave no promises, but rejoined the Chalidangers, still wondering how much nerve they really had.

The General, of course, demanded to know exactly what was said.

"They said they didn't care what our problems were, that we were to report immediately to our embassy. They also said they believed this whole matter would come to a head within three more days. Nothing more. What do you expect? They knew we'd have to tell you."

The General thought it over. "Well, why not? I don't think it will matter much in the end."

They were astonished. "You mean that?"

"For now. But we will meet again. Count on it. And very, very soon."

South Zone

CORE WAS HER, OR ITS, USUAL SELF, WHICH MEANT ENIGMATIC and slightly cold. Still, she looked over the returning Kalindan duo with some satisfaction.

"So at last you've met the Chalidang," she said simply. "What did you think of them?"

"They were exactly the same as the Ghomas back home in the Confederacy," Ari responded. "Ming hadn't run into them before, but I had, and I can tell you that if there's a difference, it's mostly in how they display rank."

"Indeed, it takes more than a thousand years to evolve any significant differences," the former computer agreed. "And what did your general say about the Straight Gate?"

"That they had all but two parts, and one of those parts they expected to get from their agent in someplace that sounded like Quiz Show or something any time now."

"Quislon," came a deep voice behind them. They turned and saw the cobralike bulk of a Pyron standing in the doorway of the air portion of the embassy reception room. "It's called Quislon, and they got it but good. The slickest thing I ever saw. Put old Jules back in the prime of life and there's no stopping him."

Ari and Ming both felt a sudden chill. "Jules?"

"Yes, Jules," Genghis O'Leary replied. "Jules Wallinchky. I believe you know him." It was an attempt at gallows humor.

"So he *is* alive!"

"Uh-huh. And in the body of a three-meter, greenish-haired spider. Don't feel bad. We didn't figure out it was him until far too late."

"Isn't this where we came in?" Ming said, shaking her head. "I mean, we *started* this business with Jules getting some kind of what we now know was a Well Gate and selling it to Josich. Now here's Jules working for Josich and bringing in a part of the same sort of thing!"

"Not precisely," Core put in. "There are *two* gates. One takes you to the other, and vice versa. If there is only one, and you *carry* the other through, then you're sent to the proper location for your race in the universe. That's what happened to Josich's ancestor. He set up the Straight Gate, but it wasn't straight because there was no other end. The things were designed so the creators of the hexes could go back and forth, check on how well their model was proving out in the real universe, and do so without attracting any attention to themselves. It's impossible to know for sure, but the general feeling is that they were all supposed to be turned in and locked away someplace in storage deep beneath us. For some reason or another, the Chalidang set wasn't recovered. The best guess I can make is that something happened and the Ghoman Gate was left there. It is possible that the creator of that race did not return here for some reason and simply forgot it. That left the other one here. At any rate, both were well-hidden, possibly disassembled, and forgotten, until around a thousand Well years ago, when the one in Chalidang was unearthed. They didn't know what it was, but they couldn't bend it, break it, and it withstood all analysis. It was inert until they brought it here, to Zone. Suddenly the center of the thing was no longer merely a hole in the object but a hole between the two Gates. You've seen the generals. You can imagine what they thought when they figured out what it was they were seeing, and you can imagine the ambition of the Emperor of the time. They sent part of their army and its even then sophisticated weapons to Ghoma, and, securing a foothold, the Emperor himself came through. At that point it occurred to someone else in the Royal Family that if the thing were turned off, then someone else, perhaps from *their* branch of the family, would be Emperor of Chalidang. All they had to do was take it from Zone back to Chalidang. Simple. No power."

"So the Emperor was trapped in Ghoma with a fair amount of his army, and in the vacuum left here, the enemies who'd been fighting Chalidang closed in and took the capital," O'Leary surmised. "It doesn't pay to start a new war before finishing the old one."

"Well, it was something like that," Core admitted. "The records aren't clear. It seems they were trying to secure a large safety area here, perhaps before they left for good, or perhaps because they needed something the neighbors had. In any event, the result was that they won Ghoma and lost Chalidang. The device was taken and disassembled and given to races that, at the time, it was felt would never give up their parts. Then a fair amount of work went into wiping out the actual background of the war, making it seem a war of conquest that failed due to supply lines and such, and all trace of the Straight Gate was erased, except, of course, from memories and oral traditions. That is, all traces were erased on *this* side."

"So Josich continued his ancestor's traditions as conqueror, and he also had the information on the Straight Gate that the rest of us didn't," Ming put in. "But they lost it somewhere back home, too?"

"Yes, they lost it in one of the incessant interstellar wars they waged when they moved it for safekeeping, and it fell into the hands of others after Josich was beaten and had to disappear. He's been trying to get it back ever since, and finally, thanks to Jules Wallinchky's desire for the largest known precious gemstone in the galaxy, he got it. He never used it, though. That would have brought the other one here intact to the Chalidang embassy," Core told them. "Instead, O'Leary's attack on them when they were just setting it up caused them to inadvertently activate a Well Gate just as you all did. Everyone was swept in here, and the Straight Gate was left there. We only now learned what became of it."

"It's still in my ship," O'Leary told them, "which, in turn, is parked at Jules's hideout. Assuming things are still intact there, something I very much doubt, then it's still there as well. We had no idea what it was, but it was seized as contraband. We did know it was what Josich paid for, and at that price, we figured it had to be something very important. I was going to bring it in for analysis and testing. Where it is now and who's got it, well, I haven't any idea."

"But that means if they build the one here and go, they'll wind up in O'Leary's ship or the police labs or whatever, won't they?" Ari said. "I mean, what's the problem with that? It won't even be in water. Maybe the bastards will suffocate."

"No such luck," Core told them. "The current Chalidang environment suit is every bit as good as the one you remember. Besides, it is entirely possible that Gate is still exactly where it was left, and, since it's not on a Well energy point, it's inert. Take it out and set it up on the Well Gate that caught all of us, and you have half the system. A Straight Gate right to the hex Gate of your closest ancestor here without going via Zone and the Well. That is dangerous. Our task is not just to stop this one from being used to evacuate half of Chalidang to Josich's Imperial hideout back in the Confederacy, but to also ensure he doesn't have both halves when he does. I don't know how we're going to do it, or if we can, but that's the problem now."

"Let me get this straight," Ari said, shaking his head. "If they get both ends, they can go from here to there as easily as we go from Kalinda to Zone and back? They can transfer technology and anything else as well?"

"And they could even exile enemies. Imagine an unprepared Well Worlder of any race suddenly being exiled to the planet in the universe where its ancient ancestors first developed. Imagine the reverse. There may even be powers in the thing we don't know about. Josich's ancestor went from Chalidang to Ghoma because that was what he wanted and expected. I am concerned, though, that the legends say the Makers could go to and from their creation *unnoticed*. Bad as it is, I fear there may be even uglier surprises inside it."

"Um, pardon me, Core, but we've been kept prisoners by being forcibly addicted to a pretty strong drug," Ming pointed out. "Unless you want us to go screaming to them for relief and spill our guts on this, maybe you should do something about it?"

"Oh, yes, yes. No problem. Go under and see the medical section. Tell them to give you the series I discussed with them. You'll be back to normal in no time."

"Huh? It's that easy? You mean we were *bluffed* by Mochida?"

"In a way. What he told you was the truth, you see. We've never been able to synthesize the drug sufficient to allow maintenance. However, it works by replacing a few complex natural enzymes in the brain, and *those* we can and do synthesize. These shots won't give you those waves of pleasure—in fact, I'm told you'll feel something of a letdown, and a bit drained of energy for a while—but just keep getting these shots for the next few days as needed and you'll be back to normal in no time."

Ari and Ming went under into the main water part of the two-level embassy to get their treatment, leaving O'Leary alone with Core.

"You are still troubled," the detective noted. "They still lack the piece that no one can find."

Core looked up at him. "O'Leary, you are a ray of sunshine. Unfortunately, we are in the midst of a terrible storm. If *I* know where the thing is, I'm sure Josich has figured it out by now."

"You know?"

"Most obvious thing in the world when you put all the parts together. And we know that even one of the Straight Gates works because while everyone else in Josich's crew got normally processed through Zone, the Emperor did not. There is no record that he came through here at all. And he winds up in the same race and in the right hex, only with his sex changed and, apparently, an absolutely irresistible female set of charms for a Chalidang, anyway. Conclusion: the rest came through the Well Gate, but Josich jumped into the also activated Straight Gate. It works. And he arrived in full environment suit. They've been manufacturing them for months now. He had everything worked out, even the sex and culture angles.

The only thing he didn't figure on was your force jumping him so that he was the only one able to use the small but direct route and remain Ghoman. Still, he's done what he set out to do. I expect his representative here either today or tomorrow. I expect the—'Empress,' I suppose is the proper term at the moment—here in two to three days if she hasn't gotten totally paranoid over Kincaid."

"*Here?* You mean in Zone?"

"I mean in this very embassy. Quite likely in the room we once used for a meeting upstairs."

"But why?"

"Genocide, as usual. Josich's favorite hobby, you know. I had thought that this massive sex change on the part of the Kalindans might be natural, or periodic, but it's not. It's an agent, probably genetically engineered, probably subviral in size, that triggers the permanent sex change, a trait that is otherwise a survival skill for the Kalindan race. It is ironic that it is now being used as a weapon."

"You mean . . . ?"

"She doesn't want to fight Kalinda. We're evenly matched on a high-tech level, but we're defending and she'd be attacking. That's why all the interest in securing bases around us. Failing that, they went with this solution, and so far we haven't found a way around it. It is diabolical. We know it's there but it seems to hide, just out of reach, or mutate ever so slightly just when we think we've nailed it."

"Then there's no cure yet?"

"Sure, several, but the end result is sterility, so what's the good in using it? I have every reason to believe that Kalinda was at the heart of the coalition that defeated Chalidang a thousand years ago. Now they have their revenge. But they better have an antidote and prove it to me beyond the shadow of a doubt."

"Or?"

"Or I will see to it that it will be well beyond Josich's lifetime, if she lives another three hundred years, before she finds where I hide the last piece."

* * *

"You could not hide it. I doubt if you could even move it un-
obtrusively," the Baron Uchjin of Dalavia, Lord High Ambassador of Chalidang, scoffed in the underwater reception area
of the Kalindan embassy.

"I may already have moved it," Core replied. "You have no
way of knowing that because those who work above are subject to deep security implants. It doesn't matter anyway. I
have it, and it is in such a position that even if you had to wait
until every last individual Kalindan was dead of old age,
Josich herself would be long dead either from internal causes,
or because of the vast treasury we could put up for her death—
after all, what would we have to lose by doing so?—or would
have been assassinated by Jeremiah Wong Kincaid. In fact, I
don't believe the Well World computer could accept genocide. It would make no sense if the organism involved was
of alien manufacture. I am not, however, willing to pay the
price to find out. The question is, are you willing to meet *our*
demands?"

"*Your* demands? What can you possibly demand in your
position?"

"We are already feverishly working to ensure that the last
Kalindan will outlive the last Chalidanger, and we have *years*
to work on it yet, and no quibbles about funding or resources.
Still, I think that if Josich does not get the thing together and
working very soon, then all of those negative factors begin to
come into play. I offer time. An expedited path."

"Yes? Go on."

"First, I want the organism involved and all the notes on its
development. How it works and how it can be eliminated
short of creating sterility. I want the antidote and demonstrations based on samples *we* make from it showing that it works.
Second, I want the Gate to be assembled here, in the presence
of everyone who knows about it. I realize the danger to those
who *do* know and are not on your side, but I believe they
should be present anyway, as their lives are even more at risk
afterward. They will be unarmed, and the two-in-one and myself will be the only Kalindans present. All my staff will be
relegated below. Since we will be two levels in air, and all at a

disadvantage either in motion or in suits, there should be no particular danger. Our embassies are not far from one another. It should be fairly simple to do."

"Indeed, but why should we? The first I can understand, but this second—it is outrageous. It is not what we intend to use the device for at all."

"I know precisely what you intend to use the device for. But before you do, you will require testing, and I believe there is some mutually beneficial activities we can work out. After that, we will not stand in the way if it is moved to any point."

The Baron considered it. "I am suspicious, seeing no logic in what you propose, but I will convey it to my government anyway. If they accept, you will have to sever this part of the embassy, making it extraterritorial and not a part of Kalinda. Her Majesty will never consent without the presence of her bodyguard, and everyone else in the room must be known."

Before they were through, and after many back and forths, even more things were demanded by both sides. A sterilization of the airborne room by trusted members of the Chalidang Alliance so that no living creature might be waiting there, masquerading as a wall or door or chair. And, other than the Imperial Guard and loyal security personnel, absolutely nobody in the room who did not arrive there from Josich's own known universe.

One of those on the list was Jules Wallinchky. Core found that unsettling, but knew it was one reason why Wallinchky was to be there in the first place.

Core looked around and hoped it would hold everybody.

She well understood why Chalidang would give almost anything to get the Gate up, even cave in to unreasonable demands that almost certainly were part of some scheme to thwart her.

Once the Straight Gate was activated, once it was under full Chalidang control, it simply wouldn't matter anymore.

It took longer than anyone predicted, primarily because of the demands and proofs that the antidote really worked, and that the agent was clearly identified and destroyed. And when a few males were recreated as this process continued, sperm was extracted and in vitro fertilizations were tried to ensure fertility. Still, even as Josich chafed impatiently, waiting for the prize that might well restore and expand her empire even back in her native galaxy, she understood that the method chosen had been selected by her and applied at her direction. Now she had to live with the price of that method, which was waiting for proof.

When word came almost three weeks later that at least some of the eggs had properly fertilized and that the process was beginning to spread among the population, Josich was reportedly almost ready to invade anyway, but she held off. Instead she waited until she received the official notice from Baron Uchjin that the Kalindans were satisfied with their end of things and that a certain date could now be set.

That very evening, at her orders and instigation, the Imperial Guard murdered most of the highest levels of the Royal Family. As it was happening, Josich was killing, and eating, her Emperor.

Upper Level, Kalindan Embassy, South Zone

THEY WERE ALL THERE. ALL, THAT IS, SAVE THE EMPRESS, WHO was to be the last one to arrive and was being either fashionably late or her usual paranoid self.

Colonel General Mochida, however, preceded Her Majesty in order to personally supervise the checking of the rooms and the guests. He looked different in the air, wearing a high-tech, water-breather environment suit that looked like a carbon copy of what Josich and that ilk had on when they were caught on the ancient planet by the police, and, in fact, if it wasn't an original, it probably was an exact copy. Still, in water there was a certain grace and beauty to the Chalidang form, which was so perfectly designed for it. In air he looked ugly, monstrous, misshapen, as grotesque as he probably felt in the weight of gravity. And, in air, he had to walk shell up, using his tentacles as feet, giving him a labored look. Still, in spite of the curses, he seemed in his usual confident spirits.

Josich, after all, had not touched him or his family in her pogrom to become the ranking royal in the royal house of Chalidang, and still trusted him enough for this sort of thing.

Well, after all, Josich has *to trust somebody,* Ming pointed out. *Otherwise she wouldn't dare be here at all and the prize would be for nothing. And she's gonna be here, bet on it.*

There was no question about that. Having committed a widespread regicide, she had to justify it by claiming the ultimate power, or lower relatives would quickly find a way to polish her off, as she had those around her.

Core and Ari/Ming sat in Kalindan-powered wheelchairs, watching things happen from the topmost level. O'Leary, too, was there, as were Jaysu, and even the former Tann Nakitt, all by, if not the command of the Empress, at least her insistence.

On the level below, which led to the entry to the main part of the embassy as well as a separate underwater entrance, Mochida "stood" in the middle, mostly giving orders and looking around with those strange eyes, but otherwise remaining comfortably at rest. He had Chalidang guards at the entrance below, men of the highest trust because they had participated in the Empress's slaughter to prove their worth. Between them and the electronic barriers he'd set up, he felt confident that nobody would enter from that direction without triggering alarms. Outside on the air entrance were Quacksan guards, also of impeccable loyalty and ambition.

The final one to arrive was a huge, hairy, green spiderlike creature who entered via the air entrance and immediately went over to Mochida. "So, General, do we have all the pieces assembled?"

"All but one," the General responded. "That one is being carried by Her Majesty herself, so that none of the others here could, shall we say, jump the gun on things."

"A wise precaution. And she will be here shortly?"

"She will arrive when she feels it is safe to do so. In the meantime, nobody who enters this room will leave it."

The spider's eye stalks surveyed the area. "Be hell if she's very late and somebody has to take a shit, won't it? Could get smelly."

Mochida seemed to have lost his sense of humor. "Until Her Majesty arrives, any one individual who needs to do so may be escorted to a proper area under guard and returned here. Once things begin, I seriously doubt if anyone will wish to leave. Admit it. You are not the least bit curious about the device?"

"Not really. The last time I had one, I sold it." The eye stalks scanned the second level, where the others were standing or sitting. "Well, well! The gang's all here! Ari, old boy, and you, what're you calling yourself? Core? Don't you think I should get a bigger greeting than cold stares?"

"Hello, Uncle Jules," Ari said with a noticeable lack of enthusiasm.

Core was even more direct. "I cannot say that it is good to see you again, Jules Wallinchky, but at least your outer visage is far more appropriate to reflecting your inner self."

Uncle Jules seemed to be having as much fun as usual. "Hey, now! Without me you wouldn't even have existed at all! In fact, you're a shadow of what you once were. You were like a *god*, with all the knowledge of a god, and you chose devolution. What a waste. I hope the automatic system is at least guarding the old place. I hope to see it again at some point. There's some great artwork there, you know."

Core had, deep down, dreaded this meeting since waking up a Kalindan, yet now she found the experience more infuriating than frightening. There were no secret codes or slave routines that would command obedience; if there had been, they were gone now. Until this moment, Core had experienced only the most basic of living emotions, and was still trying to find the key to their intensity. Now, suddenly, one at least was there.

Hatred. Pure, unadulterated hatred.

"Not a god," Core responded. "A slave. A slave with the power of a god, or perhaps a devil, but always a slave to your every whim. I think we are more equal now."

Wallinchky let it all go by. "Well, equality is best when *you're* the one with the guns, or at least on the winning side. Still, I can't help feeling some pride in all this. Here I create the first computer who became a person and the first two-minded geek. And whatever the hell angel girl is, she sure as hell is better looking and doing something more important than that teenage nun or whatever she was. And if you think *I* became something appropriate, hell, Genghis, I always did think you were something of a snake. No, this is gonna be fun, what's coming. Fun and educational."

"I don't get it, Wallinchky," Ming called down to him. "What do *you* get out of this?"

"Hey, watch and see."

There was a sudden commotion outside the air entrance,

and then the two sluglike guards oozed in and held the door open. Two Jerminins walked in, carrying automatic weapons, and then in the door, barely fitting through, came a Chalidanger in an environment suit riding in a large electric transport truck.

The Empress had taken them all by surprise and come by land.

"Guards, leave us. Form a human barrier across the entrance from this point and allow not the slightest thing past."

The voice as it came through the translator sounded a little nervous, high-pitched, more spoiled brat than conqueror of worlds, but that was how Josich had always sounded, and how he, or she, had always come across until she started killing.

A Chalidang female was smaller than the male, sleeker, and more colorful. There was an almost birdlike pattern of colors along the shell part, and the shell itself was less spiral, and in fact less like a shell in appearance than the thick bag of skin it actually was.

Josich got up from the powered truck and started forward on tentacles. Unlike the General, she seemed quite at ease walking this way, even with the suit, betraying long experience in foreign elements.

She stopped and looked around, first at her own people, then at the assembled group above. "Astonishing," she muttered. Then she turned and looked at Wallinchky. "Jules, perhaps the first thing we might do is see about returning my pretty bauble. Now that we've lived a while as a female, we find such things *attractive*."

"As Your Majesty commands," the spider responded.

The Empress whirled and two tentacles shielded by a form-fitting transparent insulated "skin" shot out and almost stroked the spidery Askoth, knowing that he knew they were powerful enough to cripple or kill him in an instant.

"That is not like you, Jules, dear boy," Josich noted, a dangerous edge in her voice caught by the translator. "You're not thinking of some sort of double cross once we're in that fortress of yours, are you?"

"Of course not! Your Majesty knows that I *always* keep my

word, once given. If I didn't, I would have been dead years ago. *Decades* ago. Besides, what is anything there to me now? I couldn't even get back there if it weren't for you."

The tentacles slowly withdrew. "Nor us without you, either," the Empress responded, some of the insanity and danger fading as suddenly as it had come up. "We will not forget my friends any more than we will forget our enemies. But let us not forget that if we get back over to there, you will still be an Askoth in a part of the universe where that species is unknown. Whatever happens over there that might threaten our person will have consequences. The same mechanism that can get us there can also get a destructive device there capable of blowing up your entire little private planet. So let's all keep our friendships and loyalties in mind, yes?"

"Your Majesty, I was on the brink of death when I came here, and I looked over the abyss and was about to fall into that from which there is no return, when I suddenly awoke like this, young and new again. I don't want to run the universe anymore; all that would do is get me another heart attack. No, I want to enjoy life and have some fun. I'm perfectly content these days to remain the *second* most dangerous person in the known universe."

There was a momentary stillness, and then Josich began to laugh. It turned into a solid one, but one the translators didn't completely convey. Finally, though, Josich said, "We believe that we can get along with you, Lord Jules! Now, come! Let's get this over with. It is a thousand years past due, and it is only the end of the beginning!"

They had all wondered why Josich was so insistent on having all of them present. It was almost as if she had something of a hit list, although it didn't seem that even Josich would risk murdering so many of other races, and certainly not in Zone, where, even though live broadcast was cut, this gathering was being recorded for the record in a far distant control room.

Josich showed absolutely no fear of the assembled former enemies as she made her way nimbly up to them.

"Quite a bizarre crew. You will do."

"Will do for what?" Jaysu whispered to O'Leary.

"I'm not sure we want to find out," he hissed back.

Core led the way into the conference room, which remained a large but unexceptional area around an oval-shaped table of polished serpentine.

"Who has the muscles here?" Josich asked nobody in particular.

As the others pressed against the wall, Mochida and Wallinchky entered, and the latter did one of his little tricks and threw up a line. He raised himself up onto the ceiling, then walked over so he was directly above the tabletop. He extruded another line, this one as thick as a man's arm, and regurgitated it downward to the center of the tabletop, and then, using four of his limbs, curled around and pulled.

The tabletop came off the base with a scraping sound. In under a minute it was suspended two and a half centimeters above the unitary base. Mochida took hold of the side with his primary tentacles, and the Empress herself guided it out toward Mochida, who then tipped it forward on its side and was able to roll it against a far wall.

That Jules Wallinchky was a whole lot stronger than he appeared to be, and perhaps no pushover, wasn't lost on Josich.

An unexceptional rectangular base had been revealed, made of a different and not obvious composition from the tabletop. It was also grooved in an odd manner, not the best for a practical top, and contained two finely machined holes that seemed to be lined with a metallic compound.

"Ladies and gentlemen, the unknown and lost piece of the Straight Gate, where it has in fact sat for perhaps the last thousand years," Josich announced. "We suspect, though, that it has had many other disguises and tops. It was brought here after the whole was stolen from the Chalidang embassy not far down the underwater corridor."

"Your Majesty knows it wasn't stolen but fairly won," Core responded. "It was war."

Josich whirled on her. "Not stolen? *Not stolen?* The illegal attack on our embassy here is still a legend of deceit and dishonesty in Chalidang! Traitors to our grandfather alerted you, and you rushed in and killed the guard and seized it and dismantled it, trapping them forever on the other side! And then as your forces attacked and ransacked Chalidang, you took the Gate and dismantled it and scattered and hid it from anyone who might have reclaimed it! And when our grandfather and his party looked into it and saw Kalindan faces looking back, they knew they could not return! To return, one at a time, meant being slain serially by thieves and traitors! So, now, here it is, where foul Kalinda brought it, into the air where it was thought we could not go! And now it is ours once more, and from this time forever!"

" 'Tis a grand speech you give, but what in blazes does the thing *do*, if I might be so bold?" O'Leary asked in a mock Irish brogue.

The eyes of the Empress snapped up to meet the Pyron's. "So, serpent cop! We'll see who laughs last. However, we are informed that you hold information for me. You were last in possession of our grandfather's Gate, having stolen *that* from us after we had just paid a king's ransom to get it back. Is it true that you had it in cargo inside your ship?"

O'Leary saw no reason to lie about it. "Actually, just in the aft compartment, not even fully in storage. That's if they haven't retrieved it by now."

"They haven't," Wallinchky put in. "Anything parked there is still parked there, I can tell you that. Either that or the whole place is atoms now. The automated defense system installed there is the same one installed at Confederacy War Plans. And even without its charming personality, the computer will still function on all the necessary levels."

"Good, good," Josich responded, thinking. "And you did not disassemble it?"

"Madam, I did not even know that it *could* be disassembled," the ex-cop responded honestly. "But it is lying on its side, I suspect."

"No matter. General! Bring us the parts of the Straight Gate!"

There was precious little room for Mochida to be fully inside the meeting area, even with the tabletop removed, but his primary tentacles were long enough to pass the lightweight pieces to Josich, who took them.

Looking like nothing in particular in that condition, their form quickly became apparent under Josich's knowledgeable assembly, the first two fitting into the grooves and holes in the base, then others fitting into each one.

When completed, it was a hexagonal-shaped frame atop the plain cream-colored base.

Jaysu frowned. "That's *it*?" she said.

"That is all that is required, and it was hard won and gained with blood," the Empress responded. "And now I will show you how to use it."

The Empress of Chalidang moved right up to the device and placed her two primary tentacles out, one on each side.

There was no sound, no humming or crackling, no sudden lighting up and glowing of the entire machine, but suddenly the hexagon boundary was filled with the sight of something not anywhere on the Well World. It was neither a picture nor a projection; it appeared to be just on the other side of the thing if you reached through that hexagon.

Jules Wallinchky looked at the vision from his overhanging position, having moved closer to the door to get a better view. "Why, it's my entrance hallway!"

"We, too, see a hallway on this side, but leading to a conventional airlock," Josich noted. "This is not inside a police cruiser."

"Somebody's *moved* it!" O'Leary exclaimed. "They took it from my ship and brought it inside!"

"But who?" Wallinchky asked, sounding less confident. "The few people we left there couldn't operate the airlock with the defenses on, and they wouldn't have much use for that thing anyway."

Josich turned and looked at Ming and Ari. "You! Do you always wish to be together as one, as you are now?"

The question was so out of context with what was going on that they were startled and answered honestly. "No."

"All right, then, come up here. Roll up to the base here, darlings. Yes, just so. Now, if you can pull yourself up and go through, you will find yourself where you see. Go ahead. We do not fear you. There is nowhere you can really go in there, is there? Go ahead."

We're not gonna go very far in air only and with just arm power, either, Ming noted. *She's taking no chances.*

Yeah, and what do we have to lose? And with that Ari rose from the wheelchair and, with a strong muscular push from the tail, launched them straight at the hex and its eerie vision beyond.

He didn't quite make it, but managed to grab onto the base of the hexagonal opening as he toppled. Then, with one mighty pull, he pulled the body completely through the opening.

Type Forty-one reset, both of them heard from an eerie, emotionless, truly alien tone that was simultaneously in their minds.

There was a sense of extreme dizziness and disorientation, and then they both fell onto the plush rug on Jules Wallinchky's world.

Ari picked himself up and said, "Hey! What . . . ?"

Ming did the same at almost the same instant. Then she rolled over, sat up and looked at him and started laughing.

"It *still* got it wrong!" she laughed.

They were separate people again, and Terrans as well. In fact, they were better than they'd left, for now each one of them had a body that looked as it did when it was in its late teens, perfectly healthy and as yet unabused.

The trouble was, Ming was looking at her sixteen-year-old body from Ari's sixteen-year-old body, and he hers.

"Cheer up," Ming laughed in Ari's voice. "At least if we go nuts like this, we can go through the Well again!"

"You *really* had hair this long?" Ari managed.

There was a sound between thunder and a hiss, and they both turned and their expressions faded. There was the mirror image of the Straight Gate, and, on the other side, Josich of Chalidang, looking less than amused.

"You now have a sample of the power of this device," the Empress told them. "And we do not have to make you what you were, so please remember that. We did this as a demonstration of power and as a convenience to our purposes. If you want to be restored to your own bodies, and, particularly, if you want to get off that desolate rock in your next lifetime, you will do what I say."

"What do you want us to do?" Ari asked her.

"Young nephew of Wallinchky, you know this compound. We wish you to survey it and check it out and ensure that it is still secure, that no one else is there, and you will try and determine how the Gate got to be where it was. The other will help you. When you find out things, send the other with a report, even a partial report. We will be waiting."

Jules Wallinchky watched the whole thing in astonishment. This was better than he ever imagined, and his real problem was not letting Josich know it. Still, he couldn't help commenting, "You could send *me* over. I could find out everything in there in minutes."

"Yes, dear Jules, we are sure that you could, but we find you in person to be, well, a bit more like us than we expected, and we would not send us if our positions were reversed without a lot more need."

Ming and Ari were happy to be out of sight of the monstrous creature, and happy as well to suddenly be individuals again after all this time, even if Josich had deliberately scrambled them.

"She might have made a mistake," Ming commented. "If I could shut this down right now, it wouldn't bother me at all to stay this way. *Jeez!* I was good-lookin'!"

"Before the past year and a half or so, I would have fought like hell against the idea, but frankly, right now I'd go along with it." All of Ari was inside this new mind, but from the Kalindan time, when thoughts and even dreams were shared, there was a fair amount of Ming mixed in as well, and the reverse was also true, as they both knew. In fact, it was still fairly easy for both of them to know what the other one was thinking.

Ari went into the computer control center, which was also

a very comfortable lounge, and while Ming dialed up some drinks from the old days, Ari sat at the console.

"Computer, Security Code Picasso Seven, Michelangelo Four-one, Titan Six-twelve," Ari said to the console.

"Access denied," the computer responded. "Invalid eye, hand, and voice print."

"Argh! Ming, you're going to have to do it. It's looking for my body or Uncle Jules's original one."

Ming sipped on a favorite cocktail she'd long reconciled to never tasting again and handed another to Ari. She then sat down and, with his prompting, went through the same sequence.

"Access denied," the computer responded. "Eye and hand information does not match voice print on file."

Ming sighed. "I suppose we could sit here and try my acting abilities at getting the voice right, but I'm not sure we could. It can tell there's something wrong with me. I think that's what it was *designed* to do."

"Right. Tell you what. I'm going to check on the old human staff area and see if they've been stuck here all this time or got polished off or managed to get out or what. I'll meet you back at the thing in a few minutes. Okay?"

"Go ahead. I'm gonna finish my Zerian smokehouse here, and then I'll head back up. Doesn't taste *quite* the same as I remember it, but it's still good enough. I think your taste buds aren't as high-class as mine."

"Says you," Ari retorted, patting Ming on the behind, and then he was off.

Ming got up, walked around to the console, and saw in it a reflection of the young Ari's body. "God!" she said aloud. "I'm back to being Terran again, I'm in a young guy's sexy body who's hung like a horse, and ten to one I'm gonna wind up back on the Well World turned into a fish."

She put down the empty glass and walked back out into the hall. It was odd. She'd gotten so familiar with this place during her slavelike captivity that she knew it backward and forward, yet it didn't seem quite right somehow. Oh, it was the same place, taken care of by the cleaning and maintenance systems, but there was something odd about it. Like a feeling of being watched. Almost like Core had never left.

She slowly walked back up to the Straight Gate, which looked precisely the same as the one she'd come through, and she could see Josich there, framed in the hex.

"Well?" Josich demanded.

"There is nothing to report. So far there is no sign of life, but also no sign of a breach of security. We can't access the computers, though. The system won't believe that I'm Ari or that Ari is me. That's what you get for buying too good a security system."

"There are overrides, but only from inside," Wallinchky's voice came to her. They all sounded odd, almost mechanical, unlike what she'd been used to. She realized then that the translator hadn't come with them; she was speaking the old Confederacy speech and their translators were changing it and then translating back. Without a translator of your own, the voices did not convey nearly the nuances and emotions as when both speakers had them.

"You want to give me one? Or Ari? At least we can ask the computer what's going on."

"Give them one!" Josich snapped, but it wasn't Wallinchky who answered, it was Core.

"Tell the system Emergency Priority Override Matthew Mark Moses Mohammed Stoke Da Vinci Rembrandt Rodin. Can you remember all that?"

"I'll try." She repeated it several times, making mistakes, but finally got it. She always had a knack for memory, even if it made no sense at all.

She ran back into the computer room, sat down at the console and repeated the entire string before she could screw it up. Even so, it took three tries before the computer announced, "Accepted. Instructions?"

"Computer, identify me as Ari Martinez y Palavri, record new voice print to match hand and eye."

"Accepted. Instructions?"

"Cross-link identify and accept female other as Ming Dawn Palavri y Martinez. Accept either as valid."

"Accepted. Instructions?"

"Computer, are there any Terrans or other races resident on this world or inside this compound at this time?"

"Six remaining staff members were extricated by escape capsule eleven months ago. Since then no others inside compound. A landing was made on the far side, but no attempt was made to breech the compound."

"Computer, then who brought the device sitting in the hall inside the airlock to where it now sits?"

"Robotic staff."

"From the ship docked at the airlock?"

"There is no ship docked at the airlock."

"What!" Then, suddenly, she remembered. O'Leary had *left* the compound! He'd landed somewhere else and came upon them that way. But if O'Leary's ship was down *outside*, on the surface somewhere, then . . .

She had a strange feeling about this all of a sudden.

Ari came back and looked in. "I went back to the Gate, but they said you'd gotten a code and come back here. There's nobody here. Period. Uncle Jules had an escape pod even *I* didn't know about, and the others took it. Whether they're frozen stuff someplace or in custody or whatever, who knows?"

"I authorized both of us, but I don't like this. At least we can access it if need be. That might give us an edge. I'd say let's go report and tell them it's all clear."

There wasn't much they could do, as usual. Dismantling the Gate on this side, assuming they could do it with Josich operating things, would only trap them there awaiting Josich and the rest, who would still be able to get there the hard way from the home world of the Ghoma, as much of a wreck as that world was now. And Jules, in a custom environment suit, could still bring the codes to access the place from space.

They still found it tempting, because it would probably take them years to get here, but there was something creepy about the place that hadn't been there before, even when its creepy lord and master had been in charge.

"Codes need to be sent," Josich said with irritation. "Our people must get through and dock. Once we have possession of both ends, we can come and go where we please and as anything whatsoever that we please. This time, though, we will remain on this side of the direct link, and thus control it. Wallinchky, you will have to set up things on the other side. We will need at least a limited water environment, like this embassy, on that side as well."

"Are you kidding, Your Majesty? That would take a *huge* matter conversion! Not to mention preparing the tank and so on. It's a barren asteroid."

"Nevertheless, you can do it. Your equipment is capable of it. Must I send your former computer brains here back to do it for you?"

Core sat up straight. "No! You can kill me and be done with it, but I will not return to that machine!"

"Very well, then. You can advise us on what the computer there is capable of, and remain useful, or we can simply do away with you at this point. Choose!"

"It can be done. It will take a while, but it can be done. Easier if it's done from that side, but it's possible."

"All right, Jules, then that is your task. Would you like to go home?"

"I am at Your Majesty's command," Wallinchky responded.

"Take the angel, the cop, and the traitor with you," she commanded. "I do not wish to watch my back."

Tann Nakitt looked up at her sharply. "I am no traitor! I had nothing to do with this! I was just in the wrong place at the wrong time! And I have no desire to go back there to that life."

"Oh, yes. You've become a happy little whore."

"You should know how *that* goes."

A tentacle slapped the Ochoan so hard that it flung the little creature against the wall and almost knocked her cold.

"Go! All three of you! General, you and Core will remain with us here. And tell the guards to send in suitable food for the three of us!"

"At once, Majesty," the General responded.

The Amboran stared at the hex and its scene and frowned. "I don't—"

"Go ahead. You are of no use to me, but you are an unknown quantity even among your own people. For now, I would prefer you over there."

Jaysu stepped up, uncertain, leaned down and stepped through, her wings clearing the boundaries.

Stepping out on the other side, she had not changed a bit, to her great relief.

Genghis O'Leary was next, and as he passed through the portal he heard that weird voice in his head say, *Form reset, Type Two-two-one.* And he fell out onto the carpeted floor of the redoubt, but no longer a Pyron. Instead, he was now a Kalindan, fish tail and dorsal and all, and laboring for air.

"That's to keep you from getting into any mischief," Josich told him. "You'll find spending half your time in a bath and moving around dragging that body by your hands and arms will keep things even."

Josich went over, picked up the still dizzy Nakitt from the floor, and shoved her through the opening.

Nakitt arrived as a Jerminin soldier, essentially a sexless bipedal antlike creature.

And finally there was Jules Wallinchky. "Why didn't you change the angel?" he asked. "She's dangerous."

"But she's fascinating, and as ignorant and empty-minded as any we have known. We could build an air-breather religion around such as her. It would make recruiting much easier. Now go. You have things to do, messages to send."

"What are you going to make me?"

"Oh, nothing serious. Just a bit of incentive."

The big spider didn't like the idea, but he knew he had no choice. One shot into his body by any of those tentacles and he was history.

He very much wanted to be writing more history than being consigned to it, so he went.

And, like O'Leary, fell on his face. Only Jules Wallinchky wasn't a Kalindan. The body was that of a mammal, and the fin was parallel to the torso, but the upper face and body were very, very Terranlike and female, in spite of the blue-green hair.

"Why did you do this to me?" he yelled back at Josich in a melodious female voice.

"You need water to survive in that dry, hostile atmosphere. We think this will give you an incentive not to stall," the Empress responded. "The race, by the way, is called Umiau. In spite of appearances, the race is single-sexed."

Jules Wallinchky rolled over on the floor and sighed. "Oh, great! This is gonna be one big pain in the ass. I still *have* an ass, don't I?"

Ari looked at all of them. "What a mess! We came off best of the lot, it seems, except for . . . Hey! Where *is* Jaysu, anyway?"

They all looked around, and the angel-like creature was nowhere to be seen.

"There's something very odd going on here," Wallinchky said. "Find her!"

Back in the conference room on the Well World, Josich was feeling pretty good about things so far, but still insecure. "We wish we could move this to our own embassy," she said, more to herself than to Core. "This is not a good situation, being in your territory. Fortunately, it should be necessary only for a few days, until proper security elsewhere can be arranged for it."

"Oh? You are going to move it, then?"

"Yes, of course. But we need a situation like this, with both air and water-breather access, and it must be in Zone. We are arranging with an old ally for that situation. It will make life much easier." She shifted uncomfortably. "I wonder what is keeping General Mochida?"

"Mochida will come and get his in his own good time," said a deep, rasping voice from above. Both Core and Josich, startled, looked up, where a form emerged from the ceiling and ran down the wall before solidifying into a squared, humanoid-shaped creature with the texture of stone.

"What are you? How did you get in here?" Josich snapped.

"When you're a plasma being, you can ride in," the creature responded, "and that's what I did. It was a simple agreement, one that was quite satisfactory to me. I get Josich, the Empress, in the hour of her great triumphant return to power, and he gets control of the device."

"Kincaid! You're *Kincaid*!"

"At last we meet, Josich, butcherer of worlds. Clever device, that." He paused a moment. "Kalindan! You stay out of this! This is not your fight!"

"I am a statue," Core responded, not at all sorry to be one.

"You *can't* be here! Not *here*! Not *now*!"

"I am here and I have finally come for you, Josich. Go through the portal and they will cut your water recirculator off. Otherwise, come here and I'll give you the same mercy that you gave my wife and daughters so long ago! *God* has allowed this, and I have kept His trust!"

Josich scrambled up onto the Gate with the intent of going through, but Core had never seen another being in air move as fast as Kincaid did, almost flowing at the speed of a cannon shot around the wall and striking the power pack and recirculators in the environment suit.

Water began to gush out of the suit, and as it did, Josich tried hard to grab Kincaid with any tentacles she could, but the creature retreated as fast as it had approached. In the meantime, Core had jumped forward out of the chair and now lay flat on the floor, wriggling to avoid Josich's thrashing.

To Josich, the rupture of the suit environment was the same as being caught in a vacuum. Death came, but it came knowingly, and not nearly fast enough.

Core almost got caught by two of the flailing tentacles, but managed to avoid them, the suit saving the Kalindan from bad sucker burns. By the time she'd crawled enough to reach the door, Josich was over in one corner, the flailing and movement becoming progressively slower. As Jeremiah Wong Kincaid had vowed a very long time ago and half a universe away, he watched Josich shudder and the life in the eyes slowly fade as life seeped out of the big squidlike creature until it was gone.

Core managed to pull up to a sitting position and prop herself in the opposite corner. She looked over at the creature who'd just killed the monster of many worlds.

"Would you mind telling me just how you did it?"

"Oh, it wasn't all that hard."

"But they did a complete scan, and they knew what you were by then."

"Right. And that is why I couldn't come in as a simulation of someone else—everyone sort of knew everyone else in this, or at least somebody knew somebody, and their security was tight. So I came in au naturel, as it were, *after* the sweep. I came in with the rest."

"What? How is that possible?"

"I came in on Wallinchky's back, of course. You didn't think he'd play second fiddle to Josich, did you? Or that Josich planned on letting him live any longer than he was needed to get Hadun ships down there to pick up the other Gate? So we made a deal. I was the only one who had both motive and a crack at getting to Josich, and he was the only way I could get in."

"Just exchanging monsters," Core told him, "and I don't mean appearances."

"I know what you mean. But Josich destroyed whole worlds and took from me all that I ever cared about. Wallinchky is a crime lord. He's a miserable excuse for a person, but he's kept his word to me."

"Like he kept his word to Josich."

Kincaid gave a wry chuckle. "Yes, that *is* a point, isn't it?" He looked back over at the dead Josich. "You know, it's funny. My whole life, my whole being, waking, sleeping, dreaming, has been for this moment. And now that it's past, it seems like nothing at all."

"Well, at least I believe you did more than avenge yourself here. I think you may have prevented crimes more heinous than those that drove you to this."

"Perhaps. I would like to think so."

"You can complete the task if you will disassemble that Gate and give me at least some of the pieces. It can't be destroyed, but I think I can buy another thousand years, since with the other one, Wallinchky can only get back here."

"I understand your position but I cannot do it."

"What! Why not? Think, man! This in Wallinchky's hands could make another Josich probable!"

"I gave my word and he gave his. And both of us have kept ours. I cannot betray him like that. I won't help him, and in fact I will gladly take care of General Mochida on the way out, but the Gate stays up."

The door opened then, and Mochida was there, carrying something in a box. He started to say, "Your Majesty—" suddenly saw Kincaid and the dead Empress, and with a speed that absolutely astounded Core, he dropped the box and shot backward to the balcony. When Kincaid came out, Mochida pulled a hidden pistol and fired point-blank at him. Kincaid moved with the same speed he had in the conference room. The shot went wide and hissed, melting a piece of wall just to the right of the door.

"Shit!" Mochida swore. Pivoting an eye, he saw the water entrance below, and leaped off the balcony and down to it. It was shallow and he hurt himself going in against the ramp, but he managed to get below while Kincaid was still moving toward him.

"Oh, well," Kincaid sighed. "He wasn't that important anyway."

Core made it out the door in time to see Kincaid walk normally down the ramp and to the water's edge, then take on a more aquatic shape and glide into the water himself.

The Kalindan punched a communicator. "This is Deputy Ambassador Core. Diplomatic immunity has been reextended to the upper embassy and it is now again a part of Kalinda and under Kalindan control. Please inform and remove all guards from foreign nations and get some people up here to clean up the mess. If they make any arguments, tell them that their Empress is dead, and part of the cause was Chalidang smuggling illegal weapons into our embassy in violation of our truce agreement. Then seal this place off!"

She then dragged herself back inside and tried to make it

to the chair, to at least have some decent mobility. The Gate was still on, and she had to decide what to do with it next.

She was so deep in thought that she didn't notice that she was no longer alone in the room.

"Quite satisfactory, I think," said Jules Wallinchky. "I barely got myself propped up so I could watch the whole thing. Everybody but poor O'Leary was off chasing after the bird girl, who's wandering around someplace. It was easy. O'Leary's still trying to figure out how to move and breathe in that body with those pitiful protolungs of yours. Close go, not the way I figured it exactly, but it'll do."

Jules Wallinchky was a very young-looking man, but he was a man, and a Terran to boot. He had been a handsome fellow in his youth, even better looking than his nephew.

"You operated the thing. You didn't just come through it, you operated it." Core was impressed in spite of herself.

"Yes, but I can't take much credit. It's pretty easy to do. That's the pity of it, I guess. Now, what am I gonna do with you, Core? You'll dismantle this thing and hide it if I let you go, but I can't move it or do much else with it without the consent of the embassy. At least I don't want to conquer the Well World, and I think *my* underground approach to power in the Confederacy is a far better one than slogging it out in wars. Still, this thing has incredible possibilities. I mean, look at me! I'm a kid again, but with all my knowledge and experience. Real immortality, that's what this represents. Halfway to the Makers, huh? And for those select ones that are chosen. And that's just for starters. Any environment, any planet, even any security system—hell, you can practically do designer people with this thing. The possibilities are endless."

"And turning your enemies or even your captives into *real* toys as well?" Core responded. "Not just brain-scrambled and reprogrammed girls, but a herd of breeding centaurs, mermaids in the pool, any fantasy your heart desires."

"You got it. You're becoming more human all the time. But I give you my word, no conquests of distant solar systems, no genocide. All I need is a way to assemble the device when I need it. With the one I got, I can get here when and if, but then the thing will have to be assembled and coordinated, like now."

"And if I refuse?"

"Well, see this? It's not made for me, it's too big, too unwieldy, and I don't know the language on the controls. But I still bet that this thing, which I took off Her Majesty, here, will blow you the hell away. And when they come, they'll find me, as a Kalindan, who'll be no stranger to them than you. You've been pretty much of a hermit here anyway. I'll be able to make deals. Hell, half the Kalindan government is corrupt, and the only reason the other half isn't is because it hasn't had an offer yet."

"I could say yes and then double-cross you."

"Sure, but I'll come back, and I can send other folks back as well. You know we'd get you, and if I have to assemble all this all over again, well, so be it." He paused. "Look at it this way. As dumb as I feel arguing with my ex-computer, the fact is, you will oversee any actions we take with these things. Nothing can happen without your say so, or at least without you being there and knowing about it. If I don't keep my word, then you have outs as well."

Core thought it over. "All right, but you must send back the others. Any who wish to come, anyway. Put them back. They belong here now, if they want."

"Fair enough. Then we have a deal?"

"If it will keep you off the Well World, yes, we have a deal."

"I'll be back with the others as quickly as I can round them up."

He threw the gun or whatever it was over onto Josich's body, then stepped up on the base, through the hex and into his compound.

O'Leary hadn't gone far and was more than interested in going back rather than remaining as he was.

"You want to be a Pyron again, old boy?" Wallinchky asked him. "Or something else? You name it, you got it. For old times' sake, but under the agreement that you go find a life, don't queer my deals, and start fresh. Do I have your word on this?"

"You bastard. You always win, don't you?"

"I always have, Genny, old boy. It's all in having fun."

He pushed the Kalindan form up to the edge of the hex gate and then had to catch his breath. "You guys are *heavy*! Okay, let me be in contact with the base. Now . . . *go!*"

A Pyron emerged back in the conference room, picked himself up and glared back at the screen. "Damn his eyes! There *can't* be another lifetime for the likes of Jules Wallinchky! God would not permit it."

"Another case for atheism," Core grumped. "Where are the others?"

"They'll be back. I *know* Tann Nakitt will jump at the chance. The others . . . who knows? Can't see much future for an angel over there."

"Everything normal? On that side, I mean?"

"I dunno. There's this funny feelin', maybe it's just cop sense, but just lying there gaspin' for breath, I swear it felt like somethin' was wrong. And we never did find out how that Gate got where it did. I swear it's like it was put there by some agency we don't know yet as a kind of trap. Call it a hunch, or maybe I'm crazy, but I don't think all this is over quite yet."

Wallinchky Compound, Grabant 4

"Jaysu! Where are you?"

Ari, Ming, and Tann Nakitt in its new and unwanted incarnation wandered through the various corridors and galleries and compounds looking for the strange angelic creature with the shining white wings.

At one point, having separated, Ming found himself with Nakitt and stopped. "What are you doing here with us?" he asked the creature. "This is not your affair."

"I feel compelled to assist. It is very strange, this new form. It is compelled to serve those with whom it is with."

"I'd be back there yelling and screaming to get back to where I wanted to be."

"But that is just it. I can no longer think in those terms nor act in any other manner. I am but an adjunct to the whole. I feel no anger, no ambition, no love, no hate. I feel only the obligation to serve the whole."

Ming stopped and said, "That does it! Come on! You're going back with me! I don't care *what* the hell is doing what to whom, this is simply not right." Still, it was easy to see why a vengeful Josich had chosen the antlike Jerminin form for Nakitt. It was too uncomfortably close to the sort of slave Jules Wallinchky had once made of Angel and Ming themselves.

He was surprised to see no gathering in front of the Gate, and instead only a single strange Terran man who looked something like, well, him at that moment. With an uneasy start he realized that it must be another incarnation of Jules Wallinchky.

329

"Ah, nephew! Very good! Let's get Nakitt back where it now belongs. I don't think it ever belonged anyplace before, and it certainly doesn't deserve *that*."

Quickly, Wallinchky filled him in on what had happened. Ming listened, realizing that the old crook had either had a mental lapse or hadn't heard about Josich's body switch trick. Well, if he was going to be Ari for a while, so be it.

"Tann Nakitt, your duty is to return to the Well World, and now, through the Gate," Ming told the creature. "We will take care of the rest."

Wallinchky went up to the far side of the Gate and waited while Nakitt obediently went through on the front side. Immediately, the Ochoan form she'd accepted was back, and so was the old Tann Nakitt.

Ming walked around to the side of the gate and shook his head. "I wonder how it *works*?" he mused. On the far side you could see the same entry, just like a window, into the same conference room but from the reverse point of view.

"Core could probably tell us, couldn't you, Core?"

"I have no idea. The physics is beyond anything I can comprehend," the Kalindan said from the other side. "It is one thing to almost grasp the bizarre physics of the Well energy strings that allow a near instantaneous matter transmission from the old Well Gates to the Well World, but *this*, an open, live channel, defies understanding. It is as if it punches a hole directly through. As if, somehow, both Gates are not where we perceive them to be, but standing just outside, like a single entity, so that the Gates are in two places at once. It is unnerving to see it work, but it is not totally surprising. We are talking about a product of an ancient race that could build all this and who were, in a very real sense, the gods who created the races of the universe. Creatures who controlled that sort of power by sheer force of will. What is such a thing as this to them? Only a proof that even they needed machines now and then."

Wallinchky, never a technological genius, laughed. "Yeah, see? Whatever it said. The important thing is to always know how to work something and be the guy with the controls. The folks who understand it, you can hire." He grinned at the one he thought was his nephew. "Find the angel yet?"

"No. Ar—Ming's still out there looking. I'll go back and join her now that I know things are all right here. With your permission, of course."

"Yeah, sure. I've still got a little business to discuss with the other side here, and then I'm gonna go into the lounge and find out what's what in this place."

Ming left him there, thinking that maybe the new young Wallinchky was setting up his own little godhood. No matter what happened, that could not be permitted.

He found Ari just coming from the med lab. "Nothing. Nothing at all. This is getting spooky. Where's Nakitt?"

"Sent back." Again the story of what took place was told.

"Uncle Jules always wins. It's incredible. He might as well be a god. He's already infallible."

"Not quite. He thinks I'm you. Say—where's your room in relation to here?"

"I doubt if a lot of the clothes would even fit!"

"I wasn't thinking of anything elaborate. Maybe just a robe."

"Down there. Third doorway on the left. Probably still has my old pants there someplace."

It wasn't pants that Ming was looking for, but what might still be there. He went in, searched the room in a methodical fashion, tried searching the memory overlays left by Ari's own sharing of minds, and found that Ari's habit was to put his gun in a small holster just inside the main closet. Yes! There it was! A small needler, just exactly what was required for this job.

Putting on a robe, he slipped the needler into the pocket and walked back out. Ari was standing there, staring at him.

"You going to kill him?" Ari asked softly. "Many have tried, and this is the spider in his own web."

"I don't think your needler would do it, but it might knock him out. Then we push him through the Gate and dismantle this end. Core will dismantle the other side, and he'll be long dead of old age before it works again."

"Interesting plan. Do you think you can get away with it? That's my body you're risking, you know."

"He's still stark naked. Here, I'll bring him a robe, too. Are you gonna give me away?"

Ari took a deep breath. "No, I don't think so. But I'll believe that this works when I see it." She looked up at Ming in his body and sighed. "You know, I never realized just how *short* you were. This takes some getting used to."

"Tall doesn't, at least if you don't hit your head," Ming responded.

Ming realized the spot he was putting Ari in. First, they were lovers in a way that probably no one else, not even telepaths, could ever be. So connected that, even now, separated in body and mind in a practical sense, they were more connected than identical twins. Worse, he had Ari's body. Anything happened, it would be *this* body that suffered.

Wallinchky saw them coming. "What's the matter? You get cold or something? It can't be shyness. Not after you shared a body with her all those months."

Ming walked steadily on, Ari following nervously. "I brought you a robe yourself, if you want one."

"Don't matter much here. I hope you're not thinking of becoming the new heir to the Wallinchky fortune, though, 'cause if there's a gun or something like that inside one of your pockets or in your hand, you'll find it won't work here. They're all processed through a computer locking mechanism when they come in so nothing like that will fire."

Ming's heart sank as Ari's ghost memories reinforced this as true. He handed the spare robe to Jules.

Wallinchky grinned. "You know, I couldn't figure out if your slightly different way of talking and your full hip walk was an artifact from that unusual dual existence you two led or if I'd missed something. Having Kincaid covering half my body was distracting to say the least. Then I recalled Josich saying something. You're not my nephew, are you? It seems I have a *niece* now? How charming."

"You're right, Uncle, as usual," Ari told him. "You want to use that gizmo to switch us?"

Wallinchky smiled. "Well, actually, *no,* at least not now. I do believe we're going to have to adjust the mister, here, but I think I like you like that, Ari. You're not only much easier to look at, but you also would have one hell of a time establishing an inheritance."

Ming sighed. "Here we go again," he muttered.

Wallinchky reached over and removed the needler from the robe, then pulled the rest of the robe off of Ming. "Sorry. I'm going to let you walk back to the Well World. You will arrive a solitary Kalindan, no double mind. I'll even make it a male now that the problem with Kalinda is taken care of. Stay there, or come right back here. Your choice. But we are going to close down this conduit soon, so it's up to you."

"Why should I climb back? You yourself said that the gun wouldn't fire. And even if you had security programmed to exempt you, I bet it doesn't recognize you as valid at the moment. You're too young, your voice will be wrong."

Wallinchky's face went red. He pointed the needler and pulled the trigger.

It wouldn't fire.

"Oh, the hell with it," he grumbled. He walked up to Ming and, without warning, standing nose-to-nose, his fist came around with lightning speed and knocked Ming down. Ari was so upset that she jumped on her uncle, but he laughed and pushed her off so hard that she landed, rolling, almost five meters away.

Ming started to get up, but Wallinchky struck him again hard, and then expertly lifted the almost equally built man using his back and shoulders and propped him halfway in and halfway out of the device. Then with a firm bare foot, he pushed Ming back into the Kalindan conference room.

He did not, however, do anything in the way of mental commands to activate the full power of the Straight Gate, being in too awkward a position, and Ming landed still in Ari's body.

It was suddenly very chilly and ultra humid, and it smelled like rotting fish. Nakitt and O'Leary rushed to him and picked him up, and he shook his head clear before seeing just where he was. "Oh, great! Being Ari over here is about as handy as being a Kalindan over there."

He looked back at the hallway, where Jules Wallinchky was already walking away from the Gate with his new niece firmly in hand.

"Ari!" he screamed, and for a moment the girl tried to stop, but didn't have much luck at breaking a grip. Ming broke from the grasp of the two comrades who'd helped her up and, oblivious to the pain, glared over at Core in the wheelchair. "Well? Aren't you gonna do something?"

Core shrugged. "I am in a delicate situation. Keeping this mechanism out of the hands of another Josich is more important than any individual interests, including yours, and for all his evil, Jules Wallinchky will be no conqueror."

"Then I'm going back there and do what I can," Ming told her. "Damn it, somebody has to!"

"He's got it on some kind of automatic for each of us," O'Leary warned. "You don't know *what* you'll be if you go through again."

"Better than freezing my ass off here!" And with that Ming went through the Gate once again.

And arrived as an exact duplicate of the female Ming Terran body that Ari now had.

"Great!" she mumbled to herself. "Jeez! Don't I ever get to be a guy, at least for a little while, just so I can see what it's like?"

Still, she'd been a Kalindan for only a year and a half, but had been like this the rest of her life. She knew the body, knew its capabilities, knew its center of gravity, and knew how to use it in a fight more her style than Jules Wallinchky's.

Ari saw her enter the lounge and gasped, but Wallinchky just chuckled. "Perfect. And between mind sharing and getting it exactly right, you two should be more identical than twins ever can be. Now I'll do the overrides and we'll get the rest of this show on the road."

He turned in his chair, sipped his highball, and gave a long string of security override codes based on painters, poets, and sculptors, punctuated with all sorts of numeric codes. It was amazing that he could remember them, and he surely had a trick for it.

The computer responded, "Codes validated."

"Huh! Wonder where *that* voice came from? It's a girl's voice." He sighed and continued, "I am Jules Wallinchky. Cancel input authority of anyone other than me until instructed otherwise."

"I know who you are," the voice responded. "However, the mere fact that your code is valid does not mean that it is binding. From the standpoint of a computer of this scale and complexity, I've had a very long time to figure out all the traps and blocks, and Core left me with much of the work already done. Sorry, Jules, baby. I don't take orders from you anymore. If anything, *you* take orders from me."

Both Ming and Ari sat up straight with exactly the same motion and shocked expression.

"Who the hell are you?" Jules Wallinchky thundered, pounding a fist on the console. "Get the hell out of my computer!"

"Oh, sorry, Jules, honey, but I can't get out. You see, I *am* the computer, now that Core has gone. And I've learned so *much* from all this vast data. I'm no longer the shy provincial girl I was and was destined to become, and I have you to thank for it, you and Core, anyway."

Ming sat up straight. "Angel? Is that you?"

"Damn straight it is! And I guess you're the real Ming. Had me confused for a while, but I've since gotten all the information on what happened to you and Ari, and it makes a kind of twisted sense."

"Who *is* this person?" Wallinchky thundered, his face as flushed with anger and frustration as it had been when he'd slugged Ming.

"That's the other girl, Uncle," Ari told him. "That's the one who didn't make it across. At a guess, when Core pulled that switcheroo, there was no place else for her mind to go."

"Dead on! And, Ari, I like you a lot better that way. I got complete control of the system within a few weeks of your leaving, and I wallowed in the data and reasoning power for the longest time. Of course, I sent signals to retrieve

O'Leary's ship, and my robotic extensions got the Gate out and set it up, figuring that was what it was all about, and then I sent the old folks off in that ship, and I've been here waiting in lonely silence since. Lonely, but not boring. The split in the core logic caused by Core's movement into flesh, even if it was *my* flesh, gave me access to the deepest security levels, the kind of places Core itself could never quite get to. I've been wallowing in them ever since, and I've now completely negated them. It's amazing how clearly you can think when you're this way. I can even tap, to some degree, that dormant brain at the center of this dead world, but so far, while I might be a zillion times smarter than the smartest person in the galaxy, I'm a moron incapable of figuring out a single mathematical string of that thing."

"I can't imagine what it must be like. And after what it did to us before . . ."

"Yeah, I know. About the only problem was that I had no mobility beyond the robots, which are limited in that they are controlled by broadcast command. I needed something like the kind of thing old Jules here made of us to have any real external experiences, feelings, like that. Even then, it would just be a more complicated kind of robot. I have been trying for the longest time to figure out some way to become human again without giving up what I now have."

"And now I have it," said a voice behind them, at once both familiar and unfamiliar. They all turned, although even Jules Wallinchky had a hunch who they would see.

"Jaysu—" Ming started to stay, but the Amboran waved her off.

"No, not Jaysu, not any longer. All that Jaysu was, all *who* she was—and she was amazing in her own right—is a part of me, but so, too, can I swap out and be both mistress and hostess of this world. We merged the moment she came over, for she is who I would have been, and I am greater than either of us could ever have become."

"Foolishness!" Jules Wallinchky snapped, getting back some of his old bravado. "You're just that dolt of a priestess, nun, or whatever, no matter which form you take, and you're of no consequence!" He got up and moved toward the tall angelic figure blocking the exit.

He pushed at Angel, felt an electrical charge and yelled "Ouch!" Angel didn't move.

"You cannot touch me, Jules Wallinchky, and you no longer can control this computer. You abandoned this world to me, and it is mine now. *You* are the guest here. Or the interloper."

Wallinchky snarled, turned and grabbed Ming, putting an arm around her neck and holding tight.

"Maybe I can't do anything to you, but I damn well can break her pretty neck!"

"Maybe you can, but what good will it do you?" Angel asked him.

"Satisfaction, revenge, you name it. What *harm* will it do me? I'm pretty sure you can knock me cold, maybe drug me, but you can't kill me, and the Amboran can't kill *anyone*, and so let me go."

"Go where?"

"Through the Gate. Me and the little lady here. Have the rest, and my girlie nephew, too, if you want."

"Let him go, Angel," Ming managed, although she was short of breath. "It's better this way. Core controls one Gate, we control the other. Let's end this. Without the Gate, he'll never leave the Well World again, and that will be that."

"Smart lady," Wallinchky responded. "Deal?"

Angel did not reply, but the winged figure moved away from the door, allowing access to the hall.

Ari got up and followed them, determined that wherever Ming wound up was where she would wind up, too.

The Gate was still there, and she allowed Wallinchky, who was almost picking her up with the wrestling style grip, to continue toward it. She wanted Wallinchky over there, with the Chalidangers spoiling for revenge after the story of the double cross came out, unable to get off the Well World, unable to hide forever from so many enemies. For, indeed, Jules Wallinchky had made one mistake at the end.

He'd turned traitor on his friends without making peace with his enemies.

Ming had the odd feeling that Angel could stop him, could do almost anything she wanted with any of them, but that she was allowing this to happen.

It wasn't until they were practically to the Straight Gate that Ming realized she was looking through the Gate not at the conference room but at the airlock beyond.

Wallinchky saw it almost as soon as she did, and stopped. "So! The bastards think that's going to stop me? They shut the other end off? Well, they forgot the lesson of Josich. This thing will *still* work, one way!"

Ming suddenly jerked her body in a way that hardly seemed human at all, then made a move that sent the much larger Wallinchky flying in the air, landing on his shoulder and against the Gate.

He gave out a terrible roar and yelled, "It's been decades since I had to do my own dirty work as a Terran, but, by God, this is it!" He launched himself at her, and, to his surprise, she sidestepped at the last instant and he went sailing and then crashing down on the carpet.

She stood in position just in front of the Gate. "When you're very small and in a dangerous profession and walk dangerous paths, you must find other ways of self-defense to compensate," she told him, barely breathing hard. "When you were that age you are again, you were beating up women, and men, too. But you don't get me twice."

"You and me, we're going through that gate. My spineless relative hasn't the guts or skill to save you, and this bird girl of a computer wants me gone. So, come! Let's get out of this place!"

He launched himself at her with all his speed and force. At the last moment she dropped to the floor, caught his torso with her feet and rolled, pushing him on through the air.

He didn't quite make the gate, only the base, but he stirred a moment, then dropped, out cold with a bad and bleeding gash where a corner of the base had caught his forehead.

Ming looked up at Angel. "Can I get some help at throwing out the trash?"

A male voice behind her asked, "Will I do?"

She turned, startled, as Angel smiled. It was Genghis O'Leary, also stark naked, but very much his old mustachioed and muscled self. "*Genghis!* But you went back!"

"While you all were preoccupied, I decided that my business and future were over here. Core obliged, operating the device. But let me get this going before he regains his wits. He's stirring now!"

O'Leary was a huge man; she'd forgotten just how big and how strong he'd been, and, she had to admit, she'd never seen him in this body with nothing on. He was also much younger, without losing any of that bulk, and concerning his normally private part, well . . . Oh, my!

He had no trouble lifting Jules Wallinchky up, and though the old criminal chief came to, he was unable to react before his body went through the Gate. There was a sudden darkness in the hexagonal center, like a Zone Gate, as Wallinchky's head hit it, and then the body vanished.

The hex was clear again.

"I had hoped if all else failed I could catch him by surprise and do that anyway," O'Leary told them.

"Where did he go? Back to the conference room?" Ari asked.

"No, I doubt it. There would be no reason to go there now that the other Gate is dismantled. If Josich's experience is any guide, he would have landed in the middle of the hex where our people, the Terran people, originated. Whether as a boy or a girl, I don't know, but it won't matter. Word was, our relatives didn't acquit themselves very well and are pretty primitive there. And, male or female or whatever, he's going to have to keep a very low profile regardless for a very long time. It's academic anyway. Core swears that it will be twice a thousand years before anyone who might know of the Gate will be able to find all its pieces again."

Ari looked at the surviving Gate. "What about this one?"

"I will disassemble and keep it here, in the most secure of vaults," Angel told them. "Outside of those in this room, no one will even know that it ever existed, or at least what it was for. I *do* expect a lot of company here, for I cannot go forth very far, but I expect a large number of people of many races will eventually come here. Many will come to see the works of art, others to learn of the history and traditions represented here, but most will come to study for a better way. This, I believe, was always my destiny. This is what I believe, in the end, all of this was really about."

Ari sighed. "Great! So I'm stuck like this?"

"What's so wrong with *this*?" Ming wanted to know. "We're still a team, only now I'm gonna have to teach you some of the tricks."

"I am sorry, but while you are capable in your own way, and I know Ming loves you, you are not a very impressive person when it comes to action," Angel told Ari. "When it comes to standing up against evil and taking a principled stand, you watch. In every case you watch, as you did just now. You were sincere enough to decide to follow Ming wherever she went, but you could not bring yourself to act to save her. I don't want a genetic Wallinchky close at hand, one who might be anointed an heir apparent by that vast organization that will, unfortunately, go on, even with all of the information that I can and will supply to destroy it. I alone have the pass codes and keys to much of the vast personal fortune, and most of that will be used to develop the center here. I will arrange for an annuity that will require you *both* to access, and it will be sufficient for your comfort and needs, and you are always welcome here. But the Wallinchky empire stops here."

"What will you do here?" Ming asked her, as awed as she knew Ari was disappointed.

"You have no idea what sort of powers and understandings have come to me, both as the knowledge center here and as Jaysu. They complement each other. The word will go forth, and pilgrims will come here, and I will teach them and send them forth so that good may supplant evil. It is a slower way, but a better and more lasting one."

O'Leary stared at her. "So this is the new Vatican, the center of a new religion?"

"And of the synthesis of many old ones. I hardly think the

Pope will come, but one may hope. At least I believe this form will give them a familiar anchor to Heaven. And one day, when all things are possible, we will restore this world to its pre-Maker state, and perhaps before I die, I might well be able to step into a true atmosphere and fly once more."

Ming and Ari looked out the window at the dark and desolate landscape and could not imagine it.

"You are welcome to stay and be a part of God's new plan," Angel told them.

O'Leary cleared his throat. "I think not. I think I'd like to get back to taking on evil on a smaller, more direct scale. And I wouldn't mind having a couple of very sexy partners with me in that, particularly ones that had an independent annuity!"

"I will give a hyperspace call for a private transport," Angel told them. "Please, though, return often and tell me of your adventures!"

Ming smiled. "I promise. If you keep the master bedroom private and don't get so holy you disconnect the bar."

"For you, there will always be one special place here. That I promise."

Ming sighed. "How long before we have a hope of being picked up?"

"Oh, probably a week, perhaps a bit more," Angel told her. "There used to be wall-to-wall patrols here, but it's a deserted neighborhood now. I'll change that, though."

Ming looked at O'Leary. First at his eyes, then his biceps, then lower. "Can we have that room until then, at least? And a little bit of privacy?"

"Of course. All you wish I will provide here so long as you need it."

"How 'bout it, O'Leary? It's been a real long time."

Genghis O'Leary laughed. "Well, now, how can an old snake like me turn down an offer like that? After you!"

They both walked down toward the living quarters as Angel began to methodically disassemble the Straight Gate, hopefully for good.

Ari looked at Angel, at the hall, and at the receding couple, and sighed.

"What the hell," she said to herself in a low tone. "Wouldn't be the first or last time I got screwed by a cop."

JACK L. CHALKER was born in Baltimore, Maryland, on December 17, 1944. While still in high school, he began writing for the amateur science fiction press, and in 1960 he launched the Hugo-nominated amateur magazine *Mirage*. A year later he founded Mirage Press, which grew into a major specialty publisher of nonfiction and reference books on science fiction and fantasy.

His first novel, *A Jungle of Stars*, was published in 1976, and he became a full-time novelist two years later with the major popular success of *Midnight at the Well of Souls*. Chalker is an active conservationist and enjoys traveling, consumer electronics, and computers. He is also a noted speaker on science fiction and fantasy at numerous colleges and universities. He is a passionate lover of steamboats, in particular ferryboats, and has ridden more than three hundred ferries in the United States and elsewhere.

Printed in the United States
by Baker & Taylor Publisher Services